About the Author

C J Taylor began her career in journalism in 1961, spending over fifty years as a print journalist and feature writer in Sussex, Gloucestershire and South Wales.

Following her retirement, she embarked on an academic journey, achieving a first-class honours degree in Religion, Philosophy and Ethics, and then a master's degree focusing on eco-feminism and Goddesses at Greenham Common women's peace camp and in Extinction Rebellion.

She has four children, including the daughter who was adopted when she was an unmarried mother in the sixties, and with whom she was reunited in the nineteen-nineties: thirteen grandchildren and a great-granddaughter.

Her personal interests include learning Italian and playing the guitar. She also dedicates part of her time to volunteering with a group that provides breakfast for the homeless and those in need.

Living Live Backwards (The Continuing Story of The Two Js) is the second book in a trilogy. The first, *Perfectly Imperfect (The Story of the Two Js)* was published in 2024.

Also by C J Taylor:

Perfectly Imperfect
(The Story of the Two Js: Book One)

Living Life Backwards

(The Continuing Story of the Two Js)

C J Taylor

First published in 2025 by Fuzzy Flamingo
Copyright © C J Taylor 2025

Author photos: Paul Nicholls Photography

C J Taylor has asserted her right to be identified as the author of this Work in accordance with the Copyright, Designs and Patents Act 1988.

ISBN: 978-1-0684468-0-1

All rights reserved.
No part of this publication may be reproduced, stored in a retrieval system, or transmitted in any form or by any means, electronic, mechanical, photocopying, recording or otherwise, without the prior permission of the copyright owner.

Editing and design by Fuzzy Flamingo
www.fuzzyflamingo.co.uk

A catalogue for this book is available from the British Library.

For June, who shared so many of my most important adventures through life; and Georgina, who was my inspiration.
Also for my grandson Archie, who offered many 'bon mots' while I was writing this book – some of which I have used.

*Remember:
Age is just a number;
it's never too late!*

Catching Up

> *"Time present and time past are both perhaps present in time future. And time future is contained in time present. If all time is eternally present, then all time is unredeemable."*
> TS Eliot, 'Burnt Norton'
> in 'The Four Quartets' (1936)

MY NAME is Clarissa and I am adopted. My parents Ken and Audrey Phillips picked me up from a foster mother when I was six weeks old.

My birth mother Juliet Campbell was twenty when I was born in nineteen-sixty-four and because she was unmarried she had been forced to give me up for adoption. According to my birth certificate, my father was a gardener called Mike Bennett and he was thirteen years older than Juliet. Juliet had named me Vittoria. My adoptive parents changed that to Clarissa.

I was told from an early age that I was adopted, in fact I can't remember a time when I didn't know. My adoptive mother used to talk about it long before I understood the words she was saying.

While I loved my parents, I often used to think about my birth mother, telling myself she was probably a beautiful princess who was so busy with her 'princess-ing duties' that she was unable to look after me.

Three years after I arrived in the Phillips household my sister Bea was born. She is the natural child of my parents but we had a very close and happy family, so I never felt I was treated any differently. Our parents loved us equally.

I was twenty-seven when I decided to search for my birth mother. That decision had been a long time coming, with the very gradual realisation that Juliet was a gap in my life which I needed to fill.

After a few futile attempts to find Juliet by myself – looking for her name in the London telephone directory probably being the most time-consuming and useless – I concluded that I needed some help. My parents, who totally understood my need to find the woman who had given birth to me, suggested I should use an accredited counsellor to assist with my search.

Western House in Hampshire was the address on my birth certificate and the counsellor Liz Morgan quickly discovered that Juliet had worked there as a nanny for the Morrison family while she was pregnant.

A letter to the Morrisons resulted in Juliet, who had kept in touch with the family over the years, contacting Liz and hey presto, I had found my birth mother. Liz said it was the easiest and least troublesome connection she had ever made.

Exchanging letters and photographs, I learned that Juliet was now married to Ted Jackson and that I had a half-sister called Rosie, who was two years younger than me, and two teenage half-brothers Felix and Michael.

I met Juliet at Liz's London office the following weekend and after the astonishing realisation that we looked alike, there was an extraordinary awareness that we 'recognised' each other and had a deep natural bond.

Juliet and Ted lived in Brighton and within a couple of weeks I travelled to Sussex to meet the family. It was fascinating to discover that Juliet had chosen to use the name Campbell-Jackson when she married Ted, believing that taking the man's name on marriage was patriarchal and old fashioned. So, while Ted was still

Ted Jackson, Juliet and the children were all Campbell-Jackson.

I thoroughly approved; being an ardent feminist myself I had kept my maiden name when I married my husband Tony, although both our daughters have their father's surname.

If this all sounds as if finding my birth mother and the subsequent connection was trouble-free, it really wasn't. Part of the problem was a feeling of guilt that I was somehow being disloyal to my adoptive parents. So, I held back a bit, reluctant to fully connect with Juliet and my 'other' family.

Luckily, my parents were gently sympathetic towards my need to get to know Juliet better, and totally understood my feelings of guilt. Their love and support, with the added bonus that Juliet was the least pushy person I had ever known and was quite happy to let me set the pace, meant that we gradually grew closer and eventually I was able to accept that I had parents and a birth family and that they could co-exist in peace and harmony.

★★★

I had always been adamant that I wanted no information about my birth father Mike, believing that as he had left us both in the lurch, I'd rather not know him.

All Juliet had told me was that Mike had proposed when he knew she was pregnant and that he had called off the engagement shortly afterwards. She did stress that Mike had been caring, saying that although he no longer wanted to marry her, he did offer his support.

Big deal, I can remember thinking. He still left you as an unmarried mother who had to have her baby adopted. How caring is that?

However, and here's the rub, shortly after Ted had died of a sudden heart attack, Juliet dropped the bombshell that Mike was almost certainly not my father.

We were in the kitchen of the seafront flat in Hove which Juliet now shared with her lifelong friend June. June's husband Brian had died of cancer two years earlier, so after Ted's death they decided to sell their respective family homes and buy the second-floor balcony apartment.

"As girls we were known as The Two Js because we were always together. We've been more like sisters than friends throughout our lives, so it seemed to make sense to spend our old age together," Juliet had explained.

Juliet was bustling around, switching on the kettle and getting out teacups and saucers, when she said *apropos of nothing*: "I need to talk to you about your father."

"Really?" I was surprised. We never talked about Mike. He had dumped us and walked away when Juliet was pregnant with me. What more was there to say?

"Thing is," said Juliet slowly, "I don't think Mike was your father."

"What!" I sat down on the nearest chair, feeling I had been felled. Juliet put a hand on my shoulder.

"Sorry Clarissa. I've wanted to tell you for ages but just couldn't find the right moment. But I guess there is never a right time, so I've decided to tell you now while there's no one else around."

She sat down on the chair beside me and took my hand.

"Poor Mike, he was amazing, really, although he's had a really bad press for years. He called off our engagement because he was adamant he was not your father and wasn't prepared to bring up another man's child. But because he had made love to me once, he accepted responsibility, allowing me to name him on your birth certificate. He knew how difficult it was in those days to have 'father unknown'.

"It was a kindness I will always be grateful for, otherwise I would have been labelled a loose woman who went with loads of men and couldn't pinpoint the one who made me pregnant.

"I did feel it was dishonest to let you think Mike was your father when I knew in my heart that he wasn't, but in the eyes of the law he had accepted paternity and so I left it at that. There was, after all, the faint chance that he had fathered you, even though I always thought it was Enzo."

Hey, hang on a minute. Enzo? Who the hell was Enzo?

I was now in my fifties and had known Juliet for more than two decades; there had never been a mention of anyone called Enzo. Juliet gave me a long look, biting her lip as if deciding how much she was able to reveal.

"Enzo de Martins was a ridiculously handsome Italian singer I lived with on the island of Capri for four months in the nineteen-sixties. I believe he is your father," she eventually confessed.

As I digested this mind-boggling information, Juliet added: "I honestly did love Ted very much. He was my other half; we were together for half a century and had three wonderful children. But he could never be Enzo; what we had together was alchemy. I knew I would never find anyone else in my whole life who would make me feel like he did."

So, what happened? Why didn't Enzo marry her? Why… My God, there were endless questions.

"Enzo and I were going to get married," explained Juliet as if she was reading my mind, "but my parents wanted me back in England because they were obviously worried about me marrying a foreigner they had never met and going off to America with him. Enzo was booked to sing in Las Vegas just before Christmas.

"As I was still under twenty-one, I needed my parents' consent before I could marry, and there were other complications because Enzo was a Catholic, so the religious thing had to be sorted.

"Anyway, Enzo couldn't come to England with me; he had to stay on Capri because he was contracted to sing at a local bar for another six weeks and then he had commitments in Rome. So, I went home alone, and then I was too scared to return to Capri."

"Scared?" I was totally perplexed. This all sounded crazy.

Juliet settled back in her chair. "Okay, here is the full story.

★★★

"Mike gave me the trip to Capri as a birthday present. Because I was training to be a florist, he thought that a visit to Italy for botanists would be an ideal gift.

"Despite huge opposition from my mother, who considered it totally out of the question for a teenage girl to go abroad alone, my father gave me his blessing and so I joined an organised tour of gardens especially for botanists, painters and photographers. It was wonderful and, incidentally, my first flight in an aeroplane, which was very memorable."

As Juliet poured out the tea and handed me a cup, I wriggled into a more comfortable position, this seemed like it was going to be a long story.

"Here," Juliet offered me a cushion, "put this behind your back. "I'm afraid this is a bit of a saga, but it is important you understand. So here goes."

Taking a deep breath and looking a bit pensive she said: "I have to admit I already had a bit of a thing about Italian men. When I was fourteen, I went out with a lovely Italian boy called Mario for a couple of weeks. I had to keep it a secret from my mother, who would immediately have put a stop to it if she had known, so it was a friendship that was never going to last. I had also discovered the movies of the Italian film star Marcello Mastroianni who, in those days was an iconic screen lover, and consequently I became totally besotted with Italian men.

"So, when I met Enzo, it was not surprising that I fell for him. Head over heels. He was on Capri for the summer singing in Bar Russe, but he had an international following and spent most of his time travelling around Italy, France and all over Europe and America. Crowds of fans used to turn up every night to listen to him sing on Capri.

"Really Clarissa, he was just so incredibly attractive with black curly hair, a deep gravelly voice and intense dark blue eyes – you have the same eyes, which gave me quite a jolt when I met you – and he spoke almost perfect English with a slight American twang. He was, in fact, the first man I slept with."

I raised a questioning eyebrow at her, and Juliet said: "He had been given a beach hut by an American fan – yes, I know it sounds crazy, but these rich American women were always giving him gifts. Anyway, he installed it on a deserted island just over the water from Capri. It was a beautiful place, wonderful golden sand and very private. Enzo simply called it The Island. He took me there the afternoon after I went to Bar Russe to hear him sing and he…"

"Seduced you," I chipped in, finishing her sentence for her.

"Well, yes and no," said Juliet blushing. "He did take me there to make love to me, but it wasn't really seduction because I wanted him to. I wanted Enzo to be the first man I had sex with."

Juliet was beginning to look a bit upset, but she ploughed on. "To cut a long story short, I fell in love with him and stayed on Capri when the botany trip was up. I moved into Enzo's apartment and we had been together for four months when he asked me to marry him.

"I returned to England to pacify my parents, intending to return to Capri within a week, and then go with Enzo to Rome before travelling to the States."

I nodded. There were endless questions on the tip of my tongue, but I decided to hear Juliet out before voicing them.

"Once home, I got the wobbles," continued Juliet. "I realised that our affair had been a wonderful dream which was really not sustainable. Just imagine…sexy Italian singing star marries ordinary English girl training to be a florist and they travel all over the world together and live happily ever after. Unlikely don't you think?

"I was so lacking in confidence that I was sure that once we left Capri, he would soon become bored with me and move on to another girl as he always had done in the past.

"He was a gorgeous red-blooded Italian who liked women for goodness' sake, flirting was in his genes. He would never be able to stop. Although he constantly assured me it was not important, I was sure it sometimes went further. He was a man who could have any woman he wanted. Why did he want me?

"Although I was passionately in love with him, I realised that Capri had been a cocoon which shielded us from the real world. I was convinced I would never be able to compete with all the glamorous and gorgeous women Enzo met on his international travels. There were a lot of women who fancied him and would try to tempt him into bed. Before he met me, they had usually succeeded. Would that stop just because he was married?

"There was no way I could share him; I could never have coped with him having an affair or even brief flings. I had to give him up, painful though it was. If I had gone back to him and he left me for someone else, I would have died of a broken heart."

There were tears on Juliet's cheeks as she added: "It was self-preservation that stopped me from returning to Capri. I knew that the pain of leaving him was nothing compared to the agony I would suffer if I went back and he eventually left me and moved on.

"The point of all this is that I had only been home a short time when Mike made love to me. It was a mistake really and it only happened once. I was feeling low, desperately missing Enzo, and Mike made a move…one thing led to another. I didn't mean it to happen, in fact I didn't even notice that it had, I was deep in a dream about Enzo at the time."

"Did he rape you?"

"Rape?" Juliet looked shocked. "Well, it never occurred to me that it might have been rape but…" She took a deep breath. "It certainly wasn't consensual, I was in no state to agree to anything; but at the time I definitely didn't think I had been raped. Putting a label like that on something that happened fifty years ago is definitely a twenty-first century thing. It might sound like rape now, but it certainly didn't feel like it at the time."

I looked at her with tears in my eyes. "Nevertheless…that's quite shocking."

Juliet, also looking tearful added: "So, when I realised a few weeks later that I was pregnant with you, I had no way of knowing whether Enzo or Mike was your father. If it hadn't been for Mike I would have returned to Capri and Enzo in the hope that he would accept us both. For your sake I was willing to risk the consequences.

"Back in the sixties being an unmarried mother was a sin of enormous proportions and almost all girls in that situation were forced to have their babies adopted. To avoid that, I would have taken the chance that Enzo would be pleased to be a father.

"But not being absolutely sure if Enzo *was* your father, I couldn't do that. There was no DNA testing in those days so no way I could prove paternity. And Mike, after initially agreeing to marry me because I was pregnant, had second thoughts after deciding it was very unlikely that you were his child."

Juliet stopped and gave me a worried glance. The shock of realising I might be half Italian was making me feel sick. I didn't know who I was any more.

She put an arm around my shoulders. "Are you okay? I'm sorry sweetheart, this must be quite a shock for you. But I really felt I needed to explain, that you deserved to know the truth. I hope I've done the right thing. Would you have preferred that I left you in the dark?"

I considered. "It's always better to know the truth, however unsettling."

"My thoughts exactly," said Juliet with a hesitant smile. "So there you are. I can't prove it, but I am as certain as I can be that you are Enzo's child."

She looked at me intently. "So, do you want me to go on, or have you heard enough? The only thing I can usefully add is that Ted knew the whole story, I told him before we married."

"I have questions," I said.

"Go ahead, I'll be as honest as I can."

"Did you never try to find Enzo? Forgive me if this sounds a bit rude, but it seems a rather pathetic and extremely remiss to just leave it at that."

"Hmm. Well, you're probably right. But I decided that it was best to leave things as they were, especially as I met and married Ted very soon after you were adopted. I felt it wouldn't be fair to him to pursue a previous love. And then the children came along and things got hectic and family life took over everything for years."

"Did you ever go back to Italy again?" I asked.

Juliet frowned. "Rosie and I went shortly after Ted died."

"Yes, of course, I remember you telling me, that had slipped my mind. But you didn't say anything about Enzo."

"Well, I wasn't saying anything about him to anyone. Not even to Rosie. She knew I'd spent some time in Italy when I was younger, but that's all. Enzo was deeply buried in the past.

"We stayed in Amalfi and took a day trip over to Capri, but things had changed considerably in fifty years. I went to look at the Faraglioni rocks, but I felt quite distraught I couldn't find Bar Russe, which I was sure used to be quite close by, and Marina Piccolo looked totally different from the way I remembered. Not surprising I suppose, things change a lot in half a century, and it made me realise that you can't turn back the clock.

"I did think of going to Naples, where Enzo's grandmother had a house. But she must be long dead and anyway, I only went there once and had no idea of the address. Naples certainly isn't the kind of city where you would want to wander aimlessly around and get lost.

"I realised that what had happened in the sixties couldn't be resurrected now. So that was it. I said my goodbyes to Capri and laid my short time with Enzo to rest. But even after all these years I still love him. I still have an ache deep inside me."

I was silent for a while, contemplating the audacious thought that had suddenly popped into my head. Eventually I moved over and took Juliet's hand in both of mine. "Juliet…I don't quite know how to put this…would you mind if I tried to find him?"

She stared at me, her face white with shock, two bright red patches on her cheeks making her look like a Dutch doll.

"Enzo? You mean you want to look for Enzo? After all this time it will be virtually impossible. Where will you start? He…he may be dead."

The tears were running down her cheeks now and I felt dreadful, but I knew with absolute certainty that this was something I had to pursue.

"Well times have changed a great deal in fifty years, Juliet," I said with a confident smile. "We have something called the internet nowadays. All things are possible."

★★★

My name is Clarissa and I am adopted. Having found my birth mother almost thirty years ago, I am now setting out on a journey to find my Italian birth father.

Chapter One

> "You can't really understand another person's experience until you have walked a mile in their shoes".
>
> Mary Torrans Lathrap,
> 'Walk a Mile in his Moccasins' (1895)

CLARISSA'S FIRST port of call after Juliet's bombshell revelation that her birth father was an Italian, was to her parents who still lived in their old family house in West London. She travelled up from Sussex, where her husband Tony had his flourishing architectural practice.

Clarissa and Tony had sold their London town house and bought a garden flat on the outskirts of Brighton when both their daughters left home. Amy, an up-and-coming actress, continued to live in the messy shared house in Hammersmith which she had moved into when she first went to drama school in her teens; Charlotte, an A&E nurse, had shared a flat with a girlfriend until two years ago when she joined her doctor boyfriend Malik in a minute rented house in Victoria.

Clarissa arrived at her parents' home just before eleven, when she knew they would be settling down for morning coffee. It was a ritual they had stuck to throughout the years and never varied. Whatever they happened to be doing, everything stopped at eleven for 'Tiffin' as Ken always called it, so they could sit and chat over coffee and biscuits.

Now in their eighties, Ken and Audrey Phillips were unfazed

when their daughter walked in and announced she was going to look for her birth father. She always had a project of some kind on the go.

"We'd always thought that looking for your father was a strong probability," admitted Ken. "We just didn't imagine we would still be around to see it."

"Ah," said Clarissa with a wry smile. "Things have moved on a bit now. According to Juliet my birth father is an Italian called Enzo de Martins."

"What?" Both Ken and Audrey stared at her in amazement. Clarissa laughed. "Your faces look exactly like Juliet's when I told her that I intended to try and track him down."

"For goodness sake sit down for a minute and explain. What happened to Mike?" gasped Audrey as she grabbed her walking stick and moved slowly across the sitting room to sit in the special chair which supported her arthritic joints.

After she had helped her father carry the coffee pot, mugs and a plate of petit beurre from the kitchen, Clarissa related Juliet's story. There was a stunned silence. "Well," said Ken eventually, that's a turn up for the books!"

"So are you proposing to go to Italy to look for him?" asked Audrey, thinking to herself, silly question, of course she is.

"Yes, eventually, depending on what turns up on my internet searches. I have a lot of work to do before I buy a plane ticket to Naples."

"Do you think you have enough information to find him?" asked Ken with interest. "How much do you know about him?" Clarissa recounted what Juliet had told her about Enzo.

"Heavens," said Audrey. "He sounds fascinating. But tell me my love, how do *you* feel about finding out your birth father may not be who you thought he was?"

Clarissa took a deep breath and briefly closed her eyes. "It was an incredible shock," she admitted. "A bit of a bombshell. I didn't know what to think at first. I really felt I didn't know who I was any more. But now I've mulled it over and got used to the idea, I'm quietly thrilled. It's quite exciting to think I'm half Italian."

"Definitely rather exotic," smiled Ken. "A bit different from having an English gardener for a dad."

"Poor Mike," said Audrey. "He was more of a good Samaritan than we thought. And that does throw light on why Juliet called you Vittoria. She knew you had Italian blood. What a secret to have kept for half a century."

"Did you ever know what happened to Mike?" asked Ken. "You always said you wanted nothing to do with him because he left Juliet unmarried and pregnant, but I often wonder if you heard any gossip."

"He's dead," said Clarissa shortly. "Burst aorta in nineteen-eighty-four."

Both Audrey and Ken looked at her with surprise. "You never mentioned it."

"No. Well I actually heard from Juliet's brother Alan via a friend of a friend. Mike married shortly after I was born and had two children. I've never spoken of it to Juliet, so I have no idea if she knows or is remotely interested. But as he is *not* my father, I wouldn't think she would be. He is nothing to do with us."

Her parents looked at each other with raised eyebrows but said nothing. Clarissa sounded slightly peeved. "Have you told Bea you're looking for Enzo? asked Ken hoping to move their conversation onto smoother ground.

"Not yet but I will. It's on my long list of things to do," replied Clarissa, making a mental note to ring her sister the following day.

Coffee finished, she jumped up and kissed her parents. "Sorry to rush off so quickly but I must love you and leave you. I need to get home because Tony and I have to host another of those ghastly dinners for some clients tonight, and I have to get on with my sleuthing. There's a lot to do. Don't get up, I'll see myself out."

Ken laughed. "I'm sure you're more than capable of coping with one of Tony's client dinners. You've been doing them long enough."

"Indeed," replied his daughter making for the door. "I can cope, of course, but it doesn't make them any less ghastly."

"Well, your mother's off gallivanting too this afternoon," said Ken.

Clarissa stopped and turned round in surprise. "Gallivanting?" Since her arthritis had become more troublesome, Audrey hardly ever went out.

"You haven't heard about her new obsession?"

Audrey laughed. "Your father's winding you up sweetheart. It's only charity bingo at the church hall along the road. I go for an hour every week and I love it. Instead of taking home any winnings you donate them to charity."

"Bingo?" Clarissa was speechless. That didn't sound like her mother's sort of thing at all.

Shaking with mischievous laughter Ken said: "This week she's been promoted – to caller! And the caller chooses the charity, so all the winnings will be going to Crisis, you know, that charity that helps homeless people." Clarissa shook her head. Whatever next.

"It's not easy being the caller," said Audrey seriously. "You have to know all the correct terms like 'Legs Eleven' and 'Number Four knock at the door' and then 'Number Thirteen unlucky for some' and so on. We all take turns to do the calling. This week it's me."

"But did you know," said Ken with twinkle in his eye, "you can no longer say 'Eighty-Eight, two fat ladies'. It's considered unacceptable nowadays in case you offend someone."

As Audrey picked up her stick to walk over and give Clarissa another goodbye kiss, Ken added: "And 'Eighty-One, fat lady with a walking stick' is a definite no-no."

"I should think so too," retorted Audrey, who was slim and graceful. "Have a thought for those of us with arthritic limbs who have to use a stick, even if we are not fat ladies. Bingo calling is fraught with danger." Kissing her parents Clarissa said: "Enjoy your gallivanting Mum. Now I really must dash."

"Keep us in touch with how you get on looking for Enzo," called Audrey as Clarissa left. "This is an excitement we didn't expect at our age. It's even more riveting than charity bingo."

★★★

Driving back to Brighton Clarissa pondered her plan of action. Where to start? First of all, she'd make a list of the people Juliet might have told about Enzo to see if any of them could shed fresh light on where he might be. Then, she'd trawl the internet to see if she could find any mention of him. Even if he was not an international star, he should be well known enough to have a posting somewhere.

If she could discover roughly where he might be living, she would try to track him down in person. I just hope he's in Italy, or at least Europe, and not in America, she thought. Tony might try and stop her if she told him she was travelling alone to the States to try and find a man she had never met who might, or might not, be her birth father.

Once home Clarissa set to work. She wrote 'CONTACTS' in large black letters at the top of a sheet of copier paper. Underneath she wrote 'June'. After five minutes of wracking her brain and chewing the top of her pen she had to admit she couldn't think of anyone else who might be able to help.

The most likely people who would have known about Enzo, apart from Ted, were Juliet's parents Mary and Dennis Campbell but they had died some years ago. Mary had died in nineteen-seventy-seven of an unspecified illness. Juliet had said she wasn't really sure exactly what it was as her father never wanted to talk about it. Dennis had met Clarissa and welcomed her into the family, but he had died of a heart-attack in the late nineties and Enzo's name had never been mentioned.

Clarissa sat deep in thought. Wait a minute though, there were Juliet's brothers Alan and Bertie, surely Juliet had spoken to them about Enzo? And of course, she'd totally forgotten about her own half siblings – the girl and two boys Juliet had with Ted. Clarissa recalled Juliet saying she had told them when they were children that they had a half-sister they had never met. Would Juliet also have told them about Enzo being Clarissa's father?

Under 'June' she added the names 'Alan and Bertie' and then under that 'Rosie, Michael and Felix' with a question mark.

That was looking a bit better, Clarissa thought with satisfaction. Hopefully at least one of them would be able to give her some useful information to work on. She had a couple of hours before having to get ready for that evening's dinner so she decided to quickly pop over to Hove to see if she could speak to June.

★★★

Juliet had gone shopping in Brighton when Clarissa arrived at the seafront apartment.

"I thought I might see you," June smiled as she opened the door. "Come in and have a cuppa. I knew you'd want to track down Enzo when Jules said she was going to tell you about him."

As Clarissa sat down at the kitchen table, Juliet and June's dog Florence plonked herself down on Clarissa's feet. "Just move Flo if you don't want her sitting on your shoes," said June. "She's miffed because Jules has gone out without her."

"No, she's fine here," said Clarissa, bending down to stroke the dog's wiry coat. Florence gave a huge sigh, just to ensure Clarissa knew how much she was suffering.

"In theory Flo belongs to both of us, but in reality, she has attached herself to Juliet and can't bear it when Jules leaves her behind," said June handing Clarissa a cup of tea. "Now, tell me about your plans. You must have been a tad surprised to say the least when Jules told you."

"It was a huge shock to learn that Enzo and not Mike was my birth father, but now I know about him, I need to find him," Clarissa explained. "I'm hoping you might have some information which might help me."

June nodded. "Well, of course I have known about him for fifty years, but I have never met him and I have absolutely no idea where he might be now."

"Mmm, okay," said Clarissa, "but did Juliet ever tell you where he lived?"

"I think he spent most of his time on the road touring, but when he was back in Italy he usually stayed with his grandmother in Naples. No idea of exactly where his grandmother lived though. Naples is a big city and she must be long dead, she was in her eighties when Juliet met her in the nineteen-sixties.

"Anyway, I think almost all the talks we have ever had about Enzo was how Juliet *felt* about him," said June. "She definitely still loved him but she never expected to see him again, so exactly where he might be in the world was irrelevant. Sorry sweetheart, I don't think I am being much help."

Clarissa looked so disappointed that June added: "Shall I tell you what I would do if I were you? I think I'd go to Naples and see if I could find the house where his grandmother used to live. From all I've heard he loved that place; I somehow doubt he would have sold it."

Clarissa smiled. "Yes, I think that's what I'll do. I'll check out the internet first to see if I can find any reference to him. Then I'll get myself a ticket to Naples and try to find the house."

"The only other place I can think of is Capri, where Juliet met him and where he used to sing during the summer season," said June. "Someone on the island might have an idea where he is now.

I think he had a friend there who ran a hotel. It's a long shot but it might be worth a try if all else fails."

"Yes, thank you so much," said Clarissa, getting up and kissing her cheek. "I really feel you're pointing me in the right direction. Sorry, this is just a flying visit, but I must go home because Tony and I have a dinner tonight."

June put a gentle hand on Clarissa's arm. "The only thing I would add my love, is a warning that you must be prepared for the fact that he might be dead."

"I have factored that in," replied Clarissa. "But I have a very strong feeling in the depths of my being that he is still alive."

★★★

It was while she was shopping in Brighton that Juliet heard the music. She was at the end of Western Road on her way to Churchill Square when the strains of someone playing the guitar and singing filtered through the crowds of shoppers.

Looking around she saw him opposite the Clock Tower; a lone busker with his open guitar case in front of him ready to receive any coins that might be tossed his way by appreciative passers-by.

As Juliet drew closer, she realised with shock that he was singing 'Can't Help Falling in Love', the Elvis Presley number which Enzo used to sing to her after they had made love. It had become their special song and hearing it now, Juliet was once again lying on Enzo's bed in his Capri apartment as he sang to her.

She stood still in the middle of the street just listening to him singing, totally unaware of anyone else around her. Deeply moved, she felt very emotional and a little light-headed as she confronted the past and her longing for Enzo, which was always lurking just below the surface.

As if he could read her thoughts the young man immediately sang the song a second time. And Juliet, tears streaming down her face, dropped a five-pound note into his guitar case and went home without buying any of the things she had on her shopping list.

"It's prophetic," declared June giving her a hug as a distraught Juliet explained why she'd returned home without the shopping. *"A good omen for the future. It means Clarissa is going to find Enzo."*

★★★

Back home, Clarissa decided to make quick phone calls to Juliet's brothers, and to Ted and Juliet's daughter Rosie, but they were unable to add any useful information.

"When we found out Juliet was pregnant with you, both Bertie and I believed Mike was your father," explained Alan. "Juliet never spoke of Enzo. Hearing about him has been a huge surprise for us too."

Bertie agreed. "We knew there had been someone in Italy that she had wanted to marry, but she came back to England alone and we all thought Mike had fathered her baby. Neither our parents nor Juliet ever mentioned Enzo."

Clarissa's half-sister Rosie hadn't known about Enzo either.

"From a very early age, Michael, Felix and I knew about *you*, and along with Mum we celebrated your birthday every year. She was always talking about you, so we thought of you as a distant cousin we had never met. But Mum certainly didn't mention either Enzo or Mike. As children it never occurred to us that you had a father as well as a mother."

Clarissa sighed. Enzo had definitely been a well-kept secret. She was about to ring off when Rosie said: "Oh, golly!"

"Yes?" said Clarissa. "Have you thought of something?"

"Well, I don't know how helpful this might be," said Rosie hesitantly, "but you remember Mum and I went to Italy just after Dad died?"

"And…"

"And we went on a day trip to Capri. Sadly, it wasn't a great success because everything had changed so much since the sixties and Mum got quite distressed when she couldn't find the places she used to go to, there was a bar where she used to hang out and a particular beach. We also took the wrong bus and ended up on the far side of the island, which was very stressful.

"Mum didn't mention Enzo but she did say there was a friend she wanted to look up. Apparently he ran a hotel on Capri and she was really upset when she couldn't remember what it was called or exactly where it was."

"Did she tell you the name of the friend?"

"She did, but stupidly I can't remember, except it began with M – Mario or Matti or something like that. Why don't you ask her?"

"I definitely will," said Clarissa. "Thank you, Rosie. "You've been incredibly helpful."

Chapter Two

"Can we ever really know another human being?"
     Gabriel Byrne, 'Walking with Ghosts' (2020)

CLARISSA WAS just about to trawl through the internet to see if she could find mention of anyone called Enzo de Martins when Tony came home. He was horrified to find his wife sitting in front of the computer still dressed in jumper and jeans.

"Darling, haven't you had your shower yet? We have to be out in an hour."

Oh God, in the excitement of trying to find out about Enzo, Clarissa had totally forgotten to keep an eye on the clock.

"Sorry my love. I'm going up right now, won't be five minutes." Regretfully closing down her laptop, she put all thoughts of Enzo aside until the next day.

One of the many things Clarissa had in common with Juliet was that they both resented spending precious time with people they didn't know and didn't particularly like. Clarissa knew that the evening ahead was not only going to be difficult, but also unenjoyable. She sighed. She'd much rather be at home searching for Enzo, but duty called.

On this occasion Tony was entertaining prospective clients in a private room at a Brighton hotel and Clarissa had to play the hostess, being charming and chatty to everyone in order to support her husband in his bid for new contracts. She knew that much of her time would be spent fending off the unwanted attentions of rich but deeply unattractive men who had drunk far too much alcohol.

When she arrived back in the sitting room after her shower Tony gave her an admiring look. "Really lovely, darling! You'll knock 'em all for six tonight, you look a million dollars."

Clarissa had drawn her long dark hair back from her face in a chignon and was wearing a floor length black skirt that swished when she moved and a high-necked silky black jumper, with huge pearl studs in her ears.

She had learned from bitter experience not to wear anything too revealing to these dinner events. Low necklines often resulted in someone ogling or even trying to touch her breasts, while short skirts usually meant the man sitting next to her would put a sweaty hand as high on her thigh as he could, groping still further if he got the chance.

In the early years when they lived in London, Clarissa used to get really upset. "It's beyond what's reasonable," she ranted at Tony when they were back at home after a particularly unpleasant evening.

"I'm really pissed off with dirty old men touching me up. That dreadful Billy Ford-Jones actually goosed me. They make me feel just like a tart. What is it about rich men that makes them think the normal rules of civility don't apply to them."

Tony had put his arm around her. "Come on darling, it can't be that bad. You are more than able to cope with a couple of blokes who have just had a bit too much to drink. You're an excellent hostess and a great help in bringing in new clients." Tony knew his attractive and clever wife was very popular with the clientele, and that was good for business.

Eventually Clarissa gave up. It was pointless talking to Tony about it and she didn't want to whine. He really didn't understand or if he did, he pretended he didn't. In his mind, anything that bought in more business was worth the effort.

She recalled a trip to Barcelona some years ago when Tony had stood around chatting, just yards away from Clarissa who was combatting unwelcome advances from their host's brother-in-law. When the Spaniard, who was admittedly quite attractive in a dark, arrogant way, called across to Tony and said in immaculate English: "I am taking your beautiful wife out for a walk to show her the stars. I hope I have your permission," Tony just gave a nod and a wave of his hand hardly pausing his conversation.

Clarissa was so furious that Tony had totally abandoned her to goodness knows what in a foreign country, that she ground her stiletto heel into the man's foot, and as he winced with pain she hissed "Fuck off!" and walked away. She could feel his astonished gaze following her as she crossed the room to join another group. That was quite satisfying, she said to herself with an inward smile.

The only problem was it had made the Spaniard even more keen for her company. This beautiful English woman had not only violently spurned his advances but also used a forbidden expletive. He didn't often experience rejection and it had, frankly, increased his desire. During the rest of their visit Clarissa had to use all her ingenuity to ensure she wasn't left alone with him.

Clarissa often wondered why her husband never came to her rescue. She knew he loved her so why didn't he protect her? Truth was Tony had complete faith in his wife's ability to cope with any eventuality. She was a strong, feminist woman and a huge asset to his career. After all, the substantial amounts of money raised by his company paid for Clarissa's comfortable lifestyle. It was a joint effort. He knew she understood and appreciated that.

Eventually Clarissa marshalled her own defence system. Wearing modest and impenetrable clothes and being charming but extremely firm, she kept everyone happy while protecting herself from drunken gropers.

"Well done, darling," Tony had said when they had arrived home after yet another exhausting evening. "We're signing up at least two new clients and a lot of that success is down to you. You really charmed Richard tonight."

Clarissa thought about Richard's young wife who had looked so stricken as her fairly new husband played the field. She had gone across with a glass of champagne and given the girl her 'Feminist Solidarity in the Face of the Enemy' pep talk.

The girl was beautiful, with long honey hair and a flawless figure. Nevertheless, Richard had left her to go and grope any stray woman who would let him get close enough to her. "It's just a game," Clarissa had assured her. "It doesn't mean anything."

Interestingly, most of the wives seemed quite unperturbed by the behaviour of their menfolk, and Clarissa sadly speculated that the young girl she had been talking to would soon become hardened to her husband's drunken flirtations.

Nowadays, with years of experience behind her, Clarissa was very adept at dealing with difficult clients. Back at home that night in Brighton, Tony said how delighted he was with the way the dinner had gone. "You were great," he said gleefully, reflecting that his beautiful wife had the enviable ability to effortlessly charm everyone.

Untying his bow tie and pouring her two fingers of brandy he added: "You coped really well with old Cyril. I know he's a bit of a lech, but he is loaded and we need his business. He tells me he is planning to build at least a dozen new properties in those fields on the way to Saltdean and I'm pretty sure I will be appointed architect, so that's going to be very lucrative."

Clarissa sighed. Well at least all her hard work to keep the disgusting Cyril Parsons at bay but nevertheless happy had been worth the effort. She still thought it was ridiculous that if men fancied her it meant they would do business with her husband, but heigh ho that, it seemed, was the way of the world. Kissing Tony on the cheek she said: "I'm pleased it's worked out well, my love. Sorry, but I must go to bed, busy day tomorrow."

Tony opened his wallet and held out some notes. "Recognition of all your hard work. Why don't you go and buy those Louboutin shoes you were lusting after."

Clarissa took the money with a smile of thanks and put it behind the clock on the marble chimneypiece. She felt like a prostitute, but if she said that to Tony he would merely look bewildered. Hard work equalled pay in his world; he was just giving her what she was owed.

★★★

Clarissa had a fascinating conversation with June about these corporate dinners. June, who until her husband died had been a rich man's wife for five decades, totally understood what Clarissa was talking about.

"I never go to dinners like that anymore, so I can't talk about how things are now; but back in the days when Brian and I used to go to these events there were always men like that who were persistently touching up women. You know, serial gropers.

"Of course, their wives knew what was going on, but they were probably hoping to pull one of the more attractive guys themselves, so they were quite happy for their husbands to be otherwise engaged.

"I have to admit that I actually met quite a few dishy men at dinners like that while Brian was off…how shall I put it…pursuing his own interests." Clarissa laughed. "And you didn't mind what Brian got up to?"

"Not at all! As long as he was discreet and didn't make a fool of himself, I was quite happy to let him get on with it. We had a fairly open marriage so we both had other partners at various times. I know this kind of thing is not for everyone, but it worked well for us, and we were together for fifty years. Mind you, it must be far more difficult for those women who actually love their husbands."

June laughed when Clarissa mentioned Tony giving her money. "Brian used to do that too, but I always took it without a qualm. I reckoned I deserved it."

Biting her lip thoughtfully Clarissa said: "Yes, but June, cash isn't a gift, it's just…money."

"We may think that my love, but to men like Brian and your Tony, cash is very important. Remember businessmen don't think the way we do. They are giving you money to buy something you really want. Tony is giving you something he has earned and values; something important to him. So, take it with gratitude."

Giving Clarissa a hug goodbye she said: "Buy your lovely shoes. You've earned them."

Clarissa went thoughtfully home. She had no doubt that Tony loved her and was completely faithful, and as he hardly touched alcohol he never got drunk and misbehaved.

Nevertheless, she was pretty sure that he knew what was going on at the dinners he hosted and just turned a blind eye for the good of his business. And he obviously appreciated all she did to help him so like June said, she deserved the thank you money he gave her. She would enjoy wearing her Louboutins.

Chapter Three

"Don't judge each day by the harvest you reap but by the seeds that you plant."
Robert Louis Stevenson,
Scottish novelist and essayist (1850–1894)

AFTER A quick trip into town to pick up some groceries from the supermarket, Clarissa had the rest of the day to herself. Settling down with her laptop and a cup of coffee, she typed 'Enzo de Martins' into her search engine.

There were half a dozen matches, but none of them could be Juliet's Enzo. She dismissed four of them immediately because they were the wrong age, Enzo must be approximately eighty years old now.

There was no indication that either of the two remaining Enzos had worked in the music business and one of them lived in China which, while not impossible was most unlikely, Clarissa decided. Nor could she find any mention of him on various entertainment websites.

So, she had drawn a blank. Clarissa was beginning to regret her breezily confident 'we have something called the internet now' comment to Juliet. Finding Enzo was not going to be as easy as she had imagined. Maybe she needed to approach the problem from a different angle.

Walking around the garden to get some fresh air, deadheading roses as she went, Clarissa admitted that she had naively expected to track down Enzo quite easily. She was by no means a computer whizz, but she had expected to find him without too much difficulty. Even if he wasn't a big star, as an international entertainer Enzo surely merited some reference somewhere. It was odd that she couldn't find any mention of him at all.

Dropping the faded blooms into the compost bin, Clarissa dusted off her hands and decided to try Plan B. She phoned Juliet to ask for the name of Enzo's friend who ran a hotel on Capri.

"He's called Matteo," said Juliet. "Can't really remember his other name though, but maybe it was Rossi, or was that the name of his manager? No, I think the manager was called Lorenzo Russo and the friend on Capri was Matteo Rossi."

"That's a great help, thank you," said Clarissa.

"Are you making any progress?" inquired Juliet, trying not to sound too eager.

"A bit," said Clarissa deliberately off-hand, anxious not to raise Juliet's hopes.

"Oh well, good luck. Let me know how you get on."

Clarissa was just about to end the call when she said: "Oh Juliet, one more thing, can you by any chance recall the name of the hotel Matteo ran?"

"I've been desperately trying to remember that too, confessed Juliet. "When I went to Capri with Rosie, I just couldn't bring it to mind, which was really frustrating, but I have been giving it some thought and I'm pretty sure it was called Villa Valentina.

"I knew it was an alliterative name, which you would think would make it easier to recall, but it completely slipped my mind, I suppose because I didn't imagine I would ever need to think about it again.

"The hotel was quite small and it was owned by Matteo's family. His sister and a couple of his brothers also worked there if my memory serves me correctly. Are you thinking of trying to contact them?"

"Mmm, I might if I can't get any further with finding Enzo via the internet."

"Well, I think you have set yourself an almost impossible task. But I love you for trying," said Juliet, and rang off.

★★★

Clarissa spoke to Tony about her fruitless internet search for Enzo.

"It does seem a bit strange. If everything Juliet has told me about him is correct, and why wouldn't it be, then there surely should be some reference to him somewhere. I'm definitely going to contact the hotel on Capri, but I would be much happier if I could find some mention of Enzo first."

"Hmm," said Tony. "Let me mull it over for a while."

Twenty minutes later he asked his wife: "Exactly what did you type in?"

"His name," said Clarissa.

"Right, and where did he sing, apart from Italy?"

"Oh, all over Europe and the States I believe."

"Well try again, but use different words," suggested Tony. "Instead of 'Enzo de Martins' put 'Italian singer 1960s' or 'Italian singer Las Vegas'. I've read that Vegas was the go-to place for live music in the sixties, so it's very likely he sang there."

"Okay," agreed Clarissa, "I'll give it a go."

She tried 'Italian singer 1950s-1960s' and there were dozens of them, but none was Enzo. Feeling she was once more coming to a dead end, she tried 'Italian singer Las Vegas' and suddenly, there he was…an old newspaper story about young girls throwing their underwear onto the stage as a relatively unknown Italian singer and guitarist Enzo de Martins played a supporting set at the International.

"Is this the new Elvis?" asked the reviewer, reminding his readers that Elvis had been 'cancelled' in the fifties for exciting the sexual appetites of young girls. The story was accompanied by a picture of Enzo, but it was so grainy that it was difficult to decipher exactly what he looked like. Clarissa could just about see that he was tall, with dark curly hair and a charming smile.

She then found another snippet further down saying that the new Italian singing sensation Enzo de Martins had cut his first record *Canzoni d'amore (Songs of Love)*, and then a further piece to say that Enzo had been 'mobbed by screaming teenage girls at Naples airport when he flew home after the Las Vegas tour'.

That was it. She could find no other mention of him. But it was enough to keep alight her hope that she might find him. It was exciting to have some substantial evidence that her birth father existed.

★★★

When Clarissa typed in 'Villa Valentina, Capri' there was an immediate match. It was, said the website, a small hotel on the eastern side of the island, which had been run by the Rossi family for over half a century. Bingo! thought Clarissa with elation. Something concrete at last. Now she could start to plan a trip to Italy.

After checking with Tony, she decided to buy a return flight to Naples but leave the date to come back fluid. "You might track down this Enzo de Martins immediately, or it might take a bit longer," he advised, so there's no point in having a fixed flight back."

Looking at her seriously he added: "Whatever happens, Clarissa, whether you find him or not, I really don't want you to be away for longer than a week. Are you sure you don't want someone to go with you? I am in the middle of settling some contracts, otherwise I would join you: but you could take one of the girls…"

"No," said Clarissa. "I'll be better on my own; this is a bit of a pilgrimage for me."

She laughed. "Even Bea offered to come with me, which was totally amazing because as you know she never travels, certainly not abroad. I told her what I've told you. This is a very personal journey and I'd rather do it alone. Anyway, I've agreed that Bea can take me to the airport, so she's happy with that."

"Goodness." Tony looked astonished. "Your sister offered to go with you? To Italy?"

"Mmm. Surprised me too," said Clarissa. Bea lived on a smallholding outside Lewes and rarely left home. Giving Tony a hug and a kiss on the cheek she promised: "I won't be longer than a week, darling, hopefully it will get sorted fairly quickly once I'm on Capri. And I'll phone you every evening to let you know I'm okay and how I'm getting on."

Booking herself into Villa Valentina for two nights Clarissa toyed with the idea of ringing the hotel and asking to speak to Matteo Rossi, but she thought that might seem odd, and she didn't know how well he spoke English. Anyway, she would rather confront him face-to-face in case he was evasive, so she made a booking via the internet, before buying her plane ticket.

She was off to Capri in three days' time.

★★★

During the drive to Gatwick, Clarissa explained her plans to her sister.

"So, when I arrive in Naples, I'm taking the train down to Sorrento, I gather it's a fairly straightforward journey, and then the ferry across to Capri. Once I've seen Matteo, I'm hoping I'll catch up with Enzo fairly easily and then…well, it's in the lap of the Gods."

"It sounds a really exciting trip," said Bea, who never went anywhere, claiming she couldn't leave her numerous animals to be looked after by someone else.

Now in her late sixties, Bea had neither husband nor children, preferring her four-footed friends to most humans. Slim as a wand and still attractive with platinum-blonde hair, she'd had a number of admirers over the years, but none had stayed around for long, totally unable to compete with the demands of Bea's menagerie.

"I've never met anyone who would put up with me," Bea always told those who enquired about her decision to remain a spinster. "I may not be married, but I've been taken off the shelf and dusted a few times," she would say jokingly. "And I'd rather be left on the shelf than end up in the wrong cupboard. I'd rather live with my animals than a man any day."

Thinking about her sister's solitary lifestyle, Clarissa looked at Bea and smiled. "Just as well you're not coming with me. You would hate it; it's not your kind of thing at all."

Bea nodded. "I know, but I would have done it for you. I don't like to think of you going all that way on your own; I worry about you." Clarissa touched her hand in gratitude: "Thank you, sweetheart, but honestly, I'll be fine. I'll call over to see you when I get back and tell you all about it."

"Well, take care of yourself and don't get swept off your feet by a handsome Italian like Juliet did." She gave her sister a hard stare and Clarissa laughed. "Very unlikely," she said. "I'm a happily married woman."

"Huh," snorted Bea, "whatever that means!"

As Bea dropped her off outside 'departures' at Gatwick, Clarissa felt a tingle of excitement as she contemplated the adventure ahead. How wonderful if she could find Enzo for Juliet.

Chapter Four

"Je t'aime…moi non plus" ("I love you…me neither")
Serge Gainsbourg and Jane Birkin,
French pop song (1969)

ONCE AT Naples Capodichino airport, Clarissa took the shuttle bus service to the city's Centrale railway station, catching the Circumvesuviano train for the hour-long journey to Sorrento.

Settling into her comfortable seat Clarissa could feel the beginning of nervous tension in her stomach. She had been so busy planning this trip that she'd had no time to really reflect on what she was doing. She knew her destination and was very clear about her objective but had deliberately given little thought to any hiccups she might experience along the way.

Now she was allowing her mind to wander, she began to feel slightly anxious about the reception she might receive at Villa Valentina on Capri. If Matteo Rossi was still around, would he be willing to talk to her about Enzo? What would she do if he was no longer there, or he refused to engage with her?

Ever practical, Clarissa decided to file those worries to the back of her mind until she had to face them. Anyway, at the moment she was fully occupied coping with a young man who seemed intent on showing her pornography on his phone. It was a while before she realised what he was doing.

Clarissa was sitting alone in the aisle seat at the end of the carriage, and he was in the seat immediately in front with his back to her. Leaning out slightly, he held up his phone so she couldn't fail to see the video of a naked couple grunting and grinding against each other. Very faintly she could hear strains of '*Je t'aime…moi non plus*', the French pop song by Serge Gainsbourg and Jane Birkin which had been banned by the BBC and several other countries including Italy in the late sixties because of its explicit content.

The guy with the phone wasn't Italian, probably Eastern European, thought Clarissa, and he was young, certainly quite a bit younger than her daughters. She peered down the carriage. The train was busy and almost all the seats further down were occupied, so there was little chance of finding somewhere else to sit.

Clarissa took her bag off the seat beside her and moved across from the aisle to the window seat. Realising that she'd changed places and he no longer had her attention, the youth stood up and sat down beside her in the seat she'd just vacated.

As the couple in the video groaned, explicitly twisting themselves into ever more impossible positions while Jane Birkin's heavy breathing and panting was becoming increasingly insistent, a thoroughly exasperated Clarissa decided it was time to take control.

Right, she thought, I have two options. I can make a fuss and call the train guard or deal with this myself. After years of coping with drunken gropers at Tony's client dinners, not to mention the amorous Spaniard on the trip to Barcelona, she felt sure this was a situation she could competently diffuse. He was only a boy for goodness sake.

Clarissa consulted her Italian phrasebook before looking the smirking youth squarely in the face, pushing his phone away and saying a very firm "*No*." As he looked at her with an insolent smirk she said: "*Basta! Basta!* Enough!"

"*Cosa?*"

"*Andare via. Non sono interessato.*" And just in case he didn't speak Italian: "Go away. I am not interested."

He grinned. "You are very beautiful *signorina*. More beautiful than her," he said in passable English, pointing to the woman on his screen. "You would be better than her at doing that."

Oh dear. Clarissa sighed. Here goes. Giving him an unblinking stare which she hoped dripped pure contempt, she said brusquely: "Just fuck off!" adding for good measure: "Stupid boy!"

The universal language seldom fails thought Clarissa as the boy, for that was what he was, looking decidedly red around the ears got up and walked rapidly away. She sounded like his mother, and he wouldn't want *her* to know what he was doing.

Clarissa breathed a sigh of relief; gone off to torment some other lone woman no doubt. She suddenly realised she was shaking. It's times like this I wish I still smoked; I could do with a cigarette to calm my nerves. Pulling herself together she knew that even if she did smoke, she wouldn't be allowed to on the train. She dived into her bag for some Rescue Remedy instead. That should hit the spot. Clarissa settled back down in her seat and thankfully, the rest of the journey passed peacefully.

★★★

Having negotiated the Piazza Tasso steps from Sorrento train station to the port to catch the hydrofoil ferry for the eight-mile journey to Capri, Clarissa once again began to feel anxious. She ought to be enjoying this trip and the glorious scenery of the Amalfi coast, but she had too much on her mind. What kind of reception would she get from Matteo Rossi?

Capri's spectacularly beautiful Marina Grande had been a port since Roman times and its ancient fortifications were still visible, but its beauty was lost on Clarissa. I'm not here for sightseeing, I have a job to do, she told herself firmly. Checking her guidebook, she decided to take a taxi for the short journey from the port to Villa Valentina rather than use the funicular and then have to seek directions once she arrived at the Piazza Umberto.

Villa Valentina was a low, white painted two-storey building set on a hillside, surrounded by a small garden and terraces offering glorious views of the Tyrrhenian Sea's calm turquoise waters. The ubiquitous bougainvillea and colourful geraniums were much in evidence as were olive and lemon trees.

It was beautiful place. If it wasn't for the task she had set herself, Clarissa had a feeling she could spend a happy and relaxing holiday here.

Chapter Five

"The only comfort about being a woman is that one can always pretend to be more stupid than one is and no one is surprised."
Freya Stark, twentieth century explorer (1893-1993)

PUSHING OPEN the glass front door of Villa Valentina, Clarissa saw a beautiful young girl with long black hair and smiling brown eyes behind the reception desk.

"Good afternoon. You are" – she consulted her list – "Mrs Phillips?" Clarissa smiled. "*Si, grazie. Buon pomeriggio.*"

The girl laughed. "We are speaking each other's language."

"Oh no," said Clarissa. "That's all the Italian I know except for *'Ciao'* and *'Per favore.'* Or of course *'No'* said very firmly. Your English is so much better than my Italian. I'm not at all sure I got the 'good afternoon' bit right!"

The girl laughed again showing a set of dazzling white teeth and a very pink tongue. "*Perfetto,*" she assured her. Handing Clarissa a room key she said: "Will you please sign the register, *signora.*" As Clarissa signed where indicated, the girl said: "Welcome to Villa Valentina. I am Isabella. I hope you will enjoy your stay with us."

"Thank you. May I ask, is Signore Matteo Rossi here this afternoon?

Isabella looked startled. "Matteo Rossi? He is my aunt – no, I mean my uncle. *Scusi.* But he does not work today. He will be here tomorrow morning."

"Right. Thank you," said Clarissa picking up her bag, politely refusing Isabella's offer of someone to carry it to her room. "I will hopefully see him tomorrow."

She could feel Isabella's curious gaze following her as she made her way to the lift. Bother, that's annoying. Now Matteo would be alerted to the fact that she was wanting to talk to him.

★★★

In the hotel dining room that evening, Clarissa was enjoying an excellent fish stew accompanied by a glass of remarkably good red wine, when a grey-haired man dressed casually in jeans and a white linen collarless shirt with the sleeves pushed up to the elbows, came to her table and without asking permission, sat down opposite her.

"Good evening *signora*," he said in very good English, "I understand from Isabella that you are looking for me."

"You are Matteo Rossi?" she said in surprise. She hadn't expected him to turn up out of the blue to speak to her on his day off.

"I am. How may I assist you?"

Clarissa gave him an assessing look. He was probably in his seventies, about the right age to be Enzo's friend. Although not particularly handsome he was, thought Clarissa, nice looking with twinkling brown eyes and fairly short crisp grey hair.

Matteo was what her daughters would call 'fit', which Clarissa had discovered meant attractive rather than healthy. He also had a deep velvety voice and there was something very appealing about his mouth. He'd be nice to kiss…

Realising she was scrutinising him, Matteo said rather rudely: "I'm sure you haven't come from England to check me out so what do you want?"

Trying to delay the questioning until she was mentally prepared, Clarissa said politely: "Would you mind if I finished my delicious meal before we talk, *signore*?"

He looked at her frowning, his dark brows drawn together, his eyes staring accusingly into hers. "You are the one who came to my hotel asking for me. If *you* don't mind, I'd like you to tell me what this is all about. *Now*."

Clarissa bristled. She had no intention of being browbeaten by this bad-tempered man who was now glowering at her across the table in a rather menacing way. His eyes were no longer twinkling but dark and brooding. Quite scary in fact.

After a brief pause, she said: "I'm not prepared to have a serious conversation while I am eating. I will be about another half-hour. Then I will meet you in the lounge and we can talk. Hopefully in a well-mannered way."

Clarissa calmly carried on eating her meal and Matteo stared at her incredulously. He wasn't used to a woman speaking so firmly and frankly or in such a self-assured way. She seemed totally unruffled by their exchange. Most women he knew were far more acquiescent, especially when he was being assertive.

Looking at him Clarissa thought, how shall I do this. Either I flatter his masculine pride and pretend I am a dim woman needing his help, or I can be forceful and refuse to let him bully me. As she considered the options, Matteo continued to watch her, brow furrowed.

Eventually Clarissa put down her fork, saying: "I'm sorry Signore Rossi but I won't be intimidated by you. Please don't sit there scowling at me, you're spoiling my meal. I will speak to you after dinner. Meanwhile, if you would like to do something useful, please will you ask someone to bring me another glass of this very good wine."

With a thunderous look, Matteo stood up and went over to the bar, returning with a glass of red wine which he put down on the table in front of her. "This one is on the house, *signora*. Now if you will…"

"Half an hour," said Clarissa in an uncompromising voice.

Matteo chewed his lip and looked as if he was going to protest at being so summarily dismissed. But rising abruptly from the table he said shortly: "Half-an-hour. I will wait for you in the lounge."

As he left Clarissa called out: "Thank you for the wine, *signore*."

★★★

Forty minutes later Clarissa walked into the lounge and found Matteo sitting in an armchair with a bottle of red wine and two glasses on a low table in front of him.

"I hope this is better timing for you *signora*," he said with thinly veiled sarcasm, pouring her a glass of Chianti. "So tell me, what do you want from me?"

"Some information," said Clarissa, settling down in the chair opposite him.

"Information? About what?"

"I'm trying to find Enzo de Martins. I'm sure he lives in Naples, but I don't have his address. I think you can help me."

If Matteo was surprised he showed no sign of it. His face was completely dead pan. "Enzo who?"

"Enzo de Martins. I know he is a friend of yours. Juliet told me."

"Juliet?"

Clarissa sighed. "This is going to be a very long evening if you are going to keep repeating everything I say."

Matteo let out a sharp breath. Looking wary he asked: "Who is this Juliet?"

"Juliet Campbell. My mother. She lived with Enzo de Martins for four months on Capri in the nineteen-sixties. I am her illegitimate daughter and I believe Enzo is my father."

There was a long silence. Then Matteo, looking very hostile, said sternly: "That's a very grave allegation to make, *signora*. Do you have proof? Have you brought your birth certificate with his name on it? Is there a DNA test? You must prove paternity if you are alleging it."

Clarissa was disconcerted. This was going to be a lot more difficult than she had imagined. She hadn't contemplated coming up against such a vigilant gatekeeper at the very start of her journey, before getting any information at all.

"Look," she said at last. "I didn't come here to argue with you. I just want to find my father. I don't really care if *you* believe me or not. It's not you I am in Italy to see. If you just tell me his address I will go away and leave you alone."

Continuing to give her an unblinkingly stare, Matteo pursed his lips and frowned, rubbing his chin reflectively, but saying nothing.

Thoroughly irritated, Clarissa added provocatively: "I have already paid for two days in your hotel, so you won't lose any money if I leave tonight…with Enzo's address of course."

Matteo's lips tightened but he didn't reply, just continued to look at her though narrowed eyes. Unperturbed, Clarissa stared back at him.

After glaring at her for a few more moments Matteo said quietly: "Do you know how many women have come to this hotel over the years looking for Enzo, claiming that he had either made them pregnant or that he was their father? Dozens. More than dozens. I've lost count. Not one of them had a claim they were able to prove. Why should you be any different? I am very suspicious of any woman who comes here and says Enzo de Martins is her father."

Clarissa nodded. "I can understand that," she said reasonably. "But I am different because I do have the proof you need." Taking a smartphone out of her bag, she scrolled down to some recent pictures of Juliet.

"Here, I know you met Juliet a few times when she was with

Enzo. These are pictures of her now. Even after fifty years, you must surely recognise her and," she opened a wallet and pulled out a creased and rather dog-eared black and white photograph. "Here is a photo of Juliet when she was twenty, just after she had returned from Capri. Now tell me you don't recognise her."

Matteo looked at the pictures and then at the woman sitting in front of him. As Clarissa gazed calmly back at him, he looked into her dark blue eyes – Enzo's eyes – and knew she was telling the truth.

This was undoubtedly Enzo's daughter. She not only looked like a mixture of *Giulietta* and Enzo, but she also had his dogged persistence and tenacity. He smiled. Who would have thought it: Enzo's daughter walking into his hotel after half a century. The first woman ever to turn up with any credible proof.

Exhaling deeply, Matteo pondered what to do for the best; he needed to talk to Enzo urgently before he took this any further.

He looked again at the pictures. Of course he remembered her. The black and white photograph was definitely *Giulietta*. In the pictures on the phone she was fifty years older, but she still had those mesmerising silvery green eyes and was still a beautiful woman.

When *Giulietta* hadn't returned from England, Enzo had been devastated and Matteo was worried that he might never recover from the loss of her. Enzo had compensated by having sex with almost any woman who offered herself to him. And there had been plenty of them over the years, reflected Matteo, he'd even married three of them.

An endless stream of women and *Giulietta*, the only one he had ever loved, had left him and never returned. Now, miraculously, her daughter – Enzo's daughter – had literally turned up on his doorstep. What an extraordinary situation.

Matteo turned back to Clarissa. She didn't have her mother's red hair, she was dark like Enzo with those incredible deep blue eyes, but she had *Giulietta's* beauty.

Like all Italian men, Matteo had the inborn ability to charm and flirt at will. Now he gave Clarissa a beaming smile and said: "I am sorry to be so unpleasant to you. But I had to be sure that you are who you say you are."

"Yes, I understand," said Clarissa feeling a weight lift off her shoulders. "But you can be rather intimidating, you know. Very unnerving. So, you do believe I am Enzo's daughter?"

"I do," said Matteo slowly, "but it will obviously be up to Enzo to make the final call."

Raising the bottle to refill her glass he asked: "More wine or would you prefer a *digestivo*?"

"I'd love some Limoncello, please," said Clarissa, and he went off to the bar, returning with two glasses of the tangy lemon liquor which is a speciality in southern Italy.

"You will accept," he said, "that I have to check with Enzo that it is alright to give you his address."

Clarissa nodded. "Yes, of course. Are you able to contact him fairly quickly? I am only booked in here for two nights so I would like it to be sooner rather than later. I must be back in England by next weekend."

"I'll try to talk to him tonight," said Matteo.

As a relieved Clarissa visibly relaxed and thanked him with a smile that lit up her face, a smile so like Enzo's, Matteo idly wondered if it was okay to shag the daughter of your best friend.

Clarissa had inherited the combined good looks of her father and her mother, both beautiful people; it was a potent mix. She was enchanting and he definitely fancied her. Like Enzo, Matteo had slept with an endless number of women and girls over the years, but his best friend's daughter…was that crossing a line?

Although the idea excited him as it trickled through his mind, he almost immediately dismissed it. For fuck's sake, whatever was he thinking. Enzo would never forgive him. If she had been anyone other than Enzo's daughter he might have tried his chances, even if she was a hotel guest and it would be going against all the rules. A night with her would definitely be worth the risk.

★★★

Matteo tried several times to contact Enzo without success. He just wasn't answering his phone. Eventually he rang Enzo's housekeeper, who said he was on the final leg of his Italian tour.

"I'm not quite sure where he is at the moment," she told him. "Probably Roma, but he is due home this week, Thursday evening at the latest. I'll leave him a note to say you're trying to contact him urgently."

She paused. "Is it anything I can help with?"

"Oh, no, thank you," said Matteo hastily. "It'll keep until he gets home."

Ending the call, Matteo wondered what to do. Clarissa could get to Naples in a day. Should he give her the address – or wait until he'd spoken to Enzo?

It was a dilemma. But honestly, given Clarissa's determination, she was going to track Enzo down anyway so he might as well give her the information she needed and be done with it.

★★★

The next morning after the hotel's breakfast service was finished, Matteo wrote the Naples address on a sheet of Villa Valentina's headed writing paper and handed it to Clarissa with an affectionate smile. She looked at it silently and then leaned over and kissed him on the cheek. "*Grazie.*"

Catching a suggestion of her scent – possibly Chanel he thought – as she leaned towards him, Matteo once again felt the slight stirring of lust. Don't be an idiot, forget it, it's just not going to happen, he told himself sharply.

Trying to sound as normal as possible he said: "I haven't been able to speak to Enzo. He's away at the moment but should be back in a day or so. By the time you have travelled to *Napoli* he will hopefully be home. I will try to get hold of him and tell him you're on your way to see him."

Today Matteo was more formally dressed in a dark suit with white shirt and blue tie looking, thought Clarissa, very attractive; more kissable than ever. 'Stop it!' She firmly shook herself; the scenario she was imagining had 'disaster' written all over it.

Returning quickly to her room she went onto the internet to find a bed and breakfast in Naples. Having booked herself in and paid for three days' accommodation, Clarissa rang Tony. "Good news. I'm almost sure I have found him. If all goes according to plan I hope to come home on Thursday, Friday at the latest."

Tony was pleased. He'd always accepted that his wife was an independent woman and was perfectly capable of looking after herself. Although he was used to her doing her own thing he would, nevertheless, be happy to have her safely back home. "Let me know when you're due to arrive at Gatwick and I'll come and pick you up. We'll stop and have something to eat on our way home and you can tell me all about your adventures."

Clarissa tidied her room, packed her bag and went to find Matteo to thank him again and say how grateful she was for his help. He offered her coffee, reluctant to let her go; Clarissa accepted, equally keen to spend a bit more time with him. They sat together in the empty bar chatting as if they had known each other forever.

"Enzo and I met at school, and we spent all our teenage years together," said Matteo. "We grew up in a rather rough part of *Napoli,* so we always looked out for each other, and we still do. He's my best friend." He gave a cheeky laugh. "We know one another really well. I protect him from women, and he protects me from myself!" He gave her a thoughtful glance. "I can be a bit impetuous at times."

This morning it was like talking to a different person, thought Clarissa. Calm, cheerful and with a dry wit, Matteo's true personality shone through, and Clarissa realised that he was actually a really nice man. She admired his loyalty to Enzo and accepted that his behaviour the night before had been to protect his friend.

Feeling the fluttering of desire, Clarissa knew she found Matteo very attractive, and she could tell from the look in his eyes that he fancied her. Despite the twenty-year age gap, there was an almost tangible frisson between them, and Clarissa was tempted to stay for the second night and see what happened. She was only too aware, however, how dangerous that would be. Playing with fire. Just as well she was leaving now; no point in deliberately putting herself at risk. Experience had taught her how quickly things could get out of hand.

Feminine intuition is a useful thing she thought as she firmly shook Matteo's hand rather than giving him a kiss on the cheek to say goodbye. It wouldn't take much…better safe than sorry. She was keen to leave Capri as quickly as possible now, furious with herself for the unbidden rush of longing.

Walking out to reception, Clarissa said *"Ciao-Ciao"* to Isabella, who called a taxi to take her down to Marina Grande to catch the hydrofoil to Sorrento.

While Clarissa was waiting for the cab to arrive, Isabella said shyly: "Is it true what Matteo says…you are Enzo's daughter?"

Clarissa nodded, "Mmm, I am." If Matteo had told his family that Enzo was her father, then he must believe it was true.

Blushing, Isabella said: "Oh, lucky you, Enzo is lovely. All my girlfriends fancy him." As do you, thought Clarissa looking at the girl's pink cheeks and sparkling eyes. "We like his music too," added Isabella hastily. Clarissa smiled and reiterated her thanks as the taxi swung into the driveway.

Once in Sorrento Clarissa retraced her steps to the railway

station and bought a ticket for the train to Naples. It was late Monday afternoon. Everything being equal she should be able to see Enzo tomorrow and be back in Brighton on Thursday as she had promised Tony.

During the return journey to Naples, Clarissa couldn't get Matteo out of her mind, still feeling the stir of desire and wondering what kissing him would have been like. She had really fancied him and part of her regretted not staying for the extra night, but she knew…

Relaxing back in her seat and closing her eyes, Clarissa allowed her mind to flutter back to a moment soon after she and Tony had moved to Brighton when she had been less cautious.

Chapter Six

*"There is no such thing as a mistake – there are things you
do and things you don't do."*
'Unfaithful', film directed by Adrian Lyne (2002)

SHE'D MET him at one of Tony's client dinners and he stood out immediately; not only because he was unaccompanied and insanely good looking, but also because he was drinking orange juice.

When she went over to introduce herself, he shook her hand with a firm grip, looking at her with a steady gaze as he smiled, saying in a very matter of fact tone: "Pleased to meet you, Clarissa. That's a very pretty name." There was nothing flirtatious in his eyes or voice, but he held her hand rather longer than necessary before adding: "I'm Colin Barnett."

When Clarissa asked if he would like some champagne to go with his orange juice he smiled ruefully and said: "I don't drink alcohol."

She was surprised. Most of the men who came to these dinners drank to excess. Although Tony drank very little, she didn't know anyone who didn't drink at all. Colin looked like a guy who should have a gin and tonic or a glass of red in his hand. Seeing she was slightly taken aback, Colin added softly: "I'm a recovering alcoholic."

"Oh." Clarissa grimaced, feeling acutely embarrassed. "I'm so sorry. I didn't know…I wouldn't have…" Colin patted her hand.

"It's alright. There is absolutely no reason why you should or could have known. Don't worry about it."

"Thank you. Well, enjoy your evening," she said, reluctantly moving on to speak to other guests.

As an unaccompanied man Colin had been put next to Clarissa at dinner. The only other solo diner Bob Baker, a successful and prosperous property developer, was on her other side. Everyone else had brought plus-ones with them – wives or husbands, significant others and in one case a mistress.

While Tony held court at the top of the table, Clarissa was asked to keep an eye on Colin. "He's a lawyer and would be a great asset to our team," Tony told her. "I'd be grateful if you would look after him as he's on his own and hasn't been to one of our dinner events before."

Tony gave his wife an apologetic glance. "I'm afraid you've also got Bob with you because Janet couldn't come this evening. Sorry about that."

Clarissa wrinkled her nose. Bob Baker was a pain and, quite frankly, a lecherous bastard. In the short time she'd known him he had made several clumsy passes at her, not only during Tony's dinners but also when they'd met elsewhere, even when his wife was with him.

He was a 'legs man' and loved it when she wore knee-length skirts, especially if she wasn't wearing tights, so he could ruffle up her skirt in an attempt to reach her thigh. He never seemed that turned on by breasts, so he wasn't one of those who would try to do 'boob grazes' – deliberately brushing a hand against her breasts, pretending it was accidental. Oh well, she smiled at her husband, she'd cope with the ghastly Bob, she always did.

Luckily, she had Colin to lighten the load and they chatted easily to each other during the meal. He told her he was a widower, his wife having died of cancer three years ago, and he had a five-year-old son who lived with his grandparents.

"It was shortly after Toby was born that Diana discovered she had breast cancer. That's when I started drinking. I was totally unable to look after Toby, so he went to live with Diana's parents in Devon and he's still there. He's happy and at school where he's got lots of friends. I thought it was wrong to uproot him and bring him to live with me in Brighton. I'd have to get a nanny for him anyway, so there seemed little point."

He stopped. "Apologies. I never talk about my family and personal problems, certainly not to people I have only just met." Clarissa touched his hand sympathetically. "That's alright. I don't mind listening and I'm truly sorry," she said. "How awful to lose your wife like that."

Changing the subject Clarissa said: "Tony tells me you're a lawyer. That must be interesting."

"It is," agreed Colin, "but lawyer is a rather fancy word for what I do. It is much more mundane than it sounds." They carried on chatting, discovering they had a mutual love of art, music and books, and that *Brief Encounter* was a favourite film – "bit of a guilty pleasure," admitted Colin sheepishly.

Their conversation was abruptly cut short when Bob, who had become increasingly drunk as the meal progressed, put an arm around Clarissa planting a slobbery kiss on her cheek, reaching across to put his other hand high on her thigh. Because it was a client dinner, she was wearing one of her long-skirted dresses so thankfully he didn't get to touch her flesh.

"Clarissa my angel, you look ravishing tonight. I would definitely like to ravish you and find out what's under that *rid-rid-ridiquloushly* modest dress. Why aren't you wearing a short skirt to show off your gorgeous legs?"

As Colin gasped with shock, Bob gave an enormous burp and slumped his considerable bulk against her. "D'you *fan-shy* coming home with me tonight, angel?" he slurred. "The wife's away and I'll make it okay with Tony."

Colin began to stand up but Clarissa put a restraining hand on his arm. "It's alright, Colin, really. I deal with this kind of behaviour all the time. He's three sheets to the wind and won't remember any of it tomorrow, thank goodness."

"Everything okay, Clarissa?" called Tony from the other end of the table where he was deep in conversation with Wendy Marshall, the wife of his accountant.

"All under control," she replied with a smile. "I think Bob's ready to leave if someone could contact his driver." She beckoned a waiter who hurried off to consult the manager about getting an almost comatose Bob back home.

"At least Farik will make sure he gets safely indoors," Clarissa said to Colin, who was looking with undisguised distaste at Bob, now snoring on Clarissa's shoulder. "I dread to think what would happen to him if it was just an ordinary taxi and he was dropped off outside his house."

★★★

They bumped into each other again a few days later at the post office. Colin saw her first and came over while she was queuing to post a parcel. "Have you recovered from the other night?" He sounded anxious and Clarissa laughed. "Oh, yes, thank you. I have dealt with worse drunks than Bob Baker over the years."

Colin bit his lip. "Are you busy or do you have time for a coffee?" he asked with appealing diffidence. Clarissa looked at her watch. "I have an appointment at twelve, but I've certainly got time for coffee. Thank you." He waited while she dealt with her parcel and then took her to a small café in The Lanes.

"I must confess I was worried when that guy hit on you," he said. "I've been wanting to call to make sure you were okay. It must have been quite upsetting."

"I'm perfectly okay, thank you," replied Clarissa. "Bob is

pretty harmless really, mostly all silly talk. It's only when he gets totally drunk that he's a real problem. What is it about free alcohol that makes the richest of men overindulge? It's not as though they can't afford to buy whatever they want for themselves whenever they want it. Bob's lucky, he's got Farik to look after him, and most of the men have wives who will drive them, but I do wonder about the guys who have to get themselves back home when they're wasted."

Colin regarded her gravely. "And do you often get propositioned?"

"Oh, all the time," she said laughing. "I've helped Tony to run his client dinners for years, in London and now here in Brighton, so being chatted up is like water off a duck's back."

He frowned. "You really shouldn't have to put up with shit like that. I'm surprised Tony allows it. That kind of behaviour is totally unacceptable."

Clarissa almost replied that there were times when she was surprised that her husband didn't intervene on her behalf but decided that it would be disloyal to say so. Instead, she said: "Oh well, he knows I am able to cope with most things that crop up. He would definitely be quick to respond if anything really got out of hand."

Colin stared at her silently for a few moments before saying "Hmm. I'm not surprised men fancy you. You're very beautiful, where have you been hiding…why have we only just met?" Before she could reply he said: "Actually, I have to go. I'm so sorry. Please do stay and enjoy your coffee. I'll pay the bill on my way out." He started to walk away before turning round and saying: "Your eyes are extraordinary. I've never seen navy blue eyes before."

"No one has navy blue eyes," protested Clarissa blushing. "You have," he replied. And he was gone.

The following week he phoned her. "Will you have lunch with me tomorrow?" She hesitated. A small voice in her head was telling her to refuse, 'say you have to work'. Instead, she heard herself replying: "That would be very nice. Where shall we meet?"

"Why don't you come here to my house in Kemptown. I'd like to show you pictures of Diana and Toby."

He's probably lonely, thought Clarissa, ignoring the warning voice which was now telling her that going to his home really was a very bad idea indeed. 'I'd like to show you pictures' is just a modern take on 'Come and see my etchings' said the voice. But Clarissa felt sorry for Colin. Poor man, with his young wife dead and his small son living in Devon, life must be difficult for him.

For some reason she couldn't begin to articulate, she didn't mention Colin's lunch invitation to Tony. Thinking about it, she hadn't told him that they'd had coffee together either.

★★★

Clarissa found the house quite easily. It was a smart end of terrace with steps from the pavement leading up to a scarlet-painted front door. He'd been watching out for her through the large bay window and opened the door as she arrived. "Welcome."

She smiled. "I haven't been to Kemptown before. I had no idea it was so trendy around here."

"A bit too trendy these days," he said laughing. "It's becoming very popular with actors and artists and members of the LGBT community. I'm told it's cool to live here, but I'm not so sure it works for me anymore."

Colin held out his hand. "Come on in, lunch is ready." He'd laid the table in the dining room and had prepared quiche with new potatoes and a green salad, saying regretfully, "Sorry, no wine. Is water okay?" Clarissa nodded. "I rarely drink at lunchtime anyway. It makes me sleepy all afternoon."

As they ate Clarissa said: "Did you make the salad dressing yourself? It's delicious." He laughed. "I made the quiche too...not that I'm bragging, but I'm quite handy in the kitchen nowadays; I actually enjoy cooking. Didn't grow the potatoes or the salad though, but I am considering getting an allotment."

Once again, they chatted away amicably. He offered no explanation for his swift departure from the coffee shop but produced an album of photographs of his wife and son, reminiscing about the holidays they spent together in Devon when Toby was a baby and Diana was in remission from her illness.

Clarissa let him chatter on, thinking that it was probably good for him to be able to talk freely about them. Eventually he looked at her and said seriously: "Thank you. I needed to do that. It was good therapy and you're a really sympathetic listener."

She helped him to clear the table and carry the dirty dishes into the kitchen and as she bent to load them into the dishwasher, he grabbed her from behind, turned her round and kissed her. With only a moment's hesitation Clarissa relaxed into his arms and returned his embrace. He was very attractive and a quick snog wouldn't hurt; it was extremely pleasurable in fact. She couldn't remember when she'd last been kissed so ardently by anyone other than Tony.

After a while he took her hand and silently led her upstairs. Thinking about it afterwards, Clarissa had no idea why she hadn't protested; instead she went with him, feeling detached as if in a dream. It was when he gathered her into his arms and kissed her again that she drew back saying: "Colin, this is wrong; I shouldn't be here. We shouldn't be doing this."

"We're just continuing the therapy," he murmured. "You'll be doing me a favour; I haven't slept with anyone since Diana died… well, quite a while before Diana died to be precise. I desperately need to find out if I can still do it."

"*Really?* Not for more than three years?" Clarissa was astonished. She couldn't imagine many men going so long without sex, especially someone so gorgeous looking. "That's amazing," she said. "There must be an untold number of women more than happy to sleep with you and give you what you need."

"Yes, I have had offers, but never any I wanted to accept. I was waiting for someone extraordinary; I think I was waiting for you." Looking into her eyes, Colin said: "I never found anyone I fancied fucking until I met you. I really want to take you to bed. Will you help to continue my healing therapy? Seeing her hesitate Colin added: "It's just sex…"

"No," replied Clarissa. "Nothing is ever just sex. There's always more to it than that."

"Not in this case," he replied firmly. "It will be just sex. I'm not asking for anything more."

★★★

The spectacular Italian countryside was a blur as Clarissa stared out of the train window recalling the crisis of conscience she'd had standing there in Colin's bedroom.

While kissing him had left her feeling excited and slightly unsettled, she also felt extremely guilty at the prospect of being unfaithful to Tony. It was the first time in their long marriage that she'd actually given in to temptation. There had been several times through the years when she'd fancied guys, and one memorable occasion when she was poised on the brink of recklessness but had managed to disengage before it was too late.

Colin looked at her, his eyes full of longing. "Will you help me, Clarissa? Please. Just sex, no strings." As he kissed her again he started to unbutton her blouse and Clarissa felt herself melting. He really was a very handsome and sexy man, and she definitely fancied him even though he was at least fifteen, maybe even twenty, years younger than her.

She wasn't totally convinced that he hadn't had sex for three years; that could just be a very successful chat-up line; but she had now reached the point of no return. What harm could it do? Like Colin said, it was just sex, not a love affair.

Overcome by lust and casting caution to the winds, Clarissa removed her top, unbuckling Colin's belt and pulling down the zip of his jeans as they moved towards the bed. Impatiently tugging off each other's clothes, they were suddenly swamped by uncontrollable desire and the sex was intense, uninhibited and very exciting.

"Oh my God, Clarissa," groaned Colin, "that was wonderful. Absolutely amazing."

"Well, you can no longer have any doubts about your ability to perform in bed," she replied, kissing his cheek.

Afterwards Clarissa had a shower while Colin went downstairs to make a pot of tea. He had asked if she wanted him to join her, but she told him she'd never enjoyed sharing a shower or a bath with anyone.

"You should try sharing a bath in the dark with seductive music and candles," he said. "That will change your mind, it's very erotic. Sex in the shower is pretty good too."

"I use the shower as 'me' time," replied Clarissa. "I think and plan and work through stuff. I don't need distractions."

"Well don't think too hard," he said smiling. "I don't want you thinking of all the reasons why you shouldn't be here."

As the warm water flowed over her, Clarissa admitted to herself that sex with Colin had been a totally incredible experience, but one that could never happen again. It had to be a one-off. Going into the kitchen, she gently put her arms around him. "That was absolutely amazing, Colin; you were fabulous, and it was wonderful. But you know we can't do this again."

Gazing at her speculatively he suggested: "Maybe we could become friends with benefits."

"No!" Clarissa was adamant. "No, I can't…we mustn't. You have to understand that enjoyable though it was, it was a mistake."

"A mistake?" He looked hurt. "That was not a mistake Clarissa. It was something we did together because we both wanted to, and it was sensational. There is no such thing as a mistake. You either do something or you don't. And we did." He looked at her meditatively and asked quietly: "What are you afraid of?"

"I'm married," she replied. "I have a husband I love and two daughters: I'm not looking to have an affair. Also Colin, you're quite a lot younger than me and I'm no Mrs Robinson. Now you're up and running again you're soon going to want to find someone nearer your own age."

"I don't think age has got anything to do with desire. You're a very beautiful and sexy lady and I fancy you like mad," he said, adding with a cheeky smile "especially now I know how good you are in bed."

"But we can't…" protested Clarissa. Colin continued: "I'm not asking you to move in or to fall in love with me. I just want to have a casual sexual relationship we can both enjoy. Absolutely no strings attached. Something we do together just for us that no one else will know about. There is no reason why anyone…why Tony… should ever know."

Clarissa felt a moment of panic shoot through her. Had she got herself into something she was unable to handle. Picking up her bag and coat she said firmly: "It was a one off, Colin. I have helped you, now you have to help me. We must never do this again."

★★★

On her way home Clarissa called into Waitrose and bought steaks, posh salads and a bottle of red wine for supper.

"Steak on a Tuesday?" said Tony when he returned from work to find Clarissa lighting a candle to put on the table. "What's the occasion; are we celebrating? Please tell me I haven't forgotten our wedding anniversary!"

Clarissa laughed. "No, it's nothing special. I just wanted us to have a nice supper together."

She went over and wrapped her arms around him, pushing herself up against his body and kissing him passionately. "I missed you today. I really want you to make love to me," she whispered, putting her hands inside his shirt.

"Mmm, that's nice," said Tony closing his eyes as he held her close and stroked her hair. "Which shall we do first, supper or bed?"

"Probably eat first, don't you think? Otherwise, we'll fall asleep and miss the meal altogether."

"Okay." Tony, poured her a glass of wine. "Food then bed. It's a date, my darling."

While Tony was delighted at the unexpected opportunity to make love to his wife early on a Tuesday evening, he was feeling slightly puzzled. Over the many years they had been together, sex had always been instinctive; he couldn't ever remember either of them actually asking for it. What had happened to make Clarissa want him so urgently?

Lying beside her husband Clarissa knew that the meal and the sex which she had initiated, were an attempt to ease her guilt. A way of saying sorry. She felt thoroughly ashamed. Tony loved her; he was kind, generous and trusted her absolutely. Now she had broken that trust.

The awful thing was that having had incredible sex with Colin only a few hours earlier, she'd had to fake her orgasm with Tony. Girlfriends had told her that they often pretended, but Clarissa had never done so before. She'd never needed to…Tony had always satisfied her completely. Although she was wracked with remorse and hated herself for making comparisons, Clarissa couldn't stop reflecting that being in bed with Colin had been so very much more exciting than any sex she had ever had with her husband. Totally unaware of what Clarissa had done that afternoon, Tony slept peacefully.

★★★

Despite her good intentions, Clarissa visited the house in Kemptown several times over the coming weeks and waves of guilt were constantly washing over her as the sex she and Colin enjoyed together became increasingly intense.

"What about work?" she had asked Colin, wondering how he managed to have so many free afternoons. "Oh, I'm working from home on a particularly intriguing case," he answered, looking at her with a straight face. "Intriguing?" she had asked smiling. "Definitely intriguing and very absorbing. It's all I can think about at the moment, it fills my mind and it's taking a bit of time to discover the best way to proceed."

"But don't people in the office ask questions?"

"Ah well, I'm very lucky because I'm a bit of a free agent and my wonderfully efficient secretary fields all my calls and deals with most things while I'm working from home, so I can devote all my energy to the case in hand," he said laughing.

A week later Clarissa said: "This really can't continue, Colin. Someone is going to find out. Not only that, but this situation… with the difference in our ages…is not sustainable. It's sure to end unhappily."

"Shush," said Colin pulling her into his arms, "stop fretting about age. You're as young as the man you feel, which makes you thirty-one. Everything is fine. We are both very discrete, no-one will find out. We're really good together; I'd forgotten that making love could be so exhilarating. Tell me you're not enjoying it."

Thinking about the way he excited her, Clarissa sighed. The sex was fantastic: wild and carefree, making her feel young and desirable. Of course she was enjoying it. The only problem was, it was becoming compelling and her afternoons in Kemptown were increasingly frequent.

Clarissa knew that the longer her affair with Colin continued, the harder it would be to give up. But give it up she must, sooner or later. At the moment she still had a fragile grip on her emotions, but it was increasingly difficult to stop herself falling over the precipice and becoming totally besotted with him. She had firmly closed her mind to the disastrous consequences if she allowed that to happen.

Yet here, in this empty house with just the two of them, the outside world ceased to exist and there was nothing but Colin and long afternoons of amazing, exciting and addictive sex, followed by companionable chats over endless cups of tea. It was reckless and foolish, but inconceivable that such intense pleasure could be taken away from them.

★★★

It wasn't long before Tony sensed there was something wrong. Feeling uneasy but unable to immediately put his finger on exactly why, he began to gently question his wife. When he asked her for the umpteenth time if there was anything wrong, Clarissa once again replied offhandedly: "No of course not, darling. Everything's fine. Why?"

"I don't know, I wondered… it's just a silly feeling. You always seem to have something on your mind nowadays. You're different somehow." He regarded her with a worried frown and Clarissa blushed guiltily. She knew why he was becoming increasingly suspicious. Two nights ago, for the very first time in all the years they had been together, she hadn't really wanted to have sex with him and had pulled away very slightly as he started to caress her. She'd quickly recovered her self-control but Tony, so acutely tuned-in to her emotions, intuitively knew something was amiss. He had also become aware that Clarissa had changed her classic Chanel scent for something he didn't recognise; something more edgy…younger.

My God, thought Clarissa, this can't go on; it's exhausting. I'm not cut out to live a double life. While I can pretend, I can't control my spontaneous reactions; and I hate lying.

The instinctive pulling away when Tony had started to make love to her had been disturbing because she knew that for a split second she hadn't wanted him to touch her. The only person she had wanted in that moment was Colin.

Although she loved her husband, Tony's performance in bed which until now had always completely satisfied her, did not compare with Colin's thrilling lovemaking. It wasn't only because the sex was illicit that it was so immensely exciting. Colin had shown her new ways of making love, different ways of getting satisfaction which were incredibly pleasurable and addictive.

Clarissa had been married to Tony for over two decades and had enjoyed even more years of candid and intimate conversations with girlfriends – yet she'd never known about the coital alignment technique or many other exhilarating positions and movements until she had sex with Colin. It was mind-blowing.

If she started doing any of that in bed with Tony, he would surely wonder why, and how she knew about it. Maybe she could buy a book, a sex manual, and tell Tony she had picked up new ideas to put a bit of extra fizz into their love life.

★★★

Colin's name cropped up while Clarissa was having coffee with Wendy, who was married to Tony's accountant Bill Marshall.

"I saw you were with the gorgeous Mr Barnett at dinner the other evening."

"Yes," agreed Clarissa, "it was compensation for having to put up with the lecherous Bob Butcher. Did you see how drunk he was?"

"I did," said Wendy, "and you coped with him very well as usual. But come on, tell me more about the adorable Colin. Have you two got a thing going?" Clarissa stared at her in horror, trying to suppress a feeling of rising panic. "What do you mean? Of course, we haven't got a thing…or indeed anything… going."

"Oh? I heard on the grapevine that you were seen together having coffee in Foresters. Not only that, but you left separately. That's a typical ploy of people who are doing something they shouldn't."

"My God! Is it impossible to go anywhere in this town without being spotted by someone who immediately jumps to the wrong conclusion and starts gossiping about it?"

"You better believe it, honey," said Wendy laughing. "You can't get away with anything, especially if it's with someone as stunning as Colin Barnett. He's so hot, we girls are all beside ourselves with envy."

"Just as well it was quite innocent then," retorted Clarissa. "We met by chance in the post office, and he asked me to have coffee with him. I think he really needed to chat over a problem he has; you know, the wisdom of an older woman. He left before me because he had an appointment. So, I can definitely assure you that your envy is misplaced." She added snappily: "Not that I should have to defend myself."

"Don't be spiky, dear," countered Wendy placidly. Looking at Clarissa sceptically she asked: "Are you sure it was simply coffee and advice? I must say he would only have to notice me once and I'd be dragging him into bed within minutes…with or without the coffee!" Clarissa gave a disbelieving gasp. "Wendy…down girl! You're joking, right?"

"Not at all, I so would! Are you blind? He's gorgeous. Not only is he incredibly handsome and sexy as well as being very nice…and how often do you come across a guy like that…but he's also a widower and totally unattached. He must get lonely and need some company and I'd be more than happy to oblige. I'm sure I could find an opening for him."

Feeling acutely embarrassed, Clarissa took a deep breath and crossing her fingers behind her back said: "Well, what are you waiting for? Go ahead if you're so keen. I can see the attraction, but I'm not interested."

Wendy sniggered. "Well, of course *you're* not interested because you've got Tony who is also very fanciable and, if you don't mind me saying so, doubtless good in bed. So, spare a thought for me. I'm stuck with good old dependable Bill, who thinks foreplay is something to do with golf, and believes that if we have sex once a fortnight, he is fulfilling our marriage vows."

Smirking, she added: "Colin definitely looks like a bad boy to me so maybe he wouldn't turn down an older lady looking for a trip to the stars. I can assure you that fantasising about a sexy night in bed with Colin Barnett stops me from going mad and throwing things."

As Clarissa giggled and said: "Oh come on, you don't mean that," Wendy added: "Certainly I do. If you were married to Bill, you'd feel like that too. Unless I take a lover, sexual fantasies may be all the excitement I have left for the next twenty or thirty years. How depressing is that!"

Clarissa remembered June telling her that when she was married to Brian, she often used to pretend she was in bed with someone else. "Loads of men are hopeless in bed, absolutely no technique, it really is 'wham, bang and thank you ma'am', so the only way to get any pleasure at all is to fantasise," said June. "More women do it than you would imagine. I used to go to bed with Sean Connery, Paul Newman, or even the wonderful Elvis and wake up in the morning to discover I was with a completely different man…occasionally my husband."

Wendy was still chuntering on about Colin. "Okay, so I guess we may be a bit out of the lovely Colin's age range, although I must say I do fancy the idea of having a sexy toy boy. He's what, thirty? Thirty-three at a push? Nodding sagely, she added: "Just you wait and see, some lucky girl will soon catch his attention and snap him up. He's far too gorgeous to be on his own."

If only you knew, thought Clarissa with a guilty inward laugh.

★★★

That afternoon after another session of electrifying sex, Clarissa told Colin: "This has got to stop. I'm sure Tony suspects." Recalling her conversation with Wendy, she thought I wouldn't say he's a bad boy, but he's certainly a lot of fun and very exciting…and definitely not averse to an older lady! I don't want to have to bring this to an end.

Stroking her hair as she lay in his arms Colin said: "That's impossible. How can Tony know? We only ever meet here, and we're never seen out together. There's no way he could have found out." Clarissa frowned. "He might not know about us, but he *does* know there is something not quite right. I am not prepared to risk my marriage for…a few moments of pleasure."

He looked at her steadily. "Is that all it is to you. A few moments of pleasure?" Sighing Clarissa said: "It's your therapy Colin, remember? No strings attached. It was supposed to be only once."

"Yes. Well, that's how it started, but now it's more than that and I want it to continue. I want more than a brief encounter."

Clarissa put up a hand to stroke his cheek. He was so young and handsome and so utterly amazing in bed, there was nothing she would like more than to continue their afternoons of exciting sex. But Tony was going to find out sooner or later, especially as they'd been seen together having coffee and Wendy was asking questions, however flippantly. The consequences of anyone, not to mention her husband, finding out were too nightmarish to contemplate. "It has to stop, sweetheart," she said. "We've been lucky so far but believe me, it can't last."

She realised he was staring at her longingly. He looked

touchingly young and very vulnerable as he murmured: "I really enjoy being with you, Clarissa, and I don't want to give up what we have together, not only this amazing sex but also the way we get on, the friendship and companionship."

He paused before adding: "I'm not only talking about these afternoons in bed but also about us as a couple. You're everything I want. After Diana died, I thought I would never want anyone ever again. Now…" As he kissed her, Clarissa could feel herself drowning. If only she could live two separate lives, half with Tony and the other half with Colin.

Holding her in his arms Colin said fervently: "These afternoons are not enough. I want more…I need more; I want to be with you all the time. I have found the person I want to spend the rest of my life with. I have fallen in love with you."

Clarissa was shattered. She knew it would be all too easy for her to fall for him too – if it wasn't for Tony; there was absolutely no way she could turn her back on him and destroy the life they had so carefully built together. "Oh Colin, I am so sorry," she said gently.

Moving out of his arms and taking a deep breath, Clarissa pulled herself together and with every shred of resolve she possessed said firmly: "You know it's impossible for us to ever be a couple. I am a lot older than you – when I'm seventy you will be more or less the age I am now…will you still feel the same about me then? I am married to Tony and we have a settled life which I have no intention of sacrificing. I won't come here again. If we see each other, it will be simply as friends."

Looking pale and shaken Colin had tears in his eyes as he watched her getting dressed. "I feel you've used me," he muttered. He sounded like a sulky child. Clarissa looked at him aghast. "Me? Did you just say *I've* used *you*?" He nodded. "Yes. I did."

"How come? This all started with *your* therapy. I was doing *you* a favour as I remember and therefore, surely you were using *me*."

Colin's handsome face was clouded with bitterness. "We've been fucking each other like bunnies for weeks in ways that you had never dreamed possible. I've opened your eyes to intense pleasure you didn't know existed, and I've given you satisfaction and fulfilment that Tony could never give you. And you've enjoyed it all just as much as I have; you didn't know what hot sex was until I showed you. Now you're saying it's all got to stop so you can go home and use those new skills to titillate your husband."

Clarissa gave a shocked gasp. "Fucking like bunnies…?" Suddenly she was uncharacteristically angry. It would be funny if she wasn't so furious with him.

"For Christ's sake, Colin! This all started with *you* wanting me to have sex with you after three years of celibacy. I do admit I've enjoyed it tremendously and yes, you have shown me different and exciting ways of making love. But from the beginning we agreed there would be no strings. If you now feel differently, I'm sorry, but I love Tony and I value my marriage. So, this is where our arrangement ends."

She turned to look at him as she reached the door. He was staring at her mulishly and there were tears on his cheeks. "I suppose it's just been a bit of fun for you to fuck a younger man," he said resentfully, "but for me it has become so much more than that. I admit I said no strings, but I didn't know then that I was going to fall in love with you. I didn't mean to…"

"Oh sweetheart," sighed Clarissa sadly. "I don't want to hurt you, but I do love Tony and I can't change that. I'm truly grateful for everything and it has been unbelievably wonderful, but I can't give you what you want; I can't give you more."

She ran quickly downstairs and out of the house, hoping he hadn't noticed that she was crying too. Affairs never ended well: inevitably someone always got hurt.

★★★

Warning bells had sounded for Tony when Clarissa initiated sex on the Tuesday evening she'd decided they should have a 'nice supper' together. In all the years they'd been together, Clarissa had never asked for sex. Their lovemaking always happened organically and had been, as far as Tony was concerned, wonderful and totally satisfying.

Tony loved Clarissa unconditionally. They had met and married while they were at university, working together afterwards to build up his architectural practice. In the early days, she had efficiently run the administrative and secretarial side of things, but as the business became increasingly successful Tony had employed staff and Clarissa had taken a back seat, concentrating on bringing up their daughters.

Nowadays she was still a huge support, providing a constant sounding board for problems and helping Tony to host client dinners…and very popular his beautiful wife was too. He knew she was the strong partner in their marriage. His anchor: the glue that held everything together. There was no way he could let her slip away from him.

It hadn't taken Tony long to realise that Clarissa was involved with Colin Barnett. The fact that they had been spotted having coffee in Foresters a few days after the client dinner was of no particular concern. What did worry him was that she had never mentioned it to him, not even in passing. The sins of omission. From that moment he instinctively knew there was something going on.

They were very discreet, for which he was thankful, and there was no outward indication that anything was wrong; Clarissa was just as kind and loving as usual. But Tony felt a subtle change in her behaviour, and when she had momentarily flinched when he started to make love to her, his nagging doubts were confirmed.

Knowing Clarissa as well as he did, Tony was certain that any fling would be fairly short-lived. She was too invested in their life together for it to be anything more permanent. And with Colin being so much younger than her, Tony was sure it would never last.

Nevertheless, it had shaken him up. What was it that Colin could do for Clarissa that he couldn't? Was it merely sex…or was there more to it than that? Tony forced himself to consider his own behaviour. Did he take his wife for granted? Probably. Should he be more romantic? Definitely. After so many years of marriage and two daughters, romance had rather gone out of the window and their relationship, which was always loving but never overtly sentimental, had become humdrum in the hurly-burly of work and family life.

Although Tony knew most men found his beautiful and charismatic wife very attractive, Clarissa had never really given him cause for concern before. Some years ago, he suspected she was tempted by flattering attention from a mutual friend, but nothing had ever come of it and Tony had relaxed, believing their marriage was enduringly solid.

Still trusting Clarissa's good sense, Tony decided to say nothing and see if the dalliance with Colin petered out of its own accord. It appeared that no one else knew about it so, thought Tony, least said soonest mended. Although he didn't relish the thought of confronting Colin Barnett unless absolutely necessary, Tony knew he would fight to the death for his wife if he had to.

Then suddenly, Clarissa was back. Nothing was said but once again there was a subtle change in her behaviour and Tony knew with relief that whatever had been going on had ended. Life resumed its normal comforting pattern and the familiar fragrance of Chanel returned.

The only thing that didn't go back to usual was their lovemaking. Clarissa gradually introduced small changes that were incredibly exciting and intoxicating. While he was always totally turned on by his wife and enjoyed having sex with her, Tony discovered that going to bed with Clarissa had become something he increasingly looked forward to. He was more aroused by her now than he had been in the days when they were undergrads making love on a sagging mattress in a grotty student bedsit.

Tony reflected that Clarissa's brief fling with a younger man had certainly brought the unexpected benefit of adding zest to their twenty-year marriage.

★★★

It was a few weeks later that Tony told Clarissa he'd heard Colin Barnett wouldn't be joining his firm. "I'm really quite sorry about it. He has an outstanding knowledge of property and company law, and he would have been a huge asset to the team, but he's moving away, sadly."

Clarissa jumped involuntarily. "Moving away from Brighton?" She hoped the shock she felt wasn't apparent in her voice.

"Mmm." Tony was reading emails on his phone. He looked up, his face inscrutable. "He's moving to Devon to be nearer his son. It seems the boy has lived with his grandparents since Colin's wife died, so it's quite natural for him to move down there, I suppose."

"Well." Clarissa took a deep breath, her stomach churning. "That seems like a sensible thing to do. Pity though, it sounds as if he could have been beneficial to the company." Tony looked at her, his face still impassive. "It's obviously for the best."

★★★

Clarissa jerked her mind back to the present as the train guard announced that they were approaching Naples Centrale. Thinking about Colin had reminded her, if she needed reminding, that she had done the right thing by leaving Capri when she did.

Clarissa was pretty sure that Matteo would have made a move if she had stayed, and much as she wanted him, there was absolutely no doubt that it would have ended disastrously. Recalling the stab of desire that she felt while they were having coffee in the bar at Villa Valentina, Clarissa knew that this time, there was a chance she could have been the one who got hurt. There were always consequences.

Clarissa understood herself well enough to accept that despite loving her husband, there would always be a sexier and more exciting guy who fleetingly caught her attention. It had happened occasionally through the years and although she had never succumbed to temptation, she had always instinctively known it was part of her temperament. Now she wondered if the innate need for excitement and flirtation was part of her Italian heritage. Was it in the genes Enzo had passed on to her? A case of nature rather than nurture?

Nevertheless, Clarissa also knew that no other man could compare with Tony, who loved her unreservedly and would look after her and be at her side for the rest of her life. She really should start to appreciate him more.

Chapter Seven

"I am having a relationship with this pizza – almost an affair…it's a moral imperative to eat pizza in Napoli."
Elizabeth Gilbert, 'Eat, Pray, Love' (2006)

ARRIVING BACK in Naples, Clarissa made for the taxi rank in the Piazza Garibaldi. Climbing into a cab she handed the address of her bed and breakfast accommodation to the driver.

The man looked at the piece of paper and then back at Clarissa, his brow furrowed. "*Scusi signora,* but this address, there is a mistake, *no*? This is in the *Napoli* red-light district. It is not a good place for a beautiful English lady to stay."

"No," said Clarissa, "no mistake. That is the address of the place I am staying. Will you take me there please."

The man looked confused. "You have arranged to stay there?"

"I have."

"But *signora,* across the road from here is the Hotel Starlight, a very good place, clean and quiet with a roof terrace and views across the Bay of Naples. It is very nice."

Probably run by one of his friends or even a member of his family, thought Clarissa. As I have already paid for a room for three days I am definitely going there. Taking a deep breath she said in her most assertive voice: "No, I would like to go to that address please. I can get another taxi if you can't take me."

Shaking his head the driver climbed behind the wheel. "Very good *signora,* if you are sure."

He drove for about five minutes before turning into a densely populated area near the docks. Pulling up outside a pair of oversized double security doors, the driver turned round to look at Clarissa saying: "This is the address *signora*. I will come with you until you gain admittance. If you are not happy, I will take you back to a central hotel. I am not content with leaving you here, especially at night."

He's very sweet, thought Clarissa, and she was grateful for his concern. She reasoned that as she had coped with the sleazy guys at Tony's client dinners and the amorous Spaniard, not to mention Porn Phone Boy on the train, she was sure she could deal with whatever Naples had to offer. How bad could it be?

Clarissa rang the bell and said into the intercom "*Buona sera*, I am Clarissa Phillips and I have booked a room." One of the doors opened slowly and Clarissa stepped into a cobbled quadrangle. She was just turning to say goodbye to her worried driver when the door snapped firmly closed behind her.

The quadrangle was surrounded by four tiers of balconies each accommodating several apartments. Hearing a shout from above, Clarissa looked up and saw a middle-aged man waving from the top tier and shouting "Up, up, up." He pointed towards an antiquated lift.

Skirting around a trio of very dirty small children, one wearing a deplorable nappy, who were playing with an old car tyre, Clarissa stepped carefully into the dilapidated elevator, which was more like a swinging cage. At least it was clean. After several attempts she managed to get the two sliding doors to click together and the lift started creaking upwards, swaying slightly as it made its way to the top floor.

Well, this is certainly an unexpected adventure, thought Clarissa, hanging on tightly to the brass handrail running around the interior and ramming her foot against her holdall to stop it sliding across the floor as the lift jerked its way upwards. Tony and the girls will never believe it when I tell them.

Waiting for her at the top was her host who helped her out of the lift, picked up her bag and shaking her hand, introduced himself as Luigi. He led the way into the apartment, taking Clarissa to a very clean, very neat room with two single beds, a cupboard and a dressing table with a big mirror. There was also a small television.

"I will bring you a breakfast each morning but you must take your other meals out," he explained.

"Is there anywhere I can get something to eat now?"

"There is a good pizzeria just along the road," said Luigi, handing her a ring with three keys, one to her room, one for the apartment and one for the street doors. "But you should be quick because it closes at ten o'clock," adding: "please make sure you close the street doors if you are going out. It is not safe to leave them open."

★★★

The lights of the pizzeria were visible as soon as she went outside. It was only a walk of a few hundred yards or so, but on each side of the street there were scantily clad girls standing on the kerb plying their trade. Hookers. What a way to learn a living, thought Clarissa with a shudder.

Hurrying along the pavement she tried hard not to look at them, but one woman drew her fascinated attention. She was not the slimmest of ladies, having what Clarissa's daughters would call 'thunder thighs' encased in black fishnet tights; her feet were, incongruously, thrust into fluffy bedroom mules with heels, and a low-cut very tight top barely covered her voluptuous breasts. A minuscule mini skirt was wrapped around her generous hips.

Men driving slowly past seemed to be shouting their choicest comments at her, and although Clarissa had no idea what they were saying, she guessed from the tone that their words were not flattering. Totally unperturbed woman laughed coarsely, calling back *"Fottiti e vaffanculo,"* showing her contempt by holding up a finger and putting a hand between her teeth.

"Crikey," thought Clarissa. She'd seen the occasional prostitute in Brighton, but this was a completely different scenario. She felt relieved to arrive at the brightly lit pizzeria which was very basic but spotlessly clean with Formica topped tables and white painted walls.

It was empty apart from a group of men who stopped eating and leered with blatantly undisguised interest as Clarissa walked in. Ignoring the comments so obviously being directed at her, she ordered a seafood pizza.

The freshly made pizza accompanied by a glass of chilled red wine was, Clarissa decided, one of the most delicious meals she had ever eaten.

The pizzeria owner kept a watchful eye on her while she ate, speaking sharply to the men at the nearby table as their comments grew more insistent and they started laughing raucously at their own witticisms. Clarissa was grateful she didn't understand what they were saying; she really didn't want to know, although their graphic gestures left little to the imagination.

As she paid, adding a rather generous tip to the bill, which was literally half the amount she'd anticipated, the owner asked in halting English where she was staying. Clarissa pointed along the road and the man said: "My boy will accompany you."

"Oh *grazie, signore,* but that is not necessary…" Holding up his hand, he said firmly: "*No*! He will accompany you."

He called into the kitchen in rapid Italian and a young man built like a tank came out wiping his hands on a cloth. Giving her a gap-toothed smile he said: "Good evening, *signora*. I am Aldo. You will come with me; it will be safer. A good woman should not be on the streets at night without an escort."

Clarissa looked at him in surprise. His English was extremely good. As if knowing her thoughts Aldo said proudly: "I learned English at school." He laughed. "Many people here speak a little English, but me, I am top of the class. He tapped his chest adding: "Gold star!"

Holding open the pizzeria door, he said: "*Andiamo*, let's go," as he ushered out her into the street. Many of the prostitutes were still dotted along the kerb and after glancing at her with concern, Aldo said slowly: "These are bad people, *signora*. I am sorry you have to see them."

Looking along the street which was busy with kerb-crawling cars and dark except for the occasional lamppost with a woman draped around it, Clarissa started to feel slightly uneasy. When Tony had given her money after a successful client dinner, she had flippantly thought it made her feel like a prostitute. How wrong she had been. She'd had to deal with a few drunken men who were Tony's prospective clients, and he had given her thank you money in gratitude. So what. Her comfortable life was a million miles away from these girls who earned a difficult and dangerous living selling sex on the streets.

The confidence Clarissa had displayed in the pizzeria was rapidly evaporating. She suddenly realised she probably was at risk – maybe not from the kerb-crawlers, but possibly from muggers or, heaven forbid, abductors – and she was grateful for her burly escort.

Her expensive clothes and glossy hair made her stand out like a sore thumb, and she carefully pulled down the sleeve of her blouse to cover up her watch, taking a firmer grip on the strap of her crossbody bag.

She now understood why her taxi driver had been worried about leaving her here. How naïve she had been. She had dealt with drunken gropers, an amorous Spaniard and a boy with porn on his phone. The dangers that could be lurking in this shadowy street were in a different league entirely.

When they arrived back at the bed and breakfast building Aldo waited while Clarissa opened the door before sketching her a salute goodbye as she stepped inside. *"Ciao-Ciao"* he said cheerfully, giving her another of his gap-toothed smiles.

Safely in the quadrangle with the door locked behind her, Clarissa relaxed. Phew! Walking around the back streets of Naples at night was not something she would be doing again. Tomorrow she'd eat out in the city and get a taxi back to the door. Lesson learned.

★★★

When a young girl knocked on the bedroom door the next morning, presenting a breakfast tray with warm rolls, peach jam and a flask of steaming hot coffee, Clarissa read out Enzo's address and asked if she knew where it was. The girl stared at her silently, before putting the tray down on the dressing table and leaving the room.

Hmm, thought Clarissa, that's odd behaviour, maybe she doesn't understand English. She'd hardly had time to pour a cup of coffee before Luigi arrived, asking if he could help. After a few moments contemplation he said he knew the area where the house was.

Thank goodness, a ray of hope at last, thought Clarissa, asking: "In which direction should I walk?" He shook his head. "Too far to walk *signora*. You must take a taxi. I will arrange for it to arrive in one hour."

Clarissa was relieved that she'd had the foresight to ask the cab driver to wait, because when she arrived at the stone villa surrounded by a fairly substantial garden on the outskirts of Naples, Enzo was not there. A middle-aged woman who introduced herself as *la governante* informed her he was away until *giovedì sera*.

Clarissa tutted with annoyance. Today was Tuesday and she

was hoping she could see Enzo and go home tomorrow. If Enzo wasn't back until Thursday evening, she was stuck until Friday and wouldn't be home before the weekend. But at least it was the correct address.

The woman was watching her distrustfully, with narrowed eyes. Although she was probably about Clarissa's age, dressed in the simple dark clothes of elderly Italian women she looked a lot older. "*Grazie signora,*" said Clarissa politely. "I will return on Friday." She consulted her Italian phrasebook, "on *venerdì.*" Nodding brusquely, the woman said "Okay" and slammed the door shut, leaving Clarissa standing on the step.

So, she was Enzo's housekeeper, thought Clarissa. Not exactly friendly but did it mean he wasn't married? That was something she had forgotten to ask Matteo. If Enzo was married it would probably make quite a difference to the reception she received. But if Enzo did have a wife surely Matteo would have mentioned it. Oh well, she'd have to wait and find out on Thursday. Getting back into the taxi, Clarissa asked the driver to take her into Naples' city centre. She was going to spend the day sightseeing.

That evening Clarissa made her daily call to Tony. "Sorry, darling, looks like I won't be home until Saturday or Sunday now." Explaining the situation she added: "Now I've come so far and have actually found where he lives, I can't leave without seeing him."

Tony agreed. "But please make sure it's no longer. I'm happy your quest has been successful, but I definitely need you back home by Monday. We have a client dinner next week."

Was that the only reason he wanted her home, Clarissa wondered; or was he missing her? She thought he probably was but wouldn't say so. Although they loved each other, theirs was still not a sentimental relationship.

★★★

Unexpectedly handed two free days, Clarissa spent them exploring Naples, visiting the ruined Roman city of Pompeii and taking a trip up Mount Vesuvius, which famously erupted in 79CE burying Pompeii, Herculaneum and many thousands of citizens in the lava.

Having only seen the city's rather dodgy nightlife, she was delighted to discover that Naples was, in fact, beautiful – the third largest city in Italy after Rome and Milan – with a wonderful ambience and friendly people who were always proud to point out that the ubiquitous pizza had originated in Napoli. Clarissa soon discovered there was much more to Italian cuisine than pizza and pasta. There were some wonderful shops for Clarissa to explore as she searched out small gifts to take home. She also bought herself a very chic jacket.

After speaking to Luigi, Clarissa extended her stay, paying for her room until Saturday. Surely, she'd have caught up with Enzo by then.

Chapter Eight

*"Be not inhospitable to strangers
lest they be angels in disguise."*
Attributed to W B Yeats, Irish poet,
and painted on the wall of Shakespeare
and Co, a bookshop on the Left Bank
in Paris. Originally from the Bible
(Hebrews 13:2)

AS ENZO walked wearily into the house putting down his guitar case and bags, Maria came out of the kitchen to welcome him, picking up the black leather jacket he had shrugged off onto the floor. "Good trip?"

"Yes, okay. The fans were wonderful as usual, but I really am beginning to think I can't tour any more, even in Italy," he said, gratefully accepting the glass of Grappa she put into his hand. "I've had enough."

"You're always saying that."

"This time I mean it. I suddenly feel too old. I'll just do the occasional gig in future. I'm definitely going to explain the situation to Elsa tomorrow."

After being with his manager Lorenzo Russo for more than twenty years, Enzo had been looked after by Elsa Garcia in New York since the eighties when Lorenzo had a spell of ill-health and retired. Although Enzo no longer did engagements in the States, Elsa remained his manager, initially organising tours across

Europe and as Enzo got older, just Italy. Now he increasingly felt that even touring in Italy was becoming too much for him. He'd talk to Elsa about doing one-off gigs. These days he rather liked coming home each night to sleep in his own bed…alone.

Suddenly realising the time, Enzo looked questioningly at Maria. "Why are you here, anyway? It's late. You should have gone home hours ago."

The housekeeper regarded him steadily. "I went home and came back. I wanted to see you. There was a woman here."

"Here? What at the house?"

"She came in a taxi on Tuesday and knocked on the door asking for you. I said you were away until Thursday and she said she'd return on Friday."

"A woman? Or a girl?" He laughed. "There is a difference you know Maria." She sniffed contemptuously. "A middle-aged woman, well-to-do, nice clothes, very polite. She was English."

"English?" Enzo looked astonished. A middle-aged English woman asking for him. So, she wasn't one of the girls who turned up every so often claiming he'd made her pregnant.

"Maria, how old was she?" The housekeeper shrugged. "Hmm. Not sure – forty, maybe fifty…"

"Ah," said Enzo. For a fleeting moment his heart had lifted thinking, as he had so often over the years, that it could be *Giulietta,* but this woman was too young. *Giulietta* must be seventy by now.

"Did she have red hair?"

Maria looked at him as if he was mad; the touring was definitely getting too much for him.

"*Capelli rossi*? Why red? No, dark hair." Enzo suddenly realised that Maria was regarding him with concern. "Oh, I just wondered…Well if she comes back tomorrow, we'll see what she wants. Anything else happen while I was away?"

"Only a phone call from Signore Matteo. He wants to speak to you urgently. He had tried your *cellulare* several times but couldn't get through. I've left a message on your desk to remind you. I offered to help…" she shrugged, "he said not to worry, it would keep. So obviously not too urgent…"

Enzo laughed. Maria was wonderful and he totally depended on her domestically, but she was the most indiscreet woman in *Napoli*. Neither he nor Matteo would ever tell her anything important; within days all her numerous relatives and friends across the city would be privy to the information.

"Well, that can wait until the morning, I guess. Everything with Matteo is always urgent." He emptied his glass and handed it to her. "Thank you, Maria. I'm off to bed, I'm exhausted."

"Too many girls," muttered his housekeeper under her breath as she put on her coat and made for the door. Turning round she said: "You be careful with that woman tomorrow. She could be anybody. Do you want me to be here with you?"

"You don't work on Fridays, Maria. I'll be fine. I'm sure I can cope on my own with one middle-aged English woman."

"She's a woman…enough said."

Enzo rolled his eyes. "*Ciao-Ciao* Maria," he said firmly. "Go home, I'll see you on Saturday and tell you all the gossip."

"Huh!" she said walking out, calling over her shoulder, "Just take care of yourself," as she locked the door behind her. Maria had been working for Enzo for ten years and she was inordinately fond of him. He might be a well-known singer and have a huge number of fans, but he was hopeless at looking after himself. Problem was he was too nice and definitely far too handsome. He drew women like a magnet.

That English woman who called didn't look like the type who was going to take advantage, but you never knew. Women always wanted something from him, usually money or sex, and sometimes both. Maria had made it her job to protect him as much as possible.

Enzo wandered around the house checking locks and windows

before going to his room and falling into bed. He was dead-tired and felt strangely deflated.

★★★

Enzo's phone rang the following morning while he was still in bed. It was Matteo.

"Where have you been? I've been trying to get hold of you for days."

"*Ah spiace*, I was in *Roma*, the final leg of the Italian tour." There was a pause and Enzo said dryly: "It went very well, thank you for asking."

Matteo grunted. "Of course it did. I didn't need to ask."

"I only got home last night, and Maria said you were trying to get in touch. I was going to ring you later," said Enzo.

"I could have grown a beard while waiting for you to contact me," grumbled Matteo.

"What's so important? I'm coming over to Capri see you in a couple of days."

"Are you sitting down?"

"I'm in bed actually."

"*Siete soli?*"

"Of course I'm alone. Give me a break, you and Maria are as bad as each other."

"You do have a bit of a track record," said Matteo laughing.

"Okay, point made! Although nowadays I sleep alone more often than not. So, what's this all about?"

"Well, a woman turned up here at the hotel looking for you."

"On Capri?"

"Yes. She was very determined. Anyway, she's English, probably fifty-ish, and says she is your daughter."

"Oh my God, Matteo…"

"Wait for this, she says she is also *Giulietta's* daughter. And quite honestly, I do believe she is telling the truth. She looks a bit like her, but also like you. She's definitely got your eyes."

Enzo fell back on the pillows, his heart pounding. *Giulietta* had given birth to his daughter. Fifty years ago. Could that be possible? Why hadn't she told him? He thought of the countless times over the years when he had regularly slept with the three women he had married and the few he'd had affairs with, as well as randomly fucking a succession of girls, always being excessively careful that he never fathered a child. And all that time he had a daughter with *Giulietta*, the only girl he had ever loved. The only girl he would have wanted to have a child with.

"Enzo? Enzo, are you still there? I said…"

"I heard what you said."

"So what do you think?"

"What? More to the point, what do *you* think? Is she my daughter?"

"I'm pretty sure she is. She has an old photograph which is definitely *Giulietta* as I remember her, but also more recent pictures of her. She says *Giulietta* is her mother, and I think you are her father."

"Fu-u-u-ck." He felt a bit queasy.

"Listen mate. She booked into Villa Valentina for two nights and asked where I was almost as soon as she arrived. It was my day off, but Bella told me about her, so I went in and confronted her at dinner hoping I could put her off. We had quite a row about you in fact, but she was very determined, and I just knew she was telling the truth. So…and I'm sorry, but I'm convinced it was the right thing to do…I gave her your address. She's on her way to see you."

"In *Napoli?*"

"Yes. Well, I couldn't get hold of you to ask if it was okay so…"

"Then she's already found me. She turned up while I was away and Maria spoke to her. She's coming back sometime today."

"*Deo Santo*! How do you feel about that?"

"If you're sure she is who she says she is, then I will be happy to meet her. Maybe I can get a little bit of *Giulietta* back." He paused as a thought suddenly hit him. "Did she say her mother was still…" he closed his eyes, his stomach in knots as he asked the question… "still alive?"

"I didn't ask, sorry. But she gave no indication that *Giulietta* had died. No, she had pictures on her phone which she said were recent. I'm pretty certain *Giulietta* must still be around."

Matteo could almost hear Enzo's sigh of relief. He had never got over that girl leaving him. Maybe meeting her rather lovely daughter would help. "Her name is Clarissa, by the way," said Matteo. "Clarissa Phillips. I had a long chat with her and she's very nice. Really gorgeous looking too; great tits. Oops, sorry mate, I was forgetting she's your daughter. Inappropriate comment."

Enzo was immediately alert. He recognised so well that tone in Matteo's voice…he fancied her. They hadn't spent their youth together without Enzo knowing when Matteo was interested in a woman. Unaware of his friend's thoughts Matteo continued: "Don't underestimate her, she is very bright and determined, not unlike you, actually. And she's also a very foxy lady."

I knew it, thought Enzo, but he just said with mild sarcasm: "Well that's alright then."

★★★

On Friday morning Luigi once again called a taxi to take Clarissa back to Enzo's house. This time the door opened as she got out of the cab and there on the step was a tall and astonishingly handsome man. Enzo de Martins. Her birth father. That old newspaper picture certainly didn't do him justice, she thought. He's very attractive.

"You are Clarissa," he said. It was a statement rather than a question. "Matteo has told me all about you. A *very* determined lady, I believe." He spoke perfect English with the slightly perceptible American twang Juliet had mentioned.

Taking her hand, he held it to his lips, staring unwaveringly into her eyes. She was lovely, no wonder Matteo was so enthusiastic. Still holding her hand, he said: "Come and sit in the garden and have some refreshments. I think we have a lot to talk about." He gave her a captivating smile. "Gosh, thought Clarissa, he is utterly charming."

Chapter Nine

"True love never dies, it is immortal and eternal, and it lives on in the hearts of those who love."

Anon

ENZO USHERED Clarissa to a wrought iron seat under a canopy of lemon trees, putting a small espresso coffee and a glass of Limoncello on the table in front of her. Sitting on the opposite side of the table, he stared at her intently. She was beautiful, rather like an older version of *Giulietta* as he remembered her, but with dark hair.

"You've got my eyes," he said at last. He still had the deep gravelly voice Juliet had told her about. Clarissa laughed. "So Juliet tells me. She says I remind her of you."

"How is she, what's she doing, is she married? I want to hear everything about her," said Enzo knocking back his strong coffee in one gulp. He shook his head. "I think I need another of those. Your visit is certainly a bit of a shock."

"Shock seems to be the word of the moment for everyone," replied Clarissa. "I was shocked to learn that you were my father and not a man called Mike, whose name is on my birth certificate. My parents and the rest of my family were also shocked to be told about *you*, and Juliet was more than shocked when I said I was going to try and find you. So, it's been shocks all round."

Enzo gave her an amused glance, crinkling up his eyes and producing a wonderful smile that illuminated his handsome face. In that moment, Clarissa could clearly see why Juliet loved him so much. Even at eighty he was incredibly charismatic. His once black hair, now grey, was still thick and curly with an unruly corkscrew curl hanging over one eye, and his expressive eyes were still dark blue and intense. For a man of his age, he was very sexy, thought Clarissa, and she could imagine most women found him exciting.

While Enzo went into the house to make more coffee, Clarissa reflected how attractive Matteo was and decided that as young men, Enzo and Matteo together must have provided dynamic and irresistible pulling power. I bet they never had to go out chasing girls, thought Clarissa with amusement. They probably just waited for the girls to come to them.

When Enzo returned with a metal cafetière of fresh coffee and slices of the Italian Easter cake *Colomba di Pasqua,* along with plates and knives, he said: "*Giulietta* sat exactly where you are sitting now when I brought her to visit my grandmother all those years ago. The lemon trees have grown a bit since then and of course, *Nonna* has passed on bless her soul, but otherwise it is the same."

He sat quietly, remembering a time long ago when a beautiful young English girl with silvery green eyes and a waterfall of long red hair had totally bewitched him. Pulling himself back to the present, he contemplated the daughter he hadn't known existed until a few hours ago. "You don't have her red hair; you are dark like I used to be."

"Juliet's hair is grey now, like yours," said Clarissa, "and my hair has grey streaks already. Let's face it, I'm in my fifties."

Enzo grunted. "It just doesn't seem possible that I have a daughter who is fifty. But you are very charming, *cara,* and you have such beautiful dark blue eyes. You are very pretty."

That's the innate flirting that Juliet had warned her all Italian men did without realising it. Clarissa stifled a smile as she said emphatically, "I have *your* beautiful dark blue eyes!"

Sighing Enzo said: "It's all very long ago and many, many years have been wasted. Life is so short; I need to make up for lost time." He sipped his Limoncello. "Tell me about her. I want to know everything. Matteo says you have photographs. And what about you? Are you married? Do you have children? Am I a *nonno* – a grandfather?"

There were so many questions as father and daughter settled down in the bright Italian sunshine to share with each other their lives over the past half a century.

Chapter Ten

"A picture is worth a thousand words."
Henrik Ibsen, Norwegian playwright (1906)

ALTHOUGH SHE was overcome with curiosity about the man who had fathered her, Clarissa offered to start the conversation. Enzo was so obviously incredibly anxious to hear about Juliet, that she felt it was only fair.

Scrolling through her phone she pulled up the recent pictures of her birth mother and handed the mobile over to Enzo. She also gave him the black and white photograph of Juliet aged twenty.

Clarissa was touched to see tears in his eyes as he gazed down at the face of the woman he had loved and not seen for fifty years. He was silent for several minutes before looking over at Clarissa and saying softly: "She is still very beautiful. Her hair might be grey but her eyes are just as I remember them."

Going back to study the pictures, Enzo murmured: "I wanted to marry her and I waited for her but she didn't come back. I blame myself. I should never have let her go to England without me. I'm sure we could have sorted out any worries she had. It's been a lifetime of not knowing why she didn't return. She wrote me a letter, but I didn't understand it; it made no sense to me. I would never have left her for anyone else. She was my soulmate. There was never going to be anyone else for me. Despite all my singing commitments, I should have gone to England to find her."

Holding up the old black and white photograph he said: "This is exactly as I remember her. Would you mind too much if I kept it?" Clarissa nodded silently and Enzo carefully tucked the photo into his shirt pocket.

Clarissa felt tears pricking her eyelids. She knew Juliet still loved Enzo and now it seemed that he felt the same about her. A cloak of sadness enveloped her. All those wasted years. Drawing a deep breath she continued imparting the information he so desperately wanted.

Enzo listened intently while Clarissa told him the story of Juliet's life after leaving him and Capri. She explained about the situation with Mike and how Juliet didn't know for sure who had fathered her baby, resulting in Clarissa being adopted. She then spoke about Juliet's long marriage to Ted, telling him that they had three children, all now grown-up with children of their own.

"Ted died of a heart attack, and it is only recently that Juliet told me about you," said Clarissa. "Until then I thought Mike was my father because his name was on my birth certificate."

Clarissa looked at Enzo who had put his elbows on the table, head in hands, almost as if in despair. "It was when she told me about you that I decided I needed to track you down." Enzo shifted his arms off the table and leaned back in his chair. "Thank goodness you did," he said simply.

He looked very nervous as he asked: "Do you think she'll want to see me?" When Clarissa nodded and said: "I'm absolutely sure she will be delighted to see you," he gave her a devastating smile of sheer pleasure. Gosh, she thought, he still has the movie star smile Juliet told me about.

She gave him a moment for reflection before saying: "But now, you must tell me your story."

His face was serious. "So, I was married as well – three times." Clarissa regarded him with surprise. "Three times?"

"Mmm. Two were American and one Dutch. Each was a disaster. It was my mistake, I guess. I was looking for something

I was never going to find. Another *Giulietta*. All three marriages ended in disappointment."

"That is so sad," said Clarissa. "I'm truly sorry. So, you are not married now?"

"No. Not for many years. After the third marriage I accepted that I was never going to find anyone else who was remotely like *Giulietta*." He sighed. "I can't change what has happened, but I am hoping that I can now meet *Giulietta* again and make up for lost time."

Enzo told Clarissa he had spent more than fifty years singing and playing his guitar, travelling around America and Europe. "I was always on the cusp of breaking into stardom but didn't really make it, except maybe in Italy. Elsewhere I was only mildly famous, never a big name. I did cut a few records over the years which were moderately successful, and I kept myself in the spotlight by touring and doing gigs. He gave his engaging smile. "Being in the music business has been a good life though, enjoyable and quite lucrative.

"When *Nonna* died – oh, many years ago now – I kept this house as my base. Now I am sort of retired although I still play gigs and do the occasional tour, but only in Italy. All that constant travelling takes its toll, and I am too old to do it now. A musician's life on the road is not compatible with old age." He laughed roguishly as he added: "All those young groupies are *so* exhausting." I bet they are, thought Clarissa, recalling Isabella's blushing face. I'm sure he has no trouble at all pulling women whatever their age.

Giving Clarissa the mischievous smile that had so captivated Juliet, Enzo said: "That's not to say I wouldn't happily travel to England if *Giulietta* agreed to see me."

He may be eighty, thought Clarissa, but he certainly doesn't look it. Despite his dissolute lifestyle, the years have been kind to him.

Clarissa explained that Juliet now lived with her lifelong friend June.

"Ah, the friend she wanted to show the mini dress to," interjected Enzo. "Mini dress?" queried Clarissa. Enzo laughed. "Oh, while she was with me on Capri, I bought *Giulietta* two dresses. One she liked so much she took it back to England with her to show June. The other she left with me together with a couple of other things. I still have them."

"Goodness, that's amazing, what an extraordinary memory you have."

"I remember everything I did with *Giulietta*." In the face of such devotion Clarissa was lost for words. He still really loves her, she thought in wonder watching him blinking back tears. Hoping to lighten the mood, Clarissa continued telling him about Juliet.

"Well, both Juliet and June are widows now. They bought a seafront flat together in Hove after their husbands died. Their flat doesn't have a guest room but if you want to come to England you could always stay with me. I don't live too far away from Juliet, and I'm married to Tony, he's an architect and we have two children – two girls, grown-up now – so yes, you are a grandfather."

Enzo gave a huge sigh. "Of course, I would love to meet your family – my family now – and get to know you all properly. But you know, *cara,* I think I would prefer to take a room in a hotel. There are hotels in… did you say Hove, *no?* Because I have a feeling *Giulietta,* and I may need some privacy."

There was a slight blush under his tan as Clarissa watched the years fall away from him. He looked like a young man again, incredibly handsome and with a very sexy twinkle in his eye.

Chapter Eleven

*"Sometimes you have to let go of the picture
you thought life would be like,
and learn to find joy in the story you're living"*

Anon

ENZO SUGGESTED they went to a local restaurant to eat a late lunch. "You really don't want to try my cooking," he said.

"I do have a housekeeper, Maria, a local lady who comes in each morning and puts the house to rights, picking up empty wine bottles off the floor, doing the washing and any shopping I might need, that sort of thing…of course, you met her when you came on Tuesday." With a teasing smile he added: "She was *very* suspicious of you! She is extremely protective, especially when an unknown woman knocks on the door asking for me."

"Does that happen often?" Clarissa asked with interest. He grimaced. "It has been known over the years." Clarissa smiled. "In *Fifty Shades of Grey,* Christian Grey makes women sign a non-disclosure agreement before he sleeps with them. Maybe you should have done the same."

"Maybe," agreed Enzo, amused. "But that never occurred to me at the time. In the…um…heat of the moment, I never thought of whipping out paper and pen!" Feeling slightly embarrassed, Clarissa gave a flustered smile. "Mmm, I see what you mean." Recovering her composure, she asked: "So, where is Maria now?"

"Oh, Maria's not here on a Friday. And as I wasn't quite sure who you were until Matteo phoned this morning, I didn't ask her to prepare anything. I didn't know you would be staying long enough to eat lunch."

"Oh, I'm sorry," said Clarissa.

"No problem. I am delighted you showed up and"…he stopped mid-sentence, tapping a finger on her Cartier watch. "You really shouldn't be wearing this while you're walking around the city." She looked at him, her brow furrowed in surprise, and he added: "You should wear a cheap watch while you're travelling. This is inviting trouble." He smiled: "I have a rather nice Rolex which I gave myself as a present when I made my first record. But I never wear it when I'm *in viaggio*. I always wear an imitation on my travels just in case it gets lost."

Clarissa nodded, remembering her feeling of concern as she was walking back from the pizzeria with Aldo. "Yes. I realised that the other night. I'll leave it at home another time."

Enzo took her hand. "That's my first piece of fatherly advice to you. Not worth the risk to have an expensive watch while you're travelling, although it is beautiful and you must enjoy wearing it."

★★★

Enzo's reference to making his first record reminded Clarissa about the lack of information about him on the internet. She mentioned how difficult it had been to track him down and he gave an inscrutable smile. "Mmm. I've been told this before."

He paused, as if unsure how much to say, before adding: "I rather think that was down to Lorenzo Russo, who was my manager in the early days before Elsa Garcia." Enzo gazed into the distance for a few moments, gathering his thoughts.

"It started with girls throwing their underwear onto the stage while I was singing in Las Vegas," he said slowly. "I was by no means the headliner, just a support act, and getting so much attention didn't go down well in some quarters, especially as there were tentative comparisons to Elvis. It seems very amusing now thinking back, but actually at the time it caused a lot of trouble.

"There was a good deal of adverse publicity in the papers about this unknown Italian singer being too sexy and leading young girls astray. Elvis had been accused of 'crimes of lust and perversion' and Lorenzo was seriously worried that I might be blamed for something similar." He stopped, smiling at the memory. "All the exposure ultimately made it easier for women to track me down. At first I didn't mind," he said with endearing honesty. "I was flattered by all the attention, and it provided me with a constant stream of girls to… um…hook up with. But eventually it just got too much. There were girls throwing knickers and bras with telephone numbers attached onto the stage every night, not only in Las Vegas but elsewhere too; and I used to get some very pornographic stuff in the post."

Locking his dark blue eyes onto hers he said earnestly: "Honestly, *cara*, I wasn't deliberately trying to be sexy. I was just singing and being *me.*" Clarissa smiled. He was just the same now, half a century later, still sexy without trying.

Enzo frowned. "I became seriously worried that all the fuss would ruin my career. Then, Lorenzo stepped in and sorted it out. I have absolutely no idea what he did or how he did it. He had been in the business for a very long time and had contacts all over the place. I never asked for details and he never mentioned it – but suddenly the flow of information about me in the papers stopped. There was the occasional story in the music press when I cut a record, but that was all. I have been told that as a result there is very little nowadays on the internet."

He smiled. "And that suits me just fine. I never wanted to be famous to the point where I couldn't go anywhere or do anything. Look what happened to Elvis, it ruined his life. "I just wanted to sing…to perform. I kept my name in the public eye by doing

American and European tours and gigs and, frankly, it's been enough. It has given me everything I wanted.

"I have always spent my summers singing at Bar Russe on Capri while living with Matteo's family or here with *Nonna*. When I met *Giulietta* I was renting an apartment on Capri for the season which gave me…us…more privacy. The rest of the year I toured. It is only very recently that I have felt retirement creeping up. I would hate to stop singing altogether but I am becoming very fussy about what I do."

Enzo explained that he had just spoken to Elsa about not touring anymore, but she had said that there was talk about reissuing his first record *Canzoni d'amore* along with some newer material, so he might have to continue for just a bit longer.

"She says those love ballads are becoming popular with a whole new generation of fans, so…" he shrugged. "If *Giulietta* and I can pick up our relationship, I don't think I care that much about touring, even if a new album does need promoting. I'll just stick to gigs. I've had my career, now I want happiness."

Chapter Twelve

"The path of true love never did run smooth."
William Shakespeare, A Midsummer Night's Dream
(Act I:i)

RETURNING TO the question of lunch Enzo said: "Let's go and eat. The restaurant is run by friends of mine, Giovanni and Elena, and they will be utterly astonished to find out who my charming companion is. I hope you like seafood, it's their speciality."

"Absolutely love it," said Clarissa.

The restaurant was only a short walk away and after being introduced to Giovanni and Elena, who were surprised and delighted to meet Clarissa, father and daughter continued to chat over an extraordinarily good dish of spaghetti with shrimps and scallops washed down with glasses of Chianti. "This is the only wine Juliet drinks," Clarissa told him. "She said she first had it at Bar Russe and has drunk it ever since." Enzo looked pleased. "It is so good to know she hasn't forgotten her time on Capri."

"Forgotten it? She relives it every day. She also listens to *Can't Help Falling in Love* all the time." Clarissa saw the sadness in his eyes. "That was our special song," was all he said.

"There's something I need to ask you," said Clarissa, when they had finished their meal and Enzo was urging her to try a glass of Grappa saying: "It is very good for the digestion."

Enzo looked deeply into Clarissa's eyes. "Why do I feel nervous at the prospect of this question?" Dark blue eyes stared intently into dark blue eyes as they regarded each other unsmilingly. The atmosphere suddenly felt heavy. "Well?" asked Enzo at last. Clarissa took a deep breath and plunged in. "Do you have any children? As well as me, I mean?"

He looked at her thoughtfully as if wondering how to answer. Then, sliding his eyes away from hers, he said slightly evasively: "I don't really know."

Clarissa was astounded. She was prepared for almost anything but not 'I don't know.' Looking her birth father squarely in the face she said firmly: "I'm sorry, but that's ridiculous. You must know." Enzo looked at her through narrowed eyes. "Well, I didn't know about *you*, did I?"

"But that's a bit different, don't you think? You've been married three times. Were there any children from those marriages? It's a simple question."

Enzo regarded her unsmilingly. "I didn't want them."

"You didn't want children?"

"No."

"What did your wives think of that?"

Enzo gave a wry smile. "We weren't together long enough for it to be a real issue."

"They were short marriages?"

"They were. Very short really, but as all the women received money, they weren't unhappy. They would have been far more unhappy staying with me and discovering I didn't love them."

Clarissa was intrigued. What did he mean? But she couldn't be sidetracked and fall down a rabbit hole. She went back to her relentless questioning. "So, what would have happened if Juliet had gone back to you on Capri and said she was pregnant. Would you have welcomed her – and me, as it happens?"

Enzo looked miserable. He leaned across the table and took her hand. "Clarissa, I really can't say how I would have reacted. At that time in my life my singing career was flourishing, and it was very important to me. I have to admit it would have been difficult to do all the travelling I had to do with a baby in tow. Although I loved *Giulietta* very much and I wanted to marry her, I don't know how I would have felt if she became pregnant. I would have been so happy to have *Giulietta* with me; but *Giulietta* and a baby, I…I just don't know."

Juliet had told Clarissa that Enzo was always very honest. "He never says anything he doesn't mean. He never pretends." Clarissa now appreciated that honesty. It would have been so easy for him to say that he would have welcomed a pregnant Juliet with open arms.

They sat in silence for a few minutes, unsure what to say to each other. Clarissa recalled that when Juliet had told June about her pregnancy, she had predicted that Enzo wouldn't hang around once he knew Juliet was expecting a baby. "You won't see him for dust," June had declared. "I don't see the playboy of the western world as a father."

Clarissa knew that June was pretty astute, and, in this instance, it would seem she was probably right. So, in a way it was a blessing that Juliet hadn't gone back to Capri. She would have been devastated if Enzo had turned his back on her because she was going to have his child.

Clarissa gathered her thoughts. She wasn't going to let him off that easily. "Right," she said crisply. "So back in those days, you didn't want to be a father and none of your wives had your children. But what about the girls you had sex with who you weren't married to? Those girls you 'hooked up' with? I imagine there were hundreds of them over the years." Enzo winced. This direct and outspoken woman was so like him that she had to be his daughter. His only child, as far as he was concerned.

"So?" Clarissa was insistent. "Did you father any children with women you weren't married to?"

"Oof! You're not giving me an easy time, are you? he said frowning.

"Nope! I really need to know. And Juliet is sure to ask."

Enzo gave a brief smile. Taking a deep breath he said: "There were women I had sex with, yes, usually only one-night stands while I was touring, although there were a few slightly longer affairs. I'm not sure there were *hundreds*." Seeing her eyes fixed on him he gave a shrug and a little grin and said: "Well, okay, maybe hundreds." Clarissa looked at him. "So many women…how can you be sure there were no babies?"

He sat silently for a moment before saying: "It is true that women did turn up out of the blue claiming I had made them pregnant, but that was a fairly typical occurrence for guys like me in the music business. It happened a lot. Still does occasionally, although today there is DNA testing, so they have to be pretty sure before they point the finger.

"I never believed I had fathered a child because I was," he paused, "I still am, very careful. Careful to the point of obsession, actually. I've always known that the consequence of a moment of recklessness will be years of regret."

"Regret," said Clarissa sharply. "So do you regret me?"

They stared at each other for a long moment, a touch of almost palpable hostility hanging between them, before Enzo said: "Oh no, absolutely not. I am delighted to discover that my beautiful *Giulietta* has given me such an outspoken daughter. Are you always like this? What does your husband – *Antonio*, is it? – think of your spirited attitude?"

"Well, his name is Anthony, so yes, *Antonio* in Italian, but we call him Tony. Tony Price." Enzo looked confused. "Tony Price? But you are his wife, and you are called Clarissa Phillips."

"Well," said Clarissa smiling, "that is all part of being a feisty feminist. When Tony and I married I planned to use the name Clarissa Phillips-Price, but frankly it was all too much of a mouthful, so I decided to stay as Clarissa Phillips. I was at university at the time, so not changing my name made things a lot easier for everyone.

"However, the girls have Tony's name, so they are both Price. Tony is well used to me being feisty, and the girls take after me, actually, so you have two feisty feminist granddaughters as well!"

"And their names?"

"Amy and Charlotte. They are both in their twenties and have chosen careers instead of husbands. Amy is an actress and Charlotte a nurse. Interestingly Amy has inherited Juliet's red hair."

"Ah," said Enzo giving his engaging smile.

Clarissa added: "Juliet was so certain that I was your child and therefore half Italian that she called me Vittoria, the Italian version of the classic English Victoria. It was my adoptive parents who renamed me Clarissa." Enzo just said simply: "Vittoria. That is a lovely name. I like it."

Clarissa stared at him calmly. "And do we need to do a DNA test so you can be totally sure I am your daughter?" Enzo threw back his head and roared with laughter. "How can I possibly doubt that you're my daughter. You are a mixture of both me and *Giulietta* in one perfect person." He went around the table and standing behind her chair, put his hands on her shoulders, dropping a kiss on the top of her head. "No test needed, Clarissa, you are definitely my daughter. I don't know if your mother has told you, but you were conceived in love."

As Clarissa caught her breath in astonishment, Enzo added softly: "Every time *Giulietta* and I had sex together it was an act of complete love so yes, I can truthfully say without any doubt that you were conceived in love."

Clarissa looked at him speechlessly thinking, oh my goodness, now *I'm* going to cry. She thought of Mike and remembered hoping that she hadn't been conceived as a result of rape. And now, here was Enzo telling her that she had been conceived in love. Surely that was what every adopted child wanted to hear. Standing up she instinctively put her arms around him in a grateful and affectionate hug. "Thank you."

They stood together silently holding each other tightly, relishing their first father-daughter embrace. Kissing her cheek Enzo said: "No, thank *you*, Clarissa. Thank you for finding me."

Silence fell between them once again. Eventually Clarissa, swallowing hard and blinking back tears, said briskly: "Well, enough emotional talk about the past. We really should discuss what is going to happen now."

Enzo sat back down in his chair. "Does *Giulietta* know you've found me?"

"I'll ring her tonight. Do you want to speak to her?"

He considered. "No," he said slowly. "I don't want our first contact after fifty years to be over the telephone. I want to see her, look into her eyes and hold her in my arms when I talk to her."

The romantic Italian again, thought Clarissa. He was extraordinary. No wonder Juliet fell for him. "So, what will you do?"

"When are you going home?"

"Tomorrow. I must book a ticket back. I left the return date open because I wasn't sure how long it would take to track you down."

"May I travel to England with you? I really need to see *Giulietta* as quickly as possible now. Do you think it will be too much of a shock for her if I just turn up without warning?"

"You don't want her to know you're coming back with me?"

He shook his head and Clarissa chewed her fingernail thoughtfully, weighing up the pros and cons. "It will certainly be a shock, but I think a good one."

They sat in silence for a while before Clarissa said: "Okay, I'll go back to my bed and breakfast place and ring Juliet to put her in the picture but not tell her you're coming back with me. Then I'll book tickets for both of us on the earliest flight out we can get tomorrow. We can find an hotel for you when we arrive home."

Enzo nodded. "Yes, we'll do that. Now, I'll ask Gio to call you a taxi back to where you're staying and then you can telephone to let me know what time to meet you at the airport tomorrow. What is the address?"

Clarissa handed him the piece of paper she had given to the taxi driver who had picked her up from the railway station. Would she get the same reaction, she wondered. She did. Enzo looked horrified. "But this is in the red-light district!"

Clarissa laughed, telling him that the cab driver hadn't wanted to take her there and the efforts he had made to ensure she was not at risk. "It's perfectly safe," she said. "I'm not planning to go out again once I'm back, so I'm sure I'll be okay for one more night."

Enzo shook his head. "You must stay here with me. I can't possibly let my daughter go and stay in such a bad area of *Napoli.*"

Clarissa insisted that she was perfectly capable of looking after herself, pointing out that she'd already spent a few days there without mishap. Her confident assertion that she was alright would have been easily accepted by Tony, but it cut no ice with Enzo. He was adamant she could not go back. Being Neapolitan born and bred, he knew about the city's red-light district. It could be dangerous, especially for a woman who looked like Clarissa.

"You will stay here," he said forcefully. "I will telephone Maria and she will come over and organise a bed and some sleeping clothes for you. Tomorrow on the way to the airport we will stop off and collect your luggage."

Clarissa was about to disagree, but looking at the uncompromising expression on Enzo's face, dark blue eyes now almost black, brows drawn together, jaw set, she stopped, realising that argument was fruitless; somehow, Enzo had taken control.

Clarissa thought she rather liked Enzo ordering her about and taking care of her. It was a curious feeling for a strong feminist who had always pursued her own path, but she felt… what was the word? … *cherished*.

She remembered Juliet telling her how excited she had been by Enzo's overwhelming protectiveness and self-assurance. Clarissa now understood what she meant. It was making her feel like a Jane Austen heroine and a bit weak at the knees. She knew just how Elizabeth Bennet had eventually felt about being looked after by Darcy.

Better not tell Tony, it might give him ideas and Clarissa was certain she didn't want such dependence to be an everyday state of affairs. Nice occasionally though, she thought looking at Enzo. He really was an amazing man. How extraordinary to think he was her birth father.

Chapter Thirteen

"Stardom isn't a profession; it's an accident."
Lauren Bacall, American actress (1924-2014)

WHILE CLARISSA rang the airport to arrange their journey to Gatwick for the following day, Enzo first of all rang Matteo to update him on what was happening, and then Maria, asking her to come over and get a bed and some nightclothes ready for Clarissa.

Enzo was prepared for his housekeeper to be a bit shirty when he told her Clarissa was his daughter; Maria was excessively solicitous and quite outspoken. However, any negative thoughts she might have had she kept to herself, arriving promptly to efficiently make up a bed and find Clarissa a nightdress and some toiletries. She also brought with her a home-made lasagna, some fresh bread and a bowl of salad. "I thought you might need something for supper as you've got a guest."

"Thank you," said Enzo gratefully. How fortunate he was to have Maria looking after him. She really was a treasure, despite her occasional interference and, of course, the gossiping. Enzo was well aware that Maria's grapevine would soon ensure that the fact he had a daughter would be common knowledge throughout *Napoli,* but he was resigned to that. Everyone had to know sooner or later.

Finally, Enzo telephoned Luigi at the bed and breakfast, firmly stating that his daughter would not be staying there that night, and they would call in the following day to pick up her belongings.

He was very authoritative, speaking rapidly in Neapolitan dialect. Luigi, suddenly realising who Enzo was, assured him that the English lady had paid in advance so there was no outstanding debt. He had no problem with them coming over first thing in the morning when he would have her luggage ready for them to pick up, and he hoped they would both stay and take *caffè* with him.

Clarissa arranged three tickets for the eleven o'clock flight. The extra seat was for Enzo's guitar: "It's a Gibson and valuable, I can't risk it going into the hold."

Afterwards she telephoned Juliet to tell her she had found Enzo in Naples. He was fit and well and longing to come to see her as soon as possible. Juliet, completely overcome, burst into tears and after a few moments June took over the call. "She'll be alright," June assured an anxious Clarissa. "Don't worry. It's just the shock. It's what she's wanted for so long, but never thought could possibly happen. A bit like when she first heard from you."

"When are you coming back? Tomorrow? What time will you arrive at Gatwick, shall I come and pick you up?" Clarissa said she expected to land about two o'clock in the afternoon and didn't need a lift from the airport. "Tony was coming, but he now has a work meeting, so one of the girls will meet me and drive over to you so I can tell Juliet everything. We should be with you before four, traffic permitting."

Juliet came back on the phone to apologise for her loss of composure. "I am so grateful to you Clarissa. Finding Enzo couldn't have happened without you." She was still crying but assured Clarissa they were 'happy tears'.

"I am really delighted I could do it for you, Juliet. I'll see you tomorrow afternoon and we'll catch up then."

"Do you have a photograph of him you can bring with you?" Juliet asked eagerly. "Oh yes, absolutely, it will be just like seeing him in person," Clarissa assured her blithely. "Lots of love," and she quickly rang off before Juliet could question her further.

"I didn't tell June you were coming back with me," she said to Enzo when she reported the conversation. "I really don't trust her not to tell Juliet. They tell each other absolutely everything, they always have done since they were girls."

"Everything?" queried Enzo. Clarissa giggled at the look of dismay that fluttered across his face. "Oh yes, everything! June is sure to know about every moment you spent on Capri with Juliet."

Enzo gave her a searching look, not quite certain whether she was teasing him. Her face was impassive as she watched his slight embarrassment. "I don't know what you and Juliet got up to in the sixties Enzo de Martins, but the past is catching up with you," she said laughing. Enzo just proffered the enigmatic smile he always gave when he was discomforted.

★★★

After supper, when Maria had gone home and all the arrangements for the journey back to England had been made, Enzo and Clarissa sat in the garden watching the fading orange sun sink into the horizon. Sitting with his feet propped up on a garden chair, Enzo was casually strumming his guitar, humming softly to himself.

"Will you sing for me?" asked Clarissa. He looked at her steadily for a moment or two before asking: "What would you like me to sing?"

"Oh, I don't know. How about *Can't Help Falling in Love*? Juliet is always listening to that."

"Ah…maybe not that one. It's a bit special to *Giulietta* and me, but I will sing you something else." He considered for a moment and then sang *Moon River*, from *Breakfast at Tiffany's*, one of Clarissa's favourite films, then the Buddy Holly song *True Love Ways*, finishing with a song by the Italian group I Pooh, *C'e bisogno di un piccolo aiuto*.

Clarissa was enthralled; she knew he had to be good to have been successful for so many decades, but she wasn't prepared for just how remarkable his voice was. "Wow!" she said. "You're incredible…that was…just amazing."

"Thank you, *cara*," said Enzo with an amused smile. "I'm sorry," said Clarissa. "I'm sort of lost for the right words; you really do have a wonderful voice." Enzo leaned across and squeezed her hand. "I'm so pleased you enjoyed it."

"I really liked the one you sang in Italian," said Clarissa. "Ah, yes," agreed Enzo. "That's just one of the many beautiful songs by the amazing group I Pooh. The title of the song means 'A little help is needed' and it seems very appropriate for the situation I find myself in. Without a little help from you I would not be going to see *Giulietta* again. So I sang that especially for you!"

They sat in companionable silence before Clarissa asked hesitantly: "May I ask you something which is absolutely nothing to do with me?"

"Of course, *cara*, I am your father, and you are my daughter. You can ask me anything."

"What did you mean when you said your ex-wives would have been far more unhappy staying with you and discovering you didn't love them?"

Enzo sat silently for a while sipping his Grappa, before saying quietly: "After each marriage I soon realised that I had made a mistake. I tried incredibly hard to conceal my feelings, but it was not easy. I know it is said there is no such thing as a mistake, there are just things you do and things you don't do." Clarissa suddenly remembered Colin saying those same words to her in Brighton. Oblivious of her thoughts, Enzo added: "These marriages, however, were definitely mistakes.

"Although I honestly believe that none of the three women realised I didn't love them…had never loved them…they left me because I was rarely at home. As soon as I knew I had made a mistake, I went off touring and wouldn't take them with me; I suppose technically, it was desertion.

"Every time, I was hoping I'd found someone who would make me feel like *Giulietta* had, but none of them did. It took three failed marriages to learn that no one could take *Giulietta's* place in my life. And how could they – what we had together was unique."

He sighed. "If they had stayed with me, these women would have quickly understood that I didn't love them. But they were not unhappy because even though they left me, I paid each of them a sum of money when the marriages ended. Guilt money, I suppose.

"Each marriage lasted only a matter of months and actually, I doubt they really loved me either. Loved the *idea* of me perhaps, but not *me*. They fell in love with stardom and celebrity but then discovered reality was something completely different."

He smiled ruefully: "Three marriages. I am not a fast learner." Clarissa patted his arm. "Thank you for being so honest. I'm sure you will be happy again when you are back with Juliet."

"Oh yes," agreed Enzo softly. "I will."

★★★

Stopping off to collect Clarissa's bag from Luigi the following morning, Enzo shook his head, dismayed that his daughter had stayed in such an unsuitable place. Clarissa smiled as Enzo said in a baffled voice: "But why here, *cara*? There are plenty of excellent hotels in *Napoli*."

After entering the quadrangle through the security doors, they crossed the cobbles, now thankfully empty of children, and stepped gingerly into the ancient lift which once again slowly creaked its way to the upper floor. "For goodness' sake," said Enzo crossly, "this contraption is dangerous." Halfway up, both he and

Clarissa were overcome by a fit of giggles at the ridiculous swaying cage, only composing themselves with difficulty as they arrived at the top where Luigi was waiting for them with Clarissa's bag.

Luigi's wife, two teenage daughters, their over-excited *Nonna*, and a couple of neighbours had also gathered to greet Enzo as he and Clarissa arrived at the apartment. The family was obviously extremely proud that the daughter of the well-known Neapolitan singer had been their guest. They were even more thrilled that Enzo had turned up to collect her luggage.

Nonna was particularly elated. She had idolised Enzo for years and was still a devoted fan. In her younger days she had travelled to gigs in *Napoli, Capri, Roma* and even further afield to hear him sing. Now she was totally overcome by suddenly being so close to him. Enzo, immediately summing up the situation, gave the elderly woman a gentle cuddle and a kiss on the cheek when they were introduced. Overwhelmed, *Nonna* could only stare at him in speechless amazement.

As Clarissa handed back her keys, Luigi was embarrassingly obsequious, offering her every good wish, not only for her journey home but for the rest of her life. He then took Enzo's hand, enthusiastically pumping it up and down before throwing his arms around him and giving him a hug.

Having posed for selfies and given another kiss to *Nonna*, who produced an original copy of his record *Canzoni d'amore* for him to sign, Enzo refused the offer of refreshments. "We'd really love to but sadly, we have a plane to catch so we don't have enough time." He eventually managed to say a final, very firm *"Ciao-Ciao"* before he and Clarissa made their way back down to the street. Clarissa was in a daze, wondering if this was the kind of rapturous reception Enzo received everywhere. When she asked him, he gave a low chuckle and said: "No, not always, but I was quite assertive when I spoke to Luigi on the phone. A little fame can be useful sometimes."

"It was brilliant to see a copy of your first record," said Clarissa, "with a great picture of you looking very young on the sleeve."

"That record is probably about the same age as you," replied Enzo. "If they do decide to do a reissue, it won't be on vinyl. The days of producing LPs are long gone. Should we tell Luigi's *Nonna* it would be a good time to sell her original and now signed copy, do you think?" Clarissa laughed. The more she knew him, the better she liked him. And once again she had that warm, fuzzy childhood feeling of being looked after and protected. Nothing bad could happen to her while she was with him.

They were sitting in the departure lounge at Naples airport when Clarissa noticed Enzo's watch. "Surely that's not the fake Rolex?" she asked mischievously. "What was it you said about not wearing an expensive watch while travelling?"

"Huh!" said Enzo, his eyes sparkling. "This is a special occasion, so I break the rule."

★★★

They arrived at Gatwick after an uneventful journey. Well, thought Clarissa, uneventful if you don't include the flutter Enzo caused among the flight attendants who kept coming up to ensure he had everything he needed and to check his guitar was still safely strapped in.

Even those blasé passengers who did a regular commute between Naples and London became caught up in the excitement of having a 'celebrity' on board, with one elegant middle-aged woman coming up to ask for an autograph. "For my niece," she said blushing. Enzo was his usual charming self. "Of course." Catching Clarissa's amused glance, he merely shrugged and gave his sexy smile.

★★★

Once through customs, Clarissa saw Amy waving behind the barrier and went across to hug her. "Hello darling, so kind of you to meet us." She turned to Enzo: "May I introduce my daughter Amy…Amy, this is your grandfather Enzo de Martins."

What a gorgeous man, thought Amy; there is no way he looks like a grandfather. What grandfather travels with a guitar strapped to his back.

Taking her outstretched hand and turning it over, Enzo pressed his lips into her palm and gazed deeply into her eyes, saying with a dazzling smile: "I am so very pleased to meet you… Amy. Thank you for coming to pick us up." Continuing to stare at her he added softly: "So, you have *Giulietta's* red hair. You look as if you have stepped out of a Rossetti picture; he painted beautiful women with long red hair."

Blushing, Amy shivered and felt her heart do a most uncharacteristic flip. Holy shit! She was totally lost for words. Nobody had ever kissed her hand like that before, and that voice…not to mention the reference to Rossetti! She was totally thrown off balance, feeling strangely unsettled. Thank goodness she was an actress and managed to hold it together, otherwise she might have thrown herself into his arms and disgraced herself completely.

"Well, the car is over there," she said breathlessly, gathering together her tattered dignity as she led the way out of the arrivals' hall.

"Where are we going?" Amy asked once they were on the motorway, "home or to Hove?"

"I think Hove," said Clarissa. Sitting in the front passenger seat she turned to look at Enzo enquiringly. "Enzo is anxious to see Juliet as soon as possible."

Enzo nodded: "Yes, please *cara*."

"Are they expecting you?"

"No," said Clarissa. "Enzo wants it to be a surprise for Juliet." Amy was shocked. "A *surprise*? Well, it certainly will be that!"

She watched Enzo in her rear-view mirror, sprawled out on

the back seat, an arm round his guitar. Wearing dark glasses, an ancient black leather jacket and with just a hint of stubble, he looked like an ageing rock star. They had offered him the front seat next to Amy, but he said he'd be fine in the back. "I expect you two have things to talk about."

Just as well thought Amy, there was no way she could have driven calmly down to the coast with him in such close proximity, subtle wafts of his cologne giving her iniquitous thoughts. He was so incredibly attractive that she had to keep reminding herself that he was her grandfather. It wasn't only the way he looked, although his wild grey curls and dark blue eyes were stunning, but also his sexy voice and just the way he *was*. His aura.

For someone who considered herself uncompromisingly feminist, Amy was finding it difficult to come to terms with her involuntary reaction to having her hand kissed. Just thinking about it made her feel hot and bothered. It was absurd.

Chapter Fourteen

"Journeys end in lovers' meeting."
William Shakespeare, 'Twelfth Night' (Act II:iii)

AS JUNE gave Clarissa a hug, she saw the man standing behind her on the doorstep and immediately knew who he was. Although they had never met, June had heard about him endlessly over the years and recognised Enzo straight away.

Having had relationships with a lot of desirable men throughout her life, June could tell just by looking at him that he was a good kisser and good in bed. Despite his age he was incredibly attractive. Wow! Lucky Juliet.

The man was looking slightly diffident as if unsure of his welcome. "Oh, now," said Clarissa wriggling out of June's embrace, "this is my birth father Enzo de Martins. He insisted on coming with me as a surprise for Juliet…and you know Amy, she picked us up from Gatwick."

"Of course," said June as Amy slid deftly past her mother and into the hall. "I'll just go and find Juliet," said Amy, kissing June's cheek and whisking herself away from any emotional upset that might be brewing. Personally, she thought it was madness not to warn Juliet and June that Enzo was turning up, but hey, nobody had asked for her opinion. She was just concerned about Juliet; she always seemed a bit fragile.

"Juliet's taken Florence for a quick walk," said June distractedly, unable to take her eyes off Enzo. So, this is the Italian Juliet had loved for half a century. She had seen Juliet's photographs of him of course, but they had been taken fifty years ago and she hadn't realised he would still be so heart-stoppingly handsome; much sexier than she had imagined.

Enzo strode over the doorstep and took June's outstretched hand. Instead of shaking it as she expected, he kissed it. "I am so very pleased to meet you, June. *Giulietta* told me all about you so I feel I know you already," he said in his deep, gravelly voice, eyes fixed unwaveringly on hers.

Heavens above, thought June as an unexpected tremor ran down her spine. How on earth did Juliet have the willpower to leave someone so gorgeous behind in Italy? If he's like this now, what on earth was he like back in the sixties? A forgotten girlish expression popped into her mind: Sex on legs!

Remembering her hostess duties, June pulled herself together saying, "Welcome. Come in both of you; Juliet will be back any minute." Still slightly flustered, she showed them into the sitting room with its long windows looking out over the English Channel and went to the kitchen to join Amy who had switched on the kettle for tea.

As Enzo and Clarissa sat down, there was a commotion in the passageway and a small hairy dog of indeterminate breed rushed into the room and came to a skidding halt, large brown eyes regarding Enzo balefully.

Close behind Florence was Juliet, her face flushed and long hair wind-swept after her walk along the promenade. "Sorry I wasn't here when you arrived, I was…" Seeing Enzo she stopped in her tracks, her face suddenly ashen, eyes wide with shock. Clarissa jumped up and moved towards her, worried she was going to faint. Oh my God, it was too much for her. They should never have kept this a secret.

With a little cry, Juliet rushed straight past her and threw herself sobbing into Enzo's outstretched arms. As they stood locked together, squeezing each other tightly, the spicy tang of his cologne immediately transported Juliet back to Capri. Tears were pouring down her cheeks as she buried her face in Enzo's chest. "I am so sorry," she said over and over again. "Oh Enzo, I am so very, very sorry."

There were also tears in Enzo's eyes as he stroked her hair and whispered: "Oh my God, *Giulietta*, so many years… but hush, *amore mio*, no more tears. We are together again, everything is alright now."

Florence gave a low growl, but Juliet didn't hear her. She was unaware of anything or anyone except Enzo. "It's okay Flo," said Clarissa quietly, "he's a friend." Florence gave a doubtful wag of her tail, her soulful eyes fixed on Juliet.

Hurrying back into the room, June picked up Florence and beckoned to Clarissa. "Let's leave them alone for a while. Come into the kitchen, Amy's making tea, although I think we could all do something a bit stronger than a cuppa, actually. It's only just gone four o'clock and the sun is definitely not over the yard arm, but nevertheless, I think I'm going to have an exceptionally large G & T and damn the consequences." Clarissa laughed. "Make that two, please."

★★★

"I did wait for you," said Enzo huskily, drowning in Juliet's eyes, still silvery green and still mesmerising. "I waited for you, but you didn't come; I've been crying for you in my heart all these years. I never stopped loving you."

She looked up at him in tearful amazement as he bent and kissed her, gently at first and then more demandingly as Juliet clung to him and returned his kiss with her heart on her lips. His mouth still perfectly fitted hers, she thought dizzily. It felt like coming home.

"*Ti amo tanto*," said Enzo tenderly. "I've always been yours. I was never going to leave you. Lying in bed at night I kept going over every little detail, wondering where it went wrong…what I had done wrong." Looking at him in wonder, unable to believe he was actually there with her, Juliet sobbed: "It wasn't your fault. It was me. I've never stopped loving you; I've always had this ache for you deep inside me."

She ran her fingers wonderingly over the stubble on his face and then through his hair, grey now…but still thick and curly and still with that fascinating corkscrew curl that fell over his eyes. She'd always found touching his hair very erotic. "You look absolutely amazing. I can't believe it's fifty years since we were together on Capri; you've hardly changed."

"Tanti anni fa tesoro," sighed Enzo. "So many years ago sweetheart…" He gave her a lingering kiss and almost instinctively they started murmuring the passionate Italian words they had used long ago while making love. Those words had become their own private language and now, as they whispered to each other, the years rolled away and they were once again a young couple deeply in love, totally wrapped up in their eagerness for each other.

★★★

After a while Amy tentatively tapped on the door and said: "Enzo, mum has booked you a small suite at the Brunswick just half a mile along the seafront, you can check in any time. She left your departure date open, so you can arrange that when you've decided what you're going to do."

"Thank you, Amy," said Enzo without moving his eyes from Juliet's face. "Do you fancy a night or two in a hotel, baby?" She nodded, smiling. "Yes please." He kissed her again, a long slow kiss full of promise. "I always want to make love when I kiss you."

Gazing deeply into Juliet's eyes Enzo said: "The last time I kissed you was at the airport in *Napoli* when we said goodbye as you left for England. I had no idea it would be fifty years before I would be able to kiss you again." Taking her hand he murmured:

"Let's go. I can't wait another second, it's already been far too long. I need to take you to bed, you're driving me crazy." She nodded, kissing him, still unable to believe they were together. "I want that too." They were so absorbed in each other there was no one else on their radar.

Amy, who had been loitering in the doorway, rushed off to find her mother. She was intensely embarrassed, feeling like a voyeur. It was made worse because she could see how incredibly attractive Enzo was. She still felt a ripple of excitement when she recalled how he had kissed her hand when they had met at Gatwick.

Having collected her coat and bag Clarissa popped her head around the door. "Are you two ready to go? If so, Amy will drive you to the Brunswick. She has to take me home and it's on the way. I must go back and see Tony after being away for a week, and Amy has to return to London this evening because she has an audition tomorrow morning."

Enzo looked directly into Amy's eyes: "Thank you, that is very kind. We would very much appreciate being taken to the hotel." Amy blushed again, and as she scrabbled in her bag for the car keys, Enzo touched her arm. "Please let us know how the audition goes. *Giulietta* and I wish you the very best of luck."

He hesitated and then asked: "Amy, do you play any instruments in addition to your acting?" Amy shook her head. "No, not really, well a bit. Both Lotte and I were forced to learn piano when we were children…" Clarissa chipped in: "Not *forced* sweetheart."

"…and I did play the recorder and violin at school for a short time," Amy continued, pursing her mouth and squinting at her mother. "The piano actually turned out to be quite useful because it meant I learnt to read music. But I am not really competent."

"And you didn't have to play an instrument at drama school?"

"Only singing," said Amy, "and I wasn't brilliant at that either!"

"Ah, I was wondering if you'd inherited my love of the guitar. You've got such lovely long fingers; I think you would be good at it."

"No, I've never tried guitar."

"Well, if you fancy learning, I'd be quite happy to give you a few lessons," offered Enzo. "It's not difficult. Think about it."

"Thank you, I will," said Amy. Guitar lessons with Enzo; that was quite a thought. Could be a useful skill to have, though.

"I can confirm he's a very good teacher," said Juliet smiling at Enzo. "Not that he ever taught me to play the guitar, mind you." Enzo raised his eyebrows at her and gave an amused chuckle.

Juliet turned to Clarissa. "How can I ever thank you? It's the best photograph you could have given me!" Clarissa laughed, and Enzo put his arm around Juliet's waist, saying: "No *tesoro*, how can *we* ever thank her. What our daughter has done for us is beyond anything either of us could have hoped for. It is a huge kindness that *Giulietta* I will never forget," he added, beaming at Clarissa and kissing her cheek. "The pleasure is all mine," she said sincerely. "You both deserve to be happy."

As they walked out into the hall June silently handed Juliet the small overnight bag she had packed for her. "Anything else you need you can pick up tomorrow." Juliet threw her arms around her, "I'll phone you." June patted her arm. "Go. Don't worry about anything. Florence will be fine with me, and I'll see you whenever."

Juliet suddenly noticed Enzo's guitar case propped up against a chair by the door. "You brought your guitar with you," she said with delight. He gave her a loving smile. "*Ovviamente, sì!* How can we possibly have sex without me singing *Can't Help Falling in Love* to you afterwards?"

Amy, who was just behind them, went scarlet. Fucking hell! She wouldn't expect to hear her parents talking like that, let alone old people like Juliet and Enzo.

Chapter Fifteen

*"Ageing is not lost youth but a new stage
of opportunity and strength."*
Betty Friedan, American writer and activist
(1921-2006)

THE SUITE at the Brunswick was perfect for two people who didn't want to be disturbed. On the third floor with long windows opening onto a private balcony with a view of the sea, it had a king size bed and a small sitting room with a well-stocked bar. Dropping their bags on the floor as they walked in, Enzo and Juliet made a beeline for the bedroom.

Lying on the bed with Enzo holding her so tightly she could feel his heart beating, Juliet was thrilled to discover that the pleasure of kissing him hadn't diminished over the years. The touch of his lips on hers had always excited her. "I see you haven't forgotten the art of French kissing," observed Enzo with a smile. It was one of the many skills he had taught her when they were on Capri.

Juliet wished, as she had wished all those years ago, that she could just lie in his arms with his mouth on hers for ever, but she knew as she always had, that although Enzo enjoyed kissing, like all passionate men it was for him just a stepping stone on the way to complete fulfilment.

After a while Enzo pushed himself up off the bed, and as he began to unbutton his shirt Juliet felt a moment of panic. "Darling

Enzo, I'm not a teenager anymore; I'm not the young girl you knew all those years ago. My body is full of lumps and bumps and I've got a lot of wobbly and saggy bits nowadays," she admitted shyly.

Taking off his shirt Enzo wrapped his arms around her. "You will always be nineteen to me, *Giulietta*. Whenever I look at you, I always see the girl you were when we first met. When you truly love someone, they never change in your eyes. They are always frozen in time." Giving her the long sexy look she remembered so well he said softly: "Love at first sight and the meeting of souls, remember. This is not just about two bodies coming together but the connection of souls, emotions and minds.

"*Ti amo tanto*. I have always loved you; nothing has changed. I still want every single bit of you. Remember I'm even older than you, *amore*. Age and years of touring have certainly left their mark."

Juliet gave a huge sigh of pleasure and closed her eyes, melting inside and feeling the almost forgotten surge of lust and desire as he slowly undressed her, gently kissing her as he did so. She was intoxicated by the smell of him and the feel of his breath on her body.

"*Sei bellissima, amore mio*," he murmured. "You should know how beautiful you are. This body has produced four children, it's wonderful, don't apologise for it; it is a map of your life. You are more beautiful now than you were when you were nineteen and I want you just as much, if not more, than I did fifty years ago." Juliet was overwhelmed with love for him. Heavens, what a man. He'd always made her feel cherished and desired.

"But Enzo, darling," she paused. "Also…"

"*Si, tesoro?*"

"Well… I haven't done this for a long time. Had sex, I mean. I'm a bit nervous."

Giving her an adoring look he said: "You may be surprised to learn that I haven't been with anyone for a while, so I am anxious too. Let's enjoy it and learn together."

Putting a hand each side of her face he kissed her, whispering the words he had said all those years ago when she was about to make love for the first time. "Relax *Giulietta*. Trust me, baby. There is no rush, we can take our time. Nothing is going to happen unless you want it to." As they held each other they once again began murmuring their special passionate words of love and desire.

Later, after they had joyfully discovered that making love together felt exactly the same as it had fifty years before, Enzo murmured in her ear, "It's still perfect, isn't it. There was no need to worry." They lay quietly in each other's arms, totally content with just being together again, before Enzo sat up, grabbed his guitar from the side of the bed and propped against the pillows sang *Can't Help Falling in Love,* the wonderful Elvis Presley ballad which he always sang to her after they made love. Juliet recalled hearing the busker in Brighton singing the same song, and June saying it was prophetic.

His voice was just as she remembered. After fifty years of concerts and gigs it had lost none of its deep mellowness and still thrilled her.

Putting his arms back around her, Enzo said softly: "You know *amore,* after all those years of having to be so very careful that I didn't make a girl pregnant, I can now once again relax completely when I am with you, which means our lovemaking is incredibly instinctive and spontaneous. I can't tell you how liberating that is."

They lay together in companionable silence until Enzo eventually said: "Perhaps we should get ourselves dressed and go down to the restaurant, otherwise I am going to have to make love to you again and we'll never get dinner."

After showering and dressing…June had thoughtfully packed her favourite black trousers and new lacy top…Juliet rang to book a table in the hotel restaurant.

When Enzo came out of the bathroom rubbing his hair dry with a towel, he had an indecipherable look on his face and Juliet gazed at him contemplatively. She used to be quite good at interpreting his expressions, but she was obviously out of practice.

"What is it?" she asked. "What are you thinking?" He gave her an impudent grin. "I was wondering if you remembered making love in the bath?"

"Of course I do. It was the morning after we'd had that really rough sex." He laughed, his eyes twinkling. "And that was when I knew I wanted to marry you. Anyone who could cope with sex like that without complaining was the girl for me."

"I bit the top of your thigh, and you gave me love bites," said Juliet, recalling the night when they had both been in a state of such extreme excitement that they had wantonly submitted to raw animal passion. They had both really enjoyed it but agreed it wasn't something they wanted to do too often, although Enzo had pointed out that as they hadn't actually planned to have sex like that, it was possible it could randomly happen again at any time if the mood was right. It never had.

Looking into her eyes Enzo added: "And then the next morning I nearly drowned you while we were making love in the bath." They laughed as memories came flooding back.

"The other thing I have to tell you is that I still have those things you left in the drawer of the Capri apartment," said Enzo. "A mini dress, some sexy underwear and a bottle of Chanel perfume. Would you like them back?" Juliet was astonished. "You've kept them all this time and taken them with you every time you moved? That's amazing."

"They're all I had left of you." Juliet looked at him, her eyes beginning to fill with tears. "That's how I felt when Clarissa was born. She was all I had left of *you*. But I couldn't keep her, I had to give her away. I felt so guilty." Enzo kissed her damp eyes. "No sadness today, baby," he murmured, "we have so many happy memories, let's enjoy them." He began to pull her back towards the bed.

"Uh-uh, no, my love," said Juliet firmly, regaining her composure. "No time for that, sadly. We have a table booked for nine o'clock and I'm starving; sex makes me hungry and I can't remember the last time I ate…I've been distracted since you arrived. I asked if our table could be somewhere out of the way, and I think they understood what I meant."

Enzo stroked her hair. "Well, at least I'll have you to myself for once and won't have to share you with Marco."

"Marco! I haven't thought about him for years."

"Sadly, he died of AIDS back in the late eighties," said Enzo. "He was so promiscuous with boys as well as girls that it was always going to be a possibility; and of course, years of smoking weed and goodness knows what else added to his vulnerability. Quite apart from the sadness of losing a friend, he was a talented guitarist and could have continued playing for many years to come if he had looked after himself better.

"Happily, Raf is still with us. He is married and quite the family man nowadays. He's in his nineties and still playing drums, although with slightly less vigour than in the Bar Russe days. I saw him two years ago in Vegas and he looked really well. He keeps in touch; you know cards at Christmas and things."

"Poor Marco. I really was fond of him," sighed Juliet, thinking back to the days at Bar Russe when Marco and Raf were Enzo's backing musicians and Marco used to regularly turn up for jamming sessions with Enzo after performances. "I know you were," said Enzo with a sideways glance, "and I did sometimes wonder if he could tempt you away from me."

"No! Surely not," gasped Juliet. She was genuinely surprised. How little we know what goes on in other people's heads, even those we are close to. "You were always so full of confidence, I never imagined there was room for self-doubt. And I thought you knew how much I loved you."

"Mmm. I did really," said Enzo. Juliet put her arms around him. "I liked Marco very much and, to be honest I probably fancied him a bit; he was very sexy and an outrageous flirt. I always thought he was like a handsome pirate, but he could never compare to you." Enzo laughed. "I'm pleased to hear it. Now, if I can't make love to you again let's do the next best thing and go down to the bar to see if they have a bottle of Chianti."

★★★

The barman produced a bottle of Juliet's favourite Italian wine saying, "We don't get much call for it here."

"In that case," replied Enzo, "we'll have two glasses now, and please may I order the rest of that bottle and maybe another to be served with our meal."

Enzo was still as confident as he had been half a century ago, thought Juliet. Whether it was in Italy or England, or presumably the States too, he seemed completely in command of every situation.

Watching him, Juliet knew her love for him was as deep now as it had ever been. She was finding it really difficult to recall the compelling reasons she had dreamed up for not returning to him on Capri. It seemed nonsensical thinking about it now. What a silly young girl she had been. How much unhappiness her decision had caused for both of them.

Putting the glasses of wine down on the table, Enzo enfolded Juliet's hands in both of his. "I was distraught when you didn't come back to me on Capri and now we have found each other again, I am never letting you go," he said softly. "We belong together. You're my soulmate; the love of my life."

Dinner passed in a blur for Juliet. Light-headed with happiness and the knowledge that she would be spending all night with Enzo, she chatted away but later had no recollection of anything she had said. Nor was she aware of what she was eating, except that there were several courses, all delicious, and at least two bottles of wine.

When she leaned back in her chair, unable to swallow another mouthful, Enzo trapped one of her feet in both of his under the table, just as he had that time they were having lunch with his manager Lorenzo Russo at La Campana in Rome. "I don't know about you *Giulietta,*" he said quietly, "but I need to make love again. Let's go upstairs." She could see love and desire shining in his eyes.

Pulling her into his arms as they walked into the empty lift, Enzo kissed her passionately. "I can't wait any longer, I have to ask you now. *Mi vuoi sposare?* Will you marry me?" Groggy with love, Juliet repeated the words she had whispered all those years ago: "*Si, per favore, anch'io ti amo.*"

"And this time," said Enzo firmly, kissing her ardently as the lift doors opened, "I am not letting you out of my sight until you *have* married me. *Ti amo.*"

The four people who were waiting to get into the lift burst into a spontaneous round of applause. Juliet blushed as one of the women said to her companion: "What is it about lifts…? Sniggering like children, Juliet and Enzo walked swiftly down the corridor to their suite.

Chapter Sixteen

"Love – true love – is a precious thing. It is painful, uncomfortable, and makes fools of us all, but it is what breathes meaning and colour and purpose into our lives. Love is the one thing that lifts our common experience into the extraordinary."
Kate Mosse, 'Sepulchre' (2007)

LYING IN bed after another very satisfying session of lovemaking, Enzo told Juliet about his three ex-wives – "They were a huge mistake, *amore*" – and various affairs over the years. He also told her why he didn't have any children apart from Clarissa.

"To be honest, I didn't want babies while I was touring, and I definitely didn't want to father a child until I found someone who would make me feel the way you did. Of course, that never happened. I have never felt about anyone the way I do about you."

In turn Juliet explained why she hadn't gone back to him. "I was so scared that after we left Capri you'd get bored with me and go off with someone far sexier and more glamorous, and I would die of a broken heart. You could have any woman you wanted. Why did you want me? Not returning to you was self-preservation. The grief I endured by leaving you was nothing compared to the agony I would have suffered if you had left me for someone else."

"Oh *Giulietta*," said Enzo sadly, "if only you had confided in me. There was never going to be anyone but you." Juliet nodded.

"I know that now." Running her fingers through his curls she thought once again that touching the hair of someone you loved was a huge turn-on.

Frowning she said: "But Enzo, I still don't really understand why you wanted *me*. I was young, totally inexperienced and unsophisticated, and you were so gorgeous, confident and charming with beautiful women of all ages queuing up for you."

Holding her in his arms Enzo said earnestly: "There is far more to love than physical attraction. I admit it was your beauty that caught my attention when I first saw you at the harbour in Sorrento, but there has to be something much deeper than that for the initial surge of desire to last.

"Boys make love with their eyes," he said gazing deeply into hers. "They can only see physical beauty and they are led by lust. Matteo and I were like that. We'd see pretty girls, flirt, make advances and then fuck them and leave, moving on to the next. We were only interested in the sexual gratification we could get, there was nothing else in it for us."

"Did you make love to a lot of girls?" Juliet was reluctant to ask, but something inside was forcing her to put the question, although she was thinking that she didn't really want to hear the answer.

Enzo paused and gave her a careful look before saying slowly: "Well, yes, there have been a lot of women over the years, but I never made love, I always fucked. It wasn't until we were together…that very first time on The Island…that I knew I was really making love. It had a profound effect on me.

"You are the only one I have ever made love to; only you. After you left I went back to fucking again. And you are the only one I have *ever* had sex with without using protection. It happened only a couple of times when we were being completely spontaneous – like the time we had rough sex and that last afternoon we spent on The Island – but I guess that's how we got Clarissa!" Juliet gave a shocked gasp; she had been so naïve she'd been unaware that there had been occasions when he hadn't used a condom.

Looking at her intently, Enzo said: "Clarissa asked me how I would have reacted if you had turned up on Capri and said you were pregnant with our child. I said I wasn't sure how I would have felt – touring with a baby would have been extremely difficult and it wasn't something I wanted to do. That was true.

"What I *didn't* tell Clarissa was that deep inside my heart I always knew that if you had become pregnant I wouldn't have minded; otherwise I would *never* have taken the risk of having unprotected sex. I have always been excessively careful that I didn't make a woman pregnant. With you it was different. You are the only one I have ever loved; the only one I ever really wanted to marry and yes, the only one I wanted have babies with…even if it did make touring difficult."

Juliet burst into tears. She could have gone back to Capri after all, if only she'd known. All those years…

Gently stroking her hair, Enzo said: "Every time we had sex together it was an act of unconditional love for me, and I think it was the same for you too." Juliet, quietly sobbing, whispered: "Oh yes. It was always love for me, right from the very first time."

He looked at her soberly. "When I first saw you, I immediately knew there was something special between us; it was much more than a fleeting physical attraction. I felt I had always known you. That feeling I had for you then has remained strong throughout the years; that bond was never broken. I still love you with all my heart, soul and mind. That will never change."

Juliet lay quietly, unsure what to say. Her love for him had always been unwavering but knowing that he had always loved her too, affected her deeply. She had known from the very beginning that what they had together was alchemy.

Through the mists of time Juliet recalled their first meeting on Capri when he had invited her to hear him sing at Bar Russe, and she'd had to fight an unaccountable urge to reach out and touch him. She remembered clamping her hands firmly onto the arms of her chair to stop herself moving towards him. As she thought about it she could almost feel the cold hard iron of the chair underneath her palms. She should have realised then that there was a special connection that she would never find with anyone else. How could she so carelessly have walked away from that.

Mentally shaking herself Juliet went on to tell Enzo that when she found she was pregnant, although she felt sure the baby was his, she couldn't prove it. So, after Vittoria, now Clarissa, had been adopted, she had quickly met and married Ted. "I did love Ted and he loved me. We had a good life together and there are three children and now grandchildren. But my deep love for you was always there in my heart and my soul. That never went away."

Kissing her, Enzo said: "Life is strange. We live so many different lives in one lifetime. Happily for us it has worked out well. We have found each other again and now I have not only a daughter, but a whole new family. So many people for me to meet and get to know. Once I only had *Nonna,* now suddenly I have dozens of relatives."

After gently making love again they slept: Juliet totally content in the arms of the man she had always loved so passionately, while Enzo, overjoyed that he had got Juliet back, felt like a young man again.

In the early hours of the morning Juliet murmured sleepily: "I just knew those coins I threw into the Trevi Fountain in Rome wouldn't be wasted. Lorenzo said they meant I would meet a handsome Italian and marry him. Well, I'd already met my handsome Italian and it's taken fifty years, but I *am* going to marry him. I am so happy."

Enzo opened one eye and said: "Does this mean you're awake *cara*? because if so…" Juliet chuckled happily thinking, I really do feel as if I am nineteen again.

★★★

The next day Juliet woke early, and with the thin grey light of a Sussex morning creeping into the room, she leaned on her elbow watching Enzo sleep. It was something she used to do when they were living together on Capri, and Juliet thought he was still breathtakingly beautiful.

Even in old age he was astonishingly good looking, and she found it almost impossible to believe that he had come back to her and still wanted to marry her. The rest of my life spent with Enzo, she thought ecstatically. Loving, talking, laughing…just being with him for ever.

As in Italy, Enzo suddenly became aware that she was staring at him: *"Giulietta, amore!"* Still in a sleepy haze he pulled her down on top of him, murmuring explicitly all the things he was going to do once he was properly awake.

He used the crude, rough words of the Neapolitan streets where he had grown up, and as he was speaking in dialect Juliet understood very little; her rather sketchy Italian just wasn't up to it. Nevertheless, she got the general gist of what he was saying, and it made her feel like a young girl again, sexy and desirable. She was full of astonished wonder that the gift of love had been returned to her.

Chapter Seventeen

"A successful marriage requires falling in love many times, always with the same person."
Mignon McLaughlin,
American journalist and author (1913-1983)

JULIET WAS showing Enzo around Brighton, where she had spent most of her life until buying the Hove flat with June, when he urged her across the street to a jewellery shop in The Lanes. "I must buy you a ring *Giulietta*. I want everyone to know that we are affianced."

Smiling Juliet said: "Affianced is such a lovely old-fashioned word. Nowadays we would say engaged."

"In Italian it is *fidanzato,* but it is all the same: affianced, *fidanzato,* engaged. You are now pledged to marry me, and I want all the world to know." He put his arms around her, giving her a long, lingering kiss. "Although I never stopped loving you, I have now fallen in love with you all over again," he murmured.

As shoppers walked around them Juliet suddenly remembered that they were in Brighton, not Capri, Naples or Rome, and people were not used to seeing couples – especially elderly couples – being romantic in the middle of a busy street. But fifty years without Enzo had made her count her blessings, and Juliet returned his kiss with fervour, not caring what anyone thought.

Thinking of Brian's huge solitaire diamond that June still wore, Juliet said she would prefer a different stone. After a great deal of deliberation Enzo bought her a square cut Art Deco emerald with diamond shoulders, elegant and classy: "Just like you, baby," he whispered pulling her into his arms and kissing her.

The jeweller, who had seen thousands of newly engaged couples over his long career, thought he had never seen a pair so blatantly in love. "It was wonderful," he told his wife later. "They were both elderly but so obviously besotted with each other. It warmed my heart."

★★★

Juliet had taken off her wedding ring when Clarissa phoned to say she had found Enzo and he was longing to see her. She'd stared for a long time at the pale white line the ring had left around her finger, thinking nostalgically about the fifty years she worn the ring while married to Ted. Then kissing the groove on her finger, she placed the ring carefully in a box and into her dressing table drawer.

The wedding ring had been her grandmother's and Juliet wore it because she and Ted couldn't afford to buy a new one when they married back in nineteen sixty-four.

It was a standing joke between Juliet and June that she'd had three proposals and one marriage but had never received either an engagement or wedding ring.

Looking down at the beautiful emerald, now hiding the groove left by the Victorian gold band, Juliet thought it was fitting that a ring from Enzo should be the first she had ever been given.

★★★

When Enzo had told June he was planning to buy Juliet an engagement ring, she had suggested that afterwards they should have a champagne lunch to celebrate and booked them a table at the best French restaurant in Brighton.

"My treat," she said with a smile. "I am delighted you have found each other again."

Enzo had no idea what June had told the restaurant's *maître d'* but they were given VIP treatment from the moment they walked through the door. Escorted to a quiet table well out of the way of the general bustle, they were assigned their own waiter who provided immaculate and unobtrusive service. A bottle of *Bollinger* was awaiting them in an ice bucket.

"Oh, Enzo," breathed Juliet, "how wonderful."

"Don't thank me, *cara,* lunch and champagne are an engagement gift from June."

"That's so kind of her. She's really more like a sister than a best friend."

"Today we can celebrate in style," said Enzo, "but I must warn you that this is going to be a very short engagement indeed."

"Really?"

"Well *amore,* we are neither of us… how do you say it…spring hens?"

Juliet laughed. "You mean spring chickens, my love. No, we aren't."

"And therefore," continued Enzo looking very solemn, "we have more life behind than before us. We don't know how much time is left to us."

"Oh!" gasped Juliet.

Enzo took her hand in both of his, running his finger over her ring. "I am not saying this to make you sad, but just to say that it is important we get married as quickly as possible. We have to squeeze fifty years into the time we have left together. There are many things we must discuss. Quite apart from agreeing where and when we get married, we must also decide where we will live – England or Italy?"

The waiter came over to top up their champagne glasses. "You may want to see menus, or you may prefer to have the dishes that Madame Turner has chosen for you. She said it would be a surprise."

Juliet and Enzo looked at each other. "I think we should choose June's surprise, don't you *Giulietta?*" She nodded and the waiter chuckled. "An excellent choice *m'sieur, m'dame* if I may say so."

The meal was absolutely perfect. June, knowing Juliet so well, had picked all her favourite dishes. The most delicious seafood cocktail was followed by a Chateaubriand steak, which they shared, accompanied by dauphinoise potatoes and delicate French beans. Then a cheese board offering Petit Camembert, Roquefort and Comte.

When their waiter came over to ask if they were ready for coffee, Enzo asked: "No dessert?" Not even *gelato?*"

"June knows I don't really have a sweet tooth," replied Juliet. "I definitely prefer cheese. After all these years, she really does know what I like."

"Well, I am very tempted to have a *crème brûlée,*" said Enzo. It's my favourite dessert."

"Oh, mine too, it's the only pudding I really enjoy," agreed Juliet, as Enzo beckoned the waiter and ordered two of the indulgent classic French desserts to be served before *macchiato* coffees. Every day we are finding out new things about each other, thought Juliet. The rest of our lives is going to be a wonderful journey of discovery.

Throughout the delectable meal flowed the golden bubbles of *Bollinger* which, like the nursery story of the magic porridge pot, never seemed to run out. Juliet had lost count of how many glasses she drank, feeling happy and sleepy and totally sated. Laughing at her slightly crossed eyes Enzo said fondly: "Time to go back for a siesta."

As they rose from the table Enzo offered Juliet a steadying arm. I've definitely had far too much champagne she thought woozily as she clung on to him. Looking lovingly at Enzo, she knew he would always be there to offer a protective arm and look after her. It was a wonderful feeling.

The *maître d'* said he would ring for their taxi. "That too has been arranged by Madame Turner." He hurried over to the desk to make the call, quickly returning to tell them the cab was just a few moments away. Opening the restaurant door to bow them out he added: "May I offer you our sincere congratulations on your betrothal."

"Well," said Enzo as he helped Juliet into the taxi, "that was certainly a very special meal we will remember for years to come." Sitting with her head on Enzo's shoulder, his arm around her, Juliet thought she had never felt so content. I suppose I must have been this happy at some point in my life, but I can't remember when. Enzo, leaning over to kiss her, was simply euphoric. He now had everything he'd ever wanted.

Looking at them in his rear view mirror the taxi driver muttered to himself, "Blimey, I hope the missus and I are like that when we're their age." He suddenly decided to finish his shift early and go home to make love to his wife. She'd be gob-smacked, but he thought she would be quite pleased. He'd definitely not paid her enough attention recently.

★★★

Back at the hotel, Juliet fell asleep almost immediately and it was Enzo's turn to sit beside her and watch her as she slept. She was still beautiful, he thought, as he gently traced with his forefinger the fine lines around her eyes and the tiny grooves that ran from nose to mouth.

The first time he had seen her, at the harbour in Sorrento and then on the ferry to Capri, she was wearing a pink sundress which looked stunning with her long red hair, and he not only thought she was very beautiful, but he also had that inexplicable feeling that there was something special between them. It was like suddenly seeing someone he had always known.

She hadn't been easy to pin down, he recalled with a smile. *Giulietta* had totally ignored the two notes he had sent to her hotel asking her to go and hear him sing at Bar Russe. And then when he had seen her on the piazza, she had initially agreed to go to the gig before changing her mind. He'd had to be quite forceful when he came across her unexpectedly in Capri town that afternoon. But when she did turn up at Bar Russe, he knew he was right – they had an undeniably strong connection.

He had sung the Italian love song *Quando, Quando, Quando* especially for her, and although they were surrounded by an enormous audience of fans, it was if there was nobody else in the room. Enzo knew beyond doubt that for him it had been *colpo di fulmine,* love at first sight. Looking across and catching her eye, he was sure she felt the same; their souls had recognised each other.

Afterwards he had taken her down to Marina Piccolo to see an unusually large silver moon hanging low in the sky over the Faraglioni sea stacks. Brushing his lips lightly over hers he had asked: "When will you be mine?" – a line from the lyrics of *Quando*. It had been a rhetorical question. He knew they already belonged to each other, but he hadn't expected to have to wait fifty years for them to be together for ever.

During his younger days Enzo had gained a reputation for being a charming playboy, leaving a scattering of broken hearts behind him wherever he went. When he met *Giulietta* there was no doubt in his mind that those days were over. There would never be anyone else but her. Then, of course, she had gone to England to see her parents while he still had singing commitments to fulfil on Capri and in *Roma*, and she hadn't returned.

Enzo shied away from raking over memories of the distress and sorrow he had suffered, or the many louche years that followed when he had sex with almost any woman who offered it. For a charismatic and handsome performer like Enzo there was never a shortage of offers; he could end up with a different girl every night if he wanted, and he usually did. But none of them was *Giulietta,* in the same way that none of his wives could match up to the English girl with long red hair and silvery green eyes who had left him so bereft.

Enzo reflected that there were a lot of people you could live with, but there was only one person you couldn't live without. For him *Giulietta* was that person and he wanted to be with her forever.

As he reminisced, Juliet stirred, and Enzo kissed her awake. So many mistakes, but now it was time to bury the past and concentrate on a happy future.

Chapter Eighteen

"Soul meets soul on lovers' lips"
Percy Bysshe Shelley, 'Prometheus Unbound'
(1820)

THE FOLLOWING morning June came over to have coffee with Juliet and Enzo at the Brunswick. After she had admired Juliet's ring and Enzo had thanked her again for their wonderful engagement lunch, he explained that they needed to decide where to hold their wedding.

"I intend to marry her very soon," he said with a twinkle in his eye. "I can't take the risk of her disappearing again." Juliet laughed but turning to June she said seriously: "We want you to help us to decide where we should get married."

June considered for a few moments and then asked: "What about the religious situation? I'm assuming you're still a Catholic, Enzo."

"Pshaw." Enzo made an irritated flapping gesture. "I am still a Catholic, but I have no intention of getting married in the Church. I would like a civil ceremony if that's alright with you *Giulietta*?"

"Of course," said Juliet. "I belong to the Anglican Church, but I rarely go so I am perfectly happy to get married in a register office. Ted and I didn't have a church wedding because he also was divorced and in those days, divorced people weren't allowed to get married in church. I would have chosen a register office anyway; even when I was young I didn't want a big showy wedding." She turned to look at her friend. "Sorry, June. I know you and Brian had a society wedding, but it's just not for me." June smiled. "I know."

Looking over at Enzo, June said: "I hope you don't mind me asking, but if you are Roman Catholic, how did you manage three marriages and three divorces?"

"All my marriages were civil ones, two in the States and one in Holland," replied Enzo. "I don't believe they were recognised or seen as valid by the Church. I wouldn't be surprised if I've been ex-communicated by now anyway, considering the life I have led," he said semi-jokingly, adding: "Anyway, I am definitely a lapsed Catholic."

He took Juliet's hand. "So, we want a civil ceremony, *no*? The question is where, in England or in Italy? Or would you like to do something really mad and be married by an Elvis impersonator in Las Vegas? I actually know one if you fancy that. It's your choice baby, you're the bride."

When Juliet and June had stopped laughing at the thought of being married by someone pretending to be Elvis, Juliet looked lovingly into Enzo's eyes and said: "What I would *really* like is to be married on Capri."

"Wow, Capri!" gasped June. "What an amazing thought."

Enzo gave his endearing crinkled-eyed smile and said: "Why not, *amore,* that sounds perfect. It's where we met and it completes the circle."

"The only problem I can see," said Juliet, is whether we can get all the family over there because it's …?"

"No!" June jumped in quickly. "You two go over to Capri by yourselves, get married quietly, and then come back to Sussex and have an enormous party for everyone."

"That's a great idea," said Juliet. Enzo considered. "If we do that – and it is a brilliant idea by the way," he said giving June a distracting smile – "then June should come with us as one of the witnesses. I will ask my best friend Matteo, who has the hotel on Capri where Clarissa stayed when she was looking for me, to be the other witness. How about that for a plan?

"Also, how would you like to get married at Villa Florentina, *cara,* the hotel where you stayed in the sixties? I was there last summer, and it is still a beautiful place and now a wedding venue. Sadly, Signore Fabrizio died several years ago, but the hotel is now run by his son, and as there will only be a few of us it should be fairly easy to organise.

"We could probably stay at Villa Florentina too, but if not, I am sure Matteo will find us rooms for a couple of nights. Then, as you say, we can come back here and have a party for all the family." Juliet leaned over and kissed him. "That sounds perfect. How soon can we go?"

"I'm aiming for the week after next," said Enzo. The two women looked at each other with raised eyebrows. Enzo was definitely on the case.

★★★

That night, after they had made love and Enzo had sung to her, Juliet asked where he wanted to live when they were married. Did he want to return to his house in Naples, or buy a new house somewhere else? She made it quite clear that she would happily live anywhere in the world as long as they were together. Italy, England, America, Timbuktu…anywhere, it didn't matter. "I will be content if I am with you, wherever that might be." Enzo gave her a look of pure love. "I feel just the same." he said. "I don't mind where we live as long as we are together."

He sat silently holding her in his arms, his chin resting on the top of her head. After a while he said: "I'm actually thinking we should live somewhere around Brighton. All your family are in England and there is no longer anyone in Italy for me to worry about. So why don't we buy something near to Clarissa and June. It seems silly to move away when everyone you love is here.

"We can keep the house in *Napoli* and use it for family holidays. I can get Maria to look after it for us, and I'm sure her husband Vito will be happy to cultivate the land, keep hens and grow vegetables."

Juliet turned round and kissed him ardently. "Darling Enzo, that would be wonderful. Thank you."

★★★

Juliet awoke the next morning as Enzo kissed her. "I want us to make love really slowly," he said softly as she opened her eyes. "Don't talk, don't think, just feel and let our instincts take over."

"Slowly like the first time on The Island?" asked Juliet. "I have never forgotten that. It was one of the most incredible moments of my life."

"Just like that," said Enzo smiling. "But back then I was making love to you, now we will be making love together. There is a difference. We should both experience in the depths of our being exactly what it feels like to come together in total love."

Holding her tenderly in his arms he gave her a long unhurried kiss before they slowly and carefully shared a gentle intimacy that was even more erotic than the passionate sex they'd had the night before.

"Wow!" whispered Enzo, "I just don't have the words in any language to say how it feels to make love with you. I have never ever had sex with anyone else that feels like this. It is exactly the same now as it was when we were on Capri. What we have together is unique and very special."

"*Soul meets soul on lovers' lips,*" murmured Juliet. "That's a line from a Shelley drama and I've always thought it applied to us."

"That's beautiful," said Enzo. "As I told you all those years ago, our souls recognised each other immediately. We have been apart for a long time, but we've found each other again. Now we are back together I just want to kiss and make love to you all the time."

"I think we have more sex now than we did when we were young," said Juliet laughing. "Is it normal for people of our advanced years to enjoy making love so much and so often?"

"Perfectly normal, *tesoro*," replied Enzo seriously. "It's just that most people don't."

★★★

Fifty years ago when they were living together on Capri, Juliet knew that frequent sex was an important part of Enzo's life. They had made love a lot – they still did – and Enzo always accepted it as completely normal.

He had told her that he had been sleeping with girlfriends – and sometimes their mothers too – since he was fifteen. As he moved into his twenties and started touring when his singing career took off, he routinely had casual sex with fans and groupies most nights, and that had continued through the years.

"I was remorseless," he admitted to Juliet. "It was a powerful urge and I knew it was something I needed to do. But it was only fucking…it had never meant anything except the gratification and comfort it gave me. It wasn't until we had sex together that first time on The Island that I suddenly knew I was actually making love and it was beyond wonderful." Juliet put her arms around him, holding him tight. "Oh my darling, knowing that means the world to me."

Remembering that Enzo had been orphaned during the Second World War when he was just eight years old, Juliet wondered whether the persistent need for sex was the solace of a small boy, suddenly deprived of his parents, needing a comfort blanket.

Chapter Nineteen

"I know the difference now between dedication and infatuation. That doesn't mean I don't still get an enormous kick out of infatuation; the exciting ephemera, the punch in the stomach, the adrenaline to the heart."
Anna Quindlen, 'Living Out Loud' (2010)

AMY AND Charlotte were driving down from London for the day to meet Enzo at their parents' home in Brighton.

"What's he like?" asked Charlotte curiously as she made her way through the west London traffic after collecting Amy from Hammersmith.

"Who, Enzo?"

"No, the postman," replied Charlotte facetiously. "Of course, Enzo. Our newly discovered Italian grandfather. You're the one who's met him."

Since driving her mother and Enzo down to Hove after picking them up from Gatwick, Amy had run into Juliet and Enzo a few times while she was in Brighton visiting Clarissa. Seeing him always gave her the same unsettled feeling she'd had when they first met at the airport.

She was also slightly perturbed by the way Enzo and Juliet behaved together; they couldn't keep their hands off each other. It was not at all how you expected old people to be. Not that you could call Enzo old, in a lot of ways he seemed younger than her parents.

Charlotte pulled Amy out of her reverie by demanding: "So, what's he like?"

"Stunning," replied Amy dreamily, "incredibly attractive, with the most intense dark blue eyes and lovely curly hair. In fact, given the chance I'd marry him myself."

"*Really?*" said Charlotte. "That's quite an accolade from an ardent feminist who has dedicated her life to staying single. You sound totally infatuated."

"No," Amy blushed. "Not infatuated. But he is gorgeous. Mum always said that Juliet was quite pretty when she was young, well, you've seen the photos so you know, but she must have been very special to hook a man like that and then to have him come back to her after fifty years. Apparently he is quite well known on the music scene, and he's got a huge fan base even though he doesn't do that many gigs nowadays."

"Gosh." Charlotte drove in silence for a while. She was unable to imagine any man having such an influence on her steadfastly feminist sister.

"Anyway," said Amy, "it's obvious Enzo and Juliet are totally nuts about each other. When they're together they absolutely exude lust. You can just feel it."

"Crikey!" said Charlotte, startled. "So, you reckon he's okay?"

"More than okay, fucking gorgeous," replied Amy. "And very sexy…he's ridiculously hot."

"*That* good," said Charlotte smiling. Enzo had obviously made a huge impression; she had never known Amy so enthusiastic about any guy, young or old.

"Lucky Juliet, I say," said Amy. "Oh, watch out, this is our exit coming up."

Charlotte carefully negotiated the ancient Porsche she shared with her boyfriend Malik off the A23 and onto the motorway before saying: "Well, it just shows you are never too old for love. Do you think they are having sex? I mean, she's over seventy and he must be eighty. Malik says libido deteriorates after fifty."

"Huh!" scoffed Amy. "Malik may be a doctor, but like all men he knows very little about women. I can assure you they are *definitely* shagging, and probably all the time from the look on their faces. You should hear the things they say to each other, it even makes me blush. And they whisper to each other in Italian. Even though I don't understand a word they say, it makes my spine tingle." Charlotte giggled. "Then there is hope for us all. I can't wait to meet our grandfather now!"

"Honestly, Lotte, you'll see what I mean when you meet him. I can't explain, but he sort of flirts with you without being obvious. He's incredibly charming and sexy but very understated. I thought he was just…extraordinary. I don't know what else to say."

"Gosh," said Charlotte again. "Despite what you say, I can see you are absolutely besotted. I hope Malik and I are like that at seventy."

"You reckon you'll still be together in forty years then?"

Charlotte laughed. "God knows. I obviously don't want to get married, but it would be nice to think we were still together."

★★★

Clarissa collected Enzo from the Brunswick to take him to meet Tony and the girls. "How's it all going?" asked Clarissa. "Is it as good as you hoped it would be?" One look at Enzo's face gave her the answer. He was in a state of bliss. "Oh, yes," he said contentedly. "It's just wonderful."

"And Juliet's spending the day with June?"

"Yes," replied Enzo. "There are some things they need to sort out and *Giulietta* also wanted to take *Firenze*…um…Florence for a walk."

After that first night together, Juliet had immediately moved into the Brunswick to be with Enzo. Now they had found each other again there was no way they could live apart. She visited June most days, to walk Florence or to sort out her belongings ready for the move to more permanent accommodation, wherever that might be.

As they travelled the few miles to Clarissa and Tony's home on the Downs above Brighton, very close to where Juliet grew up, Clarissa said with surprise: "You haven't brought your guitar! I think it's the first time I've seen you without it." Enzo laughed. "I didn't think your family would be expecting me to perform."

"Oh, I don't know, Lotte and Amy would probably like to hear you sing. They've heard so much about you…Ah, the girls are here already," she said as they arrived and saw the yellow Porsche parked on the drive.

"A Porsche!" exclaimed Enzo, "that's very stylish."

"Stylish, even in that cat sick-yellow colour?" Clarissa asked dubiously. "Even so," replied Enzo laughing. "Lotte shares it with her boyfriend Malik," explained Clarissa. "He's a bit of a car fanatic. I'm surprised he's let her drive it down here, to be honest."

"He'd get on well with Matteo," said Enzo. "He loves cars like that and always drives something classy. I think his latest one is an Alfa Romeo."

"Malik would definitely like to get behind the wheel of an Alfa," said Clarissa. "We must see if we can get them to meet up sometime." It was strange, but a shiver still went through her when Matteo's name was mentioned.

As they got out of the car Clarissa noticed a couple of twitching curtains and curious faces at the windows of some of the apartments. Word had got around and everyone in the building knew about their visitor, with many anxious to get a glimpse of him.

Tony had also heard them arrive and hurried out to welcome

Enzo. He wasn't quite sure what to expect. Clarissa had tried to explain what Enzo was like, but Tony couldn't quite picture an eighty-year-old man who was still, according to his wife, sexy and charismatic.

Although he had met the noisy and flamboyant showbiz people Amy occasionally brought down to the coast for a day, Tony was uncertain whether he would have anything in common with a semi-retired Italian singer. What would they talk about? Tony knew very little about music, which he supposed would be Enzo's main topic of conversation.

Shaking hands with his wife's birth father, Tony had admit Enzo was very good looking and quietly charming, nothing like Amy's loud and glitzy showbiz friends. He also looked extremely young for his age. He couldn't possibly be eighty; maybe Clarissa had got that wrong.

"You have a beautiful place here," said Enzo disarmingly, as he stared admiringly at the large Georgian house where Tony and Clarissa had the garden flat. "Clarissa tells me you are an architect, so did you have a hand in the renovation of your apartment? It must be tough to drag these old buildings into the twenty-first century; did it need a lot of work before you could move in? And I understand that it is Grade Two listed, so that must have thrown up all kinds of problems."

Tony was astonished. Not only did Enzo speak excellent English, but he also sounded really interested and quite knowledgeable about architecture and renovation. It wasn't going to be too difficult to talk to him after all. "Let me show you around," he said enthusiastically, leading the way indoors. "There are some quite interesting features that I designed myself."

"Darling," Clarissa put a restraining hand on Tony's arm. "Allow Enzo take off his jacket and maybe even have a cup of coffee before you show him interesting architectural details. He hasn't met Lotte yet nor had a chance to say hello to Amy."

Tony looked contrite. "Apologies, I was forgetting my manners. I always get a bit carried away when I'm talking about architecture. Do come in, have some coffee and see the girls. Then I'll give you the grand tour."

Enzo laughed. "Yes, I'd better see my granddaughters before I do anything else." He turned to Clarissa. "I'd adore a cup of coffee please *cara*. Just a small espresso, no sugar."

★★★

Charlotte and Amy put down their coffee mugs and stood up as Tony showed Enzo into the sunroom which had bi-fold doors opening onto a big garden. "Lotte, meet Enzo de Martins," said Tony.

Charlotte felt a frisson of excitement as Enzo took one of her hands in both of his. "I am so pleased to meet you at last," he said, giving her an unwavering stare. Lifting her hand to his lips he added: "I've heard so much about you, but Clarissa didn't tell me how beautiful you are. I can tell that *Giulietta* is your grandmother, your eyes are amazing, you know that?" Still holding her hand, he added softly: "Amy has *Giulietta's* lovely red hair, but you have her wonderful green eyes."

Charlotte blushed; despite her sister's warning she was totally unprepared for such devastating charm. "Pleased to meet you," she muttered weakly. Quickly pulling herself together and hoping that Amy hadn't noticed her brief loss of composure, Charlotte added brightly: "I've heard a lot about you too." Enzo gave a bark of laughter: "Ha! Well, I won't ask what you've been told. Better not to know, don't you think?"

"Oh, it was all good," she said simply. Enzo's lips twitched with amusement. "Ah well, that's a relief. I feared there might be some discontent that this unknown Italian had swooped in and stolen your grandmother away." Charlotte laughed. "Absolutely not. We're all thrilled that you and Juliet have found each other – and even more excited to discover we have some Italian blood in our veins."

"That's wonderful, I'm so pleased," said Enzo. Giving Charlotte his movie star smile, he turned to Amy, kissing her on both cheeks. "Lovely to see you again *cara*." Breathing in the faint tang of his cologne, Amy had to stop herself moving closer to him thinking, for fuck's sake a girl should be allowed to hug her grandfather, right?

Looking at her intently Enzo said: "How are rehearsals going. Is the part you got as good as you hoped? Amy was amazed he had remembered she'd had a successful audition and secured the role of Amanda in George Bernard Shaw's satirical comedy *The Apple Cart*. She nodded. "Yes, thank you. Rehearsals are always a bit tense at the beginning but it's going really well."

"Oh *brava*," said Enzo. "Maybe *Giulietta* and I can come and see you when it opens?"

Amy could feel her face going pink. He remembered she'd started rehearsals, which was more than Lotte had, and he was interested enough to ask about them, which is more than her father did. She smiled, trying to avoid looking straight into his eyes. "It would be great if you could come. I'll get you some tickets."

"We look forward to it. And don't forget about those guitar lessons. The offer is still open." Holding her left hand he said: "Your long fingers will be an advantage for guitar, you'll have no trouble reaching the frets."

Amy smiled and took a long steadying breath. Once again, he was making her feel hot and bothered without really doing anything; it was ridiculous. Goodness knows how he did it. Enzo was her grandfather for Christ's sake, and he was marrying Juliet. She really needed to get a grip. Leaning over she gave him a kiss on the cheek. "Thank you." Mission accomplished! It should be easier to give him a hug next time.

Thankfully her father saved the day by taking him off to the sitting room to have coffee with the promise of a tour of the flat's architectural features afterwards. "See you in a bit," said Enzo including both girls in a dazzling smile as he followed Tony out of the door.

★★★

Tony was slightly bemused. What had just happened? There had been an undercurrent in the room he couldn't quite put his finger on.

As far as he was concerned there was polite conversation as Enzo was introduced to one of his daughters and had said hello to the other. But looking at the girls' faces, it seemed there was a sub-plot to which he was not privy. Oh well, having lived with three women for many years, Tony was used to not knowing what was going on. He would speak to Clarissa about it later.

★★★

Carefully closing the sunroom door behind her father and Enzo, Amy looked at Charlotte who had a hand clamped over her open mouth. "Well?" she said with a grin.

"Good grief! Are all Italian men like that?"

"See what I mean?" said Amy.

"*Absolutely*," replied Charlotte. "Like you said, fucking gorgeous. He is so casually continental, and that wild curly hair and those dark blue eyes are really attractive. I've never met anyone like him. He looks like a rock star."

"Exactly what I thought," agreed Amy, then, with just a hint of sisterly cattiness she asked: "Will you tell Malik?"

"Tell Malik *what* exactly?"

"That you fancy your eighty-year-old Italian grandfather," said Amy giggling uncontrollably.

"Amy! You've overstepped the mark this time. That's disgusting. You can't joke about incest."

"Who says I was joking? Anyway, fancying him isn't incest," said Amy. "Come on, Lotte, admit it. You fancy him. I certainly do, so I'm pretty sure you must."

"Hmm. Alright, so maybe I do. Just a bit."

Charlotte thought about her boyfriend. All the girls envied her because Malik was so charming and good looking and had an aura of glamour because he was a doctor and drove a Porsche. But Enzo had something extra that Malik didn't have. An undefinable quality that made him special; a feeling that you could trust him completely and that he would really protect you and look after you no matter what. And all Charlotte could think was lucky, lucky Juliet to have a man like that so devoted to her.

"Mum says that Juliet and Enzo are going to live in Brighton when they are married," said Amy. "Wow," said Charlotte, that will cause excitement among some of the local ladies."

Giving her sister an irritated look, Amy said: "No Lotte. Point is, Enzo is keeping his house in Naples as a family holiday home, so you will be able to go over there and find your own fucking gorgeous Italian. In fact, I will definitely come with you. Remember we are a quarter Italian."

The girls looked at each other and burst out laughing. "We may be a quarter Italian, but we're also radical feminists," gasped Charlotte, "we're not supposed to need men apart from the obvious reason, of course. And Mum says Enzo's quite dictatorial. He has very fixed ideas about how women should be treated. I wouldn't have thought you'd enjoy being bossed around by a man." Amy just looked thoughtful and said nothing.

"Another interesting thing," continued Charlotte, is that Juliet's going to take Enzo's name when they're married. So, she'll be Mrs de Martins. Or strictly speaking Signora de Martins, I suppose."

"And that's interesting because?"

"Because when she married Ted, she was a strong feminist and wanted to continue being Juliet Campbell – just as mum is Clarissa Phillips – insisting that taking a man's name on marriage was patriarchal.

"In the end she compromised and was called Juliet Campbell-Jackson. Then when Ted died, she dropped the hyphen and became Juliet Campbell again. But now, she's not bothered about being a feminist. She told mum she just wanted everyone to know she was Enzo's wife and therefore will be called Juliet de Martins."

"I know exactly where she's coming from," said Amy sincerely. "If I can find a younger version of Enzo de Martins, fuck feminism. I'll be turning in my membership card. I can't think of anything better than being bossed around by a sexy, devastatingly handsome Italian." Charlotte stared at her. She knew her sister wasn't joking, and to be honest, she almost agreed with her.

"By the way, what was that about guitar lessons?" Amy blushed. She'd had a feeling that Lotte was earwigging. "Enzo has offered to teach me to play the guitar."

"Has he indeed. Well, if you are thinking of finding a fucking gorgeous Italian in Naples, maybe it would be more useful if he taught you to speak Italian."

Chapter Twenty

"La casa del sole"
I Pooh, on the album 'Beat ReGeneration' (2008)

"HAS GIULIETTA told you that we are hoping to live in England?" asked Enzo as Clarissa handed him his coffee.

"*Yes!* I spoke to her on the phone this morning. She mentioned it might be somewhere in the Brighton area. I am delighted."

"It rather depends on finding the right property," said Enzo. "I've rung a few estate agents, so we'll see what they come up with."

"I must admit we thought you'd take Juliet back to Naples with you. So naturally, we are all thrilled that you're planning to live close by," said Clarissa.

"I have no family in Italy now and she has all of you here, so it seems the right thing to do," replied Enzo. "We just have to find somewhere to live."

"Well, come and see what we've done to this property," said Tony, sweeping Enzo off for a tour of the flat. Clarissa laughed, swiftly rescuing the coffee cup from Enzo's hand as he walked past her. "He's hardly had time to swallow his coffee, darling," she told Tony, but her husband didn't hear her, his mind firmly fixed on architecture and renovation. Enzo smiled at her over his shoulder as he followed Tony into the hall. He was beginning to enjoy being part of a family.

"It's massive," said Enzo in surprise as Tony showed him

around the flat. "In Italy apartments are usually very compact, but this is the size of a house conveniently spread over one floor, and it has the added bonus of a garden. If *Giulietta* and I could find a place like this, it would be perfect."

"I'll ask around for you if you like," offered Tony. One of my clients might know about something that's about to come on the market."

"That would be so kind, we'd appreciate that," replied Enzo gratefully.

"Okay, leave it with me," said Tony.

★★★

As they arrived back in the kitchen, Clarissa said apologetically: "Enzo, I do hope you don't mind, but a few of our neighbours are popping in for pre-lunch drinks. They won't stay too long, but they rather want to meet you." Enzo smiled. "No problem at all *cara,* I'm always happy to know new people."

He's very affable, thought Tony as he took Enzo into garden. I've no idea how famous he is, but he's certainly unpretentious. I can see where Clarissa gets her easy-going nature…and her good looks. Both Juliet and Enzo are very attractive.

Clarissa wasn't feeling quite so sanguine. She initially had no idea how all the neighbours had found out that Enzo was visiting, but Tony eventually confessed that he had mentioned it in the pub. "I told Phil Prentice that you had tracked down your birth father and he was coming to see us."

"And did you tell him Enzo's name?" demanded his wife.

"I think I said he was an Italian singer and guitarist who was quite well-known," Tony admitted slowly. "Phil asked who, and then said Sybil had heard Enzo sing on one of her visits to the States some years ago."

"Well, if the Prentices know the whole world will have heard," said Clarissa resignedly. Sure enough, a couple of days later Sybil called round to ask if it would be possible for her to meet Enzo. "Just to say hello. After hearing him sing in Las Vegas, it would be great to actually say I've met him in person," she simpered.

After a couple more requests from other neighbours, Clarissa decided to issue an invitation for a quick drink before lunch to all the residents in the building. Now she was thinking it was just as well Enzo hadn't brought his guitar with him. Pushy Sybil would almost certainly have had the gall to ask him to play.

Charlotte and Amy were appalled to learn that their parents were exposing Enzo to Sybil Prentice. "She's an absolute nightmare," wailed Amy. "Poor Enzo."

"Poor us," said Charlotte. "We're going to have to put up with her too."

"Spare a thought for Phil, he has to put up with her all the time," said Tony. "Well, he married her," retorted Amy heartlessly. "Maybe she was different then," suggested her father, but Amy just scowled at him.

"It won't be for more than half-an-hour," said Clarissa soothingly, taking freshly made cheese straws out of the oven. "Once everyone got wind of the fact that Enzo was coming here, there wasn't much I could do. Inviting them for pre-lunch drinks seemed the best option; at least it means they won't hang around too long." She went over to the fridge, rooting around for dips, cheese and olives.

"I didn't realise he was so popular with old people," said Amy sulkily.

"Remember Enzo's heyday was back in the sixties and seventies, when people like Sybil were in their teens," said Clarissa, from the depths of the fridge. "So many of them remember him and are still fans."

"It's like Elvis," Charlotte pointed out. "He was really famous fifty years ago and he's still got millions of fans. Enzo was also hugely popular in the sixties and continues to have an enormous number of fans, like Elvis he…" Amy gave her an infuriated look. "Don't be so stupid, Lotte, I don't think he's at all like Elvis, you don't know what you are talking about!"

"Well," her sister replied furiously, "Juliet said that she thought Enzo *looked* a bit like Elvis when she first saw him in the sixties. Elvis with curly hair and without the sideburns she said, so it's you…"

"Ladies, p-*lease,*" said Clarissa wearily. Listening to her daughters' argument she recalled the old newspaper reports asking if Enzo was the new Elvis; and the screaming fans when he arrived back at Naples airport after his Las Vegas season. Then Enzo telling her about girls throwing their underwear on the stage while he was singing. Lotte's not so very far off the mark she thought amusedly.

Closing the fridge door and putting a selection of nibbles down on the kitchen island, she added: "We're in for a difficult half-hour, and I don't need you two arguing. We must all pull together. Now, Amy, will you please go to the larder and find some crisps, two of those big packets should be plenty."

There was a tap on the door and Sybil popped her head round. "Coo-ee, okay if we come in?" Clarissa gave her daughters a warning look.

"Come in, Sybil," called Amy sweetly, rolling her eyes at Charlotte and muttering, "as long as it's only for half-an-hour – but I bet she'll be the last one out." Hot on Phil and Sybil's heels were another nine neighbours, all keen to meet Clarissa's famous father.

Enzo's presence brought a touch of sparkle and pizzazz to casual pre-lunch drinks. Used to engaging with fans, he did the rounds, shaking hands and chatting to everyone, always knowing the right things to say.

Explaining that he and Juliet were planning to live in Brighton, he asked for advice and suggestions for everything from good places to eat out and entertainment facilities, to the best beaches and countryside walks. Tony and Clarissa exchanged satisfied glances. Enzo was in control and charming everyone.

"Most people coming to live here want to know about schools," said Sybil archly with a girlish giggle, "but I suppose that's not a priority for you and Juliet."

Charlotte and Amy bristled simultaneously, hissing under their breath, outraged at such impertinence. Was Sybil trying to be funny? Enzo merely laughed good-naturedly and said: "Clarissa is our only one and she is in her fifties, so you are right, schooling will not be something we are looking for."

Edging closer to him, Sybil put a hand on Enzo's arm. "I can't tell you how excited we are you're coming to live here," she said coquettishly, staring into his face.

"*Grazie mille.* That's very kind. *Giulietta* and I are really looking forward to getting a home of our own," said Enzo giving her one of his stunning smiles. "*Speriamo presto. Ci piace qui, è bellissimo,*" he added, instinctively knowing she was entranced by hearing him speaking Italian.

Encouraged, Sybil moved even closer, breathing in the fragrance of his spicy cologne. "Italian is such a romantic language," she whispered flirtatiously. "Did you know I heard you sing in Vegas? A couple of your sets were in Italian. You were absolutely amazing, and I've *always* been a huge fan. I do hope we are going to be very good friends, you must come to supper, I…"

"Come over and let me give you a refill, Sybil," called Tony from the other side of the room, holding up a bottle and waving it at her, offering Enzo a chance to escape her mindless chatter. Putting an arm around her as she reluctantly went over to him, Tony smiled and added charmingly: "Now it's my turn, Sybil. *I haven't had a chance to talk to you yet.*" Sybil slowly pulled her infatuated gaze away from Enzo and gave Tony a coy smile. "Enzo is *so* wonderful isn't he…" Tony sighed; distracting her was not going to be easy.

As Enzo went over to Clarissa, she murmured in his ear: "For God's sake don't encourage her. Speaking to her in Italian…really! That's just asking for trouble." Giving his daughter an innocent stare Enzo replied: "I was just being nice, *cara*. I feel a bit sorry for her."

"Well don't," said Clarissa firmly. "Give Sybil Prentice an inch and she will take a yard…or should that be a centimetre and a metre? Anyway, you should have brought Juliet with you; seeing you two love birds together would have shut her up." Shaking with silent laughter Enzo gave her a quick kiss before continuing his progress around the room.

As Amy predicted, Sybil and Phil were the last to leave. Sybil, giddy from the peck on the cheek she had managed to give Enzo as she said goodbye, was still burbling as her husband almost pushed her out of the door. "Remember to come and see us once you're properly settled," she called cheerily. "Don't forget to let me have your address. Next time you must sing for us."

"*Ciao-Ciao,* Sybil," called Enzo, waving goodbye. He kissed his thumb, blowing the kiss towards her. "Stop flirting with her," said Clarissa laughing. "She'll be utterly impossible now."

When they eventually managed to sit down to lunch, Clarissa said: "I am so sorry to have imposed that on you but thank you for being so accommodating. I know Sybil can be a bit…challenging."

Enzo laughed. "Everywhere I go I meet a Sybil." He grinned as Clarissa added: "And a Luigi too, I guess! Well, anyway, I am very grateful. You coped with her admirably."

"Happy to help," replied Enzo. "To be honest, I'm always slightly flattered that people still remember me." Charlotte and Amy looked at each other. "Not only fucking gorgeous but also really nice," whispered Amy behind her hand.

Chapter Twenty-One

"The older you get, the more you realise how 'happenstance' has helped you determine your path through life."
Rowan Atkinson, English actor and comedian

WHILE ENZO was with Clarissa and family, June and Juliet were spending the day together at the flat. Juliet had Florence spread over her lap, the dog's big brown eyes once again soulfully fixed on Juliet's face. "She doesn't understand what's going on," said June. "The cats are okay, but poor old Florence just can't work out why you've been missing. I know we share her, but she's always been more your dog than mine."

Juliet gave Florence a kiss on the top of her wiry head. "She's just one of the things we have to discuss. Would you mind keeping Florence with you while Enzo and I are sorting ourselves out and then we can have a proper conversation about where she lives. I can continue to come over and take her out for walks. If it's alright with you, I'd quite like to take Florence with me when we eventually settle."

June nodded. "That makes sense. How long is Enzo planning to stay at the Brunswick?"

"Not really sure, but I imagine he will keep the suite at least until we go to Capri and maybe for a while afterwards. The receptionist said it was free for the foreseeable future.

Putting an arm around June's shoulders she said: "The other thing is you. How do *you* feel about me going off to live with Enzo and leaving you alone in the flat?"

Handing Juliet a mug of coffee, June gave a sigh. "Well, like Florence, I miss you, of course. But this is something you have to do…and do with a clear conscience. When we bought this flat, we had no idea that Enzo was going to turn up again. Things have changed and you must go and live your life with him now."

Juliet smiled. "We had a long talk about the future last night, and Enzo wants to buy a house in or near Brighton. I was telling Clarissa when she phoned this morning. She is very pleased."

"Not Italy then," said June. "I felt sure you'd be going off to live in Naples."

"No. He has no family in Italy now and as all my family is here, we have decided to stay in England. We will keep his house in Naples as a family holiday home. So, you must make good use of it whenever you want."

June felt a huge weight lift off her shoulders. Despite her brave words, she had been very worried about Juliet moving so far away. "Well, that will be wonderful. It will be so good to have you both nearby."

As June gave her an enormous hug, Juliet said: "I'm hoping we can find somewhere around here fairly quickly. Because Enzo has spent most of his life on the road, I don't think he minds living in a hotel, but it makes me feel quite nomadic."

Looking at June with concern, Juliet asked: "But what about this flat? Do you feel it will be too big for you on your own, will you be able to manage?" Juliet knew that money wasn't an issue for June, she had got a very good price for the large rambling house in Rottingdean, and Brian had left her well provided for. Nevertheless, Juliet was concerned that June would be left to pay all the bills on her own. Perhaps she should offer to buy herself out of the flat.

"Absolutely not," said June when Juliet hesitatingly suggested it. "After all, it should be me paying you as you are the one moving out. Won't you need the money from your share of the flat to help buy something else?"

"Enzo says not," said Juliet. "He's an old-fashioned Italian man with unshakeable ideas about women. He says it's his responsibility to provide a home for me."

"Don't tell Clarissa and the girls," laughed June. "I don't think those strong feminist women will approve of that."

"I hear that Enzo and Clarissa have already locked horns, and Enzo won," said Juliet with a little giggle. "He refused to let her go back to a bed and breakfast in Naples' red-light district when she thought it was okay. And Amy has definitely fallen under his spell. In her words he is 'fucking gorgeous'." June chortled. "Well, that's high praise coming from Amy."

"Now I'm waiting to hear what Lotte thinks of him," said Juliet, "but I suspect he will have charmed her too. I wonder what Malik will have to say if his feminist girlfriend suddenly wants him to open doors for her, pull out chairs, and hand her into taxis; all the things that young women seem to think are so unimportant nowadays."

June grinned. "I can see the attraction of being looked after by a man like Enzo. I wouldn't admit it to anyone but you, Jules, but I certainly wouldn't mind a sexy Italian coming along and running my life."

Juliet laughed. "Enzo is lovely, isn't he? Now I've got him back again, I really can't imagine how I ever left him in the first place."

"We make some strange decisions when we're young and lacking knowledge of the world," said June. "Given a bit of life experience we can see the bigger picture. Everything happens for a reason."

Juliet sighed. "It's funny, but feminists like Clarissa, Lotte and Amy, make such a big thing of standing on their own feet and not needing men. But faced with Enzo, who genuinely likes women, is disarmingly charming, and has very firm ideas on how we should be treated, they seem to crumble. I suspect that at heart all women secretly want a strong man to look after them, even if they won't admit it."

"I quite agree," said June. "Just watch, I bet Clarissa's girls will be off on a holiday to Italy soon hoping to find an Enzo of their own. I somehow doubt that Charlotte's Malik will stand up to scrutiny when compared with Enzo." Juliet gave an amused giggle. "That occurred to me too."

"I've always thought Malik takes Lotte for granted," continued June. "He's going to wake up one day and find she's gone off with someone else, even if she does claim to be a dyed in the wool feminist."

"Mmm. I think Clarissa and Tony have come to an understanding after all the years they've been together," said Juliet, "but I agree with you about Lotte and Malik. Like many attractive men Malik hasn't realised that a woman needs more than just a handsome face and a sprinkling of compliments to keep her happy. She needs to know she is loved and above all, cherished."

★★★

After a bread and cheese lunch, which they ate casually at the kitchen table, Juliet and June went into the sitting room and settled themselves beside the long windows overlooking the sea with cats on their laps and Florence contentedly at their feet.

Looking across at her lifelong friend, June said: "There's something that has been on my mind ever since Enzo turned up. D'you know what I've been thinking about a lot recently Jules… us and boys."

"Us and boys?" repeated Juliet looking puzzled. "Yes. Think back to when we were in our teens and I had all the boys running after me. I knew I could get any boy I wanted, so I played the field and pitted them all against each other, just having fun and moving on, never caring who got hurt in the process.

"When my parents told me on my eighteenth birthday that I was adopted and then, after eventually finding my birth mother who refused to have anything to do with me, I went on that holiday to Spain. I deliberately intended to lose my virginity as a way of getting my own back, punishing my parents, I suppose.

"I met a lot of really great boys, and I had the most amazing sex for the first time with Pedro, he was pretty gorgeous too. Then I slept with almost all the boys I dated once I got back home. There is no doubt that I was a promiscuous hussy but now, with the benefit of age and hindsight, I really believe it was a subconscious reaction to the shock of learning I was adopted." Juliet looked at her intently but said nothing. Where was this going, she wondered.

June continued: "I know I've said all this before, but I need to say it again. I married Brian, not for love but for money and an easy life. When I quickly discovered that marriage to Brian wasn't that great and he had a mistress, I retaliated by having affairs, but we stayed together all those years because divorce wasn't really an option. People like us didn't get divorced, and therefore we lived in a shell of a marriage, but presented a united front to the world.

"To be perfectly honest, I don't think I have ever truly loved or been loved. Both Brian and I had loads of sex, together and with other people, but never love. I was always looking for something I couldn't find.

"The point I am trying to make is that although you were never that popular with the boys when we were young – sorry Jules but it's true – you have had three men in your life who have loved you.

"I admit that Mike was a bit of a disaster, but I do believe he loved you in his own way. Then Ted, who absolutely adored you, and finally Enzo, who more than adores you and has been totally obsessed with you for fifty years. So, what I want to know is how do you do it? How do you get men to love you so deeply?"

Juliet looked astonished. "I really don't know what to say. I never went out of my way to chase boys when I was young, I was never really that interested. I preferred to lust after Elvis and dream about Marcello Mastroianni. I was always hoping to find someone exceptional. Someone out of the ordinary.

"Although I *was* always adamant I wouldn't have sex until I was married, I do admit I made a conscious decision to sleep with Enzo on Capri. He was so 'fucking gorgeous' as Amy says, I couldn't resist him. He was the exceptional guy I had dreamed of and I wanted him to be the first man I had sex with. It was, of course my fault it all went horribly wrong, and I ended up as an unmarried mother with an illegitimate child. I know that the situation might have been different if I'd either gone back to Capri when I was supposed to, or let Mike have sex with me once he had said he would marry me.

"I know you couldn't understand why I didn't sleep with Mike, but I really didn't fancy him; Enzo had spoilt me for anyone else. I do understand how frustrated Mike was with me, but let's face it, marriage to him would have been a complete disaster. I am extremely lucky that everything has ended so well for me, even if it did take a long time.

"I think it proves the truth of destiny and fate; that life eventually works out the way it is meant to, even if there are a few hiccups along the way. But as for love, I have no answer. It just happened. I have been very fortunate."

Looking at June with tears in her eyes, Juliet added: "I really do feel that I am living my life backwards. Everything I am doing now I should have done fifty years ago. Enzo and I have wasted so much precious time, and it's all my fault."

June sat silently for a while and then said: "What goes around comes around. I think I got my just desserts. All those times when I played the field and caused heartbreak without caring when I was young, came back to haunt me years later. It's too late for me to find love now."

"June!" Juliet was dismayed. "I'm sure that's not true. Maybe you've just been unlucky in love. It's never too late."

"Ah well," said June giving Juliet a hug. "It's all water under the bridge now. All I will say is that I am delighted that you and Enzo have found each other again. It's just a beautiful love story and I am so happy it has happened for you.

Chapter Twenty-Two

"Omnia Vincit Amor, et nos cedamus amori" ("Love conquers all things, so we too shall yield to love")
Virgil, in the tenth 'Eclogue' (c42-39 BCE)

THREE WEEKS later Enzo, Juliet, June and Enzo's guitar flew to Italy. Seeing June's amazement that the Gibson had its own seat on the plane, Enzo simply shrugged and said: "It goes everywhere with me." Juliet added: "It even goes to bed with us."

June's surprise at the guitar being given a seat, was nothing compared to her utter astonishment as Enzo yet again caused a flutter among the flight attendants. "I've never seen anything like it," she told Juliet. "However does he do it?"

One extremely attractive young man, snaked-hipped and kohl-eyed with long blond hair wound into a top-knot, was particularly attentive as he shimmied excitedly up and down the aisle, always stopping to tap Enzo lightly on the shoulder and have a few flirty words, ensuring he had everything he needed.

June watched with fascinated admiration as Enzo firmly but kindly made it perfectly clear that he was with Juliet, dealing gently with the unwanted attention without hurting the young man's feelings. My God, thought June, he really is an extraordinary one-off. He seems to be able to cope efficiently with every situation. And yet again she thought, lucky Juliet.

When they arrived in Naples, there was a taxi waiting to transport them to Sorrento so they could make the crossing to

Capri. Feeling very emotional as they boarded the ferry, Enzo wrapped his arms tightly around Juliet, remembering how mesmerised he had been when he had spotted her in her pink sundress on this same journey across the Tyrrhenian Sea fifty years before.

With the help of various friends and acquaintances in high places, Enzo had efficiently and rapidly made all the arrangements for their visit. They would be staying at Villa Florentina and the marriage would be held there the following day.

"My best friend Matteo will meet us at Piazza Umberto so we can all go to the hotel together," explained Enzo. "He'll be staying with us at Villa Florentina for a few days rather than travelling backwards and forwards across the island."

★★★

Once on Capri they negotiated the busy funicular at Marina Grande and found Matteo waiting for them at one of the white painted tables in the square where Enzo and Juliet had first met all those years ago.

Matteo kissed Juliet on both cheeks and gave Enzo an affectionate bear hug and a slap on the back. "My sincere congratulations," he said. "Thank goodness you found each other again after all these years." Looking at Juliet he said jokingly: "You have responsibility for him now, *Giulietta*. I am handing him over to you. I will be happy to get rid of the burden after all these years." Enzo gave a grunt of amusement and introduced Matteo to June.

Giving her a beaming smile, Matteo carefully scrutinised June's white palazzo trousers and black silk shirt before kissing her hand, his eyes fixed on hers. "*Incantata*." That's the second time I've had my hand kissed, thought June. First Enzo, now Matteo. I'm beginning to think I quite like it.

"Welcome to Capri, June. I am very pleased to meet such a beautiful lady." Matteo's deep voice was warm and velvety. Continuing to stare into her eyes and still holding her hand, he said: "June? Is that how you say your name, like the month? In Italian we say *'Giungo'*, it sounds similar but we spell it very differently. It is a pretty name and really suits you."

Well, thought June, here's proof, if proof were needed, that all Italian men are incorrigible flirts. She felt slightly distracted by Matteo's mouth, noticing that he had a very enticing bottom lip, and thinking as Clarissa had, I bet he'd be nice to kiss.

Matteo, looking at June's smooth dark shoulder length hair, now streaked with grey, and her bright blue almond-shaped eyes, was thinking what an attractive woman. I wonder if there will be a chance to get to know her better. He noticed that her nails were unusually short, neat and unadorned, the way he liked them; he had never been a fan of brightly painted talons.

June was wearing an absolutely enormous diamond on the ring finger of her left hand, but as far as Matteo could see, no wedding band. Was she married? Enzo hadn't mentioned that she was. Anyway, she and *Giulietta* had been sharing a flat so there surely couldn't be a husband. He was also intrigued by June's throaty rather sexy laugh, which had captivated men of all ages since she was a teenager.

"I expect you would like *una pausa* before we move on," said Matteo, trying not to look at the outline of June's seemingly endless legs inside her loose trousers. "I have organised water, wine and Limoncello, or you may have *caffè macchiato* if you wish."

He looked around – "Do you have any luggage?"

"It's all gone ahead to the hotel," said Enzo.

"Very efficient," said Matteo approvingly, "but then, what else would I expect of you? *Auguri…*congratulations on your marriage and for making all these arrangements so impressively quickly."

Enzo said seriously: "Well, at our age we don't have time to lose, and I also had to make sure *Giulietta* didn't vanish again." Amid the laughter, Juliet shook her head giving him a loving look. "You know I won't."

Sitting down next to Juliet, Matteo asked after Clarissa. "How is your very formidable daughter?"

"Clarissa is well and asked me to give you her love and thanks," replied Juliet.

"Hmm." Matteo frowned, recalling the tense argument he and Clarissa had when she turned up at his hotel looking for Enzo. He also remembered, with a slight touch of guilt and a twinge of remorse, his fleeting and entirely inappropriate desire to sleep with her. Luckily, she had left before he could make a fool of himself and upset a lot of people. Ships that pass in the night…

"She is a beautiful but *very* determined lady, that one," he said chuckling, pulling himself back to his conversation with Juliet. "Quite understandable seeing who her father is. We did have a bit of a falling out, but we were friends in the end, so please give her my love too."

"I will," said Juliet smiling, having heard from Clarissa about the argument she and Matteo had over Enzo.

Clarissa had also told Juliet in the strictest confidence about Matteo's alluring mouth, confessing that she had rather wanted to kiss him and that she was pretty sure Matteo had fancied her. "I left before anything could happen," she said, looking very embarrassed, but relieved to be able to share the secret with one of the few people she trusted completely.

Studying Matteo now, Juliet could totally understand the attraction, knowing only too well how enticing Italian men could be and how easy it was to give in to temptation. The itch of desire was so seductive, even if you had a happy marriage, you were not immune. She recalled hearing a family whisper that some years ago Clarissa had a brief fling with a man who was going to work with Tony.

Juliet reflected that as Clarissa was Enzo's daughter, she had probably inherited the innate ability to charm, not to mention the Italian craving for *amore*. She sighed, thankful that Clarissa had been sensible with Matteo and not let the situation get out of hand. That would have been a complication they didn't need in their lives.

Enzo held up his glass. "*Saluti* to Clarissa! Without her determination we wouldn't be here today." Kissing Juliet on the cheek he added: "I am so proud she is our daughter."

"Me too," agreed Juliet."

Matteo called a taxi to take Enzo, Juliet and June up to Anacapri and the Villa Florentina. "I'll drive my car up but there's not a lot of room and you won't all fit in, so a taxi will be best." He was tempted to offer June a lift but decided that might be imprudent.

"Matteo has a passion for cars," Enzo told Juliet and June. "None of his vehicles are built to take passengers. He always drives something that is elegant and usually has only two seats."

"You should meet Lotte's boyfriend Malik, he's also a car fanatic," Juliet told Matteo. "At the moment he has an elegant but very ancient Porsche."

"And very stylish it is too," added Enzo.

Matteo shrugged. "I just like cars. For me they are an important part of life, definitely a passion – like food and art and…"

"And *le donne*," added Enzo with a knowing smile.

"Yes, definitely women," said Matteo laughing as Enzo nodded and added: "He likes his cars and his women to be elegant and stylish…"

"And ancient?" interjected June with an impish smile.

Matteo gave her an amused look. "Age is always a plus point for me, in cars and in women. It makes them classic and therefore desirable," he said staring fixedly at June.

Blushing slightly, she slid her eyes away from his and started talking animatedly to Juliet about the chances of shopping while they were on Capri. "It looks like there are some really chic boutiques here. Everything seems to be so much sexier in Italy." For goodness sake she thought as Matteo once again glanced at her with amusement, what am I saying, my mouth seems to be running away with me.

As they stood up after finishing their drinks, Matteo deliberately drew June's arm through his to escort her across the square to the taxi. She pulled away, jumping slightly as his skin touched hers. She wasn't sure why, but she had an unusual quiver of excitement in her stomach and was feeling a bit self-conscious. Unperturbed, Matteo threaded her arm back through his and patting her hand, strolled on as if nothing had happened.

The bells of Santo Stefano on the edge of the piazza, began calling the faithful to Mass as they passed. "I really must go, but not now," murmured Matteo. "You should visit Santo Stefano while you are on Capri. It is very beautiful and one of the oldest churches on the island."

"Are you a regular churchgoer?" asked June. "I only seem to go to church for weddings and funerals nowadays."

"Mmm, I am, although not as regular as I should be but I am a Catholic, so I do need to go to confession every so often."

June gave him a sideways glance from under her lashes. "And do you have sins to confess?" He bit his lip thoughtfully. "Usually I have many, but none just at the moment," he whispered. "Hopefully, that will change soon."

★★★

June was enchanted when she saw Villa Florentina. Juliet knew it well, having stayed there for two weeks when she first came to Capri with the botany group.

"It's so beautiful," gasped June, admiring the pink and purple bougainvillea tumbling over the pale blue washed building and the open balconies with their pots of colourful flowers. "Everything I could imagine an Italian hotel would be."

"That's just how I felt the first time I saw it," agreed Juliet. "I must say it seems little changed over the years."

Welcomed by Signore Fabrizio's son Alberto, a solid family man in his mid-fifties who was now the *patron*, they were shown to their rooms. Enzo and Juliet had the honeymoon suite on the top floor, while both June and Matteo had ground floor rooms with French windows opening onto tiny terraces, very similar to the room Juliet had been given when she stayed there in the sixties.

"It's absolutely idyllic," said June when they met for dinner that evening. "Thank you so much for inviting me. I really love it here. My room even has a little terrace with huge pots of geraniums."

"I wonder which room you've got," said Juliet. "It was at the window of one of those ground floor rooms that the gardener gave me the first note from Enzo inviting me to hear him sing at Bar Russe."

"You must come and have a look at my room when you have a free moment. Being back here must be full of memories for you."

"What do you think of Matteo?" Juliet asked curiously, linking arms with June as they walked to their table. "Seems alright," replied June offhandedly, recalling the way she had felt when he touched her. "Full of flirtatious bullshit, though." Juliet laughed. "He's actually really nice when you get to know him. Even Clarissa liked him eventually, and you know how fussy she is about men."

★★★

The next morning Matteo took Enzo off for a bachelor breakfast while June went up to the honeymoon suite to help Juliet get dressed for her big day. The room was filled with the fragrance of freesias.

June was about to ask Juliet if she was excited, but the bride-to-be was floating around on a cloud of happiness. No need to check how she's feeling, June told herself, remembering with clarity the last-minute doubts she'd had on her wedding day to Brian. It must be amazing to love someone so much and to be so sure they love you too that there is no room for worry or uncertainty.

They sipped glasses of Prosecco as June helped Juliet into a long floaty dress of soft white chiffon. It had narrow full-length sleeves, a deep V neckline and a shimmering floral appliqué at the waist. An Alice band of white freesias held back her long grey hair. "I decided I didn't need to carry a posy, so I've got flowers in my hair instead. Do you think they look okay; not too girlish? The wonderful Alberto organised them for me so they would be fresh today."

"They're perfect and I must say they smell amazing," said June.

Thinking back to the sixties, Juliet smiled at the memory of Ted suggesting they had a Flower Power Wedding "…you in a long white dress with flowers in your hair." It hadn't happened then, but now she was wearing a long white dress and had flowers in her hair for Enzo.

"You look absolutely sublime," said June, feeling very emotional. "Hold still a minute while I take a photo to send to the children. Rosie made me promise I would."

June thought what a difference Enzo's return had made to Juliet. She had always been pretty, even in her childhood days when she was slightly gawky, but now, shining with happiness, she was simply beautiful. She was also looking a lot younger, and her clothes had definitely improved.

Before Enzo came back Juliet was beginning to look a bit staid and comfortable, now her clothes were sharper and more fashionable and her whole demeanour had changed. She could no longer be called an old lady. Juliet was radiant. A mature woman deeply in love with a man who adored her.

Clarissa told June she had come across Juliet buying Chanel perfume in John Lewis. "She said Enzo used to give her Chanel No 5 and she hadn't worn it since she left Capri. Now she was going to wear it again for him." Love does miraculous things, thought June as they went down to the room that had been set aside for the marriage.

The short civil ceremony was perfect, made all the more so by the pure joy emanating from Enzo and Juliet who held hands throughout, unable to take their eyes off each other. The couple exchanged vows and rings. Enzo, who had previously always refused to wear a wedding band, insisted he wanted one this time as a sign to the world that he was totally committed to *Giulietta*. They both vowed to love and cherish each other for the rest of their lives.

June felt tears welling up. How wonderful to find love again in the autumn of life, just when you thought all romance was behind you.

★★★

Sitting next to June, Matteo noticed again her seemingly endless legs. He was also aware of the swell of her breasts in her low-cut dress and her very neat ankles and wrists. As June bent down to pick up the bag which had slipped off her lap, he felt strangely moved to see her shoulder length hair part to reveal much paler skin on the nape of her neck

Sensing again the surge of attraction he had felt when they first met on the Piazza Umberto, Matteo had no doubt he wanted to know June better. A lot better.

Remembering Clarissa, he thought wryly that June was the best friend of his best friend's wife. No rules to break this time.

★★★

After the ceremony, Matteo made a speech, followed by a congratulatory toast and the serving of Prosecco and *Croquembouche,* a patisserie pastry tower that had impressed Enzo while he was touring in France. The couple had decided it would be a delicious and lighter alternative to the traditional wedding cake and Villa Florentina's talented chef agreed to craft one especially for them. As there were only four of them in the wedding party, Juliet had asked Alberto to share the cake among guests and staff at the hotel.

Chapter Twenty-Three

"Bésame Mucho" ("Kiss Me a Lot")
Andrea Bocelli, on the album 'Amore' (2006)

WHEN ALBERTO Fabrizio announced there would be a two-hour break before lunch June, desperate for solitude, went outside and wandered to the far end of Villa Florentina's beautiful gardens.

There was no one else about and she stood in a sheltered alcove looking out over the calm turquoise waters of the Tyrrhenian Sea, hoping that the peaceful scene would help to shake off the melancholy which seemed to have enveloped her.

So, Juliet and Enzo were married at last. There could be no doubt about how much they loved each other. I do feel slightly envious of their happiness, thought June before admitting no, actually, I feel exceedingly envious.

June wondered what she and Brian had missed over the years, as she recalled their marriage more than half a century ago. What a glittering affair that had been. She shuddered to remember exactly what her couture dress had cost. Along with the bridesmaids' dresses, the wedding breakfast, photography and all the other paraphernalia associated with a society wedding, her father had probably shelled out a small fortune.

Looking back dispassionately, she knew that the only thing missing from her big day had been the most important thing of all: love. She had never loved Brian and she was certain he had never loved her. It was a marriage of convenience for both of them.

She had married because she wanted to get away from her parents, never having forgiven them for not telling her until she was eighteen that she was adopted. Admittedly she had also been slightly swayed by the luxurious lifestyle offered by her in-laws' millions.

Brian had to marry because he needed a son and heir to the family fortune and his parents had forbidden marriage to his older mistress, who was a triple divorcee. June had eventually produced Ned, who was a chip off the old block. The family had paid to send him to Harrow, his grandfather being an Old Harrovian, and he now had a prosperous career in finance. The only downside, thought June, was that Ned now lived in Australia and she rarely saw him, her daughter-in-law Penelope or her two grandsons.

She sighed. Such was life! Despite the lack of love and their unconventional marriage, she and Brian had remained together until his death. A lifetime had slipped away in the blink of an eye and love had completely passed her by.

Pondering Juliet and Enzo's transparent happiness, June decided that an expensive society wedding, a page of envy-inducing pictures in *Tatler,* and a luxurious lifestyle were unnecessary when you both had so much love for each other that all you wanted was to be legally bound together.

Engrossed in the past, June was unaware that Matteo was standing behind her. "May I join you or do you prefer to be alone." She gave a little jump as he spoke but smiled: "Please do, I was lost in thought." He stepped into the alcove saying: "I must confess I have been stalking you."

"Really?" said June in surprise. "Why?" He laughed. "The happy couple have gone to have coffee in their suite until lunch is ready, which I suspect means they are consummating their nuptials as we speak. So, I decided to seek you out so we could get to know each other a little better. If *Giulietta* and Enzo remain totally wrapped up in each other, we may have to spend a bit of time together, just the two of us."

June looked with interest at the man leaning against the alcove wall opposite her. He had been Enzo's friend when Juliet was on Capri back in the sixties, and Clarissa, who had met him a month or so ago, had told her he was very nice and definitely a fascinating character.

Matteo was shorter than Enzo and didn't have his devastating good looks. Nevertheless, his crisp greying hair and twinkling brown eyes full of humour were very attractive and he had the innate ability to charm and flirt which seemed to be bestowed on all Italian men as far as June could see.

June regarded him gravely through narrowed eyes, once again wondering what he'd be like to kiss. There was definitely something nice about his mouth; that bottom lip was tantalising. She remembered with a shiver the way she had felt when he threaded her arm through his to walk across the piazza.

"So…what would you like to know about me?"

"Oh, nothing in particular," he replied nonchalantly. "Enzo says you and Juliet live together."

"*Used* to live together," June corrected him. "After the ceremony this morning, we are obviously no longer flatmates."

"You're not married?"

"Widowed," said June, "almost three years ago." Ah, thought Matteo, that accounts for the ring. "I am sorry."

"That's okay. What about you?"

"*Divorziato*." Ah, thought June, that would account for his clothes. Wearing a crumpled loose-fitting cream linen suit and brown loafers without socks, Matteo didn't look as if a woman had oversight of his wardrobe. June found it strange that continental men tended not to wear socks, almost as if they'd woken up in the morning and discovered they had no clean ones to put on.

She remembered asking Juliet all those years ago when she

had first returned from Capri, whether Enzo wore Y-fronts or boxer shorts or went commando. Now she idly pondered what Matteo was wearing under his suit. If he had no clean socks, he probably had no clean underwear to put on either. Quite apart from socks and underwear, he wasn't wearing a wedding ring.

June let a pause fall before asking casually: "And you haven't found another partner?"

Matteo gave a rueful smile. "Helping to run a hotel is not every woman's idea of a perfect life. I've never found anyone willing to help me do it. One of the reasons I'm divorced is because my ex-wife preferred to have a social life rather than look after hotel guests. So she left me."

June turned to look at him. "How is it that you speak such good English?"

"To run a hotel it is necessary. I learnt English at school, although it was not taught well, so I wasn't very good at first, but then I took lessons and over the years it has got easier. Do you speak any Italian?"

June grimaced. "No, just the odd word. Being English means it is not really necessary to speak other languages, so we are very lazy about it. All I can say is *'Ciao'*, *'Per favore'* and *'Grazie'*. Said with a smile they seem to cover most eventualities." Teasingly she added: "Oh yes, and *'Ti amo'* but I've never needed to use that!"

Matteo gave her a dazzling smile. Moving away from the wall, he was beside her in two strides. Staring deeply into her eyes he said caressingly: "Italian is the language of love, all beautiful women should be able to speak it so they can excite their lovers. You are very beautiful, so you should speak Italian too. I will teach you; it will be a pleasure."

June said warily: "Stop flirting with me, Matteo. I am too old for flirtation."

He looked slightly shocked. "Oh no! A woman is never too old to flirt, or to be flirted with. My grandmother flirted until the day she died. She was well into her nineties, always insisting that amorous dalliance kept her alive. She had many gentleman callers right to the end."

June gave her throaty laugh. "That is so *very* Italian."

"You think so? He regarded her intently. "So how old are you June, if you think you're too old to flirt?"

"Didn't your mother tell you that you should never ask a woman's age," she replied provocatively. "Good boys should never ask a lady personal questions." June was beginning to enjoy herself. She couldn't remember the last time she had engaged in casual flirtatious chit-chat.

Matteo grinned. "Okay. Well, that's where it all goes wrong because I have never been a good boy; always very bad, I'm afraid. That is why I usually have so much to confess when I go to church."

Laughing he added: "No worry, I can work it out. You are the same age as *Giulietta,* and she is seventy-two. I will tell you before you ask that I am seventy-seven, a couple of years younger than Enzo. So, you see, we are not too old."

Too old for *what,* wondered June. Flirtation? She decided not to ask, fearing that she was quickly moving out of her comfort zone. Rapidly changing the subject, she said: "If you are seventy-seven now, you must have been very young to run a hotel in the sixties."

"It was a family business," said Matteo frowning, "and it still is. My sister, one of my brothers and a niece continue to be involved along with me." He gave her a hard stare with narrowed eyes. "You are trying to change the course of our conversation." He paused, biting his lip. "Why is that?"

June blushed. He was incredibly direct, and she felt the uncomfortable flutter of butterflies in her stomach as Matteo put an arm around her saying: "So, will you flirt with me June, just a little?" June could feel control skidding away from her. She was beginning to feel a bit jittery. "Um, I…I don't think I know how."

"Oh, I cannot believe that. A sophisticated lady like you must certainly know. Women always do, even when they pretend they don't." The blush on June's cheeks deepened as Matteo continued to stare at her. Wearing her wedge heeled sandals she was exactly his height, and their eyes were level as they gazed at each other.

"You can take off your shoes if you like, I won't mind," he murmured.

"Why should I take off my shoes?"

"It will be easier for me to kiss you."

"But I'm not…" He gave her a crinkle-eyed smile. "Remember bad boys never take 'no' for an answer."

"Oh!" June was aware of a nervous churning in the pit of her stomach. Although she had spent a lifetime teasing, deliberately arousing desire and enjoying the thrill of the chase, this situation felt very different from anything she had experienced before. Realising that Matteo had subtly taken control, she began to feel the slight stirring of lust. There was something strangely appealing about an attractive man being assertive.

June had been sleeping with men since she was eighteen and Matteo wasn't the type she usually went for, but he not only had the most extraordinary ability to make her feel gauche like an inexperienced teenager, but also rather excited. Embarrassed she said: "I'm not sure I want to be kissed," thinking, actually I'd really like to kiss that bottom lip, looking at it is driving me crazy.

"Is that so?" he said softly, "I was pretty sure you did," and before she could move he put his mouth over hers, gently pushing his tongue between her lips. June stood passively for a moment before kicking off her sandals and putting her arms around Matteo, instinctively leaning against his body.

He's an exceptionally good kisser she thought with pleasure; I hadn't expected that. She was usually able to spot a man who kissed that well at a dozen paces, but despite idly reflecting that

Matteo had a nice mouth and wondering what he would be like to kiss, his expertise had taken her totally by surprise. They stood wrapped together for a long time before he gently released her, giving the slow sexy smile she had so often seen on Enzo's face as he looked at Juliet.

Oh shit, thought June. What have I done? It was insane. She had come to Capri to support Juliet on her wedding day, not for a holiday romance nor for random sex for that matter…but wow, he was good! Now she found herself wondering what he would be like in bed.

After affairs and flirtations over many years June had learnt that there were very few men who really knew how to make love. They all knew about sex and getting satisfaction…as quickly as possible in most cases…but only a few made love sensitively, making sure their partner was happy and getting as much pleasure as they were.

Juliet had told her Enzo had always been amazing. "He is very skilful and exciting but incredibly gentle and considerate. During that time I spent with him on Capri he taught me a lot. He still is an extraordinary lover. Sex with him is as good now as it was when I was nineteen."

June had a strong feeling that Matteo would also be an accomplished and thoughtful partner, and she had to admit she was rather keen to find out. Taking a deep breath she wondered with slight panic if he could tell she fancied him. The thought that he might, made her feel awkward and anxious.

Matteo was simply consumed by lust. Kissing June had been unexpectedly exciting and he wanted to take her to bed. Feeling desire surge through him, he knew with pleasure that she definitely wouldn't be a quick fuck, but a lady who demanded a bit of time and consideration. Taking her hand, he gently rotated his thumb on her palm. June was immediately alert; the message was as clear as Morse code, transcending all language. She gave him a swift glance to make sure she had interpreted it correctly. Their eyes met and she knew she had.

Giving her an enticing smile Matteo asked: "Your room or mine?" As he led her out of the alcove he added: "We have about an hour before lunch, or we can have a siesta afterwards. Which would you prefer?"

Chapter Twenty-Four

"Love Me Like You Do"
Ellie Goulding, on the album 'Fifty Shades Freed'
(Original Motion Picture Soundtrack, 2018)

ENZO AND Juliet were in the bar when Matteo and June arrived for lunch. June had chosen a siesta, thinking that given a couple of hours' leeway she could probably find some way to extricate herself from a situation which she felt was now definitely beyond her control.

"Prosecco?" asked Enzo when he saw them.

Juliet put her hand on June's arm. "*Please* don't let me drink too much of this. It's utterly delicious but I seem to have been drinking since this morning, and when I had champagne at that French restaurant in Brighton when we were celebrating our engagement, I got totally sloshed."

Enzo laughed. "Don't worry *amore*, this is the last glass you're having. I don't want you sleeping all afternoon. We have other plans."

"You remember what happened the last time you said that," said Juliet teasingly. "When you told Marco we couldn't be late because we had other plans after the jamming session."

"Of course I do," replied Enzo, whispering in her ear, "rough sex." Looking deeply into each other's eyes they once again enjoyed the memory before reluctantly dragging themselves back to the present.

"It was a lovely ceremony," said June brightly, desperately hoping that general conversation would help to quell the butterflies in her stomach; it was a long time since she'd felt so excited by the prospect of going to bed with someone. "And I loved the *Croquembouche*. It was amazing, just perfect. A really inspired choice." She paused, taking a deep breath, and Matteo smiled as he looked at her, aware of her churning emotions.

"We thought it was perfect too," said Enzo, his hand on Juliet's knee, longing to take his wife back upstairs but knowing that there was no way they could skip the celebratory meal. Turning to Matteo and June he said: "What have you two been doing this morning?" It was an innocently asked question, but June guiltily felt Enzo's intense blue eyes were boring into her soul.

Sensing her discomfort Matteo jumped in. "Oh, I went for a stroll around these amazing gardens and bumped into June who was looking out across the sea contemplating life," he replied calmly. "So we had a bit of a chat and got to know each other better." June nodded: "Yes," adding rather lamely, "the gardens here are very beautiful…"

"Wonderful view from where I was standing," said Matteo looking wide-eyed at June with a perfectly straight face.

"Good," said Enzo, giving Matteo a curious look. Reading between the lines he was sure there was more to it than that. Knowing Matteo so well, Enzo suspected he had made a pass at June, and judging from her face, she hadn't turned him down. However, he merely said: "I am pleased you two have got to know each other."

"So am I," said Matteo smiling broadly.

★★★

Enzo and Juliet had agreed to give Alberto Fabrizio a free hand to organise their wedding lunch and he had surpassed himself.

"It was definitely the right thing to do," said Juliet. "This lovely wedding has been really low-key and the last thing I wanted was to start fussing over the menu. Much better to leave to the expert."

Alberto had designed a traditional Italian meal for them, starting with Italian Wedding Soup, followed by Chicken Sorrentino and Hot Berry Tart. *Caffe macchiato* completed what all four agreed was the quintessential wedding lunch. There were also several bottles of Chianti, which Enzo gently refused to let Juliet touch, removing her wine glass and pouring her tumblers of water instead.

Giving Alberto a kiss on the cheek after they had finished eating Juliet said: "Thank you, that was just what Enzo and I wanted. We all enjoyed it so much; a truly wonderful meal." Alberto was delighted. "I'm only sorry my father is not here to see your marriage. He would have been so proud that you chose to have it at Villa Florentina, and also very happy that you and Enzo have got married after all these years. He was very fond of both of you."

Rushing off to present his kitchen and waiting staff with the very generous tip Enzo had given them, Alberto reflected that although it had been the most unusual wedding they'd ever had at Villa Florentina, it had been an outstanding success. Hosting Enzo de Martins' wedding was definitely quite a coup for his hotel.

★★★

As they were sitting and chatting over a bottle of Grappa, there was something about the way Matteo glanced over at June that caught Juliet's attention. She looked from June to Matteo then back to June again. They were both looking…slightly shifty. I wonder what they've been up to. Have they hooked up?

June, catching her eye and picking up her thoughts, blushed; Jules knows!

Juliet gave a brief grin of surprise. I'm right, she thought, that was quick work. She couldn't wait to get June on her own to find out what had happened but knew it wouldn't be possible until the following day. Oh well, no rush, but I do hope they're enjoying themselves as much as we are.

Outside the dining room the two couples went their separate ways. Juliet and Enzo back to the honeymoon suite for the much longed-for siesta, while June and Matteo went off…where? wondered Juliet. She couldn't wait to tell Enzo that their best friends were sleeping together.

Chapter Twenty-Five

"Ai Du"
Ali Farka Touré, featuring Ry Cooder,
on the album 'Talking Timbuktu' (1994)

AFTER AGREEING to meet Juliet and Enzo for dinner that evening, Matteo put his hand firmly under June's elbow, guiding her towards his room. "My place okay?" he asked with an impudent smile.

June couldn't think of a single valid reason why not. Of course, she could just say 'No', but after kissing this rather attractive Italian she was riding a rapidly rising wave of desire. She wanted to have sex with him; wanted to find out if his lovemaking was as exciting as his kisses.

His room was a carbon copy of hers. Rough white painted walls with a cool tiled floor strewn with blue and white cotton mats and French windows opening onto a terrace. The double bed had a colourful patchwork quilt thrown over it and local pottery was scattered in various nooks and crannies. She suspected their rooms were much as they were when Juliet had stayed there in the sixties.

Matteo, picking up stray items of clothing that were lying around the floor, turned to June and asked politely: "Would you like to use the bathroom?"

"Yes please," June nodded and went thankfully in. She was shaking. This is absolutely crazy. She'd been having casual sex since her teens; she wasn't concerned about Matteo seeing her naked, her body was in relatively good shape for her age, and she was very confident of her performance in bed.

Both she and Matteo were free to have sex if they wished. There were no spouses to worry about; they were not committing adultery. So why did she feel she was *in flagrante delicto*? She was full of nervous excitement, like a young girl about to lose her virginity. Stop being so pathetic, June told herself sternly. You want this.

"Are you okay?" called Matteo. "Won't be a minute," she replied washing her hands and splashing cold water over her flaming cheeks.

There was music playing when June went out into the bedroom. Matteo was sitting on the bed wearing only a pair of very brief briefs; his body was unexpectedly firm and muscly with only the tiniest hint of a paunch. So that was what was under the loose suit. Shame to hide a physique like that, not bad for seventy-seven.

In an attempt to postpone the inevitable, June asked about the music that was playing on Matteo's phone. It was definitely African Blues of some sort and very hypnotic. "Nice music, what is it?"

"*Ai Du* by Ali Farka Touré. It's very philosophical, all about trust, self-awareness and understanding others," said Matteo. "Quite apart from that, it's the perfect music to fuck to." As June gave a startled gasp, Matteo patted the mattress invitingly and asked teasingly, "So are you planning to join me, baby?"

Rooted to the spot, June's heart was thumping and she couldn't stop looking at Matteo's mouth; the chemistry between them felt almost tangible. This is ridiculous, she thought. What on earth is happening. Casual sex should be…relaxed and fun. Not this uncomfortable feeling of intense magnetism.

Matteo was slightly surprised by June's hesitancy. Judging by the way she kissed he was pretty sure she was an experienced lover, and he knew how excited she had been at lunchtime. So why was she standing there looking like a virgin about to be seduced.

There was a long silence and June became aware that Matteo was staring at her. Eventually she confessed rather reluctantly: "I actually feel slightly shy; I don't know why, but I'm nervous. I feel a bit edgy when I'm around you."

"Oh, don't be *cara*, I know we are going to be wonderful together." Getting off the bed Matteo went over and held her close to him, gently running his hands up and down her back. He could feel her trembling. "There's no reason to be nervous baby. Nothing else matters, just us. In Italy it is all about the now; enjoying yourself in the moment," he said, breathing gently into her ear.

As they kissed June was engulfed by soaring desire. Heavens, it was a long time since anyone had made her feel like this; now she was desperate for him. Matteo, picking up her vibes, started trying to pull off her dress, carefully at first and then more aggressively. "Zip at the back," gasped June, wriggling. "You won't get it off otherwise." As he fiddled with the fastening she cried impatiently: "Oh, just tug it. Sod the zip. I can't wait any longer."

When she was down to her lacy underwear, he held out his hand. "Come with me." Lifting her onto the bed, he kissed her again with increasing passion. What was it about his mouth that was so arousing…she was turning to jelly. "Oh my God, Matteo," June sighed, "where did you learn to do that?"

"I once had a Thai lover and now it's just part of my strategy to seduce beautiful women."

"Well, it certainly works," said June faintly, quivering with longing for him. "Now for goodness' sake get on with it. What are you waiting for? I've always thought that too much warming up before the main event is simply wasting time. Foreplay is very overrated."

Right, let's get on with it then, thought Matteo with

amusement. What an extraordinary woman. He was only too happy to jump straight in, but most women usually needed a bit of encouragement. June, however, was not most women. He'd never known anyone quite like her. Lifting his head to look into her eyes he murmured: "You are quite shameless, *Signora*."

"So I've often been told," retorted June. "Now please stop talking."

Ai Du was playing on loop.

★★★

Matteo was completely blown away by June's skill in bed. Christ, she was fantastic, quite incredible and it was almost certainly the best sex he'd ever had. It was made even more pleasurable because she was so obviously turned on by him and enjoying herself. She was unquestionably a woman with a lot of experience. At one point he'd even had to ask her to slow down, whispering in her ear, "Wait for me, baby, I need to catch up with you."

Afterwards, snuggling contentedly into his arms, June asked: "Do I vaguely remember you asking me to slow down? That's never happened before!"

"A first for me too," admitted Matteo. "There I was jogging along nicely and savouring the moment when I suddenly felt you dashing away from me."

"At least we finished together," said June feeling ridiculously happy. "We'll get the timing right next time."

So there was going to be a next time! Matteo had a feeling June could easily become addictive. He definitely wanted more of her but she would be going back to England the day after tomorrow and the chances of them getting together again after that were limited.

June's thoughts were running along similar lines. Without doubt the sex had been good, more than good, utterly fantastic; they were perfectly matched. But they both had busy lives in different countries and it was unlikely that they would meet again unless he came to England to visit Enzo.

Another one-night stand, thought June, sadly. Well, two nights…three at a push if he wanted repeat sessions this evening and tomorrow, but that would be it. Pity. The sex had been so incredible that for a very brief moment she had allowed herself to believe there might be possibilities.

They spent the afternoon in bed, dozing before having amazing sex again, and then idly chatting, until June reluctantly got up saying: "I must go back to my room, have a shower and get dressed for dinner. I can't go into the dining room wearing a dress with a broken zip. It will make people think I might have spent the afternoon in bed with a sexy man who couldn't manage to unfasten my dress properly!"

Matteo laughed and kissed her hand. "Ciao-Ciao, bella, I'll knock on your door on my way down to dinner."

Chapter Twenty-Six

"If music be the food of love, play on."
William Shakespeare, 'Twelfth Night' (Act I:i)

AFTER DINNER, the wedding party installed itself in Villa Florentina's comfortable lounge where Enzo had agreed to sing and play his guitar. Alberto Fabrizio had hesitantly asked if he would be willing to give a short impromptu concert and Enzo felt it would be churlish refuse. The hotel had given them such a wonderful wedding that it was the least he could do, he told Juliet.

Word had got around that Enzo was staying at Villa Florentina and had also married there, so it was not only hotel guests but also fans and friends from across the island who turned up to hear him sing and wish him well. While Juliet was proud that he was still very popular, Enzo was endearingly surprised to discover that so many people wanted to hear him sing.

Matteo's niece Isabella and a few of her girlfriends were in the audience. Arriving early they had managed to secure coveted places right at the front. The large room was filled to capacity, with a number of people squashed in wherever they could find a space and some at the very back standing on chairs, when Enzo walked in gently strumming his guitar.

As at the beginning of all his performances whether on Capri, in Rome, Paris or Las Vegas, he stood quietly with hands on hips nodding and smiling to acknowledge the cheering, clapping and foot stamping that welcomed him. Piercing wolf whistles and a few shrieks and screams from over-excited girls were followed by resounding laughter as Enzo said self-deprecatingly: "Thank you. I don't often attract that sort of response nowadays."

Matteo had often been to gigs at Bar Russe and occasionally in Naples or Rome, but June had never heard Enzo sing before and she was simply amazed at how good he was and how much his fans loved him. Even now he is effortlessly sexy, she thought. Fifty years ago, when Jules first heard him, he must have been absolutely stunning. No wonder she had fallen for him.

Enzo was still very assured and relaxed as he sang Frank Sinatra and Elvis Presley ballads, plus a few numbers made popular by Buddy Holly, Bob Dylan, and the Italian band I Pooh, having decided that anything too upbeat wouldn't work without a backing group. Although Enzo continued his spontaneous joking with the men and mild flirting with the women, Juliet noticed that he didn't kiss and cuddle any of the girls in the audience as he used to back in the sixties.

After almost an hour of requests from enthusiastic fans, Enzo ended by singing *Quando, Quando, Quando,* the smooth romantic ballad he had sung for Juliet the very first time she went to Bar Russe. This time he dedicated the song to 'my beautiful wife *Giulietta*' and the applause was deafening as the youngest Fabrizio daughter who was in her teens, shyly presented Juliet with a bouquet of white roses.

Afterwards Enzo mingled with the audience, shaking hands, kissing cheeks, signing autographs and posing for selfies. The fans loved him because he was always willing to chat and never turned anyone away.

During his summer visits to the island, Enzo could often be seen walking on his own around Capri's narrow streets or travelling on the funicular, happy to engage in conversation with anyone who wanted to talk to him. Because of the way he treated them, they were always willing to leave him alone when it was obvious he didn't want attention; it was a two-way relationship. Enzo had star quality and enormous charisma, but never behaved like a self-important celebrity.

★★★

Isabella was almost speechless with delight when Enzo came straight over at the end of the concert and putting an arm around her, kissed her cheek.

"Thank you for coming baby. I'm hoping to visit Villa Valentina with Matteo before I go back to England, probably tomorrow, so hopefully I will see you again then."

She nodded, feigning nonchalance. "That will be great. I'll try to make sure I'm around."

Introducing her infatuated friends to Enzo, Isabella basked in his reflected glory as the excited teenage girls almost swooned when he kissed their hands.

Taking Enzo completely by surprise, Sofia swooped in and firmly planted a kiss on his mouth, slowly rubbing her tongue between his lips as she did so. Looking at her triumphant grin, Enzo smiled and shook his head at her, saying: "You are too young to kiss like that," as he moved on.

"I'm never going to wash this hand again," declared Viola dramatically. "He's just so cool he's hot!" The others agreed. "He's the sexiest man on the planet," said Mia one of the girls who had screamed when Enzo walked into the room. "The girls at school will never believe it when I tell them that not only did I talk to him, but he kissed my hand."

"Wait until I tell them that I actually kissed him on the mouth," said Sofia jubilantly. "I think you'll find lips and a tongue trump hands!"

★★★

Juliet felt like a princess as Enzo, his arm around her waist, proudly introduced her to various friends, fans and the Capri glitterati. She found her grasp of Italian was gradually improving and she was now able to understand many of the questions put to her. The biggest thrill came the first time she was called '*Signora de Martins*'. Now I really do believe I am married to Enzo, she thought happily.

When they eventually got back to their suite, Juliet gave Enzo an enormous hug saying: "You were absolutely wonderful my darling, that was the perfect end to a perfect day."

Enzo gave her an intense look. "Did you notice anything missing from the gig, apart from Marco and Raf, of course." Juliet didn't have to think about the answer. "You didn't sing *Can't Help Falling in Love*," she said immediately. "You always used to include that in the programme."

"I've decided to cut it out entirely," Enzo told her. "You are the only person I sing that for now. It means far too much to us to be included in a public performance." Overwhelmed with love for him, Juliet whispered: "Soul meets soul on lovers' lips. Let's go to bed. I want to hear you sing it to me again."

Juliet recalled that on her wedding day to Ted, she had decided that sex definitely felt different once they were married. Now she realised that making love with Enzo was exactly the same as it had always been. Married or unmarried it was just unbelievably wonderful. And how could it be any different, she thought. You can't improve on perfection.

Lying with her head on Enzo's chest, Juliet murmured: "The other thing you didn't do this evening was kiss and cuddle any of the girls in the audience." Enzo replied seriously: "Yes, well, I stopped doing that some years ago. As I got older, I thought it might seem just a bit pervy and weird." Leaning up to kiss him, Juliet thought about Isabella and her friends and how besotted they were with him. "I bet none of the girls would complain if you did!"

Chapter Twenty-Seven

"Anima Fragile" ("Fragile Soul")
Vasco Rossi, on the album 'Ti Amo' (2006)

AFTER JULIET and Enzo had gone upstairs, June and Matteo went to the bar for a final drink. "Will you spend the night with me?" asked Matteo, handing her a shot glass of Limoncello. "Not only am I desperate to have sex with you again, but I would also like to wake up in the morning and find you beside me."

June took his hand. "I'd like that too," she said quietly. "But tomorrow is my last day here and I am worried about becoming… she paused, seeking the right words… "becoming too attached to you."

Matteo's brown eyes stared into June's blue ones, holding her gaze. "Are you afraid of falling in love with me?"

"I don't know. I've never been in love so I don't know what to expect." Matteo looked astonished. "You're seventy-two years old and you've never been in love? That's not possible."

June held out her hands, palms up, in a tiny helpless gesture. "Nevertheless, it's true. Sounds mad, doesn't it? I admit I have been 'in lust' many, many times over the years, but I have never truly loved anyone. In fact, I am beginning to think I am not capable of love. I don't fall in love the way other people do."

Matteo frowned. "Were you not in love with your husband?"

"No," said June, "and he didn't love me. We had a marriage of convenience."

Matteo looked at her silently, brow furrowed as if trying to understand her words. Eventually he said quietly, "You poor, poor baby."

"I wasn't unhappy," said June briskly. "We were together for fifty years. He had a long-term mistress and I had numerous affairs and flirtations, but I never met anyone I truly loved. I suppose if I was being completely honest, I would say I was happily unhappy."

Matteo asked the question he had been wanting to ask since he met her. "So, what's that all about?" he said, pointing to June's diamond ring. She laughed. "This is the ring Brian gave me when he asked me to marry him. I took off my wedding ring years ago when I discovered he had a mistress, seemed pointless to wear it really. I kept this diamond because I like it and it is rather valuable. It has no sentimental significance."

Matteo looked at her with real compassion and said again: "Poor baby; a diamond is no compensation for love. What a waste of life." Swallowing his Grappa, he stood up and took her hand. "Come on, let's go to bed." Drawn by longing, June let him lead her out of the bar and down the corridor to his room. Feeling desire pulsing through her she really wanted him but knew only too well that lust wasn't love.

Once again, the sex was fantastic. It was more measured and gentler than the first couple of times when they had been so impatient for each other, but still phenomenal. "We're getting the timing right now," murmured June. "We're getting better at it."

"You are already incredibly good at it," Matteo whispered as she lay in his arms. "I can't remember when I have been so excited."

"Years of practice," said June with a wry smile. "Anyway," she added, "You're not so bad yourself. It's a very long time since I've been with anyone who was so aware of what turns me on."

He gave her a long slow kiss. Although they were both exhausted, he really wanted sex again and he knew she did too. "I think we are good together," he said gruffly. "We certainly seem to understand each other's needs."

Suddenly feeling very protective of her, Matteo was hit by the astonishing realisation that what they had just done together was no longer casual fucking. It was much more than that. They had been making love, not just with their bodies but also their minds and emotions. Gently stroking June's hair, he said: "You are an amazing woman. I think I'm falling in love with you."

June felt the creeping tendrils of anxiety. It was the feeling she always had when anyone began to get too close to her. Juliet was the only person in her whole life with whom she had ever been totally open and honest. Things were moving far too fast with this guy who, let's face it, she'd only just met.

Without thinking she pulled herself out of Matteo's arms, sat up and swung her legs over the side of the bed. "I can't do this anymore. I really think I should go back and sleep in my own room." As Matteo stared at her in total disbelief, June wound one of the hotel's huge white bath sheets around herself and grabbing her clothes and her bag, walked out. "Fucking incredible!" gasped Matteo. He didn't know whether to laugh or cry.

★★★

Back in her room June sank down on the bed, tears trickling down her cheeks. She had panicked and run away. How very childish, what on earth must Matteo think. They had been about to make love again and she was still jumping with desire. Christ, what a mess. This stupid flight response had ruled her emotions for most of her adult life and it couldn't continue. It really was weird shit and it had to stop.

Taking a deep breath, she decided to have a shower and take a couple of sleeping pills, hoping that a new day would bring equanimity. She urgently wanted to talk to Juliet but felt cut adrift, knowing that her best friend would no longer be available whenever she needed her. During her long marriage to Ted, Juliet had always been there for her, but June had reluctantly accepted that marriage to Enzo was going to be very different. Now Enzo would always be Juliet's first priority.

After an invigorating shower, June felt calmer. The jets of warm water blasting her body had settled her confused emotions and she was thinking with more clarity. She was definitely going to have to clear the air with Matteo. They had another day to get through before they went home and the last thing she wanted was a difficult atmosphere to spoil what had been a very special time for all of them.

Slipping into the white fluffy bathrobe provided by the hotel, June hurried the few paces along the corridor to Matteo's room and gave a gentle tap on the door. What if he was asleep? she hadn't thought of that. Just as she was contemplating tiptoeing back to her own room, the door opened and there was Matteo looking very solemn. "I'm sorry," whispered June. "I panicked."

Grabbing her hand, he pulled her into the room. "Come in before the whole hotel knows you were knocking on a man's door in the middle of the night, and…" looking down at her bathrobe which had fallen open he smiled… "with no clothes on."

Matteo poured her a thimbleful of Fernet Branca. "Drink this. It is a *digestivo* but it will settle you down." June took a sip. "Ugh this is disgusting. What on earth is it?" He laughed. "Fernet Branca isn't to everyone's taste. Here…" he took the glass, putting his arms around her as they sat on the side of the bed. "I feel really silly," said June, "rushing off like that."

"Hush baby, he murmured. "I understand, and you have returned so everything is good. *L'amore domina senza regole.* In Italy love dominates without rules. Anything goes, there are no expectations." June put her head on his shoulder. "The thought of love really scares me. Makes me panicky."

"Well, we don't have to call it love. We can call it anything you like. How about 'desire'? Or 'yearning'? In Italy we might say *'Ti voglio bene',* that's the love we have for family and friends. But hey, in fact we don't have to call it anything at all. It's just this amazing feeling I have for you." June gave a tearful smile. "Nevertheless, I am so messed up, you really don't want to get involved with me and all my shit."

"No? Well, we don't really know each other very well, although we have had amazing sex three…almost four times and I have a feeling we will see more of each other. Now, if you are feeling better, shall we continue where we left off? Then we must get some beauty sleep. We don't want Enzo and *Giulietta* thinking we've been up to no good."

June gave an unsteady laugh. "Juliet knows already." Matteo looked startled. "*Mama Mia!* You've told her?" Enzo had said that the two women had absolutely no secrets from each other. June shook her head. "I didn't have to. We've been friends since we were five years old, she knows what I'm thinking without me saying anything. I suspect our faces gave us away; both she and Enzo will know we've slept together."

"Well in that case we had better continue with the fourth session, don't you think? We don't want to disappoint them." June hesitated only slightly before nodding and climbing onto the bed. Truth was, she was aching for him again.

✳✳✳

The following morning they lay with their arms around each other, reluctant to get up and begin June's last day on Capri. They'd made love again during the night discovering with delight how to satisfy each other's deepest desires. It was, thought June, just extraordinary. They seemed to be naturally attuned and it was the best sex she'd had for years.

"Do you know what time your flight is tomorrow?" asked Matteo. "I think Enzo said we were catching the two o'clock, which is, I suppose, fourteen hundred hours for you," replied June.

"Hmm. Well, Enzo will almost certainly have ordered a taxi from Sorrento, so I guess you will be leaving here mid-morning. Anyway, I'm coming with you."

"To Sorrento?"

"To the airport."

"Oh, that will be nice."

"My pleasure. I will be sorry to see you go."

He was looking at her thoughtfully and she knew they were going to make love again. It was going to be much better than a one or two-night stand. If they had an after-lunch siesta, spent the night together again and had sex tomorrow morning, there would be about four more moments of intense passion, five or six if she was lucky, thought June.

I'm sure oldies like us aren't supposed to be constantly screwing, but sex with Matteo is so amazing I just want him all the time. It's too tempting to resist. She smiled thinking that's just what Jules had said about Enzo.

Matteo got up and wandered into the bathroom. He really has got a good body, thought June, watching him. He came back into the bedroom saying: "Are you just going to lie there staring at me or are we going to make love again?" June gave her throaty laugh. "I think I might just keep staring at you. You're turning me on!"

"Ha! Then we're halfway there already." Kneeling on the bed and leaning over to kiss her, he said softly: "I think you're becoming my kryptonite. I have no power to resist you." June laughed again. "I'm sure that's not true, although I must confess I also find you irresistible. I'm going to need complete rest when I get home. I'm absolutely exhausted, but in the nicest possible way."

He gave her a loving look. "We must take advantage of the few hours we have left together, so prepare to be even more exhausted because I'm about to make love to you before breakfast."

"Do we have time?" asked June. "Oh, I'm sure Alberto will be able to rustle us up a *cornetto* or two and some *caffè* if we are too late for the breakfast service, Matteo assured her.

"I'm going to miss you," said June blushing slightly. "Miss me or miss the sex?" asked Matteo cheekily. "Both," she replied, thinking that when she was with him, she felt surprisingly happy.

"I was just about to say *'Ti voglio bene'* but what I want to say is *'Ti amo'*, said Matteo ardently, holding her gently in his arms. Gazing into her eyes he added: "What I feel for you is extraordinary, and when something as extraordinary as this comes along you must listen to it. Never doubt my desire for you, I will always hold your heart in mine; the flame between us will always burn."

Heavens above, sighed June, how was it possible to be so romantic before breakfast! She felt a strange mixture of happiness and fear, reluctantly admitting to herself that, inexplicably, she was falling in love with him too. The thought terrified her.

★★★.

Juliet gave a knowing smile when June and Matteo turned up rather late for breakfast. "Good morning! Did you enjoy your evening?" June blushed slightly, muttering "Mmm."

Enzo looked at Matteo meaningfully and giving him the slightest suggestion of a wink said: "I would like to go over to Villa Valentina this morning. It's a while since I've been there and it would be good to catch up with Giorgio and Anna again."

"They will both be on duty because I am here," said Matteo. "I know they will be delighted to see you. I'm pretty sure Bella will be there too, whether she is on duty or not. She and her friends are huge fans of yours; they were really thrilled that you went over to speak to them at the gig last night."

Enzo grinned, remembering Sofia's impudent stolen kiss. "It's quite extraordinary, but I do seem to have a growing number of young fans. It's good to know that today's teenagers still enjoy the music of Sinatra, and Elvis…and of course Pooh, but then everyone likes Pooh!" Matteo dug him in the ribs. "I don't think it's the music as much as you, mate."

"Really? But I'm an old man now. I thought these young girls were all lusting after boy bands or whoever." Matteo was about to say that Bella had told him that she and her friends Sofia, Mia and Viola all had pictures of Enzo pinned up in their bedrooms but decided that telling him might make it slightly awkward next time they met. Instead, Matteo gave a gust of laughter: "You must be the only one who can't see it. I wish I had half your charisma. God knows how you still do it at your age!"

Glancing across at Juliet and June, who were sitting together deep in conversation, Matteo asked: "Are you bringing *Giulietta* with you?"

"No, I think the girls want a morning to themselves."

"Okay," said Matteo. He knew exactly what they would be talking about.

Chapter Twenty-Eight

'Exit, pursued by a bear'.
William Shakespeare, 'The Winter's Tale,'
(Act III: iii – stage direction)

JULIET AND June decided to walk down to Capri town to have coffee. Once Juliet had ordered them each a *cappuccino* – "make the most of it, you can't get them after eleven" – they sat at one of the white tables outside a cafe on the Piazza Umberto and settled in for a gossip.

"Why can't you get a *cappuccino* after eleven?" inquired June with interest. "It's something to do with all that dairy upsetting the digestion," explained Juliet. "The Italians take prodigious care of their digestion you will discover, and there is a lot of coffee etiquette, most of which I don't understand. You can have a *macchiato* if you want another after this."

They were the only customers sitting outside, everyone else was crowded into the noisy bar in true Italian fashion. Leaning back in her chair, Juliet looked intently at June and asked: "So? What's going on?" June looked slightly uncomfortable. "Matteo and I have been sleeping together."

"And?"

"And what?"

"Come on June, you know what I mean. How did it happen, what's it like and do you just fancy him or is it something more?"

June took a deep breath. "He came out and found me in the

garden after the wedding ceremony. I was in that little alcove right at the end, looking out over the sea. It was very quiet and there was no one else around. Anyway, there was a bit of flirty chit-chat…you know the kind of thing, I must say he's very good at it…and then he kissed me. Christ, Jules, he was amazing. It took me completely by surprise, he's an incredible kisser. Not what I expected at all.

"After that it was sort of agreed, without either of us saying anything, that we would go to bed. When he held my hand, he ran his thumb in circles on my palm, so I instantly knew he wanted sex."

"Oh my God! Enzo did that to me the first night I went to Bar Russe," exclaimed Juliet, "but I didn't pick up on it; it just stirred me up. I had no idea that it meant he wanted sex."

June laughed. "We seem to have lost the art of seduction without using words; I believe the Victorians and Edwardians were brilliant at it. Interesting that you still remember the thumb on palm thing after all these years."

"I have almost complete recall of everything Enzo and I did on Capri," replied Juliet seriously. "He says he does too." Looking at June she said: "Sorry, I didn't mean to butt in, I was just fascinated to learn what that meant. Go on…"

"*Well*, after the extraordinary kissing I was thinking the sex would probably be good, but honestly Jules, it was so much more than good, it was just amazing, really exciting, and now…"

"You're hooked," said Juliet.

"Yup! Well, certainly hooked on the sex. It was like a nuclear explosion. How these Italian men do it, I do not know. He said he learned stuff from a Thai lover, but I'm not sure I actually believe him. Anyway, I don't suppose *you've* noticed, but Matteo's got this alluring mouth with a very tempting bottom lip, and it took him no time at all to turn me into a quivering wreck. Now I can't get enough of it."

"Oh, my dear, I know that scenario so well," said Juliet fervently.

"I had a bit of a wobbly last night because he suddenly said he was falling in love with me. You know what I'm like… I panicked and hot-footed it to my room. But I had a shower, calmed down and went back to him and now… I don't know where this is going. In a way I want it to continue, but I'm really scared. I'm really not prepared for anything too emotional. He says he loves me, but I don't know if it's just the extraordinary sex he loves."

"I would imagine Enzo and Matteo are having a very similar conversation right now," said Juliet smiling. Looking June directly in the eyes she asked: " *Are* you falling for him, or is it just the great sex? I do recall that in the past whenever a guy has begun to get interested you've always made a quick exit."

June grimaced. "You mean 'exit pursued by a bear' or whatever Shakespeare's stage direction was in *The Winter's Tale*. I must confess that my affairs have always felt a bit like a comedy with elements of tragedy. I'm sure there's a moral there somewhere."

"Stop being so feeble," said Juliet brusquely. "Now tell me, honestly, how do you feel about Matteo? He's a lovely guy."

June exhaled deeply. "I can't remember being with anyone who turns me on like he does. He only has to touch me and I just can't think straight. It's unbelievable; such an amazing feeling, I just keep wanting more." She shifted in her chair, wrapping her arms across her body. "The other thing is I feel really happy when I'm with him, something I have never felt before, so maybe it is the beginning of love. Trouble is I don't *want* to fall in love with him because it would be so inconvenient."

"Inconvenient?"

"Well obviously. He lives in Italy, I live in England and we are not in the first flush of youth. We both have settled lives in different countries and a lot of baggage."

"Life is so short," said Juliet. "At our age we have to grab all the happiness we can get. It's strange but we seem to get less spontaneous as we get older; we get silenced by life. If you were twenty, you'd say, 'sod it' and stay with him on Capri regardless of the consequences, just like I did in the sixties. What is there waiting for you in England? A dog, some cats and a flat that's now too big for you on your own. You are a widow, and your only son lives in Australia."

"There's my volunteering. The Help for Dogs charity shop and the Friendship Café for Refugees would really miss me."

"June!" said Juliet warningly, "stop prevaricating."

"Okay, okay," said June. Frowning she bit her lip. "How can something like this have happened so fast? What if I give up everything, move to Capri to be with him and it doesn't work out? Seriously Jules, I *am* panicking. And it is a bit of a cliché, you know, go to Italy, fall in love with an Italian. It looks like I am copying you!"

Juliet laughed. "Don't talk rubbish. You sound like we're fourteen again and in competition with each other. If that's what's happened, then that's what's happened. Nothing to do with copying me."

Putting an arm around her, Juliet could feel June shaking. "Sweetheart, we've seen each other go through too much over the years to get hung up on who did what first. If he's right for you, then go for it. I know it's scary but if there is the slightest chance that you and Matteo have something special you should take the risk. As I said, life is too short, and we can't have that much time left to be happy."

"I…I don't know. It's such a big leap of faith. I just have a shitty feeling I'm asking for trouble. It could all go horribly wrong. Am I considering a relationship with Matteo because of the extraordinary sex? If so, is amazing sex the most important thing? More important than a secure and settled life?"

Juliet snorted. "Huh, you've changed your tune. Ever since

we were teenagers you've always insisted that sex was the most important thing in the world." June wrinkled her nose. "Yes, I know, and I have always believed that for me it was. But now I'm not so sure."

Staring contemplatively into the distance, she said slowly: "Matteo said again this morning that he loves me, but how can it be possible that he has fallen in love so quickly? I am not prepared to relax and become emotionally involved until I am completely sure he is serious and that he is not playing games. Having fantastic sex is one thing, the total disruption of my life and my emotions is something completely different. How can I be sure he won't hurt me."

Juliet put a comforting arm around her. "See what happens during the next twelve hours or so," she advised soothingly. "If you decide to err on the side of caution, you can always come out again. It's only a two-and-a-half-hour flight away."

"I just have to try to think about this dispassionately and make a sensible decision," said June looking slightly tearful. "It's scary as hell and I'm actually feeling a bit deranged."

Giving June a hug, Juliet said: "Don't make the mistake I made, sweetheart. The older I get the more I regret all the things I was too scared to do. Don't end up with a load of regrets. Neither you nor Matteo have fifty years to waste like Enzo and I did."

★★★

As Juliet suspected, Enzo and Matteo were indeed having a very similar conversation. Sitting in the garden at Villa Valentina, Matteo said slowly: "*Dio Santo,* Enzo! I've never known anyone like her. She's just amazing."

"In bed?" asked Enzo, knowing the answer from the look on Matteo's face. "Certainly in bed, the sex is epic, totally out of this world; she's so exciting I just want to make love with her non-stop. But I also like her as a person. I know it's all happened really quickly, but I've totally fallen for her. I don't think I'm prepared to let her go; I will do anything to be with her."

"Don't allow amazing sex colour your judgement," said Enzo soberly. "She may be a great fuck, but…" Matteo stopped him. "You know what mate, she's not a fuck anymore, great or otherwise. The first time I thought it was just sensational sex, the best I'd ever had. But now, even after such a short time, it doesn't feel like fucking…it feels like making love. You know the difference."

Enzo stared at him. Of course he knew the difference. Fucking was a casual sexual encounter, the only aim being erotic gratification. He and Matteo had done plenty of that over the years. Making love was a wonderful intimacy with someone you were fond of, someone you loved, when all your senses were engaged. "Christ!" exclaimed Enzo, "but Matteo, you know as well as I do that there has to be more than sex, more than making love however amazing, if you are considering giving up everything for this woman."

"You're giving up everything for *Giulietta*."

"*Lo so*. The sex was great right from the start for us but there were a lot of other things too. Although it was definitely *colpo di fulmine* as far as I was concerned, we both recognised that it went a lot deeper than just amazing sex. We were always destined to be together. Now, after being apart all these years, I am still so in love with her that I am willing to do anything just to be with her."

Matteo nodded. "*Si, capisco bene*. I do admit that the fantastic sex…June's incredible skill in bed…was the immediate pull, but now even after just a couple days, my mind and emotions are definitely involved as well. I may be having the best sex of my life, but I also love her. I just want to be with her and look after her. She seems so vulnerable."

Matteo ran his fingers though his hair, a look of bewilderment mixed with anxiety on his face. "I didn't know that sex with someone you love could mean so much. I was totally unprepared for it. She completely fills my mind all the time. I have never felt like this before, not even at the very beginning with Gabriella. Problem is, I know she is resisting; she seems to blow hot and cold. She's loving the sex too, but I think there are things in her past which are holding her back from making a total commitment."

Enzo frowned and looked at Matteo seriously. Taking a deep breath, he asked hesitantly: "Are you sure she's not just using *you* as a casual fuck while she's away from home for a few days?"

"Ouch! That's a bit brutal mate," said Matteo wincing.

"*Spiace!* It had to be said. I would be failing in my duty as your friend if I didn't say it. You've only known her a couple of days, maybe you both need some time apart to see how you feel? You will remember that *Giulietta* and I were together for two weeks before she moved in with me and it was four months before I asked her to marry me, and I thought that was quick."

As Matteo sat deep in thought, Enzo asked: "Are you thinking that June might come over here and help you run the hotel? She is incredibly efficient and would be very good at it, but how would Giorgio and Anna feel if this English woman turned up and started taking charge? Or are you planning to hand the hotel over to your family and go and live with June in England?" He paused before adding, "Do you want to marry her?"

Matteo looked slightly agitated. "I haven't thought that far," he confessed. All I can think about at the moment is finding out if she loves me because I am crazy about her and I don't know what I will do if she doesn't. I only have a few hours before she leaves."

He's really fallen hard, thought Enzo. It was the first time in all the years he'd known him that he had seen Matteo so hung up about a woman, and there had been a lot of them. Even when he was getting married to Gabriella he hadn't seemed as excited as he now was over June.

Clapping his friend on the back Enzo said cheerfully: "*Non preoccuparti troppo.* Don't worry, I'm sure it will all work out. Let's go in and see if we can persuade Isabella to make us some coffee and then I'd like to take a look at those renovations you were telling me about."

Chapter Twenty-Nine

"Augustus John was old enough to be a lot of girls' great-grandfathers – and that didn't stop him."
Jilly Cooper, 'Rivals' (1988)

ISABELLA HAD made sure she would be at Villa Valentina when Matteo turned up with Enzo. She wasn't supposed to be on duty but had persuaded Gianna to swap shifts with her. Gianna, who was married and in her forties, worked part-time and was quite happy to do Isabella's afternoon stint instead.

That morning Isabella had washed her hair so that it hung straight down her back without any kinks in it, and she was wearing her new narrow black skirt with a freshly laundered white blouse; hotel uniform admittedly but, Isabella thought, it showed off her figure quite well.

She had also sprayed herself with Thierry Mugler's perfume *Angel*…not too much because the suggestion of candy floss could be quite overpowering if used too liberally…and she was wearing her plunge bra with the extra push up, maybe not exactly the most practical thing to wear at work, but in the circumstances a girl needed all the help she could get.

Despite the fact that Enzo was now married to Juliet, Isabella still really fancied him. He was a gorgeous Italian man who had been married three times before and had led a rather unconventional life. There might well be the chance of dalliance, despite a new wife.

A woman who claimed she had once slept with Enzo while he was on tour, had told Isabella that he had been amazing in bed; absolutely incredible. Not that Isabella was hoping for sex with Enzo. Despite a snickety feeling that he found her attractive, she accepted that his close ties with her family meant that lovemaking was definitely out of the question, but there was always the hope of flirtation.

Although she had known him all her life and he was the best friend of her uncle Matteo, who was quite old, Isabella had never really considered Enzo's age. It was unimportant. Surrounded by the glamour of celebrity, he was just a stunningly sexy guy and she had a huge crush on him.

It was unfortunate that her mother Anna, Matteo's sister and the hotel's head of housekeeping, happened to walk into reception and saw her daughter behind the desk. Isabella was glowing and looking exceptionally pretty.

"Why have you changed shifts with Gianna?" demanded Anna. She knew the answer but was quite interested to hear what Isabella would say, especially as she had failed to mention the switch to Giorgio, who planned the rotas.

"Oh," replied Isabella offhandedly. "Viola and I want to go shopping this afternoon and as Gianna wasn't bothered whether she worked in the morning or afternoon, I asked her to swap."

"Uh-ha." Anna sounded unimpressed. She gave her daughter a searching look. "I suppose it wouldn't have anything to do with Enzo de Martins, would it?"

"Enzo? *No! Perché?* Isabella assumed a look of innocent surprise, feeling heat rushing to her face and desperately thinking about ice cold showers to try to stop herself blushing. "I spoke to him at the gig last night. He said he was coming over, but he didn't say exactly when."

"Well, he's coming here with Matteo this morning."

"*Questa mattina? Davvero?* That's nice. It means I'll get a chance to see him again before he goes back to England."

"Indeed," said her mother, pursing her lips as she went off to check bedrooms. She knew Isabella was infatuated with Enzo; Anna herself had fancied him for years. It was rather fortunate he had now married again and was going to live in England.

At the bottom of the stairs Anna turned and said to her daughter: "If I were you, Bella, I'd do up a couple more buttons on your blouse. You look as if you are about to fall out of it." That's the problem when you work in the family business thought Isabella resentfully, fastening the offending buttons. Your mother is always around and it's totally impossible have any privacy.

★★★

Luckily her mother was not around when Matteo and Enzo walked into reception and Enzo gave her a heart-stopping smile, leaning across the desk to kiss her cheek. "Oh, you smell wonderful. Like *zucchero filato,* good enough to eat." She blushed. He'd noticed.

Enzo looked at her intently. "*Come stai,* Isabella?"

"*Sto bene, grazie,*" she replied formally, loving that he said her name properly and didn't shorten it to Bella as most people did. Still gazing at her Enzo asked: "Did you enjoy the gig last night?"

"The gig was wonderful." She paused before adding: "*You were wonderful.* The girls were so happy to speak to you."

"*Grazie.* We aim for a satisfied audience." Isabella blushed again as she looked directly at Enzo and said hesitantly: "I'm so sorry about Sofia, she can be a bit…"

"Reckless?" said Enzo with a faint smile. "A bit impetuous," replied Isabella.

Enzo laughed. "*Non importa!* Please don't worry about it *cara.* It's okay. No harm done…but really, Sofia should be careful that she doesn't give a kiss like that to the wrong person, or she could find herself in trouble."

Isabella nodded. "*Lo so…*we have told her." She was staring at Enzo yearningly. Matteo, carefully watching Isabella, said impatiently: "*Pronto* Enzo?"

"Mmm." Enzo seemed preoccupied.

Turning to his niece Matteo said: "We're going into the bar to inspect the work that's being done there, Bella. Any chance you could make us some coffee and bring it over? "*Certo…nessun problema,*" replied Isabella happily.

"*Grazie mille, cara,*" said Enzo smiling deeply into her eyes. "*Pronto* Enzo?" said Matteo again. "Yes, ready," replied Enzo, still smiling at Isabella.

Isabella, feeling her heart flip, held onto the desk to steady herself. With her mother busily occupied checking rooms and no guests expected to arrive immediately, she thought she might even be able to hang out in the bar for a while and grab a bit of extra time with Enzo. She frowned. Uncle Matteo seemed to be a bit *miserabile* this morning; maybe a cup of coffee would cheer him up.

As they walked out of reception Enzo murmured to Matteo: "Isabella is turning into an exceptionally beautiful girl. She reminds me of Anna at that age. She'll be driving the boys wild very soon."

"She already is," said Matteo with a brief chuckle, "but for some extraordinary reason she doesn't seem interested in them. I think her affections are otherwise engaged at the moment!"

Enzo was looking pensive with the absorbed expression on his face that Matteo recognised so well. Biting his lip Matteo asked quietly: "Do you fancy her?"

"Who, Isabella?"

"Mmm. Just asking."

"*Si, naturalmente,*" replied Enzo. Smiling at the shocked expression on Matteo's face he added: "But don't worry, I have absolutely *no* intention of doing anything about it."

As they walked into the bar in silence, Matteo contemplated the fact that his niece was younger than Enzo's granddaughters... and that Enzo had only just married Juliet. Reading his thoughts, Enzo grabbed Matteo's arm. "*Ascolti!* Listen! I'm a man who likes and appreciates women, and Isabella is a very beautiful girl. Of course I fancy her, I can't help myself. I have no doubt that I will fancy many more women in the future. Being married doesn't stop the instinctive working of my..."

"*Cazzo?*" suggested Matteo helpfully. Enzo snorted. "Huh! *Molto divertente!* I was going to say 'mind'. The instinctive working of my mind. My thoughts."

Looking at Matteo steadily he added firmly: "You should know I will never, *ever*, do anything that hurts *Giulietta* or puts my relationship with her or our marriage, at risk. *Niente!* Any thoughts I may have will always remain safely in my head."

"You might find that difficult, mate," retorted Matteo brusquely. "It's not just your mind and thoughts, *lust* doesn't stop just because you are married. The combination of appetite and desire can be very seductive...you remember that irresistible urge that tells guys our age we're still alive!"

Enzo regarded him unsmilingly. "Then if that happens, I will go straight home and make love to my wife."

Matteo nodded but said nothing as Isabella walked in with a tray of coffees and a happy smile on her face.

★★★

Enzo knew only too well how Isabella felt about him. As a man who genuinely liked women he was very attuned to their emotions. Having been in the music business for so many years, Enzo understood that he aroused strong feelings in women of all ages. While those feelings kept him popular and in a job, his innate empathy and consideration stopped him from taking advantage. Yes, he had slept with hundreds of women over the years, but he had merely given them what they wanted, he had never exploited them.

When he met Giulietta his world changed, and although he had continued to enjoy casual sex after she left, his heart and soul had never been engaged.

He did sometimes wonder with a slight touch of shame, whether getting married three times to women he didn't love in a selfish attempt to find that elusive feeling he'd had with Giulietta, had been a form of exploitation. He shrugged such thoughts into the recesses of his mind; all that was done and dusted years ago.

Now he had married the love of his life, there would be no more casual liaisons, even if he was momentarily distracted by a pretty face. Giulietta was the only woman he wanted, and she consumed him heart, mind and soul.

Enzo hadn't really been surprised when Matteo pointed out that his new young fans fancied him more than his music; through the years he'd always known that girls became infatuated with him. He also knew that these short-lived passions for an older guy were teenage crushes that would evaporate once real and dependable loves of their own age came into their lives. And that, thought Enzo, was exactly how it should be.

★★★

Carrying out her tour of inspection, Anna's brain was ticking off items on her check list, but her mind had gone rogue.

The Rossi family had moved from *Napoli* to run Villa Valentina in the nineteen-fifties. Mario and Maria Rossi had seven children and all of them had worked at the hotel after school and in the holidays. As adults, only Matteo, Giorgio, Mario Junior and Anna had stayed. Matteo was the eldest and Anna, the only girl, the youngest by many years.

Mario Junior married a girl from Sicily and had moved there so his wife could be near her family. With their parents dead and their other siblings apathetic about the hotel trade, Matteo,

Giorgio and Anna successfully ran Villa Valentina between them. And it was thriving.

Anna, now in her fifties, was married to Angelo and they had three children, two boys with no interest in the family business, and Isabella, more than a decade younger than her brothers, who was showing great promise as a future hotelier. She worked at Villa Valentina on a casual basis while she was finishing school, but in a few months she would be joining the staff as a full-time receptionist.

Thinking about her daughter, Anna smiled. She was not only very good at her job, speaking competent English and really liking people, which was half the battle when you ran a hotel, but she was also beautiful and adept at charming the guests. A great asset.

Bella had no shortage of young men eager to take her out thought her mother, but at the moment she was totally fixated on Enzo de Martins, who was more or less the same age as her uncle Matteo.

Anna carefully pondered her own attachment to Enzo. She had fancied him since she was in her early teens, and he was in his thirties with his singing career at its height. When he was back in *Napoli* Enzo often visited Capri with Matteo, but although he was unfailingly kind and charming, Enzo hardly noticed that his best friend's kid sister was always watching him with love and longing.

She let her mind wander over the one and only time Enzo *had* noticed her. It was the Christmas just before Anna's eighteenth birthday and Enzo was spending a few days with the Rossi family at Villa Valentina.

After their evening meal, they played the traditional game of Sardines, where one person hides and as each seeker finds the sardine, they hide with them until everyone has squeezed into the hiding place just like sardines in a tin.

Anna, who was the sardine on this occasion, was hiding behind the long curtains in a dark, unoccupied bedroom when Enzo was the first to find her. She started giggling when she saw him. "That was quick. Were you following me?" Smiling he put a finger on her lips and whispered, "*Zitto!* Everyone else is downstairs at the moment."

Joining her behind the curtain he turned, and putting his hands both sides of her face, gave her a long, deep kiss. Gazing into her eyes he said: "You've become a very beautiful girl *cara*. When did that happen? Last time I looked you were a child."

She had gasped, totally unsure what to do or say, her love for him overpowering. Realising that she was trembling, Enzo put his arms around her, stroking her back. *"Ti voglio bene."* He added: "I'm off to the States in two days, but when I'm back in *Napoli* I'll call you. We'll go and have a quiet supper somewhere so we can spend an evening together," he paused, "alone." Anna shivered. That sounded like an invitation…to what? There was just time for another very intense and exciting kiss before Anna's brother Giorgio burst through the curtains. "*Eccoti!* Room for another sardine?"

Enzo, caught up in a successful season in Las Vegas, never did contact her and it was almost a year before he returned to Villa Valentina, by which time Anna was dating Angelo and they were talking about getting married. The suggestion of having a quiet supper alone was never mentioned by either of them. It was as though the romantic interlude behind the bedroom curtains had never happened.

Forty years later, Anna was still watching Enzo with longing. She had safely locked away in the drawer of her memory any hopeless dreams of what might have been, although she did occasionally allow herself the luxury of recalling those precious Christmas kisses.

Now Anna saw that her young daughter also felt the same about Enzo. Bella would eventually marry a nice Italian boy her own age, have children and live a happy life, just as her mother had done. Meanwhile, thought Anna as she firmly closed the door of the final room on her list, it was just as well that Enzo was going off to live with *Giulietta* in England. Out of sight and hopefully out of mind.

Matteo had said that Enzo and *Giulietta* were planning to return to Italy for Christmas. Fingers crossed that gave enough time for Bella to find herself a steady boyfriend and get Enzo de Martins out of her system.

Chapter Thirty

"Our tragedy is that we are haunted, not just by the masks of others, but by the masks we wear ourselves. We act all the time. Life makes us necessary deceivers. Except maybe when we are alone."
Eugene O'Neill, American playwright (1888-1953)

AFTER LUNCH with Enzo and Juliet at Villa Florentina, June went with Matteo to his room. As soon as the door closed behind them Matteo pulled her roughly into his arms and kissed her passionately. She immediately melted, feeling waves of desire washing over her. Oh my God, she thought, how can I make a sensible decision when he does that. It's not fair.

As Matteo tried to pull her towards the bed June hung back, saying doggedly: "We need to talk."

"*Lo so,*" he said. June hesitated, not really wanting to start the conversation, but as he just stood there silently looking at her, she took a deep breath and said: "What are we going to do?"

"Do?"

"Yes, do. I am going back to England in less than twenty-four hours. Will we be seeing each other again; will we keep in touch? Or will we agree that this just has been a mad but wonderful interlude and go back to our lives as they were before we met?"

As Matteo put a hand out towards her saying, "I don't think going back to how it was is really an option *amore,*" she moved out of his reach. "It is better if you don't touch me while we are having this conversation," she said firmly, "or I will never be able to make a sensible decision."

"And is a sensible decision needed?"

"Matteo." June sighed, trying not to look at his mouth. "We are too old to play games with each other. We are not teenagers. I have to know how you feel about…about us, whether this is something that is strong enough to continue. I can't cope with uncertainty." He moved towards her again, his brown eyes full of love and desire. "*Tesoro, ti amo…*"

"No!" said June firmly. "Having sensational sex is one thing, but I can't let my emotions go until I am completely sure you are serious. I don't want to get hurt." He gave her a devastating smile. "Does that mean you are falling in love with me?"

"I'm not sure…maybe. Can you ask me an easier question please?"

There was pause before he said: "I do love you and I have no intention of hurting you." This time she didn't resist as he put his arms around her. "For me it's like Enzo was with *Giulietta,*" he whispered, "*colpo di fulmine.* I fell for you almost…*no,* immediately I saw you on the piazza. You English ladies certainly know how to get us Italian men going."

"I think it's the other way around," retorted June. "You Italian men seem to have the power to sweep us off our feet." Matteo laughed. "Either way, it's happened; it's done. We just need to figure out how we are going to make it work. Now, please will you come to bed. I really need to make love to you again."

June gave another sigh. Nothing had been sorted out. She still had no idea if he was really serious about them having a lasting relationship. He just said that for him it had been love at first sight, which was no answer at all. Years ago, that would have been all she needed to run blindly into a foolish affair. Now, with the benefit of age and experience June knew love could be transient and easily confused with lust. There had to be more than love at first sight for a relationship to last. But how could there possibly be more when they had only just met. He also seemed to think that ecstatic sex was the answer to everything.

She stood still in the middle of the room. "Hardly done or sorted. We live in different countries and have different lives. We have only known each other a couple of days, how can you be so sure you love me and how can we know it is going to last?"

"I can't explain, *amore,* I just know. It is a feeling with the heart, not the head. I am happier with you than I have ever been with anyone. We are so good together. *Sono pazzo di te* – I'm crazy about you."

Taking her hand he said earnestly: "It is difficult, *no*, because we live in different countries and have different lives. But there is no doubt in my mind that we should be together. I love you and if you love me too, then we can make it work. Loving each other is the only thing that matters, all the rest is detail."

June was surprised and slightly uneasy to see tears in his eyes. She knew Italians tended to be very romantic and sentimental, but naked emotion always made her feel uncomfortable and once again she was aware of anxiety creeping through her.

She definitely felt a strong attraction and was enjoying the best sex she'd had for years. No one had ever made her feel happy like Matteo did, but the thought that it might be love frightened her. She was in her seventies. Did she want to disrupt her comfortable life to go goodness knows where with this man she had only just met?

She looked directly into his eyes. "Matteo, this is all going much too fast. Can we just cool it down a bit? I'm going home tomorrow. You could come over to England to visit me…Enzo and Juliet will be living nearby…and see how we feel then. Or I could come back to Capri sometime…"

"Christ, June!" Matteo's disappointment was written on his face.

"Matteo," said June imploringly, "be sensible. I have to go home. This been a wonderful few days but I have to leave and it's much too soon to make a life-changing decision."

Enzo's comment about June using him for casual sex had been playing on Matteo's mind. "You're just running away from your feelings," he said bitterly. "You English women are always running away. That's just what *Giulietta* did to Enzo."

June stared at him silently and then walked out the door without a backward glance.

★★★

Matteo was sitting alone at the table when Enzo and Juliet arrived in the dining room that evening. Looking at his white, drawn face they both knew what had happened. He was halfway through a bottle of wine. "I'm going home, I just waited to see you first."

"Where's June?" asked Juliet. Matteo shrugged. "*Non lo so.* Haven't seen her since this afternoon."

"I'll just go and see if she's alright," said Juliet, leaving the two men together.

Enzo gave Matteo's shoulder a comforting pat before sitting down and pouring himself a glass of wine. "Is this okay or do you want anything stronger?"

Matteo shook his head. He was utterly dispirited. "I've already drunk too much. I've got to drive home."

"No way," said Enzo firmly. "I'll get you a taxi."

Matteo looked at him, fighting back tears. "I fucked up spectacularly," he said sadly, his voice cracking with emotion. "Totally screwed up. Either I pushed her too hard for the answer I wanted, or you were right and she was just using me as a casual shag."

Enzo regarded him with compassion. "Do you want to talk about it?" Matteo shook his head. "No point really. I told her I loved her and said we could make it work and she just said she wanted to slow it down and suggested I visited her in England to see how we felt then. I do feel that she loves me, but she refuses to commit." He poured himself another glass of wine. "*Merda… merda… merda!*"

Enzo exhaled deeply. Shit indeed. This is what he feared might happen. He didn't know June well, but from what *Giulietta* had told him, it seemed likely that things had occurred throughout her life that had left her emotionally damaged. Perhaps some of what Matteo had said to her was lost in translation.

"Let *Giulietta* talk to her," he suggested gently. "They are so close, she will find out exactly how June feels. Don't worry too much. Maybe just give her a bit of space."

Matteo nodded. "I think I'll go home now and I'll give the airport a miss tomorrow. I don't want her to feel I'm pressuring her any more than I have already."

"Okay," said Enzo. "I'll get Alberto to call you a taxi and you can pick up your car tomorrow after we have left. I'll ring you when I'm back in England."

★★★

June was in her pyjamas when she opened the door to Juliet. She was looking very fragile and had obviously been crying. "I thought you might pop in. What has Matteo said?"

"Not a lot to me. He's in the dining room talking to Enzo. But I gather he's going home so I imagine you've called it all off."

"There was nothing to call off," said June stiffly, adding bitterly: "Didn't you get the memo?" Juliet frowned and sat down on the edge of the bed.

"He said he loved me; love at first sight he said, and expected me to drop everything and fall into his arms…or rather, his bed," continued June. "He seems to think sex is the answer to everything." Juliet laughed. "If that's so, then you are perfectly suited!"

June gave a wry smile. "*Touché.* I admit I do find him impossibly attractive, and we have absolutely marvellous sex; maybe I am falling for him just a bit, I feel so happy when I am with him. But I'm not sure I am prepared to disrupt my life to take a chance with a man I have only just met, even if he is a seductive Italian.

"I did warn him not to get involved with me because I am so messed up, but he hassled me too much for an answer. The worst thing was he accused me of running away from him like you did from Enzo."

"Well, he'd be right, I guess. I did run away from Enzo, and you are running away from Matteo, although for different reasons."

Juliet gently reminded June that she had once said she wouldn't mind a sexy Italian in her life. "Huh," muttered June, "that was then, and this is now. When we had that conversation, I was speaking hypothetically. Now it's all a bit too close for comfort."

"June," Juliet took her hand, "look at me. You are at a crossroads in your life. You have the choice to turn left or right. You've always said you have never ever truly loved or been loved. Enzo says that Matteo really loves you, and I think that you are beginning to love him. Isn't that something worth hanging on to? You have to take a chance and make the correct turning for happiness, sweetheart. Also, you did admit this morning that you were hooked. Was that just the sex?"

"I don't know…I don't know anything anymore," sobbed June, tears dripping down her face. She looked shattered. "I'm so fucked up, he's better off without me. I always choose the wrong turning, anyway, so why should this be any different."

Juliet stroked June's cheek. "Giving your heart to someone with no guarantee it will be treated gently is a huge leap of faith," she said. "I know our choices can have unexpected or even disastrous consequences, but sometimes you just have to take that chance."

Putting her arms around her, Juliet was about to ask how she would feel if she never saw Matteo again, but looking at June's stubborn expression, she just said: "Don't worry my love. It will sort itself out one way or another. All relationships can be difficult. Take a couple of pills and try to get a good night's sleep, we're off home tomorrow."

June hung onto Juliet as if she was drowning, the tears streaming down her cheeks. "I'm so very sorry. The last thing I wanted to do was to spoil your time here. My problems always seem to surface at the most inappropriate moments."

Juliet kissed her wet cheek. "You definitely haven't spoilt our time on Capri, sweetheart. Enzo and I are blissfully happy, and nothing can spoil that for us. I'm always here for you — you know that." June nodded, and as Juliet opened the door she said softly: "I don't want to be in love with him. I just want this horrible feeling to go away." She sounds as if she is a teenager again, thought Juliet.

★★★

Juliet and Enzo compared notes. "I really don't think there is anything we can do to help," said Enzo. "This is something they have got to sort out for themselves. We can't get involved."

"I know," said Juliet sadly," I just hate to see them both so unhappy."

"He really loves her, and he wants to look after her," said Enzo. "Do you know how June feels?"

"Actually, I'm pretty sure she loves him, but she's never been in love before and the way she's feeling has really scared her. I think she's looking for any excuse not to commit. She may be in her seventies, but she's feeling and behaving like a teenager," said Juliet.

Putting her arms around her husband and running her fingers through his hair, she said: "I did warn her of the dangers of running away from love.

It's the one thing in my life I regret, and I was hoping that June wouldn't make the same mistake."

"I should have gone to England to find you," sighed Enzo. "That is the mistake I will always regret."

Kissing him Juliet said: "Thank goodness we were given a second chance of happiness. We are so lucky. I only hope those two don't squander any chances they may get."

Chapter Thirty-One

"They always say time changes things, but you actually have to change them for yourself."
Andy Warhol, American visual artist and film director (1928-1987)

WHEN MATTEO wasn't at breakfast in the morning June felt a sinking feeling inside. So he really had left. She had hoped he might have changed his mind and stayed for the final night.

As they gathered in the hall to say '*Ciao-Ciao*' and '*Grazie*' to Alberto Fabrizio, June was still hopeful Matteo might turn up at the last minute just to say goodbye, even if he didn't want to travel with them to the airport as planned, but there was no sign of him.

Enzo put his arm around her. "Are you alright?" he asked gently, thinking that her pale, strained face was looking so much like Matteo's last night. June nodded. "I will be, just give me a bit of time." Juliet looked across at her with concern but said nothing.

The Villa Florentina taxi took them down to Marina Grande and the ferry to Sorrento, where a chauffeur-driven limousine, courtesy of one of Enzo's glitterati friends, was waiting to transport them to the airport. "This is nice," said Juliet, holding Enzo's hand as she settled on the comfortable long back seat. "It reminds me of that trip to Rome to see Lorenzo."

"That was a good day, wasn't it?" said Enzo, remembering how Juliet had charmed his manager, who had given his blessing and agreed she would be the perfect wife for him. It was after speaking to Lorenzo and taking Juliet to visit *Nonna* at the house in *Napoli,* that he had asked her to marry him.

Sitting at the other end of the seat June looked unseeingly out of the window. She felt totally numb. I have pushed away someone who probably loves me, she thought. Someone who makes me happy. Why did I do that? What am I trying to prove? There must be something very wrong with me. This is the consequence of the dissolute life I have led over the past fifty years or so. It has left me totally unable to commit. I am paying the price for all the hurt I have caused to others. I can't even feel anything anymore. Matteo is definitely better off without me. Better for me to have had just a brief moment of bliss with him than not to have experienced it at all.

★★★

Boarding the flight to London Enzo offered June the seat next to Juliet. "Sit here," he said. "I will be quite happy across the aisle with my guitar. You and *Giulietta* probably need to talk."

June shook her head. "Thank you, but no. I am not a good companion at the moment. I'll sit over there and keep your guitar company. I'll probably have a nap. I didn't sleep too well last night."

Juliet and Enzo exchanged concerned glances. Despite the fact that June had caused the split with Matteo, she was clearly taking it badly. "I think she does love him," whispered Juliet. "She's just gradually beginning to accept it. I really hope he hasn't given up on her."

"I'll ring him when I get home," said Enzo. "Home?" queried Juliet. "Home is wherever you are *amore*, and if you are in England, that's where home is for me."

Juliet's heart skipped a beat. This amazing, incredible man was now her husband. He was changing his whole life just so he could be with her; so they could be together. She couldn't ask for anything more.

Sitting with their arms around each other, heads together, the newly-weds were so obviously in a world of their own that even smitten flight attendants wandering past in the hope of a chat or a selfie with Enzo, left them alone.

★★★

Both Charlotte and Amy had eagerly volunteered to pick up the travellers from the airport but Enzo had organised a taxi. "So much easier," he said, "and it saves anyone having to make the journey from Brighton."

"I've never known the girls so enthusiastic to drive to Gatwick," commented Tony mildly. "Last time I needed a lift they were full of reasons why they couldn't help. Now they are falling over each other to go. I suppose they are anxious to see their newly wedded grandparents."

Clarissa laughed. "I think you'll find it's Enzo they're keen to see, my love. They're both potty about him." Tony stared at her uncomprehendingly. "Potty about Enzo? Surely not! He's their grandfather."

Men are so blind, thought Clarissa indulgently. Tony was a brilliant architect and a ferocious businessman, but he didn't have the first idea what went on in a woman's head.

He had told her about the atmosphere in the sunroom on Enzo's first visit. "I was probably imagining it but I'm sure there was something going on that I knew nothing about. It was the way the girls looked. I just couldn't put my finger on it."

Clarissa totally understood how her daughters felt about Enzo. He was an amazingly handsome and very sexy man, with the intrinsic ability to charm and flirt. His age and the fact that he was their grandfather didn't come into it.

She thought about Isabella at Villa Valentina and how she and her friends also fancied Enzo; they must be ten years younger than Amy and Charlotte. And there was Luigi's Nonna at the bed and breakfast in

Naples; she was well into her eighties and had been besotted with him since she was a teenager. Enzo's age was definitely irrelevant; it was his natural charisma they had all fallen for.

There was no way Tony could understand any of that, bless him. After all these years of living with a wife and two daughters, he was still completely unaware of what made them tick and that, thought Clarissa, was the way she liked it. She loved him just the way he was.

★★★

They had arranged to drop in on Clarissa and Tony before June went home to the seafront flat and Enzo and Juliet returned to their suite at the Brunswick. Amy and Charlotte had decorated the sunroom with hearts and flowers to welcome the newlyweds and Tony handed round glasses of fizz, making a short witty speech on the theme of *Tempus Fugit,* which Enzo found very entertaining.

After the conversation with his wife, Tony was keeping a beady eye on Enzo and his daughters, but he couldn't spot anything untoward. Enzo gave the girls a hug, kissing them on both cheeks, but then he also embraced Clarissa. All perfectly normal behaviour as far as Tony could see. Nor could he perceive any sign that the girls were 'potty about Enzo' as Clarissa had claimed. His wife obviously had an over-active romantic imagination, Tony decided fondly as he went around the room refilling glasses. "I trust we are calling a cab to take you back to the Brunswick after all this."

Having heard about the wedding ceremony, the beauty of Villa Florentina, Alberto Fabrizio's fabulous lunch, and Enzo's successful impromptu concert, Amy said she would drop June off at the flat on her way back to London. "I have a rehearsal in the morning, so I must go home," she explained. Noticing her father looking at her speculatively, she added reassuringly: "I'm quite okay to drive. I've been on Heineken Zero all evening and you will have noticed I declined the glass of bubbly you offered me."

Amy had told Enzo she would like to learn to play the guitar, and he offered to find her an instrument suitable for a beginner. "Let me know next time you're coming down here and we can organise the first lesson."

Concerned about June returning alone to an empty apartment, Juliet suggested she should stay at the Brunswick for the night so they could go back together in the morning; but June declined, saying she had to pick up Florence from the neighbour who had also been feeding the cats.

"I'll be fine," she promised Juliet. "I will have Flo and the cats for company, and I intend to get an early night. I find all this travelling is exhausting." She didn't add that she was yearning to be alone so she could try to come to terms with losing Matteo and sort out her confused feelings. Now she was back in England she was perversely wishing she'd stayed in Italy. Juliet gave her a hug as she went out to Amy's car. "I'll call over to see you tomorrow."

Under cover of saying goodbye to her sister, Charlotte, who was staying with their parents for another couple of days, whispered in Amy's ear: "Marriage hasn't made any difference, he's still fucking gorgeous." Amy giggled. "Isn't he just! If you get the chance, will you speak to them about us staying at the house in Naples. We need to start planning a trip."

"I see you have chosen guitar lessons rather than Italian conversation," said Charlotte. "Well maybe we can do the guitar lessons in Italian and kill two birds with one stone," replied her sister pertly.

★★★

When Juliet and Enzo arrived at the Brunswick, there was a pile of post awaiting them, most of it from estate agents Enzo had contacted before they went to Capri. "We'll go through these in the morning and make a list of any we want to visit," he said. "And we'll also see what Tony comes up with. We'll soon have a home of our own."

Annoyingly, the estate agents had chosen the most unsuitable properties. There were details of second and third floor flats, despite the fact Enzo had specified a garden was non-negotiable; a couple of dingy houses in the centre of town; a country house with seven bedrooms and extensive grounds; and a thatched cottage with not only a huge garden but also an acre of farmland, which they both felt was far too much to manage.

Juliet felt despondent. They were never going to find their own home. Enzo, however, was much more upbeat. "I'll ring Tony and see if he has had any ideas. He did say he'd look out for something for us. Don't worry *Giulietta*, our perfect place is waiting for us somewhere."

Chapter Thirty-Two

*"There are no strangers here,
only friends we haven't yet met."*
WB Yeats, Irish poet,
dramatist and writer (1865-1939)

CLARISSA HAD offered to organise the post-wedding party for family and friends. She had several ideas but wanted to run them past Enzo and Juliet to see which they preferred and arranged to meet them for coffee.

"The first thing we must do is agree a date and then decide where you want to hold it; there are several options, and of course, we need a guest list, so if you can start on that it would be tremendously helpful. The venue we choose rather depends on how many people you're inviting,"

Enzo put his arm around Clarissa. "Thank you for doing this *cara*. I'm just wondering if you wouldn't mind asking June to help you with the arrangements. I think she could do with some distraction at the moment." Catching his wife's eye, he added: "Now *Giulietta* is no longer living with her, I mean."

"Yes, of course," said Clarissa. "I quite understand. I expect she'll be a bit lonely for a while until she gets used to living alone. I'll be more than happy for her assistance, she's incredibly efficient."

"Thank you," said Enzo and Juliet in unison. They both knew that June was going to need some help to get her back on an even keel again.

After contemplating numerous options, it was decided that the perfect place to hold the party would be Tony and Clarissa's garden flat. "It really lends itself to gatherings," said Clarissa while she and June were discussing venues, "and with doors opening onto the garden it would be ideal."

Following detailed conversations with Juliet and Enzo it was finally agreed to have a lunchtime event which would suit all age groups. Along with the adults, there would be a number of younger children and some teenagers. Charlotte had offered to rope in a couple of her friends who worked on the children's ward at the hospital to do nannying duties so parents could relax and enjoy themselves.

"There are several little ones ranging from infants up to the age of eight," said Clarissa, "so yes please, thank you Lotte, that would be wonderful. It is rare nowadays that the whole family can get together so it will be great for everyone to get a chance to talk and mingle without worrying what the kids are up to."

"Won't it be a bit of a busman's holiday for the nurses, though?" asked June. Charlotte smiled: "They don't mind and in fact they offered their services. They're really keen to meet Enzo."

Clarissa and June looked at each other and shrugged. "It never fails to amaze me," said June faintly, shaking her head. "I know he's gorgeous, but really. He is eighty after all and these girls are in their twenties."

Recalling not only her daughters' enthusiasm for Enzo, but also the infatuation of Isabella and her teenage friends as well as Luigi's *Nonna,* Clarissa thought once again that his age was irrelevant. Enzo was handsome and sexy with a compelling charm that attracted women of all ages. No wonder his singing career had endured for so many decades. All those eager women…and yet, after fifty years it was still Juliet he adored with steadfast devotion.

Looking back at her 'to do' list Clarissa said they still had to sort out music and food. "We can manage the food between us and I'll also ask Alan's wife Emma. She's a great cook and I'm sure she'll be happy to help. We can enlist Rosie too."

"It's still a lot of cooking," said June doubtfully.

"We'll do it in batches and freeze it," said Clarissa encouragingly. "Oh, well," said June, "no doubt we'll cope."

"And we've had an unsolicited offer to provide the music," said Clarissa laughing. "Michael's youngest son River is desperate to do it. He wants to be a DJ and needs the practice. He's got all the necessary equipment."

"Good God," said June. "Do they still have DJs in this day and age. How old is he now anyway?

"I think he's eighteen," said Clarissa vaguely, "or maybe nineteen. He was telling me his music is to do with something called Spotify. I honestly don't understand it but he is adamant he can do music for the party."

"But what kind of music? Will it be suitable for all age groups? We don't want rapping or grunge or whatever the latest fad is."

"Michael's had a word with him and stressed that it's got to be very much background music which is suitable for everyone," said Clarissa reassuringly. "River is quite mature for his age, so let's give him a chance. We can always pull the plug if it turns out it's not what we want."

Hopefully it won't be African Blues, thought June, memories of Matteo and *Ai Du* drifting through her mind. Looking at Clarissa she said: "Okay then. That's the music sorted, fingers crossed."

Putting her arm through June's, Clarissa said: "All organised. Let's go and make some coffee. Tony has fruit cake hidden away in the larder. He thinks I don't know, bless him, but we definitely deserve a slice or two. I'm sure he won't mind."

She called across to Enzo and Juliet who were going through the list of people being invited to the party. "Time for Tiffin. Coffee and fruit cake?"

Enzo and Juliet were ticking off names to make sure nobody had been forgotten. There were Juliet's brothers – Alan, with his wife Emma and their children and grandchildren, and Bertie, still a confirmed bachelor, although he had asked if he could bring a friend with him. He hadn't given any details, so Juliet was curious. "A woman?" she wondered. It was unusual for her brother to want to bring any companion to a family event, in fact she couldn't remember him ever doing so. Even when he was at Oxford Bertie had never brought friends home. "He's seventy, a bit old to start having a girlfriend now. Maybe it's just a mate…"

Enzo laughed. "We'll find out soon enough, *amore*. It's really none of our business who his friend is." They were just like Matteo's family, he thought. Not having brothers or sisters himself, Enzo had never really understood the intense interest each family member took in the lives of everyone else.

Also on the list were Clarissa, Tony and Amy, plus Charlotte and her boyfriend Malik; Clarissa's parents Ken and Audrey Phillips and her sister Bea; Clarissa's half-siblings Rosie and the twins Felix and Michael, the family Juliet had with Ted, and their broods, including River, the wanna-be DJ; and of course, June.

"I'm afraid this party has rather been hijacked by my family," said Juliet, perusing the names that were hovering around the thirty mark."

"That's why we are living in England, *Giulietta*," said Enzo placidly, "all your family are here, and I have no family in Italy now. There are good friends, of course, but it's too far to expect them to come for a party. We'll have another one in *Napoli* when we go over for Christmas."

"But isn't there anyone at all that you would like to invite?" asked Juliet. Enzo looked across the room where June was deep in conversation with Clarissa. "Well, Matteo, of course but…"

"I have a plan," whispered Juliet, but I'll explain it to you later."

She called across to Clarissa. "Are there any friends you need to invite? What about your neighbours?"

"Tony and I discussed that. We thought no neighbours otherwise we'd have to include the Prentices and I don't think I am quite up to coping with Sybil on this occasion, quite apart from saving Enzo from her amorous clutches, of course. So just family and very close friends." They all laughed as Enzo gave a huge mock sigh saying: "No Sybil then! That's a shame."

Clarissa added: "Oh, yes, and the other thing we need to talk to you about is food. June and I think we can manage it between us with a bit of help from Emma and Rosie."

"All arranged," said Enzo firmly. "We're getting caterers in and they will also provide waitresses. It's far too much work for you to do and we want you to enjoy this party and not have to worry about cooking and serving food."

Clarissa and June looked at each other with relief. End of that conversation and also a weight off their minds.

Chapter Thirty-Three

"Is it better to have had a good thing and lost it than never to have had it?"
Charles Dickens, 'Our Mutual Friend" (1865)

WITH THE party organised and invitations issued, Juliet set out to tackle the problem of June and Matteo. As she had told Enzo, she did have a plan. When she explained it to him, he had sat quietly for a while before saying thoughtfully: "Do you think it will work?"

"Well, that really depends on the success of my chat with June. Let's see how it goes before we mention anything to Matteo."

"He's still crazy about her," said Enzo.

Juliet asked June to go into Brighton with her to indulge in her favourite pastime…clothes shopping. It was a bright, sunny day and June was keen at the thought of wandering around the shops. "I know how much you enjoy a good browse, and I could really do with your advice on what to wear for the lunch party," said Juliet.

June looked at her in surprise. "But I thought you'd be wearing your wedding dress. It's so beautiful and suits you so well, it seems a shame not to give it another outing." Juliet considered. "Do you know, that hadn't occurred to me. Yes, of course I could wear the dress I had for the wedding."

"Lotte was telling me about a tradition – Jewish I think…you know Malik comes from a Jewish family – where a new bride goes to lunch or dinner parties wearing her wedding dress to show off to all the other women," said June. "I think everyone would appreciate seeing you in yours. But we can still go shopping. I need to get a new outfit for the party anyway."

"Okay, if I'm wearing my wedding dress, why don't you wear the dress you had for the wedding? It's really pretty and would be perfect for the lunch party."

"Broken zip," said June shortly, and seeing that Juliet was about to say 'well, you can get that repaired', she added: "I've gone right off it. I don't like it anymore, so I need to buy a new one for the party."

As Juliet gave her a quizzical look, June slowly admitted: "Matteo broke the zip trying to pull the dress off when we made love after your wedding. I can never wear that dress again."

"Oh sweetheart," said Juliet, noticing that June was blushing and also had tears in her eyes. "I'm sorry. Let's go and find you a new dress."

After an hour of trawling the shops without success, Juliet suggested they stopped for coffee and led the way to a delightful place she had discovered just behind The Lanes. It was half coffee shop, half bookshop with a couple of resident cats, and at eleven-thirty on a Monday morning it was relatively empty.

Juliet ordered *cappuccinos*… "you can get them all day long here, unlike Italy"… and as they settled in a window seat with the cats heading purposely towards them, Juliet carefully broached the subject that had been on her mind for a week. "Do you ever hear from Matteo?" she asked casually.

June looked wary. "Why? Should I?"

"Oh, I don't know, I just wondered," said Juliet, avoiding June's gaze as she allowed a fat ginger cat to climb onto her lap.

"Jules, how many years have we known each other?" demanded June. "Sixty, sixty-five?"

Juliet nodded. "Mmm. Something like that."

"Well," said June tartly, "definitely long enough for me to know when you are up to something."

"I don't know what you mean!" protested Juliet. "I was just thinking that Matteo might be keeping in touch."

"And that I had simply forgotten to mention it you? Come on Jules, you can do better than that. You know that if I had heard the slightest peep from him I would have told you."

Juliet sighed. "To be honest, I was hoping we might be able to talk about the two of you and…"

June looked as if she was going to cry. "There is no 'two of us' as you so elegantly put it. As ever, it is just me, on my own. Matteo and I are history."

"But sweetheart, it doesn't have to be like that. Enzo says Matteo is still crazy about you, and deny it as much as you like, I *know* you love him."

June looked stricken. "I don't know what to do," she whispered. "I can't cope with love. It's just too much. Maybe it's better to have had Matteo for just a short time and to have parted than never to have had him at all. Perhaps that is all there is meant to be for us."

"Hush, sweetheart, that's ridiculous." Juliet put her hand over June's. "Listen. The way you felt when you were with Matteo on Capri was totally natural – for a teenager in love for the first time. Excited, scared, wanting to be with him and then unable to cope with all the intense emotions that come rushing over you when you were. It's such a powerful experience. I felt like that with Rob, the first boy I ever loved. You remember, the one I practiced French kissing with; but we were teenagers and we weren't having sex.

"That's just how you felt with Matteo. And if you add the intense sex you were having into the mix of your feelings, first love was quite naturally totally overwhelming for you. Because you didn't understand those feelings and couldn't cope with them, you just ran away. The only difference is that you are seventy-two, not seventeen…but the feelings and reactions are exactly the same whatever age you are."

June sat silently for a while, idly scooping up the froth from her coffee. "Mmm," she said at last, "I can sort of understand that."

"And," continued Juliet, "when you were young you were always rushing from one boy to another, so you never gave yourself time to really get to know any of them and fall in love. Therefore, you were totally unprepared for love when it came."

There was a pause before June said: "I suppose that's all part of the ridiculous flight thing I do. Running away when I don't understand, and things get too hard to handle. I have to find a way to stop doing that weird shit. It's really fucking up my life."

Juliet went to order more coffees and when she returned June stood up and put her arms around her. "Thank you for that Jules. It does all make sense. Poor Matteo: I really was an utter cow. And of course you're right, I do love him; deep down inside I've always known I loved him, although I find that extremely difficult to admit and say aloud…even to you."

"Maybe time to do something about it?" suggested Juliet gently. "Enzo has his phone number."

June held out her hand, now devoid of jewellery. "I've taken off my ring. That's the first step."

"So you have! I'm so used to seeing it that I didn't notice you weren't wearing it. May I ask why?"

"I took it off a few days ago when I allowed myself to finally accept that I loved Matteo. I'm going to sell it and give the money to the Friendship Café for Refugees. They need it more than I do."

Juliet gazed at her. "Well, like I said, perhaps it's time to do something about Matteo. Time to let go of the past and be happy." She decided to leave it at that and give June time to think.

"Come on," said Juliet when they'd finished their coffee.

"We've still got to find you the perfect new dress. There's nothing like a little retail therapy to make a woman feel better."

June carefully put down the tabby cat that had crept onto her lap and happily followed Juliet out into the sunshine.

★★★

"I've spoken to Matteo," said Enzo a couple of days later. *"He hasn't heard from June, but he's coming over for the party. He's desperate to see her. Should we tell June or let it be a surprise?"*

Juliet considered. *"A surprise, I think. Telling her in advance will only give her time to worry about it and conjure up excuses. Maybe seeing him unexpectedly will give her the jolt she needs to tell him she loves him."*

Chapter Thirty-Four

*"Everything we hear is an opinion, not a fact.
Everything we see is a perspective, not the truth."*
Marcus Aurelius, Roman emperor
and Stoic philosopher (121-180 AD)

ONCE AGAIN Amy found herself at Gatwick airport waiting for a flight from Naples. She'd never met Matteo but her mother had sent her photos of him so she knew what he looked like and she also had a small placard with 'Matteo Rossi' carefully printed on it in large black letters, just in case.

Clarissa had planned to ask Tony to do the airport run, but then decided he was needed at home to cope with final arrangements. The last time she'd seen him he was in the lounge helping River to set up his Sonos speaker, discussing whether the music would be better over Spotify or Apple Music.

Instead, she phoned Amy and asked her to pick up Matteo at Gatwick on her way down to Brighton. "Another Italian," said Amy when her mother rang, "is he like Enzo?"

"No, not really. Totally different in fact; but be prepared for the Italian charm though. He's Enzo's best friend and very nice."

★★★

Clarissa wandered through the rooms, checking everything was in place and ready for the party. The caterers had arrived early and were busy getting the food organised. It was a peerless morning and the folded-back doors of the sunroom were open onto the garden, which was at its absolute best in its summer finery.

She went out and sat for a while on a rustic seat, contemplating the events that had led to this day and this party. It had been quite a journey but an incredibly successful one. Clarissa thought about Juliet telling her that Enzo, not Mike, was her father, and then her trip to Italy to track him down, which had happily led to Juliet and Enzo's wedding and then, unexpectedly, to Matteo's rather stormy relationship with June, and finally this family party.

Juliet had explained to Clarissa that Matteo was coming to the party, admitting that she wasn't quite sure how the meeting with June would progress. "It could go either way, really. Fingers crossed it works. But I think we must be ready to go rapidly to the rescue if it all goes badly wrong. June can be quite unpredictable. I honestly believe she will be relieved and delighted to see him; but there is the chance that she might flip if she thinks I've been trying to manoeuvre her."

Juliet had then asked rather hesitantly if Clarissa had got over the thing she'd had about kissing Matteo. "Oh absolutely. That ship has sailed." Seeing the look of relief that quickly passed over Juliet's face, Clarissa added: "It was never real, anyway. Not for him and definitely not for me. It was a kind of mind game that quickly fizzled out. It never got out of the starting blocks." She grinned and patted Juliet's hand reassuringly. "Nothing to worry about. I really hope June and Matteo manage to reconcile any differences. They will make a lovely couple."

Despite her assurances to Juliet and although she loved Tony, Clarissa allowed herself to acknowledge that she wouldn't have minded finding out what kissing Matteo was like. Just once. But she knew that it would never have stopped at one kiss. Recalling her short affair with Colin Barnett, Clarissa thought she had learned her lesson. One kiss was never just one kiss in the same way that sex was never just sex, it always led on to something far more dangerous.

Nevertheless, Clarissa still wondered what would have happened if she had stayed for the second night she'd booked at Villa Valentina and allowed fate to take its course. Quickly suppressing the flicker of desire creeping through her, Clarissa knew she had been right to leave when she did. However much you tell yourself that a casual liaison means nothing and is just a one off, these things never end well.

She remembered reading that not everyone you meet is meant to be in your future. Some people are just passing through to teach you lessons in life. Clarissa smiled to herself: she still used the arousing bedroom skills that Colin had taught her and which Tony had accepted unquestioningly. It had certainly spiced up their sex-life and provided the excitement which had previously been missing.

So, what lesson had Matteo taught her? Probably not to be greedy for things she didn't need. She had a husband she loved and who loved her, as well as two wonderful daughters. She didn't need a fleeting moment of passion with a sexy Italian, tempting though that might be. She was a happily married woman and Matteo loved June; now she and Matteo were just good friends.

Enough brooding, thought Clarissa firmly putting a lid on her memories. People were starting to arrive, and she went indoors to welcome them.

★★★

Alan and Emma were the first to show up, generously offering as usual any help that might be needed. Clarissa thankfully rushed Alan off to the kitchen where a worrying red light had shown up on the oven. "We aren't doing any cooking for the party, but I will need to use it later."

Meanwhile Emma had gone over to chat to River and

Tony, showing gratifying admiration at their competence with organising the music. "I am filled with awe," she told River. "I have absolutely no idea how you do all this computer stuff. I can only just manage to cope with my mobile phone." Alan and Emma were soon followed by a stream of other family members all keen to see Juliet and meet Enzo.

As River, who had started playing some very acceptable music, was receiving requests and basking in the admiration of a few of his teenage cousins, Tony went off to find Clarissa to see if there was anything else she wanted him to do.

With Bertie's arrival came the intriguing revelation that his companion was not a woman nor a mate but a boyfriend who was a great deal younger than he was. Bertie was a hugely successful freelance literary agent and Lance was one of his authors.

"Apparently he writes books on philosophy," Juliet informed Clarissa, reflecting that Lance was probably not much older than Lotte and Amy. "Maybe it's not a relationship as such, perhaps Bertie is Lance's patron," suggested Clarissa.

Lance was stunningly good looking, tall and slim with cropped fair hair, chiselled features and clear blue-grey eyes. Brimming with confidence, he had a charming smile and was very friendly, apparently not in the least intimidated by meeting Bertie's family *en mass*. He was wearing a startling turquoise suit with a white polo necked sweater, and had a large, crested signet ring on the little finger of his left hand.

The idea that Bertie might be Lance's patron was, however, firmly scotched when Bertie told Juliet they had been together for over a year, although they had only recently started telling people they were in a relationship.

"It's been wonderful," said Bertie, giving his sister a cautious look, unsure how she would react. "Lance has brought a lot of love and laughter into my life. The enthusiasm of youth has rejuvenated me."

Juliet sighed. What a good thing their mother wasn't still around to discover that her favourite child was gay. By bringing Lance to the party, Bertie was obviously ready at last to share his sexual orientation with the family. Mary Campbell, stuck in her stiff and starchy Edwardian past, would have been shocked to the core. To her, this would surely have been an even greater calamity than Juliet becoming an unmarried mother back in the sixties.

All the girls, excited by the unexpected arrival of this sophisticated, chatty and handsome young man, were sniffing the air like Bisto kids, looking at Lance speculatively, assessing whether he was boyfriend material. Even Emerald, Alan and Emma's precocious thirteen-year-old granddaughter, had perked up after a fit of sulking because she was being forced to go to a boring family party. They all soon realised, however, that Lance and Bertie were a couple, and their hopes were dashed.

"What a waste," murmured Felix's daughter Lucy to her cousin River. "He's really gorgeous. Why do fab looking single men usually turn out to be gay. What has Bertie got that I haven't?"

River pulled a face. "Doh! I'm assuming that's a rhetorical question, but if you really want an answer, I'd say money."

Lucy sniffed. "Well, whatever. It's still a terrible waste of a very cool guy."

Watching Lance work the room, Clarissa whispered to Tony: "He's incredibly confident for such a young man."

"Huh," scoffed Tony scathingly, "he needs all the confidence he can muster to carry off a suit like that with a modicum of success."

Chapter Thirty-Five

"Make You Feel My Love"
Bob Dylan, on the album 'The Essential Bob Dylan'
Revised Edition (1996)

BACK AT the airport a crackly voice over the Tannoy advised Amy that the Naples flight had landed, and twenty minutes later Matteo was walking towards her, carrying only a smallish backpack over one shoulder and an airport duty free bag containing bottles.

"Amy?" He took her hand and kissed it lightly. "I am so pleased to meet you. Thank you for coming to pick me up." Amy smiled. How strange that when he kissed her hand she didn't get anything like the reaction she had with Enzo.

Matteo was not as strikingly handsome as Enzo but still nice-looking with the same effortless charm, thought Amy. Maybe she was becoming used, and thus immune, to all this Italian allure. Nevertheless, she was still determined to find an Enzo of her own; she definitely seemed to have inherited Juliet's love of romantic Italians.

Driving down to the coast, Amy explained that Enzo had booked Matteo a room at the Brunswick where he and Juliet were staying until they found a house they wanted to buy. "It's only about half-a-mile away from where June lives." Matteo said nothing, but Amy noticed his hands were firmly clenched together on his lap and he was obviously on edge. Maybe stay off that subject, she thought having been warned by her mother that Matteo might be a bit touchy about June. She started chatting inconsequentially about London and her work as an actress which seemed to be safer ground. He listened politely but seemed distracted.

When they were on the outskirts of Brighton, Amy said: "The party will have just about got going. Do you want to go straight there, or would you like to go to your hotel to drop off your bag and freshen up first?" Matteo considered. "If you don't mind, could we go to the hotel first? I've been travelling quite a while so it would be good to freshen up before I see…see everyone."

"No problem," said Amy, thinking he was just about to say, 'before I see June'. She smiled at him: "Take your time. There's no rush. I'll have a chat with Amelia the receptionist while I'm waiting for you. It's ages since I've seen her and I hear she has a new tattoo."

★★★

Lunch was in full swing when Amy and Matteo arrived at the garden flat. Juliet, who had been listening for the car, rushed out to welcome them. Giving Matteo a hug she said: "How do you want to do this? Do you want to just walk in or would you prefer to see June alone?"

Drawing a deep breath he said in a rather unsteady voice: "I think I'll walk in like any arriving guest…and see what happens."

What happened was that June, after staring at Matteo in stunned silence for a few moments, put down the glass she was holding, threaded her way slowly through the groups of chattering people and flung her arms around him, kissing him firmly on the mouth. "What a wonderful surprise," she said calmly. She was totally in control. Juliet and Clarissa who were watching nervously from across the room, breathed sighs of relief. It was going to be alright.

Wrapping his arms around June Matteo whispered against her hair: "I have come because I want to marry you." June stared fixedly into his eyes and then at his mouth before deliberately bending down to take off her shoes. She stared at him again for a moment before tilting up her face to be kissed. Matteo's heart lifted, surely she must love him.

Locked together in a passionate embrace they were completely oblivious of curious glances from Alan and Emma who were standing nearby chatting to Bertie and Lance. "Another English woman who has fallen for an Italian," murmured Emma to her husband.

Bertie and Lance smiled into each other's eyes and touched hands. "I wonder what sort of reception we'd get if we did that," Lance whispered into Bertie's ear. Bertie smiled and said: "I don't think my family is quite ready for that yet. Baby steps…"

"Worth a try, Bertie?" said Lance provocatively putting his arm around Bertie's shoulders. "No Lance!" said Bertie firmly. "This is not Comptons; we are not in Soho." Lance laughed. "Oh well, perhaps another time."

Eventually Matteo said, "June…"

"Hush," she said. "Come with me," and taking his hand she led him into the sunroom and out into the garden

Chapter Thirty-Six

*"Love rules without rules.
"There are no expectations.
"It's unconditional.
"The heart decides, and what it decides
is all that really matters."*

Italian saying.

THEY SAT holding hands on a wooden bench at the very end of the garden, well away from the house, underneath a flowering cherry which was scattering pink petals around them like confetti.

After the initial delight of seeing him, June was now silent. Feeling very emotional, she was unable to talk for fear of bursting into tears. Eventually Matteo, his head on one side, leaned over to look her into her eyes. "Are you speaking to me?"

She nodded. "I'm just not sure what to say; what you want me to say."

"What I *want* you to say is 'Yes please Matteo, I would love to marry you'. Are you going to say that?"

Sniffing back tears, she said: "Ah, that's what I thought," and taking a deep breath added, "I'm sorry but I cannot marry you."

He looked stunned, his heart sinking like a stone. "You can't, why?" After the passionate way she'd kissed him, he hadn't anticipated a refusal.

"Well, I don't want to marry you."

"Oh June," said Matteo sadly. "I have come all this way to

propose to you and you say 'no'. I love you. Please will you marry me. I want to marry you and look after you."

"I know," she said. Folding her arms around her body she closed her eyes as if trying to work out the best way to deliver bad news.

"Thing is, I just don't want to get married ever again. I spent fifty years being happily unhappy in a loveless marriage. Looking back now, I can see they were totally wasted years – half a century when I could have been completely and utterly blissful with someone I loved and who loved me. That experience has left me with a deep aversion to marriage."

"I am so sorry," said Matteo stiffly. "Forgive me. If I had realised you felt like that I would never have bothered you." He stood up. "Where are you going?" demanded June. "I came to England to ask you to marry me, and you have now explained that you never ever want to get married again," he said coldly. "So, there is little point in me being here."

"Oh Matteo," said June, smiling and putting her hand on his arm. "Sit down. I may not want to get married, but I do love you and I want to be with you more than anything. I want to wake up every morning with you beside me for the rest of my life and I would absolutely love you to look after me."

Matteo looked perplexed. "You would? But you don't want to get married." Putting her head on his shoulder June said: "Can't we live together in a loving relationship without getting formally married? Living in sin is, I believe, the delightfully old-fashioned way of putting it."

He gazed at her for a long time before saying quietly: "I will do whatever it takes. I soon discovered after you left Capri that nothing is any good unless I am with you. If that means living together without being married, then that's what we'll do."

"At least it will give you something to confess when you go to church," said June with a teasing smile, wrapping both her hands around his. "This has all happened so quickly for us, we've hardly had time to draw breath. Now we need to take it slowly. Our relationship needs to evolve; we need to woo each other."

"Woo?" queried Matteo. It was a word he hadn't come across before.

"Yes, woo," said June. "We've done all this the wrong way round. Instead of getting to know each other, falling in love and then having amazing sex, we had the amazing sex first without getting to know each other.

"Now we need to start at the beginning again. We were so caught up with totally fantastic lovemaking that there was never any thought of romance. Now we have time to feel the mystery and allure of love…something I have never experienced… while still enjoying sensational sex, of course.

"We can live together and let our relationship develop naturally. We love each other, that's a good starting point. As you so wisely said on Capri, love is all that matters. Everything else is detail."

Matteo nodded. "That's true. I love you and I was so frightened I was going to lose you that I pushed you too hard for the answer I wanted. I drove you away."

"No." June put her arms around him. "It was me. I have always been afraid of letting anyone get too close. After so many years without love, I just closed my mind to it; decided it was never going to happen. So when you said you were falling in love with me, I flipped. Because I have never been in love before, I really didn't know what to expect or how it would feel.

"Jules pointed out that the exciting, disturbing but scary sensations I was experiencing were the emotions usually felt by a teenager in love for the first time. Only problem was I was a seventy-two-year-old in love for the first time and I really wasn't sure how to cope with it. So, I did my usual thing of running away."

Totally overcome by emotion, Matteo lapsed into rapid Italian.

"*Ti amo moltissimo. E tu…tu mi ami? Davvero?* Recovering, he said: "*Scusi*…in English now… I love you very much. And you…do you love me? Really?" Kissing her forehead, he added softly, "Are you quite sure you are totally happy with us being together; you're not going to run away again?"

She gave him a loving look saying: "Running away has always been my defence. But now I have no intention of running anywhere and yes, I am absolutely certain that I love you. It's something I never expected to happen, but I am just ecstatic that it has."

Picking up her left hand, Matteo said in surprise: "You're not wearing your diamond."

"No. I took it off when I knew I loved you. I don't need it now." As Matteo pulled her into his arms, June surrendered herself, heart, mind and soul to love for the first time in her long life.

After a while Matteo whispered: "It feels like I've been an eternity without you, and I desperately want to make love to you. Do you think we can go somewhere and get a room?" June gave an unsteady laugh. "Not in the middle of Enzo and Juliet's wedding bash, we can't! We'll just have wait for a couple of hours and then we can go back to the flat and have wonderful sex all night if that's what you want."

"Mmm, okay." Leaning down to kiss her again Matteo said: "If we must wait, we must, but it's not going to be easy."

After staring at him contemplatively for a while, June said slightly diffidently: "Would you consider coming to live with me in the flat? Permanently I mean. To be perfectly honest, I'm not sure I would be able to settle anywhere else…even with you." She looked very nervous as she added: "Is that too much to ask?"

"I would be happy live with you in England," said Matteo. "In fact I will live anywhere if I can be with you. I love you so much; I want to spend every day of the rest of my life with you." Stroking her hair he added: "When you said you didn't want to marry me my heart fell out of my body like a stone. I thought my life was over. I don't ever want to have that feeling again."

"Oh, my love," said June giving a serene smile," that will never happen again. Looking at Matteo's mouth she whispered: "Now *I'm* beginning to wish we could go off and find room."

Matteo, feeling quite unhinged with love and longing, said: "I really need to make love to you, but if there's nowhere we can go immediately, then I suppose we should return to the party and give Enzo and *Giulietta* the good news. I know they've been quite worried about us."

★★★

Juliet took one look at June and Matteo's faces and relaxed. They were holding hands and the aura of happiness around them was almost tangible. She went over to them and put her arms around each of them in turn. "I am delighted," she said. "Congratulations."

"Jules," said June, "Matteo and I are *not* getting married."

"You're not?" said Juliet uneasily. Had she misread the situation.

"No, but we do love each other, and we *are* settling down together. We've agreed to live in outrageously glorious sin, probably in the flat." As Juliet gave a questioning look, June explained: "I do love Matteo, but I just don't want to get married again, once was quite enough, thank you. There's still a lot to be sorted out, but I think Matteo's going to come and live with me in Hove. The rest of our lives start right here."

Catching Enzo's eye, Juliet nodded, giving a covert thumbs up sign. With a beaming smile he hurried over, giving Matteo a hug and kissing June on both cheeks. "*Auguri*! I am so pleased."

"They're not getting married, but they are going to live together in the flat," said Juliet. "Ah," smiled Enzo, "that sounds like an excellent compromise."

"I'm going to live here in England," explained Matteo. "I will hand my share of the hotel over to Giorgio and Anna, they both have children who can carry on the business, and I will live in happy retirement with June."

After updating Clarissa and Tony, Enzo tapped a fork on his wine glass, calling for silence. "This may be a party to celebrate *Giulietta* and I getting married, but I am delighted to announce that we now have another wonderful event to mark." Holding up his glass he said: "Congratulations and *Salute t*o our very good friends Matteo and June who have decided to settle down together in Hove."

A surprised and delighted murmur rippled around the room, although those who had witnessed that passionate kiss were not quite so astonished. "Told you so," said Emma to Alan with a satisfied smirk. "Women know about these things." Alan just laughed and gave her a fond kiss. "You were right as usual," he said indulgently.

When Clarissa went across to offer her congratulations, Matteo kissed her cheek saying: "We have so much to thank you for *cara*. If it wasn't for your determination to track down Enzo, June and I would never have met."

Clarissa laughed. "Well, I admit it could all have gone horribly wrong. You were so scary when I turned up at Villa Valentina that I almost gave up immediately." Matteo wrinkled his nose as June gazed at him with raised eyebrows. "Yes, I know, I'm sorry, but it was in service to a friend."

Turning to June he said: "I was trying to save Enzo from this mad woman who was insisting that he was her father!" June laughed and Clarissa said gently: "I was only teasing. I totally understand that you were protecting Enzo."

Matteo looked at Clarissa, remembering the last time he had seen her was on Capri when he had been thinking he fancied shagging her. He had been slightly concerned about seeing her again now he was in a relationship with June, wondering if it was going to make things awkward. But Clarissa showed no sign of embarrassment and Matteo realised that absolutely nothing had happened – except in his head.

With a huge feeling of relief, he smiled and said softly: "The important thing is you didn't give up and now June and I will be together for ever. I am happier than I thought it was ever possible to be." Clarissa smiled. "I am so pleased for you both. It's just wonderful. First Enzo and Juliet and now you two. I think I may hire myself out as a fairy godmother. I wonder who will be next on the list."

Chapter Thirty-Seven

"Love is an irresistible desire to be irresistibly desired."
Robert Frost, American poet (1874-1963)

MALIK PUT his arm possessively around Charlotte's waist. With these amorous Italians around he had every intention of keeping her close. Having overheard Lotte and Amy discussing not only Enzo's charms but also a trip to Naples, the sudden news of another Anglo-Italian romance had left Malik feeling unusually anxious.

He and Lotte had been living together for two years and there was no way he was going to let her to go off to Italy without him, especially as he knew Amy was hoping to find an Italian boyfriend. Goodness knows what might happen. Anyway, he was planning to ask Lotte to marry him – when he could summon up the courage and find the right moment.

Malik was well aware of Charlotte's strong feminist views and they had always suited him admirably. She wasn't one of those clinging, fluffy, helpless women but sensible, practical and down-to-earth…qualities which made her ideal for the very tough job she did so well as a nurse in A & E. However, she was also very beautiful with gorgeous green eyes and a bubbly personality. He knew many guys at the hospital where they both worked fancied her and were poised to jump in if anything went wrong between them.

With masculine arrogance Malik, who'd had an endless

succession doting of girlfriends before he met Charlotte, never doubted that she was happy to be his partner, so he'd never suffered a moment of uncertainty – until now. Although he loved her, Malik couldn't remember ever actually telling her so, thinking that because they were living together Lotte must know he did. There had always been the throw-away 'love you' at the end of a telephone call, or when they left for work, but never a serious declaration. Things had to change.

Malik had noticed how women behaved around Enzo, who was charming and chivalrous but also very protective and a tad bossy. There could never be any question about how much Enzo loved Juliet; he made it perfectly clear that he absolutely adored her, and judging by the look on her face, he probably told her so all the time.

Malik was thinking that maybe he should be more like that with Lotte. Perhaps a bit more spontaneous and tactile to make sure that she knew he loved her and wanted to marry her. He needed to talk to her, and sooner rather than later. He certainly didn't want her going off to Italy with Amy.

Taking her hand he said: "Lotte, it's getting a bit stuffy in here, come outside with me for a breath of air." Charlotte gave him a distracted look. "You go, hun," she replied. "There are people I need to talk to. I can't remember the last time I saw Michael and Sarah…" Taking a deep breath and swallowing hard Malik said firmly: "No, Lotte. I want you to come with me *now*."

She regarded him with a flicker of surprise. It was the first time she'd heard that authoritative tone in his voice and she found it unexpectedly exciting. "Oh, okay, if you like," she said casually, giving him a curious glance. What had happened to the easy going, take it or leave it guy she'd always known?

Malik led her out to the garden bench recently vacated by Matteo and June. "Lotte," said Malik, hoping she didn't realise how nervous he was and couldn't hear his heart hammering, "what with your grandmother getting married, and now her best friend announcing that she and what's his name" – "Matteo" said Lotte, "his name is Matteo" – "yes, Matteo, are settling down together, I'm thinking that it's time we put our relationship on a firmer footing."

"*Really?* We're already living together. That's pretty firm, I thought."

"Yes, but Lotte, I want something more permanent than that."

Malik looked into her eyes feeling horribly exposed. He so rarely showed his emotions, always claiming it was because of his work as a hospital doctor. "Goodness knows where I'd be if I got emotional about every sad case I came across." Now he admitted to himself that it was an instinctive mechanism to prevent getting hurt. Taking another deep breath, he plunged in. "Lotte, I love you very much and I want to marry you."

"Marry?" Charlotte felt a strange mixture of happiness and bewilderment surge through her. He'd never seriously said he loved her before, although she was pretty sure he did. And marry? "I thought you were happy with us living together. I had no idea you loved me and wanted to get married."

"Well I do. Don't you? Want to get married, I mean. We've been giving it a trial run for two years."

"Well…" Now she allowed herself to think about it, marriage to Malik seemed an appealing proposition, even though she'd always protested that as a feminist she didn't need a husband and had no intention of getting hitched. She'd really enjoyed the two years they had spent together and couldn't imagine living without him. After a short pause she said shyly and slightly self-consciously, "Actually, I think I'd rather like that."

"You would? So you *will* marry me; can I take that as a yes?" asked Malik gently with a tentative smile. "Will you marry me Lotte?" Charlotte nodded. "Yes please."

Pulling her towards him, Malik put his arms around her. "And you love me too?" He sounded so uncharacteristically unsure and insecure that Charlotte felt incredibly protective of him. Of course she loved him. How little men understood women. "I do love you. I always have – but we feminist women aren't supposed to say so, at least, not until someone has proposed to us."

Giving her a lingering kiss, he whispered: "Would a feminist woman wear an engagement ring if I gave her one?"

"I don't know about feminist women *per se*," replied Charlotte contentedly, "but I will, with love and pride."

After a while, she pulled herself out of Malik's embrace and said: "There is one thing though."

"What?" asked Malik with alarm. "Can we keep this to ourselves for just a bit longer. I don't think we can go in there and tell everyone now, right after June and Matteo have announced their news. "Let's wait until tomorrow and tell Mum, Dad and Amy. Then after you have telephoned your parents, the whole world can know."

"That seems fair," said Malik. "I am so happy and excited that I don't know how I'm going to keep quiet for twenty-four hours, but I agree with you, my darling. My lips are sealed until tomorrow."

"Not so tightly zipped that you're unable to kiss me, I hope," whispered Charlotte moving back into the circle of his arms.

★★★

When lunch was over and the caterers had collected plates and glasses and cleared the party detritus, Clarissa announced that River would be providing music for dancing.

Enzo went over to Juliet who was sitting on the sofa chatting to Audrey Phillips. The two women had met many times over the years and really liked each other, quite happily sharing the 'mothering' of Clarissa. They were discussing Juliet's dress. "It's really lovely," said Audrey, "is it your wedding dress?

"It is," said Juliet. "On the day, I had an Alice band of freesias but I thought that would be a bit too much for a family party, so…"

"*Scusi,*" said Enzo politely, "but may I borrow my wife, we have to dance."

"Dance?" Mystified, Juliet wrinkled her brow. As she posed the question, Clarissa proclaimed: "And the very first dance will be enjoyed by our newly married couple Enzo and Juliet." Audrey laughed. "Off you go!"

Juliet looked disconcerted, suddenly realising that even back in the sixties she and Enzo had never danced together. She hesitated, but taking her hand Enzo pulled her up from the sofa and led her into the centre of the room to resounding applause. "Don't look so scared *amore,*" he whispered, "we can do this."

Putting his arms around her he held her close against him as River played Elvis Presley singing *Can't Help Falling in Love.* Juliet gave a surprised jump. "Enzo it's…" He looked down at her smiling. "Our special song, which I have always sung to you after making love and which is now off the programme at gigs. Yes I know."

As they moved slowly around the floor Enzo murmered: "June told me that you felt you could never dance to this, not even with Ted, because it meant so much to us. So, it seems right that the very first time you *do* dance to this song it is with me. Now when I sing it, you will always remember that we danced to it at our wedding party."

"Oh Enzo," sighed Juliet gazing into his eyes. "I adore you. I just wish…" Enzo put a finger on her lips. "Hush baby, I know what you were going to say, and I wish it too. But we can't turn back the clock and what has happened has happened. Now we must make the most of the time we have together and hopefully that will be many, many years. *Ti amo moltissimo.*"

Overflowing with love for him, Juliet put her head against his shoulder and closed her eyes. Looking down at her contented face, Enzo whispered: "Be happy for this moment. This moment is your life." Juliet opened her eyes and said: "That's from the book of Persian poetry you gave me on our wedding day." He smiled: "*Ruba'iyat of Omar Khayyam*. The only book anyone needs in life."

As other couples began to dance, Enzo murmured in Juliet's ear: "I'm giving you a choice, baby. Either we slip out and go back to the Brunswick for an hour, or we find a room here that has a lock on the door." Knowing exactly what he was suggesting, Juliet was wide-eyed with shocked surprise. "Can we get away with that?" Enzo shrugged, giving his sexy smile. "Don't see why not."

"Then it had better be here. I don't think leaving is an option. We'll try Amy's room, it's furthest away from the lounge and I'm pretty sure it has a lock."

"Thank goodness for that! I was afraid you were going to suggest the bathroom," said Enzo. "Amy's room will be much more comfortable. I can't lean against walls or lie in a bath or on hard floors anymore. I really do need a bed to perform at my best nowadays."

Juliet laughed and as Enzo led his wife out of the room Clarissa, interpreting the purposeful look on their faces and guessing what they were up to, glanced across and gave Juliet a broad wink. Then she went over to River and his growing entourage of teenage girls and asked him to shift the music up a gear. "Time to get this party moving," she said. With a grin of delight River said: "Now you're talking."

"But River…let's start gently with a bit of Elvis, the Stones and Status Quo before you move on to Greta Van Fleet and Blink-182," suggested Clarissa. "We need everyone to get used to it before we blast their brains out."

"She's so cool," said one of River's groupies. "Wish she was my mum. Mine would think Blink was batting your eyelids!"

★★★

Safely locked in Amy's room Enzo and Juliet looked at each other, stifling the urge to burst out laughing. "This seems strangely exciting," said Juliet. "I feel like a teenager having illicit sex in my parents' bedroom."

"Did you ever do that?" asked Enzo with interest.

"Of course not," replied Juliet. "The first time I ever had sex was with you on Capri and I was nineteen. Anyway, with a mother like mine it would have been impossible. It's just the kind of thing June would have done, though."

Enzo began to pull her towards the bed. "Wait a minute," said Juliet, "I need to take my dress off. I can't roll around on the bed in this."

"Do you intend to roll around?" asked Enzo with a mischievous smile, carefully unzipping the dress and helping his wife to step out of it. "Not roll around exactly," said Juliet, "maybe just a bit of gentle rocking up and down."

"This is very improper talk for a respectable married lady, Signora," said Enzo taking her in his arms. Juliet started giggling as he gently pushed her down onto the bed.

"We have time for a quickie Signora de Martins before anyone realises we are missing and comes looking for us. Just remember, no loud moaning and groaning," said Enzo shaking with suppressed laughter. "Huh, you're a fine one to talk," retorted Juliet, as she happily prepared once again to give herself up to ecstasy. "I hope it's a strong lock on that door."

Chapter Thirty-Eight

"Of two sisters, one is always the watcher, one the dancer."
Louise Gluck, American poet
and essayist (1943-2023)

THE FOLLOWING morning Charlotte asked her parents if it would be possible to have a small family gathering over a late breakfast.

"We had a family gathering yesterday," said Tony slightly grumpily, feeling the worse for wear after too many whiskies with Juliet's son Felix the night before. "Why do we need another? God, I feel awful."

"You look pretty awful too," said his daughter unsympathetically. "Don't go outside, you'll frighten the horses."

"You can always have some Fernet Branca," suggested Clarissa, holding up the bottle of bitter amaro. "This is one of the bottles Matteo gave us. It's very medicinal and great for fighting hangovers."

"No thank you," said Tony with a shudder. "It tastes foul. I'll just have some water."

Passing her husband a glass of water and two paracetamols, Clarissa gave her daughter a searching look and asked: "I'm assuming there is a particular reason for this request."

"There is," agreed Charlotte, "but I don't want to talk about it until everyone is here."

"Then I suggest we do lunch," said Clarissa. "We all had

quite a late night and it's going to take a while for people to get themselves up and about this morning. Who do you want to be here, Lotte?"

"Well, you two and Amy. Then Juliet and Enzo, and June and Matteo. Oh yes, and Malik, of course, if he manages to get out of bed. He has the mother of all hangovers this morning."

"Can't be worse than mine," grumbled her father. "I don't think I will be able to touch malt whisky ever again. Why did I drink so much? I *never* drink that much. Maybe I'll become a teetotaller."

"Right," said Charlotte, "I can see that happening. It will last until you come face-to-face with a bottle of champagne."

Chuckling, Clarissa nodded at her daughter. She had a glimmer of an idea where this was heading. "Okay sweetheart, let's do a casual lunch, say two o'clock? Are you happy to phone around and issue the invitations?"

"Absolutely."

When Charlotte had gone off to her room to make the calls and tempt Malik out of bed with a glass of fizzing Alka-Seltzer, Tony looked crossly at Clarissa and said: "Another lunch. I was planning to go for a tramp across the Downs to clear my head."

"You can do that afterwards," said Clarissa serenely, pouring him a glass of orange juice. "I have a feeling Lotte's gathering is important."

Tony stood up and kissed her. "Sorry to be a grump, darling, but I honestly don't feel great." Clarissa looked at him with a comforting smile. He certainly did look a bit peaky. "Drink your juice and go back to bed for a couple of hours," she said briskly. "You'll feel much better by lunchtime."

★★★

Although surprised by Charlotte's invitation to lunch and not exactly brimming with enthusiasm, Juliet, Enzo, June and Matteo all agreed to be there. "It is important," said Charlotte. "And you only need to stay for an hour max, unless you want to stay longer, of course."

"Well if it's important sweetheart of course Enzo and I will be there," said Juliet. June was also acquiescent, despite her plan for a late lunch in bed with Matteo. "We'll be there," she promised, "and we'll pick up Jules and Enzo on the way."

Amy was more outspoken. "Do you *honestly* need me Lotte? It's a real bore, I had plans."

"I want you to be here," said her sister quietly. "It's important."

"How important is important?"

"Mega important."

Amy stared silently at Charlotte for a long moment before saying: "Are you doing what I think you're doing?" Charlotte looked away, biting her lip. "Holy shit!" shouted Amy. "You and Malik are getting married."

"Shush! Keep your voice down. I don't want anyone to know until Malik is up and about. We're going to tell everyone at lunch." Amy looked pole axed. "What ever happened to radical feminism and not needing a man except for the obvious? She suddenly stopped and asked: "For fuck's sake, you're not…"

"Definitely not pregnant," Charlotte assured her. "Malik proposed and said he loves me and I do love him, so…" She spread out her hands and shrugged.

"Crikey," said Amy. "I know I said I was off to find a fucking gorgeous Italian to look after me, but you have always been insistent that you were never interested in getting hitched…even if you and Malik were still together when you were seventy."

Charlotte looked embarrassed. "I want to marry him, I always have deep down inside. I want him to look after me the way Enzo looks after Juliet. As a radical feminist I am obviously a complete failure."

Amy kissed her sister's cheek. "Whatever turns you on babe," she said. "Malik does," said Charlotte crisply. "That's why I am going to marry him."

"Holy shit," said Amy again. "It's just me for Naples then."

★★★

"Lovely to be invited to lunch two days in a row" said June as she and Matteo arrived. Clarissa noticed they were still holding hands and radiating happiness. "Anything we can do to help?"

"Not really, thank you," replied Clarissa. "It's only *Vichyssoise* and leftovers from yesterday's party, so don't get too excited. We are all here at Lotte's invitation. Even Tony and I don't know what this is all about. She's telling us over lunch."

"Intriguing," said June.

Looking around, Clarissa asked: "Where are Juliet and Enzo? I thought they were coming with you."

"Oh, they did, but they have gone for a walk around the garden. They still can't keep their hands off each other."

"Those two are behaving like teenagers, bless them. They're so lovely together," said Clarissa with a fond smile. "It's difficult to believe they are my parents. They feel more like my teenage children."

"Well, if we'd been apart for fifty years, I guess I wouldn't be able to leave Matteo alone either," said June. Giving her a doting look, Matteo added: "I can't keep my hands off June at the moment; I have to keep touching her to make sure we're really here together."

As Charlotte walked into the kitchen followed by a rather fragile-looking Malik, June asked with interest: "What's the big surprise, Lotte?" Malik and Charlotte looked at each other rather sheepishly and Clarissa quickly suggested that Malik should take Matteo outside to show him the Porsche. "The fresh air will do you good."

"Heavens, Mum, once those two get talking about cars we'll never get them back in for lunch," protested Charlotte. "Yes we will, don't worry sweetheart. I'll send Amy out to get them; she won't stand for any nonsense."

"Ah," said June. "So, you really are planning a big reveal over lunch, Lotte!"

★★★

"Shall we eat *al fresco*," asked Clarissa. "It's a beautiful day." Amy and June set up the garden table under the spreading branches of an ancient plum tree, while Charlotte helped her mother gather together the food and carry it outside.

Looking at her watch, Clarissa sent Amy to break up Matteo and Malik's car talk. She then asked June to call over Juliet and Enzo who were sitting with their arms around each other on the bench where the day before, June and Matteo and Charlotte and Malik had sealed their futures; meanwhile Clarissa went to wake up Tony.

Once they were all seated around the table and Tony was pouring glasses of chilled Prosecco, wondering if he was the only one who couldn't face the thought of any more alcohol, Clarissa turned to Charlotte and Malik saying: "Right guys, you're on." Holding hands, the young couple stood up looking distinctly nervous, and Malik said a bit unsteadily: "I asked Lotte to marry me yesterday and she said 'yes' so…"

"We're engaged," said Charlotte happily. "Malik just has to phone his parents in Dubai and tell them and then the whole world can know."

As Clarissa hugged them both, Tony said: "Well, this is a turn up for the books. My feminist daughter is getting spliced." Malik gave Tony a startled look. "Oh fuck! Should I have asked your permission first?" Hearing a ripple of laughter, Malik added:

"Gosh, I'm so sorry, I didn't mean to say fuck, but…well, I hope I haven't fucked up! I've never done this before…"

"I should hope not," said Charlotte smiling lovingly at his mortified face.

As the laughter became louder, Tony got up and put an arm around Malik's shoulders. "Don't apologise. I have to confess I didn't ask Ken for Clarissa's hand in marriage. We were at university and as left-wing students we thought such niceties were old fashioned and unimportant…and they probably still are. Anyway, Lotte is a feminist and will tell you that although I am her father, I don't own her, so no need to ask permission."

Looking relieved Malik took Charlotte's hand and producing a small box from his pocket, he went down on one knee and said: "Charlotte Price, please will you marry me." Lifting the lid of the box he revealed a green sapphire and diamond ring. Charlotte gasped with delighted surprise.

"Do you like it? The green sapphire is the same colour as your eyes. I know we should really go together to choose a ring, but I saw this weeks ago and thought it was perfect. I've been carrying it around with me ever since. I'd been planning to ask you to marry me for ages but somehow I just couldn't find the right time. So once I *had* asked you, I decided to give you the ring after we'd announced the news to your family."

"Wow, I had absolutely no idea. I love it, and there is nothing I want more than to marry you." To resounding cheers, Malik slipped the ring onto Charlotte's finger and kissed her.

Pulling herself out of her aura of happiness, Charlotte turned to June and Matteo, saying: "I hope you don't think we're jumping on the bandwagon. We didn't want to announce our engagement yesterday after your big news, which is why we asked you to lunch today." June kissed Charlotte's cheek. "That is so thoughtful my love. I sincerely hope you and Malik will be as happy as we are."

Amy smiled. "Hitching up is becoming a bit of a thing in this family; first Juliet and Enzo, then June and Matteo and now Lotte and Malik."

"And," said Clarissa, "I hear that both Matteo and Malik popped the question yesterday on the bench under the flowering cherry at the end of the garden, so perhaps we should attach a plaque with the date on it."

"Maybe we could call it 'The Love Bench'," suggested Amy, laughing as her father rolled his eyes in horror, saying: "Absolutely not. Over my dead body!"

"That too can be arranged," teased Amy, now in hysterics.

As Tony refilled glasses to toast Charlotte and Malik's engagement, June looked across at Amy: "Your turn next."

"I don't think so, not just yet," replied Amy seriously. "Three is a lucky number, let's leave it at that for the moment."

"Well, you never know what might happen," said her father. "All three romantic relationships in this family were definitely unexpected."

"Hmm," replied Amy slowly. "But you know what…as soon as the play finishes, I'm booking a flight to Naples." There was a general gasp of astonishment around the table as Amy added half-jokingly: "And it's going to be one-way because with a bit of luck I won't need a ticket back." Amid gales of surprised laughter Charlotte said: "She's off to find her own fucking gorgeous Italian."

Enzo and Matteo laughed uproariously, and June looked across at Juliet, giving her a knowing nod. "What did I tell you. She's inherited your love of romantic Italians."

Wiping tears of laughter from his eyes Enzo said: "Let us know when you're going Amy, and I'll give you the keys to the *Napoli* house and tell Maria to expect you." With his arm tightly around Juliet he murmured in her ear: "Fucking gorgeous Italian, eh?"

Chapter Thirty-Nine

"The only limit to our realisation of tomorrow will be our doubts of today."
Franklin D Roosevelt, US president (1882-1945)

TONY TURNED up at the Brunswick with a florid, prosperous-looking man in his early sixties. "This is Cyril Parsons," he said, introducing him to Enzo and Juliet. "He's a property developer and one of my clients."

Juliet offered them coffee and Amaretti biscuits and they sat in the suite's small sitting room which seemed smaller than ever with Cyril's large frame in it.

Cyril gave Juliet an assessing look. So, this was Tony's mother-in-law and very attractive she was too. It was clear to see where Clarissa got her beauty; both her parents were extremely good looking.

Cyril was very fond of Clarissa and really fancied her. He'd often made flirtatious overtures during Tony's dinner events, without success. Now he contemplated her mother whom he also found extremely alluring, but with a husband who looked like that… and an Italian to boot… it was unlikely he would score there either.

Even with his considerable wealth, Cyril was finding it increasingly difficult to pull women the way he used to. An excess of good food and his liking for alcohol had helped to pile on the pounds, and his extreme girth was not helped by the fact that he drove his Bentley everywhere.

Despite dire warnings from his concerned doctor, Cyril rarely walked or took exercise of any kind. The housekeeper and gardener he employed simply made any physical effort completely unnecessary. Since the time he'd lost his licence for drink-driving, he also had a part-time driver who would pick him up from social events and also drive on those occasions when Cyril just couldn't be bothered to get behind the wheel. But he usually enjoyed driving his Bentley, it was one of the few pleasures left to him, he reflected sadly.

The only exercise Cyril took was mental and metaphorical. He still enjoyed the thrill of chasing a beautiful woman…although it always ended with him being rebuffed. His wife, a glamour model thirty years his junior, had left him and he was finding that even those girls who went with him purely for his money and the gifts he might give them, were also few and far between nowadays.

Cyril ruminated despondently that his gargantuan size meant he could no longer efficiently perform in bed. There were ways and means of course, but chance would be a fine thing. Unless he could pull occasionally, there was no hope of that either. Cyril had considered paying a call girl for her services but was reluctant to go down that slippery slope. I'm not yet that desperate, he told himself firmly. There's still hope.

Most of the effort Cyril expended was focused on his business, where he was utterly ruthless, rarely sparing a thought for those he trampled over to get what he wanted. Tony seemed to be the exception; Cyril liked him – and not just because he fancied Clarissa. Tony was also a talented businessman, and although he was much less rapacious than Cyril, the two men understood each other, speaking the same language. Thus, Cyril was happy to offer the occasional favour in recognition of sweeteners Tony had put his way.

"Now, don't get too excited," Tony told Juliet and Enzo, "because this is just a random thought, and it may not work for you. Cyril is developing those fields off the road to Saltdean, and my company has been appointed the architect. In addition to the fields, where there are plans for a dozen or so houses, Cyril has a small plot of land about a mile away, with a rather dilapidated bungalow on it. I was wondering if anything could be done with the bungalow to make it suitable for you."

"Oh!" said Juliet frowning. She couldn't see how a ramshackle building could be remotely what they were looking for, but Enzo looked interested. "What are you thinking could be done with it?"

"There are a couple options," said Tony looking across at Cyril. "Do you want to take it from here?"

"Mmm." Cyril put a hand on Juliet's knee, squeezing it caressingly. "I can see you don't look too impressed my lovely but wait until you hear the details before you decide. There may be possibilities."

Tony suppressed a grin as Enzo's gimlet eye zoomed in on Cyril's podgy hand with its ostentatious diamond signet ring, grasping his wife's knee. Juliet said nothing but shifted slightly in her chair, moving her knee from under Cyril's hand, while Enzo leaned towards his wife and put a solicitous arm around her, pulling her towards him. His message couldn't have been clearer: 'Hands off!'

"Anyway…" Cyril, looking slightly discomforted, shuffled his file of papers. "The bungalow and the small plot it stands on came as a separate parcel with the field I've bought, and I just want to get rid of it. It's really of no use to me, I do more large-scale developments.

"Whoever takes it on could either do a renovation job…the bungalow was built in the nineteen-twenties and is substantially constructed…or pull the whole lot down and build something completely new. However, if a new property was wanted, the council planners might insist on it being replaced by another single storey building."

Enzo nodded. "What would you choose to do?" he asked Tony.

Tony rubbed his chin thoughtfully. "I think if it were me," he said slowly, "I'd keep the bungalow and renovate it. It was once a very attractive building and it could be again; it's not listed, so that's a bonus. The small bit of land it stands on could be turned into a manageable garden, in fact I'm pretty sure it once was a garden."

Enzo looked at Juliet. "I think this is something we need to discuss *amore*."

"If you think you might be interested Mr de Martins you should come along and have a look at it. I really need a decision in a week or thereabouts," said Cyril, mopping his glistening brow with a handkerchief. He gave Enzo a wary glance. Mr de Martins was obviously exceedingly protective of his wife, a very different kettle of fish from Tony, who always left Clarissa to fight her own battles. It seemed that even a little gentle dalliance with the lovely Mrs de Martins was definitely off the cards.

Suddenly becoming very brisk and businesslike he added: "You have first refusal, so I won't put it on the open market until I have heard from you."

"Yes, you two have a chat," said Tony, "and let me know what you think. I can take you over to look at it and we can discuss the renovation possibilities. If you do decide to go for it, I will give you my architectural services as a wedding present."

"That is very generous," said Enzo gratefully. "Thank you," said Juliet, getting up to give Tony a kiss on the cheek.

Cyril hauled his bulk off the sofa. "Okay, Mr de Martins, I'll wait to hear from you or Tony. I haven't yet worked out how much I want for it, but I don't think it will be too expensive because I really need to get rid of it. I'll get my accountant to look at the figures and let you know by the end of play today."

"Thank you," said Enzo. "My wife and I will go and look at the site together, but she will have the final say. She has to be happy about where we live, so what she says goes."

"Right," said Cyril knowing he had been put firmly in his place.

After showing Tony and Cyril out, Enzo went back to Juliet who was still looking a bit dubious. Gathering her into his arms he said: "Let's ask Tony to show it to us, *Giulietta*. If we really can't see the possibilities we don't have to buy it. But you never know, it could be what we are looking for. We might be able to turn it into our home…but only if you agree."

"Alright," said Juliet, "as long as I'm *never* left alone with that creepy man." She laughed, beaming into Enzo's eyes. "Isn't he absolutely revolting. I was very tempted to slap his hand."

"Don't worry, *Giulietta*," said Enzo calmly. "I had my eye on him."

★★★

A couple of days later, Enzo and Juliet went with Tony to see the bungalow. "Can that price be correct?" queried Enzo. "Mr Parsons' accountant assured me it was, but I think I may have misunderstood." Tony laughed. "No, one hundred thousand pounds; that's absolutely what Cyril is willing to sell it to you for."

They stood looking at the large rosy brick building standing in about a third of an acre of land. "It's a great opportunity," said Tony. "Cyril is certainly being unusually generous. If he puts it on the market it will go for at least four or five times that amount."

"What do you think, *cara*?" Enzo asked Juliet, who was wandering around the plot looking at the weed-choked flower beds, occasionally stooping down so she could inspect a plant more closely. "I think I could do a lot with this garden; it's crying out to be saved," she replied enthusiastically.

"I think the bungalow needs saving too," said Enzo. "Shall we buy it and give it a new lease of life?" His wife nodded at him smiling. "I think we should."

"That's great," said Tony. "I hoped it might suit you when Cyril told me about it. Luckily it's on a small lane so you won't have access difficulties and it has basic utilities like water and electricity, so it's just modernisation and possibly, a new roof needed, nothing too drastic."

"I expected it to be far more rundown when you called it 'dilapidated'. I thought it might be a ruin," said Enzo. "I must say it's a pleasant surprise."

"You need to spend some time deciding the rooms and facilities you want, and then I'll set to and draw you some plans," said Tony. "As you are only really doing a very basic renovation job, there may be no need to go through the planners. I'll check and get back to you on that."

Juliet dragged herself away from the garden to join Tony and Enzo. "I really love it – the views are glorious and the whole place has a nice feel about it. I think we could live very happily here."

"Wonderful," said Tony, "I'm so pleased. Now you two go home and think about how you want the bungalow to look inside and out. When you've decided, I'll get to work."

Enzo put his arm around Juliet. "We're going to have a home of our own at last, *amore*."

Chapter Forty

"By three methods we may learn wisdom: First, by reflection, which is the noblest; Second by imitation, which is the easiest; and third by experience, which is the bitterest."
Confucius, Chinese philosopher (c551-479 BCE)

ENZO AND Juliet were having Sunday lunch with Clarissa and Tony. Amy, who was staying with friends in Brighton for the weekend, had joined them so she could have a quick guitar lesson before returning to London for a rehearsal. The play was opening in a week.

It was lesson number six and Amy was slowly becoming more confident, although she had very sore fingers, which had occasionally stopped her from practising. "You'll quickly get over that," Enzo assured her breezily. "It happens to everyone. Your fingers will soon toughen up." Amy was not so sure. Enzo had been playing the guitar for more than sixty years. He'd doubtless forgotten how much even nylon strings could hurt delicate fingertips.

"She's doing extremely well," Enzo told her parents when Amy had left for London. "We'll be jamming very soon."

After lunch, Enzo and Juliet took Tony and Clarissa to look around the bungalow. Essential renovation had been completed in record time and the builders, plumbers, electricians and carpenters were about to depart so the decorators could move in and work their magic.

Juliet and Enzo had spent a lot of time discussing exactly what they wanted in their home. "I think simple and practical would work best for us, *Giulietta,*" said Enzo as they prepared a list of rooms for Tony to include in his plans. Juliet agreed. "Practical, simple and easy to care for are my thoughts," she agreed.

Thus, they asked Tony to provide two bedrooms. The master was to have an ensuite wet room: "We don't want to be stepping in and out of a bath or shower at our age." said Enzo, adding dismissively, "anyway, our days of making love in the bath are long gone so we don't need a bath." The guest room would have its own ensuite shower, thus making a family bathroom unnecessary.

The kitchen needed to be a good size with a dining area; and a very necessary utility room would provide not only all laundry facilities, but also have an extra loo and a shower – "for washing muddy dogs and boots," said Juliet practically. The biggest room would be the sitting-room with bi-fold doors opening onto the garden. There would also be a small snug, with a screen and music system, where Enzo could keep his collection of guitars, and which would double up as an office.

Although they both wanted a fireplace in the sitting-room… so nice to have a log fire at Christmas…Enzo had requested underfloor heating throughout the bungalow, knowing that English winters could be much colder than the temperate climate of southern Italy. He had occasionally suffered cold hotels while touring, an experience he had no wish to repeat.

Planning the garden had been totally left for Juliet, and she had spent many happy hours working with a handyman who cleared bushes, weeds and brambles to reveal flower beds, an area of lawn, a vegetable patch, an apple tree and, most surprising of all, a beautiful flag-stoned patio. "A perfect blank canvas," she told Enzo happily, flicking through gardening catalogues in her quest for a greenhouse. "D'you think we could also keep some hens…?"

Most of the decisions about internal decoration had also been left to Juliet, Enzo's only proviso being that he didn't particularly like bright colours on walls. With June and Clarissa's help, Juliet had chosen paint, wallpaper and fabrics in neutral and pastel palettes, checking with Enzo before making a final decision.

Some pictures and other art, together with small pieces of furniture had arrived from the house in Naples, but only things Enzo felt he couldn't live without. "I don't want to move it all to England because we are going to be spending holidays in *Napoli* and it will be nice to see familiar friends when we visit."

As they proudly showed Clarissa and Tony around their new home, Enzo said: "All the workmen have been very efficient. If the decorators keep up the pace, we're hoping we can move in within a few weeks."

"After living in the hotel for several months, we have got to the point where we definitely need a place of our own," said Juliet firmly. "I want to cook meals for Enzo in my own kitchen, and I would like to have Florence living with us, if June agrees; we're even thinking we might also get another dog to keep her company."

It was less than three months since Cyril Parsons had offered them his unwanted plot of land.

Putting an arm around his wife, Enzo said: "The people at the Brunswick have been wonderful and very understanding, constantly renewing our reservation. They've done everything possible to make us comfortable, but nice though it is, it isn't a home."

Juliet added with a chuckle: "I actually think most of the help has come because the receptionist has a huge crush on Enzo and doesn't want him to leave. Why would she when he flirts and gives her flowers?"

Enzo gave Juliet his enigmatic smile, a sure sign he was slightly discomforted. The girl was extraordinarily attractive and he knew she fancied him. In a previous life he would have fucked her by now… "Her name is Amelia and she's very sweet and probably not much older than Isabella," he told Clarissa and Tony. "She has done a lot to make our stay at the Brunswick more comfortable. She is the one who arranged for us to have a microwave oven in our suite. The flowers were just a thank you."

"I'm eternally grateful to her for the microwave," agreed Juliet. "Having it has definitely improved our quality of life."

Knowing how easy it was to fall for a sexy and charming Italian, Clarissa sympathised with Amelia. Enzo flirted innately but she knew he would never be unfaithful to Juliet. Clarissa could only hope he hadn't raised the girl's expectations.

Italian men are so complex, she thought, looking affectionately at Tony, who was solidly English and phlegmatic, and really didn't understand the need for dalliance. What you saw was what you got with Tony.

★★★

Totally secure in Enzo's deep love for her, Juliet was completely unperturbed by any flirtation. She knew her husband did it instinctively and that it meant nothing.

A few days ago he had walked into their suite at the Brunswick and putting his arms around her said urgently: "Giulietta…amore, come to bed with me." It was ten o'clock in the morning and Enzo had been out to pick up some milk on his way back from a stroll along the beach. Looking at the familiar absorbed expression on his face, Juliet knew he had been aroused by flirting with Amelia.

She kissed him and he almost dragged her into the bedroom. Their lovemaking was exciting and very passionate. Afterwards, as they lay quietly in each other's arms, Enzo gently kissed her lips whispering: "Ti amo tanto – I love you so much. You know I belong only to you."

"Anch'io ti amo – I love you too," murmured Juliet. And she did. More than anything in the world.

With age and experience comes wisdom, she thought. As long as he comes home to me every time he is turned on by a pretty face, I have no problem with him flirting. If only I'd had such understanding and awareness at twenty, what a very different life I might have had.

Chapter Forty-One

"Beauty perishes in life but is immortal in architecture."
Leonardo da Vinci, Italian painter, sculptor, architect, draughtsman, engineer and scientist (1452-1519).

MOST OF the family turned up for the opening night of Amy's play which was staged in a remarkable Art Deco theatre in East London.

Clarissa and Tony were joined not only by Enzo and Juliet, Matteo, June, and Charlotte, but also by Alan, Emma, and Bea. The only one missing was Malik, who was on night duty at the hospital. Bertie and Lance turned up unexpectedly, and having bought their own tickets at the last minute, had seats in the stalls instead of the dress circle where everyone else was sitting.

Tonight Lance's suit was a pale pinky-orange. Quite extraordinary, thought Tony with a shudder as he went over to speak to them. "I hope you'll join us for supper later," said Tony. "We're going to this amazing Italian restaurant Enzo has found near Tower Bridge. They always seem to be able to find a table for walkers-in, so fitting in a couple of extras at our table shouldn't be a problem."

Tony was enchanted by the theatre, which had been recently restored. "What an amazing building," he said as they arrived, totally captivated by all the original features that had been thoughtfully kept during renovation.

Clarissa had to call him back as he obsessively wandered off to inspect more closely a particularly ravishing geometric arch and some decorative panels around the windows. "Don't disappear sweetheart, we're going to have a drink in the bar."

"Do you think they'd mind if I took some photographs?" Tony asked Clarissa enthusiastically. "Maybe make some sketches," suggested his wife gently. Tony, pulled out the small notepad and fine line drawing pen he always carried with him for just such a situation, and wandered off again.

"A pre-show drink is definitely beckoning," said Juliet, leading the way to the beautiful red and gold bar on the first floor. Tony, who had returned from his wandering, once again went into a paroxysm of delight over the bar décor, peering closely at the windows and the decorative stained-glass panels.

Matteo bought a round of drinks and they sat at one of the wrought iron tables, idly chatting while waiting for Tony to calm down and join them.

"The loo is pretty amazing too," said June, returning after a trip to 'spend a penny'. "Please don't tell Tony," begged Clarissa, "or he's more than likely to gatecrash the ladies toilet and cause utter chaos!"

As they settled into the front row of the dress circle where Amy had procured seats for them, Tony was again in raptures, this time over Art Deco features in the auditorium, including delicate plaster ornamentation, the antique chandelier and the *trompe l'oeil* safety curtain.

Although he was very proud that his daughter was about to make her London acting debut, Tony would much rather have spent his time exploring the theatre and admiring the stunning architecture than watching the play. He didn't, however, relish the thought of Clarissa's response if he suggested it. Perhaps he could return another time on his own and maybe get permission to take pictures.

★★★

Everyone thought Amy was perfect as Amanda Postlethwaite, the fiery Postmistress General, in Shaw's satirical political comedy *The Apple Cart*. Although it was only a supporting role, she commanded the stage whenever she was on, earning enormous applause. "I know we are biased, but she really was brilliant," said Clarissa proudly. "Brilliant," echoed Tony, dragging his eyes away from the decorative plasterwork on the ceiling.

Both Enzo and Matteo admitted that despite their fluent English and efficient grasp of the language generally, much of the subtlety of the ironic satire were lost on them. "To be honest, I just didn't understand it," Enzo confessed to Juliet and June afterwards. "But I could definitely see what a good actress Amy is."

Matteo agreed. "Lost on me too," he said with a grin. "Went completely over my head; absolutely no idea what was going on. Really enjoyed seeing Amy doing her thing, though. A talented young lady. Do you think she will really give it all up to go to *Napoli?*"

"Not just to go to *Napoli,*" Enzo reminded him. "Go to *Napoli* to find a fucking gorgeous Italian!" The ensuing laughter continued until they were out in the street and hailing cabs to take them to the celebratory supper. Amy would be joining them later if she could drag herself away from the first night party – and a young stage technician called Milo, who seemed to be taking up more and more of her time."

"Bring Milo to supper with you, sweetheart," urged Clarissa. "We'd all love to meet him."

"Mmm," said Amy, "maybe not. He's really just a friend. We're dating but we're not exclusive. I don't want him getting the wrong idea."

Her mother looked perplexed. "What exactly does that mean? Dating but not exclusive?"

Amy tutted and rolled her eyes. "Well, we see each other

casually so it's non-exclusive dating; we're not in a relationship and certainly not committed. We're both free to see other people," she explained patiently.

"Goodness." Clarissa frowned. "That sounds complicated. It was a lot easier in my day. Then, if you met a boy you liked, you dated and you didn't go out with anyone else while you were with him. Otherwise you would be two-timing. If he eventually dumped you, then you would mope around for a while before going out with someone else until you met someone you wanted to marry. It was so simple."

It was Amy's turn to look startled. "Marry? Oh there are no thoughts of marriage. If you are in a committed relationship – and please note that Milo and I are not – you are then exclusive and don't go out with anyone else. Exclusivity means you both agree not to date or pursue other romantic relationships *pro tem*. So I don't want to invite Milo to meet the family or he will start to think I want to be exclusive, and that's the last thing I want at the moment."

Knowing she was off to Italy before Christmas, Amy didn't want the complication of a boyfriend in England. That was definitely not part of the plan…especially a guy like Milo whom she suspected could be a bit serious and clingy given half a chance.

Clarissa shook her head. She really didn't understand. "Well, I'm sure you know what you are doing but it all sounds very odd to me." As Amy scowled at her she added: "And I would still like to meet Milo…even if he isn't exclusive."

"Huh, don't hold your breath," replied Amy.

Chapter Forty-Two

"He took me in his arms and settled me there gently, with my head against his chin. We danced. I was conscious of his body against mine... I loved him. I should have thought of that, or at least thought what love might be like, this obsession, this painful lack of satisfaction."
Françoise Sagan, 'Bonjour Tristesse' (1954)

THE HOUSE warming party was a huge success. Enzo and Juliet had invited not only all the family but also staff from the Brunswick who had become friends during the many months they had been living there. The workmen who had renovated the bungalow and the garden flat neighbours, including the Prentices, also received invitations. It was, said Juliet, a dress rehearsal for the party they were planning to throw in *Napoli* for Italian friends at Christmas.

Tony, Clarissa, Amy and their neighbours arrived *en masse* in a mini bus, which would return to take them home again, while the Brunswick staff travelled in transport organised by the hotel. Most family members had booked taxis or had designated drivers so they could all enjoy themselves without worrying about being stopped by the police for drink-driving on their way home. Charlotte and Malik, who had driven the Porsche down from London, had arranged to spend the night in Enzo and Juliet's guest room.

Arriving without a partner Amelia, the Brunswick's

receptionist, immediately caught the eye of several young men including Arlo, one of the electricians who had helped to rewire the bungalow. Amelia was wearing a black lacy micro-mini with thick black tights, huge silver earrings, and Doc Martin boots. She looked absolutely amazing thought Arlo, weighing up his chances of moving in on her before anyone else did.

Strange what young girls thought attractive nowadays, mused Enzo, slightly taken aback by Amelia's boots and recalling the pretty pink sundress and flat silver sandals *Giulietta* had been wearing when he first saw her in Sorrento. And that skirt was exceeding short, it hardly covered her bottom. He just hoped Amelia didn't bend over, there were enough young men showing an interest in her already.

Turning to greet Charlotte and Malik, Enzo chided himself: what Amelia wore was nothing to do with him, he wasn't her father! Shaking his head, he led Charlotte and Malik to the guest bedroom. "You're on the other side of the building to us, so you can make as much noise as you like without disturbing anyone."

Despite Juliet sending her a 'plus one' invitation, Amelia was unaccompanied because she was hoping, as Isabella had on Capri, for a few moments alone with Enzo, and the presence of a companion would scotch any chance of that. She had told her boyfriend Danny that the invitation was only for her. A lie, yes, but it was almost certainly the last opportunity she would have to get close to Enzo.

Although they had been flirting across the Brunswick's reception desk for several months and Amelia had a feeling that Enzo definitely fancied her, she knew it was unlikely he would return to the hotel now he had moved out. She had seen the way Enzo and Juliet behaved together and how Enzo *was* with his wife – he obviously adored her. There was no reason for him to come back. Nevertheless, Amelia was hoping, as Isabella had, that *something* might happen.

From the very beginning Amelia had accepted that she would never be able to compete with Juliet, but the fact that a gorgeous guy like Enzo de Martins was aware she existed at all was incredible, she told herself. Women must throw themselves at him all the time; she was amazed that he'd actually noticed her. Amelia had found she couldn't stop thinking about Enzo; he was in her mind all time and she went to pieces whenever she saw him. Was it just an enormous crush or could it be love?

A friend of her mother's had dug out Enzo's record *Canzoni d'amore* to show her, and Amelia was astounded to discover he was an international singer who had been quite famous. She had stared for a long time at the picture of Enzo on the album sleeve. That record had been released in 1964…was that how he looked when Juliet first met him? He was very sexy now, but back then he must have been absolutely sensational. Amelia once again felt the flicker of desire. Even a quick cuddle with him would be unbelievable and if he kissed her…she felt her stomach lurch at the thought.

***

Music for the party was once again being provided by River and as this was an evening event, he was looking forward to playing stuff that was a bit more contemporary and revolutionary, even though Juliet had requested some easy listening music while people were arriving. An added bonus was that he was getting paid; Juliet and Enzo had insisted that all his hard work should be recognised with hard cash.

River was elated. He now had a girlfriend, a sassy blonde called Tania, and as it was the first time River had actually been paid for playing music, he was thinking he might take Tania to celebrate at McDonalds or Kentucky Fried Chicken on their next date. He didn't want to splash out too much because he was saving to update his music system, but at a push he was willing to consider Yo! Sushi, which was Tania's absolutely favourite place to eat.

Tonight Tania was wearing her white one-shoulder crop top with baggy white cargo trousers and white air cushion sneakers. She looked really cool thought River admiringly. He was hoping that at some point during the evening he could keep everyone happy by putting on music from his Spotify playlist, allowing him time-out to take Tania off somewhere for a quick cuddle. He knew there was a snug with a really enormous sofa – maybe be a snog in the snug might be a possibility. River was beginning to feel a fizzing excitement at the prospect.

★★★

Sybil Prentice made straight for Enzo as she walked through the door. "*Ciao!*" Guess what! I'm learning Italian. The local Women's Institute is running classes in the village hall led by a native Italian speaker called Luca. She's a woman not a man by the way; the name Luca is gender neutral," Sybil informed him self-importantly, keen to show off her knowledge and totally forgetting for a moment that she was speaking to an Italian. "Hmm." Enzo looked unimpressed.

"So, very soon I hope we'll be able to have a proper conversation…*per favore Signore de Martins,*" said Sybil, moving in on him with a girlish giggle. Before Enzo could reply, she smiled at him flirtatiously and added: "Meanwhile, I'm hoping we can chat together and you could correct my pronunciation? If you come over one afternoon, Phil will be at work and we won't be disturbed."

She put a hand on his arm, starting to edge even closer, the familiar scent of his cologne making her feel quite skittish. Enzo smiled politely, wishing he'd heeded Clarissa's warning not to give Sybil any encouragement. He remorsefully recalled that at one point he had felt sorry for her.

"So did Phil come with you?" asked Enzo, in an attempt to deflect her. "What?" Sybil looked vague, before saying dismissively: "Oh yes, he's around somewhere. Gone off to chat to Tony, I think." Turning her obsessive gaze back to Enzo, Sybil continued: "Now which day would suit you best for some Italian *parlando*? You could come over Tuesday or Wednesday afternoon next week...we might even have a cheeky glass or two of Prosecco."

"I think my wife might have something to say about that," parried Enzo. "Oh, you don't have to tell Juliet," replied Sybil coquettishly. "I won't be telling Phil. It will be our special secret."

Santa merda! thought Enzo, she was totally brazen. He was used to women chasing him but Sybil was in another league altogether. Anyway, as an Italian man, he preferred to be the one who did the chasing. How on earth was he going to get away from her without being really rude.

Luckily, Clarissa noticed his predicament and came over saying: "Ah Sybil! Good, I'm pleased you're here. There's someone I'm really keen for you to meet. He's a professor at the university and a really nice guy. He's just back from a study tour in Florence, so I thought you'd find him interesting given your enthusiasm for Italy."

Sybil looked nonplussed: "Oh really?...oh well..." Looking longingly at Enzo as Clarissa firmly took her arm, she said "*Ciao*... catch up with you again in a moment, *signore*." Enzo grimaced; that sounded almost like a threat.

Oh my God, thought Clarissa, I only hope Bruce will forgive me for this! But she needed to get Sybil away from Enzo, and Tony's friend Dr Bruce Bell would provide the perfect distraction. He was a dear man and very charming, but being short, rotund and lacking Enzo's charisma, she thought it unlikely that Sybil would want to flirt with him. Bruce would be quite safe, thought Clarissa with a smile, and anyway, long ago he had trained for the priesthood and had chosen to be a lifelong celibate.

Leading Sybil off across the room, Clarissa turned round, mouthing to her father: "You owe me!" Enzo grinned ruefully and pressing the palms of his hands together mouthed back *"Namaste."* They smiled at each other with affection and total understanding.

Absurdly feeling he'd somehow dodged a bullet, Enzo went into the kitchen where Amy and June were putting nibbles onto plates. Having once again refused to invite Milo to join her, Amy was quite happy to be unaccompanied and was keeping June company while Matteo was animatedly discussing cars with Malik.

"I thought we were paying people to do this," said Enzo, reaching across to stab a couple of large green olives with a cocktail stick. June slapped his hand. "Stop snaffling the food. And yes, there are hired staff but we are just helping things along." Enzo laughed. "Well that's okay then. Next time we won't bother with the staff, we'll just use you."

"Sit down for a minute and have a glass of wine," said Amy. "I saw Mum rescuing you from the clutches of that dreadful Sybil, so maybe you should hang around here for a while."

"Do you miss singing and touring?" asked June as they settled themselves on bar stools. Enzo shook his head, taking a sip of wine. "Hey this is good..." he picked up the bottle..."Ah Italian red, no wonder it's good!"

"Well it's Chianti," said Amy. "Juliet's favourite."

"Yes, I know," said Enzo smiling. He turned to June. "I don't really miss touring and singing at all...well, maybe I do miss the singing a bit, I love performing, but definitely not the touring. However, I have a couple of concerts in *Napoli* when we are there at Christmas. Elsa Garcia set them up. Although technically I am retired and she is no longer my agent we keep in touch and apparently there has been some enthusiasm for me to sing in Italy. And I'm also doing a gig at Villa Valentina on Capri. Anna and Georgio said that fans had been asking if it would be possible." Staring into the distance he added: "I guess it will have rarity value so I'm hoping a few people might turn up." Amy glanced at him, thinking once again how modest he was, very different from some of the pushy, self-promoting celebrities she'd met in theatre-land.

Looking out across the sitting room where Sybil was simpering and giggling at something Bruce Bell was saying, Amy reported: "Coast is clear. Sybil is being distracted by the lovely Dr Bell. That man is a saint."

"Come over and talk to Bertie and Lance," said June. "I want to hear about the amazing *avant-garde* photographic exhibition they went to at a gallery in Curzon Street. I was hoping to get there myself but couldn't manage it."

★★★

Tonight, instead of one of his colourful suits, Lance was wearing an elegant white tuxedo with tight black satin trousers and smooth white leather loafers. He looks far more stylish than the rest of us put together, thought Enzo, he really ought to be a model, not a philosopher. Scanning the room he asked: "Where did you say Matteo was? I haven't seen him all evening."

"Last seen in the hall talking cars with Malik," said June in a resigned voice. Enzo laughed. "Of course he is! Well I won't disturb them."

Enzo was listening to Bertie and Lance enthusing about the photographic exhibition when he noticed Sybil making her way purposefully across the room towards him. "Sorry, must go... something's cropped up," he said hastily and Amy, patting him on the arm, whispered with a giggle: "If you're quick you'll give her the slip!" Turning swiftly on his heel to join another group of guests, Enzo crashed into Amelia, who tipped the drink she was holding down the front of her dress.

"Oh, *mi dispiace, cara*," gasped Enzo, instinctively putting an arm around her shoulders. "Are you alright? What about your dress? Let me get you a cloth so you can mop yourself up, and I'll bring you another drink."

"No need, I'm fine thank you," said Amelia, feeling slightly off-balance as she stared into his concerned eyes. "No damage done; it's only a dress, it can be washed."

He'd put his arm around her! That's the closest I've ever been to him she thought, her stomach full of butterflies. If throwing a drink over myself is what it takes, then it's worth it. Her heart was pounding and she was trembling with anticipation at the possibilities ahead. Looking down at the drenched bodice of her mini, Amelia wondered if Enzo could tell she wasn't wearing anything underneath. She blushed at the thought that her nipples might be showing through the wet lace. Oh well, not much she could do about that now.

Grabbing the unexpected opportunity fate had sent her way, Amelia took a deep breath and asked with far more bravado then she felt: "Will you dance with me?" Seeing Enzo hesitate slightly she added cheekily: "Compensation for spilling my drink."

Enzo laughed. "Oh, okay, well just wait here a moment, there is something I have to do." He led her to an armchair. "Sit there and I'll be back." His eyes automatically moved to the outline of her breasts in the wet dress. Dragging his gaze away he said: "I'll bring you a towel. Are you sure you don't want another drink?" She shook her head and he vanished into the throng of guests.

As she waited for Enzo to return, Amelia breathlessly tried to imagine what it was going to be like to be held in his arms. Despite their months of flirtation, there had never been any real physical contact. Only once, when he had kissed her hand after she'd arranged for a microwave oven to be put into the suite – and that had put her in a tizzy for days. He had given her flowers a couple of times too, but she knew they were thank you gifts and suspected they may have been organised by Juliet.

After picking up a clean towel from the wet room, Enzo found his wife in the kitchen, loading the dishwasher with dirty glasses. Putting his arms around her, he said with exasperation: "*Amore,* what are you doing? Not so long ago I found June and Amy organising nibbles, now here you are filling the dishwasher. We're paying people to do these things."

"Oh, I was passing through and saw the tray of glasses. I thought I'd just pop them in; we're going to need more clean glasses very soon."

"Okay," said Enzo, " but *Giulietta,* please don't spend your evening in the kitchen."

He gave her a considering look. "I came to find you to ask if you'd mind me dancing with Amelia. I managed to throw a drink over her and she says it will be compensation." Juliet laughed. "You know you don't have to ask permission, sweetheart."

"*Lo so,* but I wanted you to know, I didn't want you to think…"

"I don't," she said firmly, giving him a kiss. "Now go and enjoy your smooch…I'm assuming it will be a slow dance. It will make Amelia's night, she's been wanting to get close to you for ages." As he turned to leave she put a hand on his arm. "But Enzo darling, remember she has a crush on you. Go carefully with her."

"I will," promised Enzo. "I think this will be a chance for me to say goodbye to her. Now we've left the Brunswick, it's unlikely we will meet up again." Juliet nodded. "Mmm, probably a good idea. Amelia needs to get on with her life."

Noticing the towel he was holding Juliet asked: "Is that so she can mop herself up. How wet is she?"

"Drenched," replied Enzo. "I turned round, not realising she was right behind me, and the drink went all down the front of her dress."

"Oh dear, that must be really uncomfortable. She will need dry herself off a bit before you dance."

Enzo took her hand, smiling into her eyes. "And will *you* dance with me afterwards *cara*?" Juliet was suddenly struck yet again by how astonishingly good looking he was. She knew Amelia was totally infatuated with him but she trusted her husband absolutely. "Of course. Come and find me when your dance with Amelia is finished and we'll dance together." He gave her a swift kiss and disappeared back into the sitting room.

★★★

"Ooh, look at that," said Lance gleefully and a tad spitefully as Enzo and Amelia joined the dancers in the middle of the room and Enzo put his arms around her. Bertie smiled and said nothing, but June said shrewdly: "Juliet will have given her permission."

"Really? Permission?" Lance gave a disbelieving snigger. "He actually asks for her permission?"

"Oh yes," replied June calmly. "Neither of them would do anything like that without telling the other first." She looked steadily at Lance. "Matteo and I do the same."

Amy watched a flush of embarrassment spread across Lance's handsome face as Bertie took his hand. "You hear that, my dear, some couples do tell each other what is going on."

I really don't want to know what that's all about, thought Amy, saying: "Please excuse me, I just need to catch up with Alan and Emma – and I've just spotted Bea, so I must go over and talk to her too. She's got a new litter of puppies and I'm hoping I can get one as a present for Enzo and Juliet to be a companion for Florence."

As she left, Lance who had been silent since Bertie's mild reproof, flounced off and Bertie, looking rather put out, said quietly to himself: "Oh dear!"

"And I must go and find Matteo," muttered June hastily. She had known Bertie since he was a boy, as long as she had known Juliet. She was slightly concerned he just might want to offload his frustration over Lance's behaviour. That was the last thing she needed; June wasn't great at dealing with other people's problems

★★★

River was playing *Love Song* by The Cure – one of his favourite tracks on the 'Greatest Hits' album – wishing he could abandon his DJ duties and dance this one with Tania, when his attention was caught by the sight of Enzo holding the hand of an astonishingly pretty young girl as he led her towards the dancing. Strangely the front of her dress was soaking wet; wonder what happened there, thought River curiously. As they reached the edge of the group of dancers, Enzo turned and clasped the girl in his arms.

Gosh! River was impressed. Despite his age and the fact he was married, Enzo could certainly still pull. And not just pull…pull an absolutely stunning girl young enough to be his granddaughter. Judging by the look on the girl's face she was totally besotted with him.

Winding her arms around Enzo's neck, Amelia felt shivers running down her spine as his body touched hers. She was exquisitely aware of his breath on her neck, and wafts of his spicy cologne were making her feel unsettled and jittery.

Amelia's attempts to dry off her dress had proved fairly ineffective and it was still saturated. I'm making your shirt all wet," she whispered. "No more than I deserve," murmured Enzo, pulling her closer. As they danced in silence Enzo could feel Amelia's quivering excitement. Just as well he was saying *'arrivederci'.* She was very captivating and he had enjoyed the past few months of playful teasing, but now it was time for it to end. He knew she was becoming far too fond of him.

The Cure track lasted three-and-a-half minutes and as it finished, Enzo decided he needed more time. Looking over and catching River's eye he made a circular motion with his finger; River nodded and played *Love Song* again.

Tightly enfolded in Enzo's arms, Amelia could feel his comforting warmth and the beat of his heart. Thrusting herself against him she felt as if her body was melting into his; conscious of his mouth just inches away from hers, she had to firmly stop herself reaching up and kissing his lips. Engulfed by longing, Amelia had a compelling urge to slip a hand inside his shirt and touch his skin. She could hardly breathe. Danny had never had such an extraordinary effect on her. So this was what love was like.

Enzo was beginning to think this dance hadn't been such a brilliant idea after all. Amelia's wet dress had soaked the front of his shirt, which was now uncomfortably sticky, and he could feel her nipples as she pushed herself against him. With a jolt of surprise, he realised that she wasn't wearing a bra. Recognising the intense yearning in her eyes and instinctively knowing how much she wanted him, he felt the familiar lick of desire spreading through him, rapidly followed by a spontaneous wave of lust. It would be so easy to take her off to the snug and fuck her…

★★★

…gazing deeply into her eyes while slowly unbuttoning his shirt, he said: "Better take off that wet dress." She nodded, bending down to remove her boots and peel off her tights before pulling the dress over her head. She was naked except for black Brazilian knickers. Neither of them spoke as he put his arms around her and pulled her down with him into the cushiony depths of the sofa…

★★★

As the music played on, Enzo firmly squashed the tantalising scenario that was running through his head, knowing he had to cool things down while he was still in control. He was on the cusp of indiscretion; this was a situation that could easily get out of hand. Amelia was far too young…she needed a boy of her own age to seduce her; more importantly, there was absolutely no way he was going to cheat on *Giulietta*.

Loosening his hold on her he said very gently: "You know this is our goodbye dance, *cara.*" Dismayed Amelia lifted her head to look at him, her eyes brimming with tears. Nuzzling her hair Enzo murmured softly in her ear: "You're a very special girl, Amelia. Remember not to give yourself away too easily; make sure you always value yourself."

She nodded, gazing up at him despairingly as he carefully wiped away the tears on her cheeks with his fingers. "I love you," she whispered helplessly. Enzo shook his head sighing. "No…no you don't *cara,* not really. It's a false feeling, a trick your emotions play on you when you are young. But you will find someone to love, and then you'll know it's real and it will be wonderful."

When *Love Song* ended and River was playing Fleetwood Mac's *Everywhere,* Enzo kissed Amelia's forehead saying: "*Ciao-Ciao* baby. I will always remember our dance together." Smiling he added: "I hope you have now forgiven me for spilling your drink."

She sniffed back tears as Enzo took her hand and led her over to River, saying brightly: "Have you met River our talented DJ? River this is Amelia. We enjoyed dancing to the music you were playing; that's a great song."

"Ooh, I'm so pleased you like The Cure," said River, a tone of slight surprise creeping into his voice. "Definitely," said Enzo dryly. "I have a very eclectic taste in music. I like Fleetwood Mac too."

"Of course, you're a musician," replied River, feeling a tad awkward. Enzo smiled. "Mmm, yes I was, but you're too young to remember."

Putting an arm around Amelia, Enzo whispered: "Thank you for everything, *cara.* Both *Giulietta* and I are very grateful for all your help." He gave her a light kiss on the cheek and added matter-of-factly: "Now if you are sure I can't get you another drink, I must go and find my wife, she promised me a dance."

Turning to River he said: "I think *Giulietta* would really like to dance to *I'm On Fire* by AWOLNATION. She loves that, but it's quite short so you'll need to play it at least a couple of times. And we would both love you to play Chris Isaak's fabulous version of *Can't Help Falling in Love*."

"Chris Isaak?" queried River, "not Elvis?" Enzo smiled. "Well the Elvis recording is very special to both of us, but on this occasion I think Chris Isaak will be perfect."

As River nodded wordlessly, Enzo added: "And then please will you play one for me; that amazing song by I Pooh, *E' bello riaverti* from *Opera seconda*?" River stared at Enzo with a look verging on respect; he hadn't met many people who knew the Italian band which had been performing since the sixties and was one of his favourites. "Wow! Yes, of course."

It was Enzo's turn to sound surprised. "You know it?"

"I do," replied River. "I'm a huge Pooh fan. Really great band and good choice of song. Not quite as good as *La casa del sole*, which I like even more than the original Animals' version, but pretty close."

"Hmm." Enzo looked at River with interest. Unusual young man. He would have a word with his friend Enrico about him; Rico was a music producer and always on the lookout for new talent. He might be able to help River advance his musical career if that was what he wanted.

"Are there any other Italian singers you like?" queried Enzo curiously. "Well Renato Zero, of course," replied River smiling at the surprised look on Enzo's face.

"You also know Renato?"

"Absolutely. I love most of his songs but one of my favourites is Piper Club because it has a touch of Bob Dylan, and I am a big fan of Dylan."

"Well, are you aware that Piper Club was a real place in Rome where Renato took his first steps in the world of music when he was a teenager? I guess that song is a tribute to those days," said Enzo. "The kids in Rome used to go there to listen to music and dance in the sixties. I saw both Jimi Hendrix and Pink Floyd perform there and I was told that Mick Jagger went there to dance while he was on holiday in Italy."

"Wow, wow and wow again," gasped River. "I'm convinced I was born in the wrong era. It would have been brilliant to have been able to go there. I feel I have been cheated."

Enzo smiled and patted him on the shoulder. "Renato and Pooh are still performing today so you could always go over to Italy for one of their concerts," he said, making a mental note to definitely mention this bright young man to Rico.

"Meanwhile," added Enzo, "*Giulietta* and I will be back ready to dance in five minutes and afterwards you must take a break and pay some attention to your charming girlfriend. I believe the snug is unoccupied…and there is a lock on the door." Giving River a knowing wink, Enzo added: "I was your age once. *Ciao*." Going off to find his wife, Enzo thought how much he wanted to take *Giulietta* to bed; holding her close as they danced was going to drive him crazy.

River and Amelia stared at him striding off across the room, and as Tania joined them with a trayful of drinks and snacks, River said: "Tania, this is Amelia, she's a friend of Enzo's."

"Oh no," said Amelia sadly. "Not really a friend, I just work at the hotel where Enzo and Juliet were living."

"He's a really cool guy," said River. Smiling at Tania he added: "He's my role model. I want to be just like him when I grow up!"

★★★

Tears dripped unchecked down Amelia's face as she watched Enzo and Juliet dancing while River dutifully played *I'm On Fire* twice, followed by Chris Isaak singing the beautiful love song that Elvis had made so famous. Locked in their own impenetrable bubble they were totally oblivious of anyone else in the crowded room.

Enzo had changed his wet shirt and Juliet was running her fingers through his hair; they were kissing as they danced and it was blatantly obvious how much they loved each other. "Christ, *Giulietta*," whispered Enzo as River played *E' bello riaverti*, "even after all these years you still drive me crazy." Gazing deeply into her eyes he murmured: *Ti voglio così tanto*. I want you so much." Holding his gaze Juliet felt a shudder of desire. "*Pure io*." She desperately wanted him too.

Amelia suddenly felt exceedingly foolish that she had even imagined Enzo might fancy her. How could she ever have thought that his interest in her was anything more than just casual flirtation. Juliet was very beautiful, she was Enzo's wife and they adored each other. End of…

Overtaken by a panicky impulse to escape as quickly possible, Amelia rushed into the hall to ring Danny and ask him to come and pick her up on his motorbike. She needed to go home; to go to ground in the sanctuary of her bedroom until she could forget the embarrassment of her idiotic crush on a gorgeous guy she could never ever have.

From the other side of the sitting room, Arlo watched her leave. Shit! He'd been about to ask her to dance. He'd seen her dancing with Enzo and thought he'd wait awhile. Now it was too late. He suddenly realised he didn't even know her name. Never mind, he'd get her name and phone number from Mr de Martins and give her a call in the morning.

★★★

Lance was sitting at the kitchen island staring moodily into a tumbler of whisky. "What's wrong with him?" *murmured Juliet as she went over to June who was ferreting for orange juice in the fridge.*

"Slight disagreement with Bertie, I think," *said June with a grin. She* was still mildly intrigued by the revelation that Juliet's brother was gay. Personally she felt like giving Lance a slap and she wondered how on earth Bertie could be bothered to put up with him.

They gazed across at Lance, who had a pouty face, bottom lip pushed out, looking very much like a cross small boy denied a treat. He appeared to be totally unaware of their presence. Lance is just a child who has never grown up, thought Juliet. "Oh poor Lance, he looks really upset," she whispered to June. "I hope Bertie's not being unkind."

"Actually, I think it's Bertie you should feel sorry for," replied June with a chuckle. "He's definitely the one who is cock-pecked in that relationship!" Juliet looked at her with amusement. June had always been able to succinctly sum up a situation. "Well I hope they get it sorted. Bertie is really fond of him."

"And therein lies the problem," said June profoundly. Laughing she added: "Now my love, if there nothing I can do to help here, I'm going to tear Matteo away from Malik and take him home. It's quite the bromance developing there – I hope Lotte knows what she's letting herself in for!" She raised her glass. "I'm driving this evening, hence the novelty of drinking orange juice."

Chapter Forty-Three

"Merely innocent flirtation – not quite adultery,
but adulteration."
Lord Byron, 'Don Juan' (Canto I:xiii)

SITTING AMONG the party detritus after all their guests had departed, Juliet surveyed the sitting room and said: "Let's leave this and go to bed. I'll make a start on it in the morning and then Mrs Wilson can sort out the rest when she comes in at ten o'clock."

The hired caterers had cleared the washing up and packed away plates and glasses, but all the rooms needed cleaning and putting back together again after the invasion of so many people.

Enzo walked over and sat down beside her. "A very successful evening Signora de Martins. I would say a triumph," he said, kissing her hand.

"Yes," agreed Juliet wearily as Enzo added: "The next thing we have to look forward to is Lotte and Malik's wedding – which thankfully *we* don't have to organise – and then we're off to *Napoli* for Christmas and another party." He pulled her up off the sofa, "but now, time for bed."

As they went hand-in-hand into the bedroom, Enzo asked urgently: "How tired are you *tesoro*?" Giving him a loving look Juliet said: "Never too tired for you, my love."

"Ahhh, good!" Enzo gave a huge sigh of relief. After the unsettling dance with Amelia, his first instinct had been to take his wife to bed – but that had been impossible in the middle of a party they were hosting. Now he was aching to make love to her; he needed sex with *Giulietta* to restore his balance.

Getting into bed Juliet asked: "Did you enjoy your dance with Amelia? I assume you had a cuddle judging by the state of your shirt. It's soaked! How big was that drink she threw over herself?"

Enzo gave her a melting look. "Can we talk about that after we've made love? I don't think I can wait any longer, I've been wanting you all evening. Dancing with you and not being able to make love was terrible…I had to stop myself dragging you off into the bedroom. In the words of Aaron Bruno, I'm on fire." Juliet kissed him. "I'm all yours. I know how you feel, I really wanted you too."

After blissful lovemaking had restored Enzo's equilibrium, he held Juliet in his arms and said with a sigh: "My dance with Amelia was pleasurable, but rather sad. We did have a bit of a smooch and I gave her a very chaste kiss. She cried and said she loved me. I felt dreadful…" Juliet looked at him sympathetically as he added: "I felt so *responsible* after teasing her for so many months."

"And that drink?"

"Ah, that was a large glass of cola, so it literally did soak her."

"I bet she was all sticky," said Juliet. "We both were," replied Enzo smiling at the memory, before adding: "And talking of sticky moments, I had a really difficult time with Sybil, who was trying to get me to go round to her place and speak Italian with her while Phil was at work. *And* without telling either him or you, would you believe."

"Well, she's another one who's got a crush on you."

"*Merda, Giulietta,* she's in her sixties!"

"There's no age limit on a woman being infatuated," replied his wife, "as you well know."

"Mmm, maybe, but Sybil Prentice…really! Anyway Clarissa rescued me, thank goodness, and took her off to annoy someone else."

Juliet grinned, saying wisely: "You're being sniffy about Sybil because you don't fancy her. Most of the women who come on to you are young and attractive, so you don't mind *them* chasing you." Enzo chuckled. "You're probably right *amore*. You understand me too well!"

After a slight pause Enzo admitted: "There was also an uncomfortable moment while I was dancing with Amelia when I was worried things might be"… he paused … "getting out of hand."

Looking intently into Juliet's eyes he confessed: "I was holding her really close to me; her dress and my shirt were wet through and I suddenly realised she wasn't wearing anything underneath. She rubbed herself up against me and I could feel how excited she was. It really turned me on."

"Mmm," said Juliet placidly, steadily holding his gaze. "I had a feeling that was going to happen."

"Anyway," continued Enzo taking a deep breath, "we got past that and Amelia understands that I'm…unavailable. I told her not to give herself away too easily. I felt that was the best advice I could give her; she is so young, and so *desperate* for love. I said *'Ciao-Ciao'* and that's the end of it as far as I'm concerned."

"Well, Amelia has had this crush on you for such a long time that smooching will have heightened all her emotions," said Juliet. "You do tend have that effect on women, sweetheart. Look at Sybil…"

Cuddling his wife Enzo's thoughts were still fixed on the dance with Amelia; it was important that *Giulietta* understood what had happened. "I *was* excited, but it was only my body responding to stimulation. I do admit that just for a moment I did wonder what it would be like…in my head I was a young man again, led by lust and wanting to fuck. I really needed you, but there was nothing I could do because of the party."

Juliet gave him a gentle kiss. Bless him, he was determined to 'confess'. She appreciated his complete honesty and the fact that he never tried to hide things from her. How was it possible to love someone as much as she loved him?

She looked at him meditatively for a while chewing her lip, before saying: "So…I've been thinking. Maybe we should deliberately have rough sex occasionally."

Enzo gave a startled gasp, mildly shocked. "Really? You think so? Have you forgotten that the one and only time we were really rough with each other was all those years ago on Capri when you bit my thigh, I gave you love bites and we both ached for days! *And we were very much younger then too.*"

Unperturbed, Juliet gave a seductive smile. "But we *have* thought about it several times recently…and remember how much we enjoyed it! Anyway, all those years ago it happened purely by chance; now it will be because we want it…*solo per amore* – just for love."

Taking his hand and kissing his fingertips she said seriously: "We have fantastically passionate sex all the time and it's perfect – absolutely wonderful and utterly satisfying. But perhaps, sometimes, it would be good for us to move out of our comfort zone and see…um…see where it takes us? We should remind ourselves every now and again how nice it feels to have wantonly uncontrolled pleasure."

Enzo felt the shudder of desire. Although they had an equal sexual partnership, with *Giulietta* initiating lovemaking almost as often as he did, her suggestion of occasional rough sex was startling and thrillingly unexpected.

Juliet saw the spark of excitement in his eyes as she ran her hands slowly down his body. "What? Now?" he whispered. "Are you sure? You're not too tired?" She shook her head. "Actually, I don't feel tired at all now; just thinking about this is turning me on."

Enzo stared at her in silence before pulling her down on top of him, completely overwhelmed by his love for her. He recalled her calm reaction to that time they had rough sex back on Capri in the sixties; it was then he knew that he wanted to marry her. What an incredible woman. Kissing her ardently, he murmured: "Hold on tight, baby, we're about to have a rough ride."

Much later, after they had enjoyed an electrifying bout of raw, rampant and totally satisfying sex, they slept happily in each other's arms, completely exhausted and totally sated.

★★★

Snuggling up to Enzo in bed the next morning, Juliet asked with a wicked smile: "How are you feeling? Are you stiff and achy? Any bites you want to show me?" Enzo laughed. "I feel very energised today, thank you Signora de Martins. That was a great idea of yours. I really enjoyed it and I don't seem to have any bites!"

"Oh right, well I'll do better next time," Juliet promised teasingly.

Enzo went off to make coffee, returning with his usual espresso along with a cappuccino for Juliet, together with *cornetti* and jam. "Breakfast in bed," he said. "I think we have earned it. Here…" he handed her a large napkin "…to keep the crumbs out of the bed!"

"What about Lotte and Malik?" asked Juliet. "They appear to still be sleeping," replied her husband. "Good thing they're over the other side of the building. I told them last night they could make as much noise as they liked and they wouldn't disturb us." Grinning at Juliet he added: "I just hope we didn't disturb them. I have no idea how much noise *we* made!"

Discussing the party as they ate their croissants, Enzo told Juliet about River's surprising musical knowledge. "I was really amazed that a nineteen-year-old English boy had heard of Pooh and Renato, let alone liked their music. "I'm going to speak to

Rico about him. You never know, he may be able to help River if he wants to have a musical career."

After telling Enzo about the tiff between Bertie and Lance and June's astute summing up of the situation, Juliet asked if Enzo had recovered from his dance with Amelia. "You mustn't blame yourself for fancying her, sweetheart. She's a very pretty girl who is totally obsessed with you. I realise how hard that must be to resist. However, I understand that Amelia has a rather nice boyfriend so…"

"Oh *yes*," interjected Enzo licking jam off his fingers, "All that shockingly wild sex with my wife made me forget. Arlo, the young electrician who worked here on the bungalow, asked me for Amelia's phone number. He seems *very* keen."

"Well then," said Juliet, "Amelia should be devoting herself to the nice boyfriend or Arlo, who is also rather gorgeous, not lusting after an outrageously sexy extra mature Italian, who has more than his fair share of admirers, not to mention a totally devoted wife."

Chuckling with amusement Enzo said: "Extra mature – that's a nice way of saying old!"

Putting his coffee cup down on the tray, he added with a puzzled frown: "But *tesoro*, I honestly don't understand why girls *still* seem to get crushes on me. I really don't give them any encouragement. I'm just being *me."* He smiled, remembering that was exactly what he had said to Clarissa when he was telling her about fans throwing underwear onto the stage in Las Vegas all those years ago.

"Ah, well," said Juliet serenely, pushing back the corkscrew curl of hair which still fell over his eyes, "you'll just have to stop flirting if you want women to ignore you."

"Flirting?" said Enzo. "I'm never aware that I'm *flirting*."

"Of course, not," said Juliet amusedly, "you're Italian."

★★★

My name is Clarissa and I'm adopted. Having found my birth mother thirty years ago, I have now found my Italian birth father. They had never stopped loving each other, and after a lifetime apart they are married at last. My family is reunited. The circle is complete.

Acknowledgments

Once again I owe a huge debt of gratitude to the many people who encouraged me to write and who supported me with love, enthusiasm and endless cups of coffee.

They include my children: Georgina, Paul, Adrian and James and their families – as well as good friends Sandra and Stella, who were always there for me and kept me on track, and Maggie and Mike, who triggered so many excellent ideas.

Thanks also to Helen, who checked the draft of this book before it went to print.

Grazie mille to my Italian teacher Gaia, who generously shares with me her love of Italy and its beautiful language and culture. *Grazie* also to my good friend Max, who sent me sublime Italian songs to listen to, and who has definitely improved my musical and linguistic education.

My sincere appreciation goes also to Jen Parker of Fuzzy Flamingo, who took on me and this book with kindness and good humour.

Printed in Great Britain
by Amazon